FEAR

of

FALLING

S.L. JENNINGS

Fear of Falling

Editing: Tracey Buckalew
Cover Design: Regina Wamba/ Mae I Design & Photography
Photo: © Tomasz Zienkiewicz Photography
Formatting by JT Formatting

ISBN-13: 978-1491006917
ISBN-10: 1491006919

Find out more about the author and upcoming books on Facebook at
http://www.facebook.com/authorsljennings

For Her.

Shit happens.

I never really understood that saying. Yeah, there were certain situations in life that were shitty, but they were just that; they were *life*. So it really wasn't the shit in life that was, well, so shitty. It was life itself.

Life happens. That was much more appropriate.

Unfortunately, many of us found that out earlier than some. We found out just how awful life could really be. We found out that monsters were, indeed, real. They walked among us. They looked just like you and me. They came in the form of the people that we loved and trusted the most. The people whose only job was to love and protect us.

Funny thing about life is that it never turns out the way you want it to. It's never fair. It's harsh and brutal. It kicks you when you're down. It makes you wish you could give up and part with it just to have a semblance of peace.

I almost felt that peace unintentionally. And if I had known exactly what I was fighting against, I would have succumbed to it. I would have traded my young, shitty life for the peace that came with death.

I should have. I would have been free.

CHAPTER ONE

I needed a drink. A strong one.

One that could possibly knock me on my ass and make me forget what I had done just 20 minutes ago. This was always the hard part. The guilt, the self-loathing. Sometimes it strangled me. I hated what I did. I hated the pain I inflicted but it was part of the process, part of what came with being me.

I hurt people, and it wasn't something I was proud of.

Pulling into the parking lot of the first bar I spotted after leaving the scene of the crime, I punched in a number on my cell phone, speed-dialing Angel. "It's done," I announced, not even bothering with a cordial greeting. Those were reserved for days when I didn't feel like locking myself away from everyone and everything. For days when I didn't feel myself breaking into a million pieces.

Angel sighed on the other end, feeling my pain through the receiver. "You okay, baby?"

"Yeah. I will be. Down to get shit-faced?" I chuckled though I truly couldn't find the humor in my own request.

"I'm always down. Where are you?"

After giving Angel the address, I fixed my smeared

mascara in the visor mirror. I could have just stopped at a liquor store and gone home to drown my troubles, but I needed an excuse to hold it together. A distraction. In public, I'd have no choice but to plaster on a phony smile and ignore the immense guilt I felt. I'd be forced to pretend.

10...9...8...7...

I started the mental countdown ritual. I could do 10. Twenty was reserved for extra shitty days. Fifty was for all-out hellish catastrophes. Today felt more like a 10: a craptastic situation.

"You can do this," I whispered to the reflection staring back at me. "It's ok. You're ok. It had to be done. You have to keep going. You can do this, Kami Duvall. You will not break. Not today."

The bar's marquee stated Dive, though it only slightly resembled the traditional, hole-in-the-wall dive bars I was accustomed to. As I scurried into the air-conditioned building, seeking refuge from the relentless Charlotte summer sun, I could tell it had been recently upgraded with modern furniture and a fresh coat of paint. I liked it already though ambiance was not a requirement for what I had planned for the rest of my evening.

I settled in at the bar and ordered a shot of tequila along with a Long Island Iced Tea chaser. When the bearded bartender raised a questioning brow at my request, I diverted my eyes to a bowl of peanuts a few seats down. I didn't need his misguided judgment.

"Damn, baby. Sure a pretty little thing like you can handle a drink like that?" a voice laced with a southern drawl called out to me. I looked up to spot a smiling onlooker across the bar. Great. Judgment *and* an asshat with my beverages.

I smiled sweetly before grabbing my shot of tequila, downing it, tossing the slice of lime to the side, and slamming the glass on the bar. When I looked back up, Asshat was already making his way towards me, obviously intrigued with my shot-pounding capabilities. Unfortunately for him, that'd be the only thing getting pounded tonight.

"Hey there, honey. I've never seen you 'round here. You must be new. I'm Craig," he smiled, extending his hand. I looked at it, scanned the length of his body and turned my attention back to my drink. It was much more exciting. Craig took the hint and pulled his hand back but still settled in the seat beside me. I rolled my eyes; he was a persistent little prick. Normally the southern charm was endearing to a California girl like me, but after what I had just been through, it was annoying as hell.

"Craig, right?" I asked after a long pull from my Long Island. He nodded and flashed a hopeful smile. I couldn't wait to wipe that dumb look right off his face. "First off, calling the wrong person 'honey' could very well get you cut. And second of all, how would you know if I was new? Do you hang out here on a regular basis?"

"Easy there, darlin'," he chuckled, holding his hands up in defense. "Just making friendly chit-chat. And yes, actually, I do come 'round here often. This happens to be my family's place."

I eyed Craig disapprovingly. With his wavy, chin-length brown hair, light brown eyes, and the bit of scruff on his chin, he wasn't exactly bad to look at. He was actually pretty cute in that young southern gentleman kinda way, but I was too far gone on the self-depreciation train to even fall for his charm.

"So what? That gives you a right to harass all the paying patrons?" I replied with a raised brow before down-ing the last of my drink. It was strong, but not strong enough to stow my bitchiness.

"You are an exotic little thing, aren't ya? Yes, indeed," Craig appraised, ignoring my jab. He finished his beer just as our empty glasses were quickly swiped from the bar. "Let me guess—you're one of those *moo-lot-toe* girls."

I nearly choked, and probably would have spit my drink right in his face just for shits and giggles if I'd had a mouthful. "Excuse me? Are you trying to say *mulatto?"*

"Yeah! That chocolate and vanilla swirl! I'm right, aren't I?"

Wow. Craig was a bigger asshat than I initially assumed. I had played this game with guys before. The whole, *"What are you? Let me guess..."* bit was not new to me. Usually I shut it down, but since I had nothing else better to do than stew about my predicament, I thought I'd humor Craig and eventually make a fool of him. I didn't think it would take long anyway.

"No, I'm not *moo-lot-toe*, jackass. Chocolate and vanilla? Do I look like an ice cream cone to you?" I snickered. Craig's eyes widened with glee at my choice of words, instantly making me regret them. Thankfully, the bartender returned with our drinks, so I could get back to the task at hand: getting stupid drunk.

I looked up to say thank you and was met with a hooded pair of chocolate brown eyes and a boyish grin. His hair was covered in a worn baseball cap, and he had just the right amount of scruff on his chin and upper lip to give his baby face an edge. His hands and arms were covered with intricate, colorful tattoos. He was different from what usually attracted me and absolutely beautiful. So beautiful, in fact, that I had to tear my eyes away before I used Jedi mind tricks to undress him. I wanted to see what else those tattoos covered. Badly.

"CJ, I hope you're not botherin' this young lady," the younger, much more enticing bartender smiled, his deep voice laced with a touch of southern drawl. His large hand (yeah, I noticed) clapped Craig on the back as he shook his head, a lock of brown hair escaping his cap and falling into his eyes. His gaze came back to me, and he winked.

Under normal circumstances, the move would have probably made me blush, and/or flash a flirty smile, but my mind and heart were still heavy with grief. I returned the sentiment with a nod and a nervous half-grin. Sure, he was attractive, painfully so, but that thought would be all I could allow myself to enjoy.

"Aw, you know me, Blaine. Always makin' friends," Craig snickered before taking a sip of his fresh beer.

Blaine.

Even his name was sexy as hell, and I resisted the urge to try it out on my tongue. He placed his palms against the bar, and leaned in, looking at me expectantly. Shit, I really didn't want the attention. But he looked at me intently, his head cocked to one side, with his mouth curled up, and I couldn't think of anything witty or even rude to say to make the guys go away.

It made me nervous. Like, *really* nervous. So I tore my

eyes away from his and nodded towards a HELP WANTED sign propped up on a high shelf. "You guys hiring?"

Blaine turned and looked at the sign before bringing those brown eyes back to me. "Yeah. Waitresses, line cooks. A bartender. Looking for work?"

"Maybe," I shrugged before taking a sip of my drink while I surveyed the room. It was a good-sized place, and it was centrally located. But, it was virtually empty aside from a few bar patrons. "Did this place just open or something?"

"Nah," he responded with a little shake of his head. The lock of hair fell farther into his line of vision, and much to my dismay, he swept it to the side, tucking it back into his cap. "Just got new management."

Craig snorted and rolled his eyes before taking a chug of his beer. He turned his attention back to me and waggled his eyebrows. "So darlin', where were we? Oh right…how about Puerto Rican? Mexican? I have to be close. Did I get it right? Or are you just gonna keep me guessing all day?"

Ignoring Craig completely, my gaze fell to Blaine's hands. They rested on the bar, just inches from mine. On one hand, he had a letter written in some type of old script on each finger. The other had a design on the back that fused into the piece crawling up his arm. My eyes followed the vibrantly detailed pattern slowly, studying every line and curl. Even shrouded in ink, I could tell his arms were magnificently cut and defined with muscle. Muscles that flexed and quivered as he leaned against the bar, causing his biceps and shoulders to strain against his fitted, plain white t-shirt.

"So are ya?" Craig asked, intruding on my thoughts and pulling me away from the splendor of Blaine's arms.

"Huh?" I sputtered, looking up with a doe-eyed expression and praying that neither of them had noticed my shameless gawking. They both chuckled, making me believe that my prayers had gone unanswered.

"Are ya a spicy Latina?" Craig asked as he leaned in closer, hoping to steer my attention to him.

I could feel my lips curve into a grimace, and I swallowed down the disgust I felt at that very moment. Without knowing what to do or say next, I looked up at Blaine, whose eyes were still trained on me, an amused grin on his face. Initially, my eyes widened as if to plead for help then settled into a dreamy stare. They wanted to continue their study of Blaine's physique and I really couldn't blame them. And who was I to deprive my peepers of the sexiest piece of man-candy they had seen in years?

Noticing the flash of desperation in my expression, his smile broadened, and he turned to Craig, releasing me from his compelling gaze. "As always, you're way off, CJ," he said, as he turned his body sideways to rest on an elbow. The move allowed me a better inspection of his torso, and revealed a chest and abs under the thin fabric that just begged for a tongue to trace each defined cut. The weight of his body supported by his elbow caused his bicep to stretch his shirt even more. I envied that damn t-shirt.

"How so, cuz?" Craig asked, pausing before bringing his beer bottle to his lips.

Blaine looked away from Craig to meet my eyes again, however, his gaze was different this time. Less playful and curious, and more… intense. Almost lustful. It held me on my barstool and refused to let me look away or even blink. It burned right into me, marking me in an uncanny way. His expression both disturbed and aroused me, and I couldn't decide which I was more upset about.

"Well, first off," he finally said, "she isn't mulatto or even Hispanic. Look at her eyes…perfectly slanted and sexy. Soulful. And her hair… so dark and thick, slightly curled. Hair that beckons you to run your fingers through it from root to tip. Maybe even pull a little," he smiled crookedly. "And then there's the shape of her lips…how they dip and curve into a full pout. Lips that you can't resist staring at for hours. Lips that beg to be kissed."

Blaine chewed his bottom lip and narrowed his eyes, as they continued to scan every part of me that he had just so eloquently described. I was nearly dizzy from the breath I didn't even realize I was holding.

"Asian. You're part Asian, right?" he asked simply, no trace of seduction in his voice. His eyes no longer smoldered or emitted the fiery passion he had displayed just seconds before.

The switch in gears nearly made me fall flat on my face. Luckily, my roommate/girlfriend/savior strolled in and successfully diverted the attention from me. Every eye turned to witness the grand arrival of Angel Cassidy, dressed in too short cut-offs, a red tank that was suggestively torn and cut to reveal her plump breasts and lace-up black platform heels. She was the quintessential blonde bombshell that filled every guy's fantasies. With her heart-shaped cherry lips, milky white skin and curves for days, she easily resembled a younger, edgier Marilyn Monroe.

I masked the disappointment of losing Blaine's attention and gave Angel a wink. She strutted over to me, a hand on her hip, and gave me a wicked smile. She clutched the back of my head, tangled her fingers in my dark brown hair, and crushed her glossed lips to mine. A moan rumbled her chest as I pulled her body into mine.

It was the kiss heard ‘round the world. Well, ‘round the bar, anyway.

Other than a few audible gasps at seeing Angel’s pink tongue dart out of her mouth, Dive was completely silent as she flicked my upper lip before pulling away. The two guys before us each wore amused grins that screamed of lustful possibilities.

“Oh, hell yeah!” Craig exclaimed, breaking the deafening silence and smacking Blaine’s chest with the back of his hand. “Lesbians! Now *that* explains it!”

“How are you, baby?” Angel cooed, tucking a lock of hair behind my ear while gazing at me adoringly.

I matched her soft smile and placed my hands on her narrow waist. “Better now that you’re here.”

“Wow! Can you believe this, B?” Craig still rambled excitedly.

I turned back around on my barstool to assess Blaine’s reaction, which was unreadable if not indifferent. Good. Better for him, and everyone else, to see that there’s no chance with me. Not that I thought he was thinking that.

“Can I ask you ladies a question?” Craig chimed in. For once since meeting him twenty minutes before, I was glad for his intrusion. I had to stop looking at Blaine. I had to stop giving him the impression that I was interested. Because I wasn’t. I couldn’t be.

“Sure!” Angel piped up, sliding her arm around my

shoulders and leaning into me.

Craig took a hefty gulp of beer and cleared his throat before leaning closer. "Ok. I know you gals are gay, and all, but *lez-be-honest*...you gotta miss that full, thrusting feeling," he snickered in a mock whisper.

"CJ, dude!" Blaine scoffed, smacking him upside the head.

"Ever been with a guy?" Craig continued, ignoring Blaine's pleas to knock it off. "Because I'd love to be the meat in your sandwich."

With that, Angel and I rolled our eyes before making our way to an empty table. Blaine was still scolding Craig for his comments, and I honestly had to refrain from laughing. Craig was certainly an asshat, but I had to give it to him—he was a funny asshat.

"So what happened?" Angel asked once we were settled.

I shrugged and looked down at the table, digging my fingernail into a nick in the tabletop. "Same thing that always happens. I hurt him, he cried, then I came here."

"He cried?" Angel grasped my hand, her sparkly black fingernails a drastic contrast to her pale complexion. "You wanna talk about it, babe?"

"No," I replied, shaking my head. I hated that part of the game. Each time, I told myself I wouldn't get involved—that I would be better off without the trouble. Yet, each time, I somehow let myself break the rules. Then came the pain.

Before I could delve deeper into my own self-inflicted misery, Blaine strolled up, giving me a clear view of the rest of his body. Worn blue jeans hung from his hips in that way that showed off his chiseled frame without being too tight. His plain white tee clung to his torso and, if I looked closely, I could see the outline of eight perfectly hard mounds, comprising his midsection. And, I could tell that there was more ink, arousing my interest even more. I forced my eyes back up to his, silently cursing myself.

"Hey ladies, sorry about my cousin. He was dropped a lot as a baby," he said with a smile before crossing his arms in front of him and leaning against a nearby table. The movement caused those luscious biceps to bulge and, once again, that lucky-ass t-shirt stretched.

"Oh wow, you're related to that tool?" Angel snickered. "My sincere apologies."

"He's an ass, but he's harmless," Blaine replied with a one-shouldered shrug and a crooked grin. The combination was incredibly adorable, and I had to squelch a rising swoony sigh. "So is there anything else I can get you ladies?"

As always, Angel commanded attention. "Well, handsome, we will have two shots of tequila to start." She peered at my melancholy expression through dramatically long eyelashes. "Actually, make that four shots. Maybe I'll get lucky," she winked.

Blaine smirked knowingly before scraping his bottom lip with his teeth. Something inside me clenched. "Was I right?" he asked, suddenly directing his attention to me.

I frowned, completely caught off guard. "Huh?"

He uncrossed his arms and took a step forward, causing me to take in a sharp breath. "About your nationality. I was right, wasn't I?"

"Um uh…" I stammered. I wasn't entirely sure why I

had suddenly lost my train of thought, but all I could focus on was that pesky lock of hair that was slowly easing its way from outside of his ball cap once more.

"Oh, Kami's nationality?" Angel piped up, her eyes darting between Blaine and me questioningly. "Her mom's from the Philippines."

With his eyes never straying from mine, Blaine smiled crookedly and nodded. Then he turned away from the table, stealing my breath and taking it with him back to the bar to retrieve our shots.

"What the fuck was that about?" Angel squeaked in her high-pitched soprano. The crude comment was a direct contrast to her bell-chime tone.

After regaining the usage of limbs and brain function, I turned to Angel. "Nothing. He and his cousin were trying to figure out what I was."

"Yeah, yeah, I get that… I'm talking about the obvious *Take me, take me now* stares. I mean, seriously, did it just get hot in here or what? I thought he was about to ask you to grab your ankles!"

I shook my head and looked down at my peeling nail polish. "No, you're seeing things. Besides, I'm not going down that road again. I'm done."

"Sure, sure, sweetheart. Whatever you say. I love you anyway," she grinned, blowing me a kiss and eliciting a chuckle from me. "There's that smile!"

Just as I was beginning to unwind, Blaine returned with a tray of shots, lime slices, and salt. With one extra. He distributed our four, then picked one up for himself, raising it in a toast. Angel looked to me with a wicked gleam and picked up the saltshaker. She leaned over, then seductively licked my neck and sprinkled a little salt on it. Feeling satisfied with my compliancy, she eased a lime wedge between my lips and picked up her shot glass. My eyes fluttered closed when her small hands cradled my face and sucked the salt from my neck, licking and nuzzling as if we were alone in the room. Then she pulled back, clinked her glass against Blaine's, and downed her poison. For the second time today, her lips pressed against mine, as they sucked the wedge of lime.

Blaine didn't even bother with his own slice; he was too busy staring at the girls practically making out in front of him. From a few yards away, I could hear Craig catcalling and cheering, yet Blaine was silent, a small smile playing on his perfect lips. It made me wonder if he was just being respectful or was gay himself.

"Ok, your turn, Kami!" Angel exclaimed. With a sigh, I nodded and began to make my way towards her neck when she grasped my shoulders, halting my approach. "Not me, silly! *Him*. He doesn't have another shot, and I want to take the next one with you. Don't worry, I won't get jealous."

My eyes instantly whipped to his furrowed brow, both our expressions full of surprise. "Um, Angel, honey, I think that is highly inappropriate. There's no way I could do something like that to him. He works here."

Blaine licked his lips and cleared his throat. Somehow it sounded more like a groan. "I don't mind if *you* don't, Kami," he said. My name sounded different on his tongue, almost dirty. The delicious kind of dirty.

I bit my bottom lip, and glared at Angel, knowing exactly what she was up to. She made everything into a game and was always looking for ways to be entertained. That attitude was embedded in her poor-little-rich-girl persona. She returned my evil eye with a wink and waved her hand towards Blaine.

Not feeling nearly drunk enough, yet warm from my previous drinks, I rolled my eyes and returned my attention back to the deliciously tattooed bartender before me. "Um, ok. I guess."

Blaine smiled sheepishly before pulling up a chair and straddling it backwards. Now he was closer to me, so close that I could smell him. And I'll be damned if he didn't smell amazing. It was a mix of mint and spicy cologne that paired with his body's natural scent in a way that made my mouth water. I silently cursed again, but directed it at Angel this time. I should have never smelled that man. It was wrong. So, so wrong. Yet so, so good.

I mustered up my courage and inched towards him slowly. Blaine kept his eyes on mine, refusing to even blink in my pursuit. I knew he had to hear my heart nearly pounding through my chest; hell, it was all I could hear. His gaze never wavered. When I was only inches from the smooth, tanned skin of his neck, he sucked his bottom lip into his mouth and tilted his head, giving me full access to the known erogenous zone. By this point, my heart was hammering double time, and I thought I might go into cardiac arrest at any second. I had to keep going. I couldn't let him see just how much he affected me. Angel and I had done this plenty of times with guys way less good-looking. This man should be no exception.

The taste of his skin caused a tiny moan to escape my throat as the tip of my warm tongue licked a trail toward his earlobe. He tasted exactly how he smelled—of mint and spice. It made me want to keep licking and suck that earlobe right into my mouth, to nibble it gently between my teeth. Aware of the spike in his breathing at the feel of my wet tongue, I pulled back to gauge his reaction. Blaine's eyes were hooded, low, and smoldering, and I knew that they matched my own. His teeth released his bottom lip and his tongue rested on it, ready for… I don't know what. But I noticed. I noticed everything about him in that moment. With the taste of him still lingering on my tongue, it was damn near impossible not to.

Angel cleared her throat and nudged me with the saltshaker, bringing me back to the here and now. I took it from her, not even bothering to acknowledge her presence, and sprinkled a bit on the moistness drying on his neck. With another nudge, she passed me a lime wedge. Tentatively, I advanced towards him again, my eyes trained on that tongue. With just an inch separating my fingertips and his lips, Blaine opened his mouth just a fraction, and I saw it. A barbell. His freakin' tongue was pierced.

I knew I should have stopped there. I was getting in way over my head. Really? Body shots with a complete stranger? Not only that, but a tattooed, pierced stranger that screamed recklessness? But I couldn't stop myself from leaning forward. I couldn't keep my tongue from darting out and licking that salty trail, sucking his skin gently into my mouth, and causing him to groan. After I downed the shot of tequila, his flavor still hadn't left my mouth. It coaxed me to cradle his face and crush my lips to his. The wedge of lime may have separated our mouths, but I distinctly felt Blaine's soft lips and the warmth of his breath. I didn't even bother to suck the lime at first. I just let my eyes close for a split second and enjoyed the intimate feeling. It was… incredible. Stupid and dangerous, yet incredible.

Remembering the task at hand, I gave the slice of citrus a suck, eliciting another groan from Blaine. Then I realized I was actually sucking his lip. His bottom lip, so soft and sweet, was in my mouth, and I had been running my tongue along it. I pulled away quickly, abandoning the lime and letting it fall to the floor between us. Neither one of us made a move to pick it up. There was too much …there. I don't know what it was that crackled between us, but it was there. And it was confusing the hell out of me.

Blaine's expression was still full of desire and question, making me believe that he was just as confused about what transpired. My lips burned and I wanted to feel that fire again immediately. The way he licked his lips signaled that he wanted the same.

"Woo hoo, cuz!" Craig sidled up, clapping Blaine on the back and breaking our trance. "Looks like you wanna be the meat in the sandwich tonight! You lucky sonofabitch!"

Blaine looked up at his cousin and blinked rapidly, as if he had been entranced for the past five minutes. Jumping from his chair with enough force to make it screech against the hardwood, his eyes darted between Angel and me before settling on my face. Then he…frowned. He frowned like I had just manipulated him and forced my tongue down his throat. Like he regretted the semi-kiss we just shared. I looked down at my last shot and threw it back, not even bothering with salt and lime. I don't think I could ever use those accompaniments again.

"Um, uh, if there's nothing else…" he stuttered, chewing that lip again. The very same lip that I had just sucked lime juice from. "Yeah, I'll be at the bar if you need anything." Then he turned and retreated back to safety, leaving us with his dim-witted cousin.

Plopping down in the chair that Blaine abandoned, Craig smiled brightly at us as if he were next in line. I rolled my eyes at him and looked to Angel who was wearing a devilish grin. I was beginning to think those were the only kinds of smiles she possessed.

"So, it's CJ, right? Hi, I'm Angel Cassidy," she announced with an air of arrogance that only Angel could pull off gracefully. She extended her hand to him and he received it eagerly.

"Yeah. Well, the name is Craig, but people been callin' me CJ since I was a kid. Real good to meet ya, Angel. Real good. The name certainly fits."

Angel held up her hands in warning before CJ could go any further. "Ugh, do not ask me if it hurt when I fell from heaven, or if I have wings, or any other dumb ass pick-up lines."

Tuning them out as they made small talk, I looked towards the bar, instantly locking eyes with Blaine who was staring intently. Several seconds ticked by before either of us could do anything but breathe. Finally, a bar patron grabbed his attention and stole his gaze from me. I was thankful and highly irritated, all wrapped into one.

"So CJ, what's your cousin's deal? Is he seeing anyone?" Angel asked, provoking me to whirl around and narrow my eyes at her.

Craig looked back towards the bar where Blaine was still helping a customer. "Who, B? Nah. He doesn't have a girl. Not anymore. Why?"

"Oh, no reason," Angel replied, darting her eyes to me. She was up to no good, which was usually the case. Before she could inquire if Blaine was a boxer or briefs guy, the older, bearded guy that served me earlier poked his head from behind a door a few yards away and summoned Craig to the back.

"I think it's time to go," I said, forcing myself not to look towards the bar.

"What? I haven't had nearly enough to drink!" And with that, Angel waved directly towards the area I was trying to avoid.

Seconds later, Blaine was in front of us, his tattooed hands grasping the edge of the table. His presence brought it all back to me...his scent, his taste, the way his body was a work of art that I wanted to paint with my tongue. All the reasons why I most definitely should not speak to him again.

"Hey Blaine, can we get a couple more? And don't forget to grab a shot for you too," Angel winked.

"He can have mine," I mumbled, refusing to look at him.

I felt a lone finger brush against my forehead, pushing a lock of hair behind my ear. Then it traced the curve of my earlobe, making me shiver. His touch resumed the pesky pounding in my chest.

"Are you sure, Kami?" he asked with a husky voice. The same voice he used with me before as he described my eyes, my hair, my lips...and what should be done to them.

Unable to string a sentence together, I simply nodded. Blaine made no move to leave. He kept touching me, like feeling my skin was the most natural thing in the world to him. Slowly, he leaned down to me, coming in so close that his scent of mint and spice filled my nostrils. We were almost eye-level, and I couldn't do more than hold my breath with anticipation. I should have been scared by his touch. I should have stopped him before he moved any closer into my personal space. But I just…couldn't.

"Hey, you don't have to pretend anymore," he said just above a whisper.

"Pretend?" I exhaled, the word coming out in a rush. What does he know of my pretending? There's no way I could be that transparent. I'd had years of practice.

"Yeah," he grinned crookedly. "CJ's gone. You can stop pretending…that you girls are together. That you're gay."

"Excuse me?" Angel piped up, her voice laced with annoyance. "What makes you think that we're pretending to be gay?"

Blaine's eyes darted to Angel for a split second, and he shook his head lightly. "Not you." Then his chocolate brown gaze was back on me, sweeping over every inch of my face. It was like he was studying every feature, trying to unveil some big mystery. "Her. She's pretending."

"How do you know I'm not a lesbian too?" I asked. The question was meant to come out with a trace of attitude, but it ended up being breathy and light.

As if the sound of my betraying voice amused him, Blaine flashed that boyish grin. My tenacity was going… going….gone.

"Because I'm pretty sure you're feeling the same thing I'm feeling right now."

Then he did something that had me yanking my purse open, throwing down a twenty, and high-tailing it out of there in 3.5 seconds.

He took off his worn cap and ran a hand through his hair, the light brown locks settling into perfectly messy "just-fucked" hair. Hair I wanted to grab and tug while his tongue slid against mine. Hair that I wanted to feel tickling my sensitive areas while he worked me over with that metal-studded tongue.

I was in my car and flying out of the parking lot before Angel even made it outside.

CHAPTER TWO

"Oooh…a little harder," Angel cooed. "You don't have to be so gentle. It won't break."

"Like this?" I hummed.

"Yes, yes. That's right. Feel it swell and vibrate…see how good it feels on your fingertips."

I gasped in surprise. "Oh yeah, you're right. Wow… that's incredible."

"Feels good, doesn't it?"

"Mmmm," I hummed, too caught up in the moment to say much more.

A flirty giggle escaped her red glossy lips. "I told you; it's the best."

I sighed with contentment then returned Angel's brand new, very expensive, top-of-the-line guitar to her waiting hands. "Well, it certainly sounds like it. Too bad I can't even think about a new one until I find a job," I frowned, diverting my attention back to the listings on my laptop screen.

"I told you, Kami; you don't have to worry about rent," Angel remarked, strumming a tune of her own. She hummed along with the melody.

I let out a breath then looked back up at her. "There's no way I am skipping out on rent. What Dom and I pay is already peanuts. Plus, I am getting sick of you two feeling like you have to foot the bill for every outing."

"Well, you know you could always dip into your money…" she said, her voice trailing off into a whisper at the end.

I gave her a stoic look. "No. Absolutely not. I'm not touching it and I don't want it."

"Kami, that money is yours. It was owed to you. You have every right to spend it."

"No," I answered, shaking my head. "It was owed to my mother about fifteen years ago. It can rot away at the bank for all I care."

I wanted the satisfaction of earning my own way, not taking something that my mother could have desperately used to raise me. But Angel Cassidy, bless her heart, knew nothing about that. She came from money—old money. And since her parents were ultra-conservative and didn't accept her sexuality, or "lifestyle choices" as they called it, they were more than happy to buy her a plush condo, car, and anything else her pretty little heart desired to keep her from showing up at the country club in her scandalous rocker motif with a busty groupie on her arm.

I went back to scouring the Help Wanted ads while Angel jotted down lyrics as they came to her. Seeing my frustration at the lack of options, she asked, "Why don't you just go back to the firm? I'm sure Kenneth would be professional about the whole thing."

I shook my head. No, that definitely wouldn't be a good idea. "I can't, Angel. You didn't see the pain on his face. I really wounded him."

"But it's been a couple weeks. Maybe he's gotten over it. I'm sure he wouldn't hold a grudge."

"Angel, honey, I was his secretary and he is a partner at his firm. And I basically told him I didn't want him anymore after he confessed to being in love with me and seeing a future for us. Does that sound like a situation that's easy to get over?" I asked with a raised brow.

"But you guys only dated for a couple months! And a guy like Kenneth...he's probably too concerned about his reputation to make a scene on the job."

I shrugged and let out a breath. "Well, it doesn't matter anyway. It was a temp job; you can't just pop up whenever you feel like it. I just hope that he finds what he's looking for...with someone capable of returning his affections."

"Sorry," Angel whispered, her lower lip jutted out.

I gave her a sincere smile. "Don't be. I made a huge mistake getting involved with someone on the job, especially my boss. You live and you learn, and I certainly won't be doing that again. Plus, I'm used to...being this way. I wish I could say I was used to hurting people but I don't think anyone gets used to being a cold, heartless bitch."

Angel propped her custom-detailed pink guitar against its stand and came over to wrap her arms around me. "Kamilla Duvall, you are not a cold, heartless bitch. You just haven't met the one worth giving your heart to. So it's just a little harder to find because you've been burying it for so long."

I squeezed her forearm circled around my chest and rested my head against hers. "Thanks, boo."

"And since you won't take me up on my offer of love,

affection and mind-blowing sex, I highly doubt we'll be excavating it any time soon," she snickered.

I gave the blonde bombshell a pinch on her thigh and pushed her away. "Ewww, Angel! You know that will never happen. I am strictly dickly," I laughed.

She made her way back to her guitar, shaking with laughter. "Well, it's been hard to tell, seeing as there haven't been any dicks coming through here in a while."

I stuck my tongue out at her though I knew she was right. "But between you and Dom, there's been plenty of pussies. Pussy galore!"

"Hey did someone say my name?" a deep voice called from behind us. We spun around to see our third roommate, and my most favorite person in the entire world, Dominic Trevino wearing only boxers and a lazy, satisfied grin.

"Depends. Is your name Pussy Galore?" Angel asked between singing the melody from before.

Dominic, or Dom as we called him, ran a hand through his jet-black bed head and gave us a sly smile. "No, but after the night I had, it sure was Pussy Galore in my room. One word: twins!"

Angel and I both cringed at the thought and let out a simultaneous *Ewwww*. I loved Dom more than anyone in this world, and he was probably the only person who had ever fully understood me and loved me anyway, but he could be disgusting. He pretty much slept with anything in a skirt, and being that he was tall, dark, and amazingly handsome with penetrating brownish-green eyes, most skirts flocked to him in droves. I knew his whorish ways stemmed from the downright horrific things he experienced as a child so I didn't chastise him too much about it. But I worried about him. And I hoped one day that he would find someone special to fill the void he kept trying to satisfy with nameless women.

"So are you staying for practice today?" Angel asked me, trying to steer the conversation from Dom's latest sexcapades.

"Nah. I think I'm gonna get out there and pound the pavement some more."

Angel sucked her teeth and rolled her eyes. "Come on, Kam! Just join the band already. You could be making money from performances and with your voice, we'd probably score even more gigs. I don't know why you keep depriving yourself and the rest of us of something you know makes sense. You were born to sing!"

I sighed because I had heard this speech before. "Angel, you know why I won't join. I don't need that kind of attention. It's…not smart. *Not safe.* Besides, I like being head cheerleader for AngelDust," I smiled, hoping to appease her.

Angel perked up and I gave myself a mental pat on the back. A little stroke of her ego and she was putty in my hands. "I just want you up on that stage with me. The world should get to experience your gift."

"Angel, you are an amazing artist! What are you talking about? The way you perform and captivate the audience …I could never, ever do something like that. And you are a much better musician than me."

Shrugging, she twirled a long lock of blond hair between her fingers. This week, she had added hot pink extensions in honor of receiving her new guitar. "But you're a better singer. And I know singing makes you happy."

"Geez, enough of the Vagina Monologues!" Dom interjected playfully. "My dick just shriveled up into beef jerky!"

Angel gagged. "Gross. Sounds like Gonorrhea. I told you about picking up those gutter sluts. Don't leak any shit on my rug. I just had it cleaned."

"Carpet muncher," Dom sneered.

"Whore," I shot back at him in Angel's defense.

"Dick tease," he spat at me.

This was us: A modern day, dysfunctional Three's Company. A lesbian rocker, an insatiable man-whore and a notorious commitment-phobe, all under one roof. Of course, that was just the tip of the iceberg when it came to our laundry list of issues. And while we may have sounded more like a raunchy joke that begins with us walking into a bar, we had somehow become a family. Dom and Angel were as close as family could get for me. And in all honesty, they were the only two people on Earth that had ever met the skeletons hanging out in my closet. Hell, they just moved them over to make room for theirs.

Angel stood up and stretched her limbs, her tight body looking X-rated in her sheer chemise and panties. *Didn't anyone wear clothes around here?* "So are you sure no one else is hiring that you know of?"

I twisted my lips as if I was in deep thought though the answer was at the forefront of my brain. "Yes. No. I don't know. Maybe."

"Maybe?" Dom asked, plopping down on the couch next to me.

"Well, um, there's that bar..." I could feel my face

heat just at the mention of it.

Dom propped his legs onto my lap and reclined, his hands behind his head. “Bar? Do tell.”

“Yeah, uh, you know…that bar that Angel and I went to…and, you know…”

“The bar with the hottie bartender?” Angel perked. She threw herself onto Dom’s body and cuddled him like a giant-sized teddy bear.

“I mean, that was weeks ago and I’m sure they’ve already filled the positions,” I said with a phony smile.

“Well, you don’t know for sure until you check. You should stop by, Kami! That’d be a pretty cool place to work,” Angel giggled as Dom tickled her ribs.

“Nah, it’s ok. I’ll keep looking.”

Angel let out an exasperated sigh and rolled her eyes. “Look, you can’t afford to pass up this opportunity. I’ll tell you what; I’ll go with you if you stay for rehearsal.”

I furrowed my brow, wondering what she was up to. “You will?”

“Yeah! I wanted to check if they have a house band booked anyway. Did you see the size of that stage? A.D. could use a steady gig.” I nodded my compliance, causing Angel to squeal with glee. For a badass rock star, she giggled and squealed more than a pubescent schoolgirl on a Pixie Stix high.

“Ok, cool, I’m gonna grab a shower,” she announced jumping off the couch. “And Dom, you should do the same. You smell like skank sex and you have cooch breath.”

After another dish of loving insults, we all showered, dressed and got ready for our day. When the other ladies of AngelDust arrived, Angel and I were already in the spare bedroom that Angel had converted into a studio. The first to arrive was the band's lead guitarist, MiMi. A pint-sized Japanese girl, no more than 5 feet tall, she played like a badass rock god three times her size.

Behind her was K.C. on bass that, quite frankly, scared the shit out of me. She wore all black from her make up to the color of her hair. She was ghostly pale and I don't think I had ever seen her smile. But from what I heard, she was a devoted wife, mother, and den mother of her local Girl Scout troop.

Bringing up the rear was the drummer, Nessa, who I could only describe as Beyonce's doppelganger. She was gorgeous, statuesque and stylish. I always felt like a wallflower next to her but she had the sweetest, most calming spirit. She was heavy into holistic living and was always trying to sell us on the benefits of veganism. I was a vegan once. Then Dom made bacon at breakfast an hour later and I said fuck it…Y.O.L.O!

To put it plainly, AngelDust was the shit. Angel Cassidy (she insisted we use her full name when addressing her in anything pertaining to her as a musician) possessed a presence that most mainstream bands were lacking. She was incredibly engaging, arousing and entertaining on stage. She captivated every eye when she performed, no matter if they were male, female, gay, straight or other. And she oozed sex appeal. It seriously seeped out of her pores whenever a mic or guitar was in her hands. I envied her confidence in so many ways. Angel Cassidy was utterly fearless.

The girls played through a few of their signature songs before working on a new piece. I smiled and sang along quietly, swaying my head and tapping my foot. Although Angel suggested I grab my own guitar and play with them, I was way too intimidated by their caliber of talent. That was one of the biggest reasons why I refused to join the band. I was too afraid of looking like a complete ass.

After rehearsal, Angel stood by her word to go back to Dive with me. I know I seemed indifferent to it all, but I was freaking out inside. *Freaking the fuck out.* I was thankful that Angel offered to drive—she didn't want to risk me getting crazy eyes again and ditching her. There was no way I could force myself to revisit that bar alone. She knew that. Between her and Dom, they had somehow managed to get me to live through most of my deep-rooted fears. They just didn't know I was afraid of *him*. Blaine. The scary-beautiful bartender covered with tattoos that I had nearly made out with weeks before. The man that I hadn't stopped thinking about since.

It wasn't Blaine's physical adornments that scared me. It wasn't even his intense chocolate-brown gaze that made me forget to breathe. It was him. All of him. My body's response to his scared the living daylights out of me.

I had been attracted to plenty of men before and had my fair share of conventional relationships. I had dated, had one-night hook ups, and even a fuck buddy or two. But with every single one of those guys, I was able to separate my body's wants from my heart's needs. Sex had nothing to do with feeling. It was quite the opposite for me. It got me out of my head. It pressed pause on the fear and doubt that weaseled its way into every other facet of my life. Sex was my band-aid over the bullet wound that was my scarred psyche.

Still, after each guy served his purpose, the guilt set in. It always did, and I knew from the first glance how long I could keep up the ruse. I could project how long we'd be in each other's lives before I broke it off without reason.

Take Kenneth for instance. When I began working at his law firm, and he locked eyes with mine, I knew he would want something more. Much more than I could give him. He wanted a wife, children, a home, and a life together. All of the above were out of the question for me, so the moment those three little game-changing words passed his lips, I knew I had to crush him. I had to hurt him so deeply that he couldn't keep himself from sobbing into my shoulder. Men like Kenneth didn't get rejected, especially not for doing something as selfless and soul-bearing as loving another human being.

With Blaine, things were different. I couldn't see the point where things would become complicated and I'd have to break his heart. I couldn't decipher what exactly it was that he wanted from me, but I could clearly see what I wanted from him. And that fact, along with the uncertainty of his motives, if any, scared the hell out of me.

I smoothed my denim skirt and ribbed tank before taking a deep breath and advanced to the door. Suddenly I felt drastically underdressed, especially for someone seeking employment, but it was hella hot in Charlotte. I know I should be used it being that I lived in Atlanta before Dom and I moved up here eight months ago, but the sticky humidity was something I could never grow accustomed to.

Just as I was formulating an excuse to turn around and get back in the car, Angel sidled up to me and gave me a kiss in the cheek. It wasn't our usual lesbian bit to prevent unwanted attention from guys. She knew I was 2 seconds from running. In the time we had lived together, Angel and I had grown extremely close. She knew when apprehension seized me to the point where I couldn't move. She had experienced more than a couple of my freak-outs. And because she was nothing but patient and understanding, I loved her dearly.

We entered Dive and made our way to the bar. Most of the afternoon crowd was seated at tables rather than at the bar and to my surprise—and, honestly, dismay—Blaine was not stationed behind the bar. I immediately let out a relieved breath but, for some reason, it sounded more like a disappointed whimper.

"Good afternoon, I was hoping to find out more about the bartending position available?" I smiled, greeting the bearded man wiping down the bar with a rag. He was the same guy from before and seeing his familiar face gave me an ounce of assurance.

The older gentleman, probably in his 50s, rubbed his beard and nodded before extending a hand to me. "Is that right? Well, I'm Mick."

I shook and smiled warmly. "Kamilla Duvall, but everyone calls me Kami. It's good to meet you Mick." I stole a peek at Angel as she walked towards the stage to check out the digs.

"Alright, Kami, let me go fetch you an application so we can go ahead and get the paperwork out the way."

Once Mick retreated to the back, I took the liberty of getting a better look at the place. It was spacious, clean and it felt inviting. I knew I could be comfortable here. Comfort was a major factor in stifling all my idiosyncrasies.

Without warning, something deep within me clenched, nearly making me gasp for air. It was as if every one of my senses were on hyper alert and humming. I could not only feel him when he entered the room, I could taste him. He was on my tongue, minty and spicy, and tasting slightly of lime. That memory came barging in like a Mack truck. And something in me didn't just want it as a memory anymore. It wanted it to be reality.

"Hi," he muttered from behind me.

Just the sound of his voice jolted me, causing every detail from weeks ago to come rushing back with a vengeance. I tried to take a deep breath without the rise and fall of my shoulders being too obvious then licked my lips before turning around. My plan was to be nonchalant. Breezy. Maybe even flash him a friendly smile. But what my eyes found when I turned to face him was something I could not plan nor prepare for. It was…him. Dressed in simple jeans and a tee that showcased the vibrantly colored body art roped around his arms, he was even more gorgeous than I remembered. And, he didn't have on a ball cap, letting his ruffled hair that screamed sex sweep across his forehead. Oh no. This would not be good. I was a whore for a good head of hair.

I struggled to swallow, my mouth completely barren of moisture. "Hey," I squeaked, my voice a bit too enthusiastic. I cleared my throat. "I mean…hi. Blaine, right?"

Blaine gave me a knowing smile, though it looked more like he was trying not to laugh. "Yeah, Kami. What brings you here today?" he asked, folding his arms in front of him and causing those biceps to flex. Once again, those lucky little sleeves hugged them tight.

"Oh, um, I…" I began, mentally scolding myself for being so easily distracted by the thin fabric.

"Here you are, young lady," Mick announced, sliding the application over to me. I hadn't even noticed he had come back.

I smiled and thanked him, then looked back to Blaine. He was frowning. It was a slight frown, just creasing the middle of his brows, but it looked like a frown nonetheless. "You want to work here?" he asked, a hint of disbelief in his voice.

I shrugged and gave him a tight-lipped grin. "Yeah, why not?"

Blaine relaxed his features yet his expression still seemed a bit perturbed at the idea. I instantly regretted coming here. It was evident that he was still upset, if not confused, by what happened between us before. His mouth moved as if he was rolling his tongue, his brows still knitted together. Then I got a flash of silver, causing my stomach to clench once again. The reminder of that tongue ring had me doing an internal happy dance. Why? I have no idea. It wasn't like I expected to feel that barbell sliding against my tongue… or other places.

He looked to Mick and nodded, snapping me out of my trance. "I'll take care of her." Then he took a step forward and grabbed my hand.

He grabbed my hand! And I yelped like a freakin' puppy.

We both sputtered apologies at my outburst, and my face reddened instantly. Damn Asian flush. Not wanting to make me any more uncomfortable, Blaine tentatively plac-ed his hand on the small of my back, leading me to the other side of the bar just as Angel approached and took a seat. I know my wide-eyed expression at his contact was evident to her.

"Good to see you again, Blaine!" she beamed, cutting her eyes at me.

He smiled warmly, one side of his mouth curled up farther than the other. "You too, Angel." He then turned his head to me, placing his palms against the bar and leaning forward a bit, regarding me intently. "Ready?"

My eyes narrowed in confusion. "Ready for what?"

"Your audition," he said, with that amused, trying-not-to-laugh look on his face. It was infuriating and adorable all at once.

I nodded stiffly and pursed my lips, frustrated with my betraying emotions. After washing my hands, I turned to him and waited for his first order. He was staring at me. Not just casually gazing, he was staring at me like he was appraising a rare piece of artwork. It was odd and intense, and that damn flush crept back up my neck and painted my cheeks.

Finally, he turned his body and pressed his backside against the bar, casually crossing his ankles, his head turned towards mine. He was close—very close. Close enough for me to get a whiff of his scent and feel the warmth of his body.

Standing side by side, I could tell Blaine was tall. He had to be at least six inches taller than my 5 ft. 6 in. frame. I liked tall men. I liked the way they could fold their bodies around mine and make me feel safe and secure, even just for a night. My mind began to drift to images of Blaine's arms around me, those big hands sliding across hips, around my ass, up my bare back…

"It's good to see you again, roadrunner," he muttered for my ears only. It was enough to startle me from my insane daydream. Just as well. It would never, ever come to fruition.

I glanced at Angel, engaged in a conversation with Mick, then turned my head back to him and raised a brow. "Roadrunner?"

Blaine's mouth twisted again, giving me another peek at that metallic barbell. He wasn't doing it to be seductive. At least I didn't think he was. It seemed more out of habit than anything else. "Yeah. The way you ran outta here last time, you would've thought a 50-ton anvil was about to come crashing down on you."

"Is that right?" I smirked playfully. I couldn't help flirting with him. It was harmless, after all. "So what does that make you? Wile E. Coyote?"

A question knit his brows. "Why would you think that? You think I'm chasing you?"

My eyes widened with embarrassment. "Oh, no, I wasn't saying…"

"Because I'm not chasing you," he cut me off. "Not yet, at least."

I didn't know how to respond. I was confused by his behavior, unsure if he was attracted to me…or not. Not that he should be. I just liked knowing where I stood.

"Oh," was all I could manage.

Blaine grinned crookedly, his warm chocolate eyes heating into a smolder. "Screaming orgasm."

"Huh…what?" I juggled the glass in my hand, almost dropping it.

He chuckled, and I had to admit, it was a fascinating sound. Husky and sexy. He ran a hand through his perfectly unruly hair. “I want a Screaming Orgasm. You do know what those are, right?”

“Oh, yeah,” I mumbled, assembling the cocktail. Yeah, I knew what they were from prior bartending jobs, but unfortunately I had only experienced them in drink form.

Once the shot was perfectly garnished, despite my slightly shaky hands, I slid the drink over to him. It wasn’t far since he had made it a point to only leave a few inches between us.

Blaine took the tall shot in his hands, appraising it thoroughly, then brought the glass to his mouth and took a small sip, licking his lips afterwards. It gave me full view of that tongue ring, and I felt I could die happy right then and there.

“Mmmm,” he groaned lightly. I had to suck my lips in to stifle my own reaction. He turned to me and held up the glass just inches from my face. “Taste it,” he breathed, the words audible only to me. Before I could take the shot glass from him, he was pressing it to my lips gently, his gaze predatory. As my lips parted, so did his, as if he was guiding the movement. He tilted it back, the sweet-strong mix of vodka and creamy liquor trickling down my throat and warming my chest.

“You like it?” he asked just above a whisper as he brought the glass down, his eyes never leaving mine.

I licked my lips slowly, probably too slow to be considered totally innocent. “Yes.”

“I like it too.” Blaine’s eyes drifted down to my lips and he began running the top row of his teeth along his bottom lip as if he was contemplating whether or not to kiss me. His breathing was just as labored and heavy as mine, anticipation flowing through our veins. This was bad. Very, very bad.

Angel's jingling laughter ringing throughout the bar doused the heated moment like ice water. We jerked apart and looked sheepishly towards her and Mick as if we had been caught red-handed. Nothing had happened, but for some reason I felt guilty and a little exhilarated. No…a lot exhilarated.

Blaine grabbed the blank application from the bar and handed it to me. "So, um, just fill that out, and someone should give you a call," he mumbled without looking at me. Then, without further explanation, he turned and disappeared through a door a few feet away.

Mick frowned at Blaine's retreating back, and the guilt crept back in, making the exhilaration I felt just moments ago go up in a puff of smoke. Of course, he must've seen our flirting. Assuming he was the boss, he surely wouldn't want his bartender canoodling with a potential employee.

I filled out the form, although I didn't have high hopes of getting the position. I knew that it was definitely for the best. I had vowed to never get involved with a coworker again, and a part of me, a part mostly comprised of hormones, was already very much involved with Blaine.

I chalked up that whole experience as being the last time I would see the scary-beautiful bartender. And that thought bothered me more than it should.

CHAPTER THREE

We were just sitting down to eat takeout sushi when our home phone rang. It was odd since hardly anyone called the house. Usually it was reserved for random parental calls which none of us received more than once or twice a month. Angel rolled her eyes and went to grab it, figuring she was due for a judgment-laced talk from Mr. and Mrs. Cassidy. I shot her a sympathetic look when she answered. However, when she paused after her greeting, her brows shot up with excitement—a reaction that would definitely not accompany a call from her parents.

"Guess what, losers?" she giggled, after hanging up with the mystery caller and rejoining us on the couch. "AngelDust just got invited for an exclusive audition at Dive! I guess a ton of other acts were inquiring about the steady weekend slot, so they're holding live tryouts this Friday. Only two other bands were invited!"

"Oh wow! That's great, Angel!" I beamed, dropping my chopsticks and giving her a hug. "So, um, that was, um, Blaine or…"

"Oh no, that wasn't your badass, boy-toy bartender. That was Mick. I'm guessing he runs the place and wanted to invite us personally."

I fought the frown creeping onto my face. "So…he didn't want to speak with me? About the job?"

"Oh shit, Kam! I'm sorry, I didn't even ask!" She squeezed my arm in apology before grabbing a tray of edamame. "I'm sure he'll get around to calling you."

I nodded, hoping she was right. It had been three days since I applied and, with each passing day, I grew more restless. I knew it was stupid to feel so anxious; I had pretty much written off any opportunity at Dive after my careless flirting with Blaine. Still, I couldn't deny the fact that I hadn't stopped thinking of him.

The reality was, I wasn't the type to act recklessly. I wasn't impulsive or spontaneous, and I was cautious to a fault. *To the point of insanity.* I couldn't risk a wrong turn. I couldn't do anything to bring undue attention to myself. And to blatantly pursue a guy like Blaine could be dangerous to me and my already delicate rationality.

We had just finished our sushi feast and were sitting cross-legged on the carpet, watching Modern Family when I heard my cell phone ringing a couple feet away. Dom reached over and grabbed it for me while I lounged on the floor, my head nestled in his lap. This was the norm for us. Affection between the three of us was effortless, yet next to impossible with anyone outside our circle.

"Hello?" I answered, chuckling into the phone, my eyes still glued to the screen.

"Hi," replied a voice dripping with sensuality.

I shot up like someone had lit a match under my ass, smacking Dom in the face in the process. "Hi," I squeaked.

"I hope I'm not interrupting anything." His voice was

deep, and slightly raspy with just a touch of southern drawl. Just as I had remembered.

"You're not." Ok, I said that way too fast. I scrambled to my feet, mouthing a half-hearted apology, and dashed to my room, earning more than a few sideways glances from my roommates.

"I wanted to tell you that you got the job. If you want it."

"Oh?" There was more than just a trace of surprise in my voice. "Really? Um, wow."

"You sound shocked."

"I…I am. I didn't think… I mean, I only made one drink for you."

"It was a really good drink," he replied with a sexy seriousness that made my tummy quiver.

I swallowed the whimper in my throat. "Yeah?"

"Yeah. So…do you want it?"

"Oh, yeah. Definitely." I had to wonder if we were still talking about the bartending position.

"Good." Blaine was quiet for a long beat, and I imagined him rolling that barbell between his full lips. I listened for the clink of metal against his teeth. "Can you start Wednesday afternoon? I'll be training you. Is that ok?"

"Sounds good." More than good. "Anything else I should know? What should I wear?"

"We've got t-shirts with Dive's logo on it. I'll give you a few. Anything for the bottom. Except, um, skirts."

"Oh. Are skirts against the dress code policy?"

I heard him suck in a breath. "No. They are just very… distracting. On you. You distract me."

"Is that a bad thing?" Oh, hell. I was flirting. No, no, no. But I couldn't seem to stop myself. Not when it came to him.

"Depends."

"Depends?" I said in my best innocently naughty voice.

"If I distract you too."

I didn't know how to respond, and the growing silence was shifting from nervous to awkward. Of course he distracted me. He had distracted my thoughts ever since I walked into Dive teary-eyed and mournful three weeks ago. But there was no way I could tell him that.

"Ok, well, I guess I'll see you Wednesday."

"Yeah. Goodnight, Kami."

"Goodnight, Blaine."

I held the phone to my chest after swiping the OFF button, then looked up to find a smirking Angel leaning against my doorframe. I was so busted.

"So, Kami, how have you been since our last visit?"

I nodded, fidgeting with a loose thread on my tank top. "Good."

"Good? So no irrational fears or meltdowns?"

I frowned at the grey-clad psychiatrist sitting across from me. Good shrinks were so hard to find, and this was my third since moving to Charlotte. I felt like I could do without them, but Dom was insistent to the point of demanding.

"Why do my fears need to be irrational?" I snapped.

Dr. Evelyn Cole raised a brow and scribbled a note on her pad. "Do you think your fears are rational?"

"I think they're understandable considering…I'm not saying they're altogether healthy, but I don't think they are irrational. I don't put anyone in danger with them."

Dr. Cole scribbled another note. "You don't put yourself in danger?"

I looked at her incredulously. "Of course not. If anything, I am careful to a fault."

"By isolating yourself."

"I don't isolate myself. I just keep a certain distance from people in order to remain…safe. There are things people do not need to know about me. If they did, I'd be alone anyway."

"And Kenneth? Is that why you broke it off with him? Because he was getting too close?"

"Kenneth let himself fall for someone who is incapable of love. I told him not to. I warned him that I couldn't get serious with him or anybody else. He wanted more of me than I was willing to give. More than I can give him or anybody else."

Dr. Cole chewed the end of her pen and puckered her brows. "And you think by holding back, by making yourself emotionally unavailable, that you are protecting yourself? That your…episodes won't be an issue?"

"That's exactly what I am doing," I murmured, yanking the thread on my shirt and snapping it. I took a deep breath and dropped my chin to my chest. "If Kenneth knew just how damaged I really am, just how neurotic my past has made me, he wouldn't stay. He'd call me crazy and abandon me. And he'd be justified to do so. I am doing him a favor. He doesn't need someone like me bogging him down with a laundry list of issues."

"And how do you know he'll run? How do you know he won't stay with you in spite of your fears?"

I looked the psychiatrist dead in her eyes with all the conviction I could muster. "Well…that's the one risk I am willing to take."

After leaving my weekly appointment, I headed straight to Dive for my first day of training. Of course, this wasn't a coincidence. I had purposely scheduled my visit with the good doctor to precede my first day of work to help combat the anxiety. But once I spied the marquee as I pulled into the parking lot, I felt ill. Clammy palms, mouth as dry as sand and heartbeat heading into dangerous territory.

"Oh no, not here. Not now. I can do this. I have to do this." But even my inner monologue wasn't convincing.

I counted down from ten, desperately trying to psyche myself up enough to leave the safety of my vehicle. I had worked plenty of jobs before without severe incident. I had played the role of a normal, sane young woman for many years and had succeeded for the most part. There had been hiccups. There had been roadblocks. But I survived them. I had my friends to help me get by one day at a time. Things were fine.

Right?

So why the hell was I freaking out inside my car in 100 degree heat over a certain inked bartender that gave me goose bumps whenever I simply thought of his name?

Blaine.

God, why couldn't he have been named something less sexy? Like Mortimer? Or Buford? Because for a name like Blaine to be attached to someone as gorgeous as that scary-beautiful man was downright cruel.

Dammit, I should have done 20.

I wiped my sweaty palms on my jeans and took a series of calming breaths to slow my heart rate. I knew I was being ridiculous. This was just a guy. Nothing was special or different about him. He represented something that I could never have: a serious relationship, companionship, trust…love. I had to keep reminding myself of that fact. Blaine needed to remain at a distance, especially now that we would be working together.

I made my way into the bar, greeted by the soft sounds of classic rock playing over the sound system. A cozy, familiar feeling filled me, comforting my nerves. I really did like it here. Maybe it was nostalgia from the music paraphernalia adorning the walls. Or maybe it was the faint smells of lemon-scented wood polish and crispy-fried comfort food from the bar's kitchen. Or maybe, just maybe, it was the man behind the bar, grinning at me in a way that made his chocolate-brown eyes look like warm pools of decadence. Whatever it was, whatever made my head swim with uncertainty, it didn't keep me from smiling back at him.

"Hey, roadrunner. Good to see you again," Blaine said on my approach. He gripped the edge of the bar and leaned forward like he always seemed to do. I didn't know if it was out of habit or if he was discreetly stretching. I knew how standing on your feet for 8+ hours could wreak havoc on your back.

I shook my head and rolled my eyes playfully. "Dude, you really gotta quit calling me that."

He crooked a knowing smile and narrowed his eyes at me. "Why? Are you done running?"

Running? *Was* I done?

"Nobody's running, Blaine. I'm here, aren't I?" I replied in a small, yet confident voice. I wanted it to be true. Oh God, how I wanted it to be true.

Silence filled the space between us, muting the lunch crowd chatter and background music. His gaze never left mine. The way he looked at me put me oddly at ease considering the intensity of his stare. He had the eyes of a man that had seen things. Eyes that were soulful and wise, yet vibrant and sultry. Eyes that made me want to run away, yet urged me to stay.

The subtle movement of his mouth working over the barbell threaded through his tongue was enough to distract my thoughts and focus on the task at hand. Work. I was here to work.

"So…where do you want me?" I sputtered without thinking. "I mean…do you want me behind the bar or, um, uh… Should we get started?"

Blaine chuckled, throwing his head back. When his eyes returned to mine, they were playful and full of mischief. "Sure, Kami. I want you back here with me."

I couldn't help but inwardly scoff at his choice of words. Then again, mine were just as cringe-worthy. I needed to put my game face on. Playtime was over. This…whatever it was…was over. It had to be. I had let too much of myself peek out from beneath the mask I wore for the general public. A mask that had only been penetrated by the two people I shared a home and any semblance of a life with. Blaine wasn't one of those people. He would never be one of those people. And if he knew the real me, not the person who pretended to be sane enough just to get by, he wouldn't want to be.

I squared my shoulders and stood next to him, careful to keep a bit of distance between our bodies. That seemed like the right thing to do. The safe thing to do.

Assessing the space between us and my unreadable, stoic expression, Blaine frowned. "What? Something wrong?"

Nothing was wrong with him. Not a single damn thing. It was me. It was always me.

I shook my head, mentally fixing my mask back into place. "No, Blaine. But I came here to work, remember? And you're here to train me. So maybe we should focus on that."

I could see his tongue rolling the metal inside his mouth, successfully thawing my cold glare and warming the space between my thighs. Shit. I was still here. The real me was still in this moment. With him.

ShitShitShit.

It was going to be a long day.

CHAPTER FOUR

Blaine

You ever get that feeling in your gut that something is about to happen? Something…big? Life-changing even? Something that would not only rock your world right off its axis but flip it upside down and shake the shit out of it? Yeah, I totally got that about three weeks ago.

I should've known the first time she came tearing into the parking lot. The first sign? She had been crying. Not drama queen, full on sobbing, but there were definitely tears. I had been just about to duck back in after a much needed break, when the screech of her tires caught my attention.

I froze.

Hell, there was no way my legs could take another step. Even with mascara smeared under her watery eyes, I could tell she was beautiful, and I think that fact made it even harder for me to turn away. I wanted to ask her what was wrong and wipe away every tear. I know it was absurd of me to want that. Shit, it was downright creepy. But she looked so…sad. And alone. And maybe even afraid. Like whatever it was that she had just run away from was bound to show up any second and drag her back to the hell she had just escaped.

After a brief chat on her cell, I watched the internal battle play across her features as she tried to get her emotions in check. That should've been my chance to escape. I could turn away from her and let her deal with her own misery. I had enough of my own and I'd be damned if I'd take on someone else.

But I didn't turn away. I didn't abandon the hellish North Carolina summer for the air-conditioned sanctuary of the bar. Nope. I took a step forward. Toward her.

She began fixing her makeup, and I could have sworn she was talking to herself. That should have been a huge red flag that this chick was bat-shit crazy. I had dealt with more crazy broads to last a lifetime, and I wasn't looking to pick up another. Not that I felt like I needed her in my life. No… definitely not.

But I continued to walk towards her. I had no clue what I would say or do, but I knew that I had to say or do *something*. Anything to erase the pain that she so clearly shouldered. But before I could—before I could do something stupid in an attempt to make it all better—her car door swung open, and I ducked back under the shade of the building before she could misconstrue my intent.

The second sign was her eyes. They seemed to pierce right through me, making it impossible to tear my own gaze away. Eyes that had witnessed grief and pain. Eyes that glazed over and tried to push all the hurt away. I should have let her off the hook then. Should have let CJ irritate the shit out of her until she was fed up enough to leave and never look back. That was what I should have done. But I'd never been good with the obvious solution.

None of those signs meant a damn thing the moment those perfect lips touched my skin. I could have been choking on the smoke signals, and I still wouldn't have stopped her. She was so…soft. There was a fragility about her that made me want to cherish and protect her. It was ridiculous and stupid and downright embarrassing. But none of that mattered. Her touch had branded me in the most permanent way, over a shot of tequila and a wedge of lime.

I didn't do drama. Not anymore at least. I had learned to let go of the bullshit and free myself of all emotional baggage a long time ago. So I surely didn't need her showing up inquiring about a job. And I damn sure didn't need to be working side by side with her, making the temptation to delve deeper behind those haunting green eyes, to reveal those hidden pains that much stronger…

"Dude, what the fuck? Did you even hear a word I just said? I swear, B, you'll scrub a fuckin' hole in the wood if you keep that up."

My eyes snapped to my cousin, CJ, then down to the area on the bar that I had been mindlessly—yet forcefully—wiping down with a rag. "Uh, my bad," I stammered, my glazed eyes blinking out of their trance.

CJ shook his head while unraveling his tie. He had rushed here from his day job as a contractor in hopes of seeing Dive's newest addition. Unfortunately for him, I had sent Kami home an hour ago, when I honestly couldn't think of another detail to exhaust. I had introduced her to the day staff, shown her the bathrooms, locker rooms, and she had mastered all the signature drinks. There was honestly no other excuse to keep her other than wanting her near me. Even after she had gone all cold and distant, I couldn't deny my attraction to her. And I could tell that she felt it too. Shit, anyone in a 10-mile radius could feel the sexual tension rolling off of us in heated waves.

"Like I was saying," CJ started, rolling his eyes at my lack of enthusiasm at whatever idiotic thought had popped into his shallow mind. "Wendy asked about you. You remember, Wendy from high school? With the big titties? Dude, I swear, I would motor boat the shit out of those double-Ds."

I narrowed my eyes at the Neanderthal known as my cousin, Craig Jacobs. I should have been used to him, being that we had lived together since the 9th grade when I was sent to live with him and my Uncle Mick. Craig and I had become more like brothers, and I was immune to his idiocy. Yet some of the asinine shit that left his mouth still surprised me. If we weren't related, I would bet money that he was a product of one of those stories you hear about where the teenage, coked-out mom gives birth in the toilet. Something was wrong with him, yet he was the only one who couldn't see it.

No matter how I felt about CJ and his rude and crude ways, I knew he was a good guy. And he was family. He and Uncle Mick were the only ones there for me when shit had hit the fan, resulting in my return to Charlotte a year ago. I could have gone anywhere else, but I needed to be with the people that knew me…that understood me. And though they were both rough around the edges, they were there for me in my darkest hours. I owed them.

CJ took a long swig of his beer before launching into stories of his latest conquests. As disgusting as he was, he somehow pulled his fair share of women. It was pretty damn surprising. Either they had to have extremely low self-esteem, the IQ of a fruit fly or they had to be deaf and blind. I needed to tell myself that to maintain just an inkling of faith in the opposite sex.

"So I pull up to one of my job sites at some strip mall and there she is, Wendy Tig-o-Bitties Braxton, looking as hot as ever. And I swear her tits got even bigger! Of course, I wanted to hit that, but before I could even grace her with the famous Jacobs charm, she was asking about you." He downed the remains of his beer and shook his head. "I swear, this whole broken-hearted-puppy-dog shit gets you more pussy than ever. Pisses me off."

I couldn't help but laugh at his analogy, as I filled an order for a nearby customer. The regulars had grown used to CJ and his mouth. And if they hadn't, they soon would. He was a permanent fixture at Dive and even filled in on occasion, though he sucked at making drinks.

"Don't blame me, CJ. Blame these clueless chicks you keep running behind. I don't ask for their sympathy or their charity."

"Yeah, but you sure don't hesitate to take it," he snorted, just as I placed an ice-cold beer in front of him. "Admit it, the whole Lonely Boy shit is all an act to get easy ass. It is, isn't it?"

"Lonely Boy?" I asked with a raised eyebrow.

"Oh yeah," CJ replied, embarrassed. "The girl I've been banging has some obsession with Gossip Girl. She makes me watch that shit with her to get her in the mood. Fucking irritating at first but it's a pretty cool show. The chicks are hot as hell, and Chuck Bass is one cool motherfucker. I might start wearing bowties."

I couldn't do more than shake my head. Yeah, Craig was family but he had about as much sense as a houseplant.

"The things we do to get laid."

"The power of the pussy," he nodded in agreement. I couldn't argue with him there.

CHAPTER FIVE

Kami

My earliest memory was at the age of two. Experts may argue that it's impossible to have memories at that tender age. But some things you just can't forget, no matter how bad you want to rip them from your memory. And I remember…everything.

I remembered the tiny apartment with the sand colored rug and the bare, off-white walls, barren of any mementos of family vacations or milestones. And I remembered my father shoving my mother's head through one of those off-white walls, leaving a large, gaping hole.

I was sitting on the floor, looking up at the two of them as he tried his hardest to beat her until she was unrecognizable. I don't remember crying though. I never remembered crying. I should have cried for my mother. I think any normal child would have at the sight of their mother's agony. She cried all the time. It seemed like that's all I remember her doing when I was younger.

That memory was revealed in kindergarten, when I was about six years old. Most girls drew pictures of flowers and hearts. I drew pictures of terrifying monsters that preyed on women. There were no flowers and hearts in my world. I didn't even know they existed. And I told stories... elaborate tales of bloodthirsty beasts that brutalized my mother and me every night. About how we would cower in my room, trying to stay as quiet as possible, in hopes that he wouldn't find us.

But he always did. My stories never had happy endings.

My teachers called me a liar. They would place me in timeout and revoke playtime privileges. I didn't cry then either. I just sat in the miniature red plastic chair and tried to savor every second away from home. Even though the kids picked on me and called me weird and poor, and my teachers had deemed me a problem child, I was safe. No one wanted to hurt me there. I wasn't afraid. My mother wasn't crying in the corner, shielding my body with hers. There were no monsters there.

252

I counted the tiny paper stars in the glass jar every night. I had been doing it for years. I had to. I had to count them all. 252. A star for every fear. Most of them were repeats but I wrote them down anyway. Just acknowledging my neurosis was enough for the time being. It was enough to get by.

I took out a skinny strip of pastel colored paper and scribbled a single word on it before my fingers worked it into a tiny star no larger than a button. Then I slipped it into the jar.

253. This one wasn't a repeat.

"What are you doing?" Dom asked, suddenly in my doorway, startling me. I really wished I could close it, but I…couldn't.

I answered with a weak smile as I stuck lucky number 253 in the jar. It had been a while since I had added any new additions.

Dominic frowned, not completely satisfied with my lack of an answer. He invited himself all the way into the semi-sanctuary of my bedroom and flopped down on my bed, rattling the glass jar of tiny origami stars. "Did you just add one?"

I shrugged sheepishly and let out a breath. "Yeah. So? No big deal."

His expression softening, Dom pulled my body close to his, draping an arm around my shoulders. "Hey, you wanna talk about it? I know you haven't added in a while."

I shook my head against the warmth of his sculpted chest. He was the only man I would ever let hold me like this. This was the one sliver of affection that I found acceptable. It was the closest I would ever come to true intimacy, though we weren't intimate in the sexual sense. We could never cross that line; I couldn't lose the only man I ever loved.

"There's nothing to talk about. Really. It's nothing." At least my head was saying that. Every other part of me screamed otherwise.

Dom sat up and grasped my shoulders, pulling my body away from his to assess my face. Even my blank expression couldn't elude his bullshit meter. He was such an experienced bullshit artist himself; he could spot a load of crap a mile away.

"It's not *nothing*. And you do need to talk about it. I told you about this, Kam. It was part of our deal. You go to therapy and be completely honest with me, and I wouldn't give you shit for your condition."

I shrugged out of his hold, giving him a stern glare. "No. That was *your* deal. I told you—I'm fine. And therapy isn't working. I'm not going back." I grabbed the jar of stars still on my bed and placed it in its designated spot on my windowsill. "And I don't have a condition, Dom. Yeah, I have issues, but we all do. Yourself included. I'm surviving the best way I know how, just like you are."

My oldest friend, the man that had become closer than a brother to me, let out an irritated breath at the mention of his own demons. Demons that still haunted him in every aspect of his life. "This isn't about me. Yeah, my life is pretty fucked up, but I'm functional. You're barely hanging on, babe. And I'm not saying all this shit to get under your skin. I want you to get better."

"What if I can't get better?" I snapped, whirling around to face him. "This isn't some illness I can just take medicine to get rid of, Dom. You of all people should know that. This. Is. Me. My situation isn't fucked up. *I'm* fucked up. Completely, irrevocably, fucked up to my core."

Dom was already on his feet and enveloping my frame with his. "Stop. Just stop it, Kam," he whispered into my hair. "The real you isn't fucked up. We just gotta dig deeper, babe. Just keep trying to push aside the bullshit and reveal the real you, ok? Your fears are not you. Do you hear me? They don't define who you are."

"But this *is* who I am," I murmured, trying to stifle my sudden surge of emotion. "It's been me for 23 years. I'm tired, Dom. So fucking tired."

I forced myself to take a cleansing breath then tucked away the conversation and all its revelations. Compartmentalizing. It had been the only way I had survived the first six years of my life. And the only thing that kept me from wasting away in a padded cell after that.

Dominic squeezed me tighter, knowing that it was exactly what I needed. He was holding me together. Hanging on to all the complex pieces that had somehow created the illusion of a well-adjusted, twenty-three year old woman. But he knew the truth. He knew the pain that festered inside of me. He knew about the memories that haunted me every time I closed my eyes. Dominic was probably the only person on Earth that understood how wholly my demons had plagued my life, because he lived with similar demons. And he loved me anyway. Our pasts, our pains, had brought us together. They were the glue in our relationship.

To be completely honest, I felt like an asshole being so needy and pathetic compared to Dom. If anyone had an excuse to break, it was him. Dominic Trevino was both the strongest, and most tortured, person I knew. We met nearly five years ago though it felt like we had known each other our entire lives. Our past pains were our solidarity; our individual hells had bonded us for life.

The day Dom found me in the parking lot of our campus counselor's office, I was a shivering, blubbering mess. I was hell-bent on making it on my own. I had run away from any and every thing I knew and traveled across the country in search of freedom from my past. I just didn't expect for my journey to leave me more afraid and unstable than ever.

Dom was attending a group therapy session for abuse survivors. I was still trying to conjure up the courage to enter the building. He took one look at me and knew exactly what to do. Tentatively, he took my hand and led me inside. He didn't say a word. He didn't even ask me my name. He just sat with me as I listened. When it was Dom's turn to share with the group, he passed, as did I. And when it was over, he led me back outside, his hand in mine. I don't know why I let him touch me. That was something I hadn't allowed anybody. But something about Dom put me at ease. As if we were kindred. I recognized something in his touch that was familiar.

He was damaged. Even more so than I was.

Dominic stroked my hair and squeezed me to him. Even after all these years, he was still holding me together. "I'm tired too, babe," he murmured, as he kissed my forehead. "But we have to keep going. We can't let them win. If we let them control us now after we've come so far, what else would we have left?"

I pulled away from his embrace, looking up into greenish-brown eyes shrouded in long, black lashes. "We'll have each other. We'll always have each other."

He smiled down at me, yet failed to hide the turmoil he dealt with on a daily basis. It amazed me that he even got out of bed each morning, let alone maintained a somewhat healthy lifestyle. Dominic Trevino was undoubtedly more tormented than me, yet somehow he found a way to live through it. I envied him, I loved him, and I wanted him to have the happily-ever-after he deserved. That we all deserved.

"Come on, I want to take you out to dinner, so you can tell me all about your first day at work," he said, brushing a stray lock of hair behind my ear.

I shrugged, but let him lead me out of my bedroom. "Nothing worth going to dinner over but, hey, a girl's gotta eat. Hmmm, I'm feeling a celebratory lobster is in order," I winked.

Dom snorted, his hand still in mine, before spinning around to face me. "Ok, I'll make you a deal. You'll get your lobster if you tell me what you wrote on that strip of paper. You know it's good for you to talk about your fears, Kam. You have to tell someone. It's been months since you've added one, and I need to know you're ok."

I was shaking my head before he had completed the last word of his proposal. "I can't tell you that, Dom. Maybe one day, but not now."

His hands were grasping my shoulders with enough pressure to get my attention, and indicate he was serious. "You can, Kam. You can but you won't. There's a difference. Saying it out loud doesn't bring it to life. It doesn't power the fear. It takes it away. It shows that you are in control."

"Does it?" I asked, a frown easing itself between my brows. "Because every time I've let my guard down, it has backfired in my face in the worst possible way. By tucking it away, by listing everything in this life that terrifies the shit out of me, I am releasing it. I need this, Dom. It's the only thing that is keeping me sane." A smirk played at my lips as I shrugged under his grip. "Well, somewhat sane."

Dominic dropped his hands and let them slide down to my wrists. "Just promise me one day. Promise you'll let me in. I need to know that you aren't crumbling inside."

"My, my…notorious playboy, Dominic Trevino has a heart of gold," I smiled, hoping to lighten the mood.

Humor was my fallback when things got too heavy, and they often did with us. To the outside world, we were normal, carefree, fun-loving, young adults. But the truth was, we were anything but. We were broken, battered and bleeding. We had depended on each other for so long that we didn't know how to survive without the other. Dom had become an appendage to me. He was just as vital to my life as my arm or leg. I not only needed him to keep moving forward, I needed him to keep the crippling anxiety from squeezing the breath from my lungs every single damn day. Dominic was my savior.

He narrowed his eyes and shook his head, totally seeing through my ploy to change the subject. But he would let it go. For now. He always did.

"Ok, Fatty, let's get you fed." He pinched the sliver of exposed skin where my jeans hugged my hipbones. I rolled my eyes. If it were up to him, I'd be a good 15 pounds heavier. I still hadn't put on the weight I had dropped after the last incident.

"I really wish you'd talk to me," he said quietly. "I don't like this, Kam. I don't want you suffering in silence." A quick flash of hurt played on his features. But that was all he would give me. He was just as emotionally blocked as I was.

"I know you want me to open up. And I will. One day." I tugged at a lock of hair nervously, trying to pull the words from my lips. "It's just… It was just a name, Dom."

Before I could explain, his eyes had widened with alarm, and he was pulling me closer to his body protectively. "What happened? Did he find you? Has he made contact? Tell me what happened, Kam."

I shook my head furiously, hoping to dispel his alarm. "No, nothing like that. A new name." I tried to give him the most confident smile I owned, which was pretty damn pathetic to his trained eye. "It's not what you think. And it's not really the person I fear. It's me. It's my reaction to him. It's the pure adrenaline that courses through my veins whenever we're near. It's the excitement I feel when he says my name. It's the way his eyes penetrate the front I put on for the world to see me for what I am. And I hate it. It scares the shit out of me because I like it too."

I would have sworn that a family of flies could have camped out in Dom's mouth that hung ajar for a good 30 seconds after my confession.

"You met a *guy*? And you're afraid of him?"

"No," I said shaking my head. "I'm afraid because, whenever he's around, I'm not scared anymore. I feel… safe. Like being near him is the most natural thing in the world."

Dominic shook his head as if he couldn't believe what he was hearing. I couldn't blame him. I couldn't believe I was actually saying the words aloud.

"And I assume you won't be sharing the name of this

mystery man that is so damn scary, yet somehow so damn appealing? I'll even up the ante with champagne," he winked.

I grinned at my little secret and shook my head. I wasn't ready to say. Not because I was afraid to tell him in fear of judgment. And not because I thought he'd disapprove. But if what Dom said was true about revealing my fears—if saying it out loud somehow made this feeling less real, then I don't think I could ever be ready.

For the first time in twenty-three years, I felt *something.* Something other than trepidation when a man touched me. Something more than the sick feeling in the pit of my stomach when I had to shatter another heart because I couldn't let anyone in. Something so much more than the emptiness that filled my chest when I thought about the normal, happy life that I would never have.

Blaine was my *more*.

CHAPTER SIX

Kami

After spending another day shift with Blaine, I was ready to brave the Friday night crowd at Dive. I wasn't worried; bartending was one of the few things that didn't make me nervous. It was fast-paced, lively, and you could be whoever you wanted to be. I could flirt and laugh without reservation. I could be a total bitch if a patron got too ass-grabby. I could exude complete confidence and self-assurance. I could be fearless.

Tonight, the girls of AngelDust would be in attendance for their live audition. If anything, I was more nervous for them. Sure, they were amazingly talented, but after seeing who they would be up against, my stomach clenched and roiled into a dozen tiny knots.

All that was erased the moment I saw his face, his mouth rolling his studded tongue in concentration as he filled an order. I tried to focus on filling the beer mug in my hand without collecting too much foam, yet every few seconds, my gaze swept to him. And every glance ignited a jolt in me, making that damn Asian flush creep onto my cheeks.

"What's that look for?" Blaine asked, suddenly beside me. Oddly, the nearness of him didn't make me feel uncomfortable. I only felt…heat.

I finished up my order of beers and slid them to the customers with a smile. "What look?" I asked innocently, simultaneously taking another order while he worked on filling a tray of shots beside me.

"The look that says you're secretly undressing me with your eyes," he answered without hesitance.

My mouth was hanging open, unable to formulate even a mutter of defense, when a familiar squeal saved me from further awkwardness.

"Kam! Holy shit, can you believe the size of this crowd?" Angel yelled over the roar of bar chatter. She leaned over the bar, her cleavage nearly spilling over into a pitcher of beer, and gave me a kiss on the cheek. I greeted the other girls with a wave before rushing to take the next order.

"So, Blaine, how's my girl working out here?" I heard her say as soon as I turned towards a group of girls who were blatantly checking out Blaine's backside.

"Oh my God, is that Blaine Jacobs? When did he get back?"

"I'm not sure but–Wow–he's even hotter! Looks like getting rid of that dead weight worked out for him because, DAMN!"

"I know! Can you believe what that bitch did to him? I'm not complaining because that means he's back on the

market!"

"Did you hear what he did to that guy? I heard they released him from prison early for good behavior."

"I don't care. I want him. Look at those arms. I can't wait to feel them wrapped around my naked body."

"Hell no, bitch, I saw him first. Mark my words, Blaine will be between my legs by the end of the night!"

"Can I help you?" I asked with more attitude than absolutely necessary. I couldn't help it; the way they were talking about Blaine had my blood boiling and my bitch-slap hand twitching.

The girls, who had to be in their early twenties, looked at me with stunned expressions. I tried to plaster on a tight smile to ease the tension, but that didn't make me feel any better. Was I…jealous? No. Of course not. I'd never been jealous a day in my life. I'd never even cared enough about a guy to *be* jealous. Yet, for some reason, I wanted nothing more than to reach across that bar and snatch those gossipy bitches bald-headed.

And what dead weight were they talking about? And prison? I knew it was quite possible that Blaine had a dark side. Yeah, he was covered in tattoos and had a particular… I don't know…swagger that spoke of his seamless confidence. Yet, he didn't seem cocky or douchey. Blaine just seemed completely at home in his ink-adorned skin.

The boldest of the flock spoke up first. "Oh, I love your earrings." (She was lying.) "Do you think you could do us a huge favor and get that guy to serve us instead? We're old friends from high school, and I know he'd love to catch up with us," she said with a sickly sweet smile that nauseated me. I returned the sentiment with one of my own before spinning around and marching across the bar.

As if he could somehow feel my presence, Blaine turned and smiled at me while ringing up a patron's order. However, it quickly faded when he eyed my irritated expression. "What's wrong?"

I shook off the annoyance and grinned. "Nothing at all. Some friends of yours are requesting you down there," I said with a nod towards the group of fan-girls.

Blaine followed my gaze and I could have sworn there was a trace of a frown on his lips when his eyes fell on the pack of hyenas. Or maybe that's just what I wanted to see. He turned back to me and nodded. "Thanks. I got this."

I followed his fluid movement towards them and could visibly see the girls light up as he got closer. Even over the roar of the crowd, I could hear their squeals and laughter, especially when he brushed his sexy mussed hair from his eyes with a tattooed hand.

"I never thought I'd see the day that Kami Duvall would get jealous over a guy," Angel remarked just loud enough for me to hear. I returned my attention to the line of waiting customers and took an order hoping that my indifference would lead her off the scent of my true feelings. I didn't want her to see just how much Blaine, or any guy for that matter, affected me. And I damn sure didn't need to witness Blaine flirting with a group of cock-hungry bar sluts.

"Who's jealous?" a deep masculine voice asked, adding fuel to Angel's accusatory fire. I turned just in time to see Dominic plant a kiss on her cheek. Even though I was annoyed that Angel was on to me, I couldn't help but beam at the sight of my dearest friend.

"Dom! You came!" I leaned across the bar to greet him so he could press his lips against mine. The greeting may have been oddly intimate to some, but he and I had always been touchy. Affection amongst the three of us was something that most didn't understand, but it was simple; it was the only show of love that we found acceptable. Outsiders didn't understand because they were just that—outsiders.

"Of course, I couldn't miss supporting my girls on their big day," he beamed, his bright white teeth contrasting brilliantly with his caramel skin. Only when his eyes diverted to my right did his smile fade. I looked to see Blaine beside me, damn near scowling at Dom.

"Hey Dom, this is Blaine. He's one of the bartenders here at Dive." I waved a hand between the two of them. "Blaine, this is Dominic Trevino."

"The most awesome guy she's ever had the pleasure to know, love and live with," Dom added playfully, shooting me a wink. Blaine nodded politely then busied himself with an order without another word. From what I knew of Blaine, which wasn't much, it seemed out of character. He'd always been so warm and friendly towards everyone. Before I could really feel the arctic temperature of his mood, boisterous laughter approached us, followed by a barrage of cheers.

"Well, well, well, if it isn't Angel Cassidy and her cute, little pussycats," Ryan Winn sneered, flanked by his band mates.

Ryan was the lead singer for The Takers, the band that Angel used to play for before she left and started AngelDust two years ago. It was a nasty split, resulting in him sparking up nasty rumors about Angel. To make matters worse, Ryan had been vying for my attention since I got to Charlotte. I knew it was to get under Angel's skin, which just made me hate him more.

"And if it isn't Ryan Winn and his load of unswallowed cum-shots," she shot back. Even I had to giggle at that one. Ryan acted like he didn't even hear it.

"Hey, can we get some service over here?" Ryan shouted loud enough to earn a murderous glare from Dom. I could see Angel and the other girls coaxing him to let it go. The bulging vein in his neck was about to explode.

I could feel Ryan fix his gaze on me even though I was down the bar helping customers. The prick had always made me uncomfortable. I knew he was just a regular, run-of-the-mill douchebag but I didn't like how grabby and crude he could be. It wasn't even funny when he did it. It just made him look like a world-class asshole, and not the sexy kind of asshole either.

I turned to reluctantly help them when Blaine intercepted me with an outstretched hand. "Hey guys, I'm Blaine. Glad y'all could play for us tonight. What can I get ya?"

Blaine served the band their beers with a slight polite smile though I could tell he was annoyed with their comments about Dive's female patrons. When Ryan made a crass remark about my ass when I bent down, I thought I saw Blaine visibly flinch, then ball his fists. I didn't even want to think about Dom's reaction. Angel and the girls had to take him to a table out of earshot to calm him down. I was thankful; I really didn't need my best friend and roommate getting kicked out of the bar I work at for fighting.

An hour later, CJ took the stage and grabbed the microphone. After greeting the crowd like only he could (I'm pretty sure at least three F-bombs were dropped), he announced the first band taking the stage.

Crux was a well-known band in Charlotte, known for their infusion of classical and rock music. They were amazing and hard to beat, but they lacked Angel's sultry stage presence. After playing a few songs, CJ took the stage again.

"Give it up one more time for Crux! What did y'all think? Let me fucking hear ya!" The crowd clapped and cheered while CJ successfully pumped them up for the next act. I had to give it to him; he was pretty entertaining to watch. "Ok, simmer down, y'all. We got more for ya. Do you want more? Do ya? Then put your fucking hands together for The Takers!"

I could tell that most of the crowd had heard of them by the way they screamed when the guys took the stage. Ryan Winn was the quintessential hot rocker front man. Hard body, great hair, and eyes that seemed to melt the panties off every woman his gaze touched. After he roused the crowd further, The Takers launched into one of their known hits, a fast paced song with a catchy melody. Ryan owned the stage, moving around, interacting with the other band mates, and flirting with anything in a skirt. His act was undeniably sexual and enticing, and I even found myself entranced by him for a second. That was, until Blaine sidled up behind me.

"They're good, huh?" he murmured in my ear. I felt his lip brush my earlobe, causing my eyes to close for a moment. Luckily, the bar patrons were busy watching the act and we were left forgotten for the moment.

"Yeah," I nodded. I could feel the heat flooding from his body, could smell his signature scent of mint and a spice that I couldn't quite pinpoint. I didn't know what it was, but I liked it. So much that I wanted it all over me.

"Yeah, they are," he remarked, his mouth still close to me. I found myself easing toward him. I didn't even know what we were talking about.

"Mmmm hmmm…"

I wasn't sure how long we stood there in lust-drenched silence before a customer demanded our attention, but I knew one thing for certain: Whatever it was between Blaine and me, it wasn't just harmless flirting. At least for me it wasn't. I wanted him. Badly. And wanting him the way I did would only end in tragedy for us. The realization made me want to rip out my traitorous heart and kick it across the floor.

"Alright, y'all, give it up for The Takers!" CJ was bellowing into the microphone as the band exited the stage. I had zoned out during their entire performance.

"Ok, this next act is the hottest, sexiest fucking band I have ever seen. Now, girls in the front, you might want to back up and let the fellas through because—I shit you not—you guys are gonna want a front row viewing of this. Give it up, Dive, for AngelDust!"

The first thing I noticed was that Angel had changed into what I could only describe as a black, strapless leotard. She paired it with fishnet stockings and hot pink 6-inch heels to match her pink extensions and glammed-out guitar. She looked flawless, and the guys of Dive more than agreed, judging by the raucous cheers.

Angel didn't even seem fazed by being on stage nearly naked. She was completely calm as she faced the crowd, her tiny fist in the air, as she began the countdown into the first song. It was a popular choice and one of my favorites, speaking of a crush that can't quite work up the nerve to come clean to the object of his desire. She enticed the crowd, rolling her hips to the beat and locking eyes with every guy and girl. She knew when to bellow out the notes and when to dip into a feather-light, breathy tone that probably had every guy adjusting themselves.

I looked over at Blaine, who appeared to be just as enraptured by Angel's charms. A tiny fragment of my heart cracked. I could never be that bold and brave. I could never be as free and confident as Angel. He'd never look at me while I performed. No one got turned on by a timid field mouse. Angel was a lioness. She ate chicks like me for breakfast. No pun intended, though she would say otherwise.

By the time AngelDust moved on to their next selection, a song about slutty chicks that ruin good guys, the crowd was eating out of the palm of Angel's petite hand, and no one was requesting drinks. That's when I realized just how enthusiastically I was singing along behind the bar.

"Enjoying yourself?" Blaine asked with an amused grin. He leaned against the bar comfortably like he had been watching me intently for a while.

I stilled my little dance moves and snapped my mouth shut. "Uh, yeah. Angel is amazing. AngelDust is one the best bands out right now," I beamed proudly.

"Well, don't stop now. I was enjoying the show."

"There's a live concert going on right in front of you," I said waving towards the stage.

"Yeah, they're great," he nodded. "But I'd rather watch you."

I couldn't stifle the warmth that flooded my belly at his confession. And I didn't want to. Blaine pushed away from the bar and closed the distance between us. Again his lips were at my ear, sending the delightful shivers of his breath down my neck.

"Can I ask you something, Kami?" Even with the pounding drumbeats and Angel's voice flooding the speakers, all I could hear was him. His voice was smooth, level and just above a whisper. Blaine didn't have to yell over the noise. He had my full, undivided attention. And he knew it too; his question didn't even warrant an answer.

"That guy that you kissed earlier…is that your boy-friend?"

I turned my head to assess his face, but he was too close. So close that his lips brushed against my forehead when he stood up straight. I took a step back, though everything inside me wanted to melt into him.

"Who, Dom? No, of course not," I said with more vehemence than necessary. I knew I sounded too eager to set the record straight, but the cat was already out the bag.

"But you live together."

"Yeah, and I live with Angel too. Dom is my best friend."

Blaine looked unconvinced, but being so close to him, feeling like we were alone on our own little island off the coast of Dive, I couldn't find the words to explain further.

"You kiss all your friends like that?" A small, playful

smile tugged at the corner of his mouth.

"Some of them," I jibed as flirtatiously as I could. I was horrible at flirting in one-on-one situations like these. I was awkward and nervous, and my palms sweated profusely. But in that moment with Blaine, with AngelDust in the background creating our very own soundtrack, everything just seemed right. Natural and seamless.

He smiled, his mouth slightly ajar, and I could see him rolling the metal in his tongue. "Can I be your friend?"

God, how I wanted that. I wanted it more than I ever wanted anything or anyone before.

"Now what do we have here?" a southern drawl interjected, causing me to swiftly move away from Blaine. He frowned at my retreat, then cut his cousin an annoyed glare.

"What do you want, CJ?" Blaine barked at him.

CJ raised his palms in defense. "Easy, B, I just need a beer. Didn't mean to intrude."

"You're fine, CJ," I found myself saying, pulling a beer from the cooler and popping the top. "There was nothing to intrude on," I said with an assured smile.

Just like that, my mask had fallen right back into place where it should have been the entire night. Yet, anytime Blaine was near, it slipped off easily. I didn't feel the need to hide or protect myself. Deep down, there was an impulse that wanted to reveal the real me. I was tired of hiding. I wanted Blaine to be the one to make it better. To make it ok to be me. And that scared the hell out of me.

I refused to look at Blaine, but I could feel his eyes burning into me. Whatever was going on between us had to stop. I knew it from the first time I saw him. Blaine forced me to let my guard down. I couldn't afford for that to happen. My sanity depended on it.

CJ looked between the two of us before shrugging off the awkwardness that hung between us like stale air. "Alright then. In that case, Blaine," he said, pointing his beer bottle towards his cousin, "you won't believe who showed up tonight. Wendy-fucking-Braxton! I told you she wanted you! I told her to stick around 'til after the show. And, dude…she looks good enough to eat. Well, in your case, go in for seconds."

I felt the bottom of my stomach tighten and drop as I tried to busy myself with washing tumblers and focusing on the music pouring from the speakers. I felt sick, like I would lose my lunch at any moment. I couldn't look at him; I wouldn't do that to myself. I knew I had no right whatsoever to feel anything but indifference about the situation. Yet, my blasé demeanor had abandoned me, leaving my emotions raw and vulnerable.

I told myself that this was for the best. This was exactly what I wanted, what I needed. No matter what my body felt, my head knew that I could never give myself to Blaine. And my heart? It never got a say. It was buried under years of mistrust and apprehension. It had been broken far beyond repair before it ever got the chance to open itself enough to love. While I felt affection for Dominic and Angel, I would never know what it felt like to be truly, deeply in love. And I was ok with that realization. At least that's what I told myself as my chest filled with sorrow and my heart did the impossible.

It broke even more.

CHAPTER SEVEN

Blaine

Even over the hellacious cheers, I could hear my heart hammering inside my chest, creating its own rhythm, complete with booming bass lines. I should have said something—done something—to make Kami see that I wasn't interested in Wendy or anyone else for that matter. I had no idea why I needed her to understand this but now more than ever, I wished that CJ would have just kept his damn mouth shut.

I couldn't quite read her, but I knew Kami had heard his dumbass comment. It had been hours and she still wouldn't look at me. I really couldn't blame her. I didn't deserve those green eyes. I was a selfish bastard for wanting them sweeping over me, just a touch of a smile playing on her pouty lips. She tried to hide what she really felt, but those eyes said it all. It hinted at the secrets she kept locked away, tempting my curiosity. I couldn't help myself; I needed to unveil her mystery. I needed to know Kami, and dammit, she needed to know me too. She just didn't know it yet.

"Dude, you ready to go yet?" CJ asked, appearing in the doorway of the back office as I counted the cash drawer after closing. He had a chick under each arm, each one tipsy, half-dressed and, unbeknownst to him, looking at me like I was a Porterhouse steak. I diverted my attention back to the money in front of me. I'd rather lick the bar's toilet seat. It'd probably be much cleaner than touching any of the girls CJ usually pulled.

"What'd I tell you about bringing chicks back here, man?" I snapped at him as I prepared the night's deposit. "I don't wanna hear shit when Mick strangles you."

CJ shrugged, but quickly began to retreat. He was well aware of his dad's fiery temper. It ran in the family. "Fine. But we're waiting out here for you. Hurry up; I'm fucking starving. Oh, and Wendy is out there too."

ShitDamnFuck.

I knew when I reentered the bar that the atmosphere had shifted. I could feel it. Kami was wiping down the sink area, wearing the same impassive guise she had donned since CJ alluded to some of my past dealings with Wendy. Still, the fact that she was affected, even if it made me look like bed-hopping player, made me feel good. I knew she cared. And if she cared enough to get pissed that Wendy was sitting at the bar, smiling while her nipples were practically winking at me, maybe she cared enough to give me the time of day. Maybe she could let me in, so I could see what all she hid behind those green eyes.

"Hey there, stranger," Wendy piped up. Kami's head

snapped to me in surprise. I thought I saw just the tiniest suggestion of a smile before her brow furrowed and she turned back to her task.

No. I couldn't have that. I wouldn't accept her attempt at brushing me off, whether Wendy was sitting three feet away or not.

I strode up to her, turned and leaned back against the bar so she would have no choice but to look at me. "Hey Kami, a bunch of us usually go out for breakfast on the weekends after closing. I want you to come with us."

She was already shaking her head before I even got my question out. "Thanks, but no. I'll have to pass. Maybe some other time."

Her mouth said the words, but her face was regretful. Like maybe she wanted to go. Maybe she wanted to be near me just as bad as I needed to be near her.

I took a step closer, letting my arm brush against hers. "Are you sure that's what you want?" I asked, catching her gaze and pinning it with my own. She couldn't look away; I wouldn't let her.

I could hear the breath catch in her throat as long moments ticked by without either of us saying a word. There was nothing left to say. The words were evident in every heated breath we took, close enough for our scents to mingle, creating our very own fragrance. Kami wanted me, and I'd be damned if I let her deny that fact.

"Why do you do that?" she scowled, her eyes narrowing into tiny slits. She took a step back, breaking the contact that bound us just seconds before.

"Do what?"

"Look at me like that. Like you're looking through me.

It's...unnerving."

I let my mouth curl up on one corner and again closed the distance between us. Something inside me did a back-flip when she didn't move away.

"I'm not looking through you, Kami," I said only for her ears. I didn't need an audience; I just needed her to really *hear* me. "I'm looking into you. I'm standing here, wondering how the hell a girl so beautiful could hold so much sadness in her gorgeous green eyes. And I'm asking myself why I want—no—why I *need* to know what's made her so sad. And what I can do to take away every ounce of that sadness. I need to know what it will take for you to let me in, so I can do just that."

Her lips parted just as her eyes grew with shock. Yet, I still continued to stare into those emerald pools. I was ready to drown in them at that point. Anything to keep her here with me.

Her throat moved as if she was swallowing a knot. "You don't know what you're talking about," she whispered.

"No? Then tell me I'm wrong. Tell me that this," I motioned between us, "is imaginary. And that no matter how hard you try to deny and fight it, you don't feel it too. Tell me that it's just me feeling this pull, and I'll leave you alone."

Kami stepped in closer, if that was possible, and met my determined gaze with a steely one of her own. "You're wrong, Blaine. I don't feel a damn thing. I never do."

She eased back and spun on her heel, retreating into the back room. I was still standing behind the bar, shell-shocked and speechless when she reappeared with her things. She made her way over to her friends who had waited for her at one of the tables, still celebrating their newly acquired weekly gig at Dive.

She never even looked back as she slid through those double doors. But I had seen this before. I had experienced her reaction when she was backed into a corner by truth's unrelenting glare. Kami was running. But I'd be damned if I let her get away.

CHAPTER EIGHT

Kami

I didn't speak until I was 5. It wasn't that I didn't know how, I was just afraid of what my words would trigger. My mother was often slapped and punched in the face whenever she spoke. Even before I even knew what her words meant, I knew the consequences of speaking. I didn't want to meet the same fate, though I knew it was inevitable. Silence wouldn't be able to spare me for much longer.

My father wasn't stupid. He knew that bruises fueled questions, and questions warranted explanations. So as much as he hated me, as much as my very existence disgusted him, he usually refrained from leaving physical scars. Instead, he chose to etch them into my young, fragile psyche. Those scars would never heal. They followed me like a bad omen, marring every relationship I had attempted since. Those scars were the security blanket that crippled my emotional growth, leaving me lost, alone, and tragically afraid. I clung to them, letting the scar tissue form a wall around my heart. They held the pain inside, so it wouldn't completely devour me.

There was a coat closet he liked. I remember that closet because it never held any garments. The only thing I ever saw strung up in it was my mother, her hands bound by rope above her head, naked and hysterical, as he had his way with her. I remember how he would laugh at her tears, how he found her weakness arousing. The things he did to her, his young daughter just feet away, were unimaginable. Except to me. I had the displeasure of witnessing every unspeakable act, bound by my own terror and unable to run and hide. That was what it felt like to be frozen with fear. How it gripped every muscle and joint, stripping all mobility and forcing you to live through your worst nightmares with eyes wide open. I knew that feeling well. I lived with it every single damn day as a child.

Sometimes when he was feeling playful, he would pour a bucket of ice water over her naked frame as she struggled to get free from her restraints. Then he'd grab a curling iron, the toaster, anything that could be plugged into an electrical socket, and threaten to throw it at her feet while she stood in a puddle. He'd bring the electrical device as close as he could to her, getting off on her blood-curdling screams, laughing at her wide, horrified eyes.

Seeing her so broken down and pleading for her life revealed something to me. It showed me what true desperation looked like.

My introduction to the closet fortunately was more merciful, though not by much. On nights when he was overcome with drugs, alcohol, and his own sickening thirst for our tears, he would lock me in that dark closet. The light switch was on the other side of the door where I could hear my mother's cries, pleading for him to let me out. Hearing her child wail in the dark, my little fists pounding the door until they were raw and bruised, tore her in two. But part of me was relieved. He would have his fun with me, my tiny whimpers sating his sickening need until his chemical high plummeted him into a coma-like sleep. She would be safe for the night.

"Ok, spill it. And don't say there isn't shit to spill."

I rolled over Saturday morning to both Angel and Dom lying on my bed, wearing their nosey-as-hell, shit-eating grins. I was pretty sure why, but I decided to feign ignorance anyway. Damn, I wish I could lock my bedroom door. It was way too early to submit to an interrogation.

"What are you talking about?" I asked with a yawn.

Angel rolled her eyes before scooting me over and folding herself around my body. Dom was close behind her, hopping over our bodies and easing down on my other side. He was snatching one of my pillows before I could protest.

"You know exactly what I'm talking about, Kam. Spill the deets about the bartender, and don't leave out a single morsel. And if you tell us there's nothing going on, Dom and I will hold you down and tickle you until you pee. We will piss the truth out of you one way or another."

"Yeah, Kam," Dom added. "What's up with you two? The sexual tension was stinkin' up the place like a fog machine. Start talking."

I rolled my eyes and sighed, pulling my comforter over my head. "Not you too, Dom. I thought we had an understanding? You don't see me questioning you about every walking vag you talk to."

"That's different," Angel interjected. "He doesn't know or care about any of those skanks enough to answer any questions."

I felt Dom shrug beside me. "True story."

"Besides," Angel continued, "this is a first for you. For all of us, really. You like him, Kam. *Like him*-like him. This is a pretty big fucking deal!"

I pulled the covers down from over my head and frowned at both of them. "Who said I liked him? I don't even know the guy."

"Ah, but you want to know him. And that's the part that counts." Angel wrapped her slender arm around my waist and rested her head on my shoulder. "Come on, just throw us a bone. Just a teeny tiny bone, and we'll leave you alone."

I felt my face heating under their expectant stares and could feel my annoyance meter rising. "Why do you two even care? It's not like I haven't ever been with a guy before. Shit, I just got out of a pseudo relationship like a month ago."

Angel let out an exasperated sigh. "But you know that shit wasn't real, Kam. Stop dickin' around, and tell us the truth. Do you like this guy or not? And remember, I know when you're lying to me. I have a bullshit-ometer. My nipples twitch whenever someone lies."

Dominic and I locked eyes before bursting with uncontrollable laughter. Big, ugly guffaws that had us sprouting tears and snorting.

"What?" Angel trilled. "I'm serious! They seriously do twitch!" And with that, she raised her camisole and flashed us her C-cups, causing us to laugh even harder.

"Ewww, get those things off me! And that is the biggest crock of shit I have ever heard, and you know it!" I squeaked just as she pinched my arm. "Ow! Don't be mad because it's true!"

Our spoiled little brat scrambled to her feet and poked out her bottom lip, glaring down at Dom and me with contempt. It only fueled our hysterics.

"Fine! I can see my special services aren't needed." And with that, she stomped off to her room.

"Dude, something is seriously wrong with her," I remarked as soon as we came down from our amused high.

"I know," he said shaking his head. Silence stretched between us before Dom wrapped an arm around me, easing my head onto his bare chest. "You would tell me, right? If you needed someone to talk to… you'd come to me, right?"

"Of course, Dom. You know I would."

More silence blanketed the words we both needed to say but couldn't—wouldn't—because they'd become more real. We had lived through unspeakable things, had defeated most of our demons the best way we knew how, yet we were both cowards when it came to facing the unknown. Our emotions, our wants, our desires… we ran from them. Our hearts had been banished to a strange land that we seldom visited. It was easier this way. It made dealing with who we were more tolerable. It remedied the fear enough to get through each day.

With a chaste kiss on my cheek, Dominic slipped his arm from under my head and climbed out of bed. I understood. It was his way of escaping the subject, though he truly wanted to be a good friend and push for more. Somehow, over the years, we had become kindred souls. And as hard as it was for me to open up, it was just as hard for him to digest those foreign feelings.

"It's ok, you know. It's ok if you care," he said just as he reached my bedroom door. "It won't make you weak or stupid. It doesn't mean he'll be like...*him*."

I nodded because it seemed like the right thing to do. But it didn't mean I agreed.

I settled into my new job, and my new life, over the next week, every day grasping a piece of normalcy and working to feel more content in my own skin. Working with Blaine had proven to be interesting, to say the least, but he had stowed the bulk of his intensity. It seemed as if my words had finally gotten through to him, and that was a good thing. It had to be, for both our sakes. I couldn't feel; feeling led to things that just weren't possible for us. And instead of dealing with the fallout, I thought it best to keep things pleasantly cordial, no matter how badly I craved for more.

"Hey," I smiled, stepping behind the bar and tying the

little black apron around my waist. Dive had just opened and was completely empty, aside from the day shift preparing for the lunch crowd.

Blaine turned from his task of refilling the soda dispenser and crooked a grin. I could only describe it as polite, and that fact tore me in two.

"Hey, Kami." His deep chocolate eyes narrowed. "You change your hair?"

I twirled a lock of my honey blonde-highlighted mane and shrugged. "Felt like I needed a change." I didn't have the guts to tell him that it was really an attempt at bribery by Angel. She knew I was a whore for spa days at the upscale salon she frequented, and used my weakness to try to get me to gush about my feelings for Blaine. It didn't fully work as she intended but I did throw her a bone: I told her I was attracted to him. It was harmless enough. Even a 90-year old deaf and blind woman would have a raging lady boner for him.

Blaine gave me the most genuine smile I had seen from him in days, and I swear I felt something in my chest swell. "I like it. Makes you look…devastatingly sexy."

I didn't try to stifle the blush that I could feel heating my cheeks. I embraced it. It was the first time I had felt anything other than regret in days. "Yeah?"

"Hell yeah," he said, closing the distance between us in three long strides.

And there it was again. The smell of mint and spice and pure male. The heat that seemed to roll off his body and enfold me like a mink blanket. Those intense brown eyes that made me forget my own name and had me imagining screaming out his.

Him. It was all him. Blaine somehow made me forget *me*. The *me* that wasn't allowed to feel all these beautiful, exciting things. The *me* that didn't believe in happy endings. The *me* that was unlovable, and in turn, could never, ever love.

"You were sexy before…unbelievably so. But the way the golden strands seem to meld with your green eyes, it just… wow. Makes it hard to look at anything or anyone else."

I sucked in a breath of air and let it out slowly through my mouth, closing my eyes in attempt to regain some sense of composure. "Blaine…" I couldn't say anymore. His name, occupying my tongue like his skin once did, was enough.

"I'm sorry," he quickly sputtered, breaking me from the sweet memories of tasting him. My eyes fluttered open to him looking sheepish, rubbing the back of his neck with a tattooed hand. Shit, even *that* was sexy.

"I think I should explain." He rolled the barbell in his mouth before flashing me a strained grin. "I have this habit of always saying how I feel, no matter how embarrassing it is. A long time ago, I didn't speak my mind. I didn't ask the right questions because I was afraid of the answers. And life fucked me over because I kept my mouth shut. So I vowed to always be brutally honest and let the chips fall where they may. I'm sorry if that makes you uncomfortable."

I looked away, seeking refuge from his penetrating stare. It didn't make me uncomfortable. His words, his presence, it made me anxious. It made that pesky flutter in my stomach evolve into a full-on swarm of butterflies.

"It doesn't make me uncomfortable," I replied, speaking my truth. For once, I didn't let fear suppress my first instinct. "But you do make me nervous."

"Nervous?" Blaine asked, crooking a brow.

"In a good way," I quickly recovered. Shit. *Real smooth.*

Blaine chuckled, and that fascinating sound chipped at the wall around my forgotten heart. "I wasn't aware there was a good kinda nervous. But I'll take it. Anything to see your cheeks get pink like that. You have no idea how it makes me feel when that happens."

Speechless. I was rendered completely speechless, and my cheeks had taken on a life of their own and complied with his wishes. The smile that spread across Blaine's lips as he took in my reddened face was undeniable and I suddenly felt completely stripped bare before him. I just wanted to cover myself and hide. But Blaine wasn't having that. Before my nerves sent me cowering in a corner, his head dipped, and his lips were at my earlobe.

"I know you said you don't feel anything," he whispered. "But can you honestly say that you don't feel *this*? That this heat, this attraction, is all in my head? Don't think about it; just answer. Tell me what your heart wants to say and not what your head keeps trying to make you believe."

I swallowed down the "no" that was already reflexively building in my throat and let Blaine's proximity push away the fear. His presence did that for me; it got me out of my own way.

"Yes, Blaine," I rasped. "I feel it." I did. I felt all of it. I felt all of *him*.

I dared a glance up at him, and my knees buckled

when my eyes met his. Luckily, he reached out to steady me before I could bite it in a big way. As his arm wrapped around my waist, an audible gasp escaped me, and my body nearly went limp.

"Don't worry," he smiled, pulling me into the hard warmth of his chest. "I've got you. I'll always catch you when you fall."

And just like that, Blaine had staked his claim on the untouched part of me that no living soul had ever moved. He had captured every fear, every reservation, and crushed them in the palm of his inked hand.

"Um, can we get some service here?"

We both spun around, my panting body still wrapped in Blaine's tight, protective grip. Even with the realization that we were no longer alone, he didn't loosen his hold on me. If anything, it only made him pull me in closer.

"Hey guys," I squeaked nervously, peeling Blaine's fingers from around my hips. "What are you doing here?" I tried hard not to sound snarky, but I knew trouble was amidst.

Angel and Dominic wore twin mischievous grins. "I thought I'd treat Dom to lunch," Angel piped up. "I heard this place has really good food. And I was craving a burger."

I rolled my eyes. "Angel, I have never seen you eat a burger, let alone carbs. Seriously?" I knew what they were up to, and I was pissed. Not so much at their presence but at the fact that I was forced from Blaine's arms. Judging by the slight frown between his brows and the way he worked his studded tongue, he felt the same way.

"I'm trying something new," she trilled, grabbing a

menu.

My gaze fell on Dom, who seemed amused by me and Angel's tiff. "And you? You let her talk you into it?"

Dom shrugged and smiled into his own menu. "A man's gotta eat, Kam."

I shook my head before stealing a glance at Blaine. He looked down at me and gave me a small smile. I couldn't help but return the sentiment. It felt like we were sharing a private joke, and that was enough to squelch my bitchiness.

"Fine," I sighed. "What can I get you two?"

My friends ordered, and by the time their food arrived, more lunch-seeking patrons had arrived, though most opted for the tables on the dining floor. Few people ordered more than sodas, making work for Blaine and I pretty lax.

"So how long have you been working here, Blaine?" Dominic asked, munching on a fry.

Blaine was leaning against the bar, his arms and legs crossed casually. My eyes zeroed in on the way the movement made his muscles stretch his t-shirt, generating fiery heat in my belly. I couldn't even hear his answer. I was too mesmerized at the way the fabric pulled and molded every delicious ripple. Though he always dressed simply in t-shirts and worn jeans, the way clothes fell over Blaine's physique was masterful. His body would be a fashion designer's dream. But at that very moment, I could care less about his clothes. Unless they were on my bedroom floor.

"Kam? Hello? Kami, you there?"

"Huh?" I asked blinking rapidly, my dilated pupils struggling to focus. Angel giggled, and I could have sworn I heard Dom snort. Assholes.

"I asked if I could get some ketchup," Angel winked. Part of me wanted to squirt it at her, staining her white, eyelet sundress.

"So how do you all know each other?" Blaine asked, pulling me from my dress-murdering thoughts. I grabbed the bottle and handed it to her with a tight smile.

"Kam and I went to college together in Atlanta," Dom replied. "After I graduated, we came up here. Angel was pathetically single in her big lavish condo and said we could room with her. I know her from high school, since I lived in this area for a few years back in the day."

"He's the guy that turned me gay!" Angel added.

"Oh, come on! Do you have to tell everyone that story? You know that's bullshit!" Dom protested, throwing his half-eaten fry at her. Angel dodged it and stuck her tongue out at him.

"It is not!" She turned to Blaine and me on the other side of the bar, her blue eyes shining with conviction. "Dirty Dom was quite the ladies man, even as a youngster. He was my first piece of peen and, thankfully, my last. Why anyone would want to stick that thing up in them is beyond me. Yuck! I'd rather fuck a frozen hot dog."

"Well, maybe that's because you haven't had the right one to turn you straight, darlin'," said a familiar southern drawl. Angel turned just in time to see CJ easing onto the barstool next to her.

"Trust me, one is enough. There is nothing soft and sensual about men. Sorry guys, but you have got nothing on the ladies," she cooed, flashing me a wink and blowing me a kiss.

"CJ, this is Kami and Angel's roommate, Dominic,"

Blaine said motioning between the two guys. "Dominic, this is my knucklehead cousin, Craig Jacobs."

"Holy shit, dude!" CJ exclaimed, leaning over to offer Dom his fist. "You actually live with these two? You are my new fucking hero!"

Dom bumped fists with him and shrugged. "Trust me, it's not as great as it sounds. This one," he said nodding towards Angel "walks around practically naked, yet doesn't like the D. And Kam…she doesn't like *anyone*. A guy can only take so much cuddling before blue balls cripples him or renders him sterile."

My eyes widened with shock as I tried to eject daggers from them. *How could he say that?* I mean, yeah, it was true for the most part. But it wasn't supposed to be public knowledge!

"So cuddling, you say? Like naked cuddling?" CJ pressed. I rolled my eyes and tried to busy my hands before they spontaneously slapped him.

"Naked enough," Dom replied. "I mean, yeah, I see them naked. Angel is an exhibitionist and Kam never closes her door."

I could tell by the way he glanced at me and cringed, he regretted the words as soon as they left his mouth. What was wrong with Dom? Why was he spilling our personal business to virtual strangers? And why was Angel shrugging and nodding in agreement? I had to be missing something.

Against my better judgment, I glanced at Blaine, who was intently looking at me. Not with disgust, or amusement, or even lust. He seemed thoughtful, and maybe even a bit embarrassed by the topic. Whatever was behind his gaze, it made me feel oddly at ease. It washed away the horror that tried to bubble its way to the surface.

"Well, kids, I gotta get back to work," Dom announced, standing up and tossing his napkin onto his plate. He looked to me with apologetic eyes before leaning over the bar. I knew I should've been slapping his handsome face right at that very moment, but instead, I pressed my lips to his for a quick peck. Dominic sighed with relief. He couldn't stand when I was angry with him, and denying him affection would destroy him. I was mad at him, but I didn't want to hurt him. He didn't deserve to ever feel pain again.

Angel left a kiss on my cheek before I could pull away, and wrapped her arms around our shoulders, resulting in an awkward group hug. It was silly and probably garnered quite a few sideways glances, but it was us. It would always be the three of us—the rejected, the abused, and the damaged. Nothing could penetrate our bond. No one else could fully understand it.

"Ok, boys, see you tomorrow night!" Angel remarked, releasing us. "Hope you're ready for A.D. to rock the house!" Tomorrow would officially be AngelDust's first night as Dive's house band. They were scheduled to play every Friday and Saturday, plus sit in and play on Thursday evening for Dive's new Open Mic Nights starting next week.

"No doubt," Blaine nodded. "See you guys later."

After the lunch crowd had diminished and CJ had begrudgingly returned to his day job, Blaine turned to me as I was drying tumblers.

"So no one, huh?"

"Huh?" I asked, genuinely confused.

"Dom said you don't like anyone."

Heat crept onto my cheeks, urging Blaine to take notice. He did, and reached up to brush his thumb against the apple of my cheekbone down to my jaw. After he had repeated the ritual with the other, I let out the breath I didn't realize I was holding.

"Pretty pathetic, huh?" I asked, not knowing how to respond with his fingers still tracing my jawline.

"No," he replied, shaking his head, yet still intently focused on the movements of his fingers. "Absolutely not. Better for me."

"Better for you, how?"

A smile curled his full lips, causing my eyes to fixate on them. "Well, Kami, I told you before that I wasn't chasing you. But now…now I am. So it's better that I know your interest isn't elsewhere."

"Oh, is that right?" I smirked. "And what makes you believe that you chasing me will be a sure bet? Just because there's no one else, that doesn't mean you win by default."

His fingertips fell from my face, but he didn't break contact. They drifted down my throat, stopping to gently fondle my collarbone before sliding down my arm. My skin heated under the soft touch, begging for more. My whole body screamed for more Blaine. It had gotten just a sweet taste, and now there was no going back.

"I know that," he finally said, making me remember that we were actually having a conversation. "But I am very persistent. I never give up on the things I want. This… you and me…it's inevitable. There's no use in fighting, Kami. It's going to happen. And when you are madly in love with me, the only thing you'll regret is not falling sooner."

CHAPTER NINE

Kami

I was never one to believe in fairy tales. I always figured that when things were too good to be true that they were just that—a beautiful lie. So after Blaine declared that he was, in fact, actively pursuing me, I knew there was a catch.

Even though Friday and Saturday came and went without incident, with Blaine remaining his usual flirtatious, incredibly enticing self, I kept waiting for the other shoe to drop. Nothing should be this good. The way he'd look at me, those brown eyes stirring something deep inside me, it was much more than I deserved. I kept waiting for something to come crashing down, shattering the perfect picture I had painted of him in my mind. But nothing happened. Not until Sunday, when a sledgehammer disintegrated my tiny slice of hope into rubble.

We had been open for a few hours and were expecting a slow day. Sundays usually brought in a few regulars, but since it wasn't football season yet, most people were out enjoying the warm weather with their families. Blaine was in a good mood. Things between us had been comfortable and easy, though I still would break out into a deep blush whenever his arm grazed mine or our eyes would lock. The past two nights had been so crazy that we hadn't had much alone time. I think we were both looking forward to the slower shift, and I was secretly hoping that Blaine would step his game up. I wanted to experience the Blaine Jacobs persistence that he so confidently believed would eventually break me down and make me fall madly in love with him. As if *that* could ever happen. But, hey, there was no harm in trying.

"Hold still just a sec," he said suddenly, as I was filling a beer order for Lidia, one of the waitresses. Luckily, the pitcher was full, and I slid it towards her. She cocked a curious brow and winked at me before heading off to service her tables.

I felt him behind me before we even made contact. There was something about his scent that drove me absolutely mad. It was masculine, natural and impossibly erotic. I could pick it out even among the sea of scents at a department store fragrance aisle. By the time I felt his hands at my waist, I was high off the smell of mint and spice, and drunk with anticipation. They were firm yet somehow gentle as they gripped my hips, drawing our bodies together. When his chest and abs were flush against my back, I felt as if I might pass out. That's when I realized I had stopped breathing.

"Kami," he whispered, his lips on my earlobe unapologetically.

I wanted Blaine's ways of persuasion, and now I was getting it. Oh, sweet baby Jesus, was I getting it.

Warm breath slid down my throat and caressed the top of my chest, spilling down into my shirt. "Here, let me help you," he rasped.

Blaine's fingers traced the edge of my jeans, skimming the tiny bit of exposed skin that my tight Dive tee couldn't conceal. That's when I looked down and realized that he was retying my apron. His hands were at the base of my spine above my tailbone, driving me insane as they slowly worked those strings into a bow. What should have taken him mere seconds was drawn out into a vicious assault on my senses. I wondered what else he could prolong with those fingers, the possibilities causing a flame to spark between my legs.

Though I knew my apron was secure, Blaine's hands never strayed. They coasted back to my front, stopping at my hipbones as he pulled me back into him. My head was leaning back onto his shoulder while his head dipped further into me, warm lips grazing my neck. My eyes fluttered closed reflexively as a low moan seeped out before I could stop it.

"God, you smell good," he breathed, running his soft lips from my earlobe down to my collarbone. "I bet you taste as good as you smell."

"Why don't you taste and see?" a voice moaned. It sounded like mine, but there was no possible way it could have come from me. It was too confident, too self-assured. There wasn't a trace a fear laced between those words.

"Can I?" he teased. He knew damn well I was ready to let him sample every bit of my body in that moment.

The gruff sounds of a clearing throat cut into our aroused senses like a knife. Blaine and I broke apart in time to catch the narrowing eyes of Mick. He glared disapproving daggers at his nephew before snorting and retreating to the back office. Mick was a man of very few words, but I could tell he didn't like his bartenders canoodling on the job.

"Shit!" I whispered, covering my beet-red face with my hands. Blaine had the nerve to chuckle, eliciting a smack on the arm from me. "Not funny, Blaine! We're gonna get fired!"

Blaine let out a pompous half-snort. "There's no way that's happening. Let me worry about Mick."

"Well, *you're* his family. Of course, he won't fire you. But I'm still new here. I don't want him to think I'm just a walking, talking set of T&A. I want to earn my place here."

I swear I heard Blaine groan just at the mention of tits and ass. *Such a man.* Yeah, he seemed like a rare breed, but I had to remember that Blaine Jacobs was a male, and therefore, could not be trusted. Yeah, that's what I should've been thinking, but my mind was still clouded with the remembrance of his lips caressing my neck. Blaine had completely dismantled me without even really kissing me.

Seeing the flush rising on my cheeks, he stepped into me, close enough for me to damn near taste the air he occupied.

"You're right. I'll try to tone it down here. But I need us to finish what we started. I need to see you outside of work. Tonight. Just us."

My breath expelled in short pants as I tried to regain

my wits. It wasn't just my nerves rising at the thought of being alone with Blaine. It was panic. Terror. *No, no, no,* this wasn't happening. *Not now, please God, not now.*

"Kami, are you alright?" he asked, all traces of seduction wiped clean from his face. "You don't look so good. Here sit down."

Blaine grabbed a stool and eased me onto it, just as dizziness claimed my balance. I quickly leaned forward, steadying myself with his body and placed my head between my legs. Then I started the countdown in my head …from twenty. It had truly turned out to be a shitty day.

After a while, the hot clamminess of my skin cooled into a sheen of sweat that blanketed by whole body. My heartbeat slowed from techno to an R&B groove. When I was sure that the dizziness and nausea had ceased, I raised my head and risked a peek at Blaine. Now he knew. There was no hiding my psychosis now. All the better; now I wouldn't have to be the one to break a heart. I'd have the privilege of being on the receiving end this time.

Blaine looked down at me with nothing but concern etched onto his handsome face. With the halogen lights beaming down directly behind his head, his light brown hair creating a halo of sorts, he reminded me of a sexy, dark angel. There was no disgust, no humiliation, radiating from him. There was only worry for me.

He stroked my cheek adoringly, not even cringing at the tiny beads of sweat that had sprouted in the last 30 seconds. Then he smiled, emitting warmth and comfort in that simple gesture, telling me that it was ok. That I was safe and he was there to, once again, catch me.

His eyes flickered up, and he held a finger up to

someone, telling them he'd be with them in a moment. Then he squatted so he and I were eye level, and took my face in his hands.

"You scared me," he whispered. The pads of his thumbs drew circles on the apples of my cheeks. "How are you feeling?"

I nodded, but I couldn't find it in me to tell him I was okay, because I knew I never would be. I would always be a nervous fucking wreck, successfully ruining any hopes of a normal relationship.

I swallowed, though my mouth was as dry and thick as cotton. "I'm sorry." It seemed like the right thing to say.

"Hey, you have nothing to be sorry about." A small frown rested between his brows. "Don't you dare apologize. You did nothing wrong."

With his hands still cradling my cheeks, I wanted to believe him. His touch did strange things to me, including making me ignore the warning signs that could have helped us to avoid this drama.

"I'm going to get you some water. Will you be ok to sit here for just a second?"

I smiled my most convincing smile, despite being completely humiliated. "I'm fine. I feel normal now." I tried to get up to prove it, but Blaine quickly dampened my efforts.

"No, sit here. Don't try to stand yet. Let me get some water and food in you first."

I sat idly, feeling like an invalid, while Blaine fetched a cold bottle of water and a basket of fries from the kitchen. He demanded I at least try to eat and drink while he apologized to the waiting customers and quickly filled their orders. I told him I could help, but he wouldn't hear any of it. I wasn't about to argue and draw even more attention to myself.

When I had consumed enough food and fluids to appease Blaine, I excused myself to the ladies room to freshen up. Mascara had settled in the corners of my eyes, and sweat-drenched strands of hair stuck to my neck and forehead. I looked like a hot, sweaty mess, and it only added to my embarrassment. I fixed myself as well as I possibly could and made my way back to the front. I needed to work my ass off and redeem myself. Plus, if I appeared busy, maybe Blaine wouldn't question what brought on the sudden episode.

However, my game plan was quickly forgotten when I spied a pair of boobs practically playing patty-cake with Blaine's face.

Neither Blaine nor his "friend" noticed when I reentered the bar until I asked a customer if they needed to be helped. It was obvious that Blaine was too busy helping himself to two Slippery Nipples.

"Oh, uh, I don't know if you two have met, but Kami this is Wendy, an old friend from high school. Wendy this is Dive's hot new commodity, Kami."

I rolled my eyes at Blaine's description of me. It was a typical *man* move—trying to diffuse the situation with flattery or humor instead of just admitting that he was a super-douche. I shook off my annoyance and quickly gave Wendy a tight smile and a wave. There was no way I was letting him know I was bothered.

"Well, aren't you just the cutest little thing," Wendy remarked in her heavy southern accent. All that was missing were daisy dukes, blonde pigtails and mid-drift top adorned with cherries. "The guys here must just eat you up, huh? I bet that CJ has been puttin' the moves on you. You certainly are his type." Her eyes ran the length of my body as she took a sip of her Appletini. Typical.

"Is that so?" I replied flippantly. "And what type is that?"

"Oh you know…the ethnic girls. The wild, exotic ones," she explained with a straight face, free of shame or embarrassment. This chick was describing me like I was some rare breed of bird, and she was totally convinced that it was ok! Wow, just…*wow*.

"CJ isn't getting anywhere near her," Blaine snapped before I could respond to her ignorance. Both our eyes were on him as his expression suddenly turned cold.

"Oh well," Wendy shrugged, waving off his odd outburst. "Anyway, Blaine, I was thinking I would hang out and wait for you until you close up for the night. You never did get to show me your truck like you promised. I guess neither one of us were thinkin' about it that night."

For the second time in the past hour, I felt sick. But it was for a totally different reason this time. It wasn't out of fear or anxiety. It was out of sheer anger and disgust. Blaine was just talking about being alone with me tonight for…I don't know what. And now he's making plans with some big-boobed bimbo?

I should have seen it coming. I knew I shouldn't have trusted the concern he showed when I nearly fainted. I knew the kindness in his smile was generic. The moment Blaine saw that I wasn't a sure bet for the night, he moved on. And, judging by the pure lust that dripped from

Wendy's glossy pink lips, he'd be moving right into her in a couple hours.

I thrust myself into serving, even offering to help out the waitresses after I had wiped down every surface behind the bar. I could feel Blaine trying to catch my gaze, but I refused to look at him. I had to admit, he was good. He'd almost made me believe that he was something other than what I had always feared. But a tiger can't change his stripes, no matter how hard he tries to mask them.

True to her word, Wendy stuck around, tossing back drinks and dancing to the music coming from the jukebox. Blaine only spoke to her when she needed a refill, but I chalked it up to him being embarrassed about getting caught. I would have preferred he be upfront about being an asshole. I would have respected him more and it would give the ache in my chest meaning. My suffering wouldn't be in vain.

After the bar was mostly empty and the waitresses had cashed out their tips, I popped into the back to retrieve my belongings. Mick was gone, delaying my plan to apologize for my behavior and assure him that I would never be caught flirting with Blaine again. Ever. When I returned to the front of the house, the lights were dimmed, and everyone had left for the night. Even Wendy and her twin flotation devices.

"If there's nothing else..." I said quietly, fixing my eyes to the exit sign. It was so close. Soon I'd be free to scream, punch pillows and eat insane amounts of ice cream. Too bad Angel and the girls had a gig out in Raleigh. I really needed one of her man-bashing sessions, and no one did that better than Angel.

"Kami, wait," Blaine said, leaning against the bar.

"Look, Blaine," I said, spinning towards him. He was keeping me from Ben & Jerry, the only other guys I loved even more than Dom, and it was annoying the hell out of me. "Whatever you were hoping for, forget it. I'm not the girl you're looking for. I'm not going to waltz in here with my tits propped up to my chin to get your attention. I'm not going to hang onto your every word like a fucking puppy. And I'm not interested in seeing your truck, hanging out after work, or being alone with you. *I'm not the girl, ok?* So whatever bullshit you were just about to feed me, save it. You're off the hook. Goodnight and goodbye, Blaine."

I turned towards the refuge of the exit, trying to keep my eyes trained on those glowing red letters to avoid looking back at Blaine's confused expression. When I hit the night air, still muggy and warm despite the late hour, I sucked in a deep breath, gulping down oxygen to combat the sob rising in my throat. Not here, not in public. I wouldn't let myself crumble.

In my devastated state, I hadn't even noticed my surroundings. Had I been paying attention, my senses not diluted with thoughts of Blaine, I would have been fisting my keys. I would have kept my head down and walked swiftly to my car. And I would have noticed a darkly dressed figure approaching me just as I was feet away from my vehicle.

"Hey, girl, come here. Whatchu doing out here all by yourself?"

I didn't answer. I just kept rummaging through my purse, praying that my trembling hands would find my car keys before fear completely washed over me. I could feel it—the building anxiety causing my extremities to lock up. I wanted to run, wanted to scream, but once the fear had seeped into my bones and attacked my senses, it was impossible. I couldn't hear the man taunting me anymore. Couldn't even hear the sounds of gravel crunching under his boots as he stalked closer to me. Finding those keys was the only thing my mind could focus on.

The moment I felt the stranger's hand grip my forearm, I yelped, causing the sob in my chest to break free. He reeked of hard liquor, dirt and body odor, and my stomach roiled in response. I froze. I should have fought, should have yelled for help, but I couldn't. I had shut down, letting my thoughts wander into the darkest places in my mind. The places I never visited, for fear that I would never be able to return...

I was just a little girl, completely helpless, useless, and defenseless. I knew fighting would only make Daddy mad. And when he got mad, he hurt me more. Every time Daddy hurt me, Mommy would try to stop him, earning the full brunt of his anger. It was better to just stay still and let him have his fun. It made him happy. Making Daddy happy was what Mommy and I always tried to do. Even if that meant slowly killing ourselves in the process.

Something began to tug at me, pulling me away from the bleak fog of remembrance. I still couldn't escape it. The memory had taken hold and refused to let me go, clawing into me, making me relive every single sordid second. But whoever was pulling me to safety, freeing me from myself, was much stronger.

I could hear his voice, asking me if I was ok, telling me I was safe. My body was crushed against his, a crumpled, trembling mess of tears and sweat. We were on the ground, the hardness of the concrete unnoticed by me, as I rocked back and forth, my knees drawn up to my chest. When he pulled back a bit to assess my face, it was my undoing. Those brown eyes, wise beyond their years, full of so much concern and fear for me, snatched me away from the hell of my memories completely and brought me back to the present.

The scream that pierced the night air sounded unnatural, like a wounded animal's cry. I didn't recognize it though it had come from me. I couldn't stop screaming, couldn't stop crying, couldn't stop rocking back and forth as I squeezed my knees impossibly tight. I bawled until there was no more agony in me to dispel. Then I cried some more.

"Kami! Kami, I need you to calm down. Look at me. Look at me and try to understand what I am saying," Blaine said urgently.

I locked eyes with his, letting his touch, his smell, permeate my senses. I needed to calm down, and I needed to trust him. I didn't know why, but that is exactly what I wanted to do.

"Are you hurt?" he asked, cradling my tear-stained face once my shrieks had quieted to whimpers. "Do you want me to call the police? An ambulance? Just tell me what to do, and I'll do it."

I shook my head furiously, squeezing my eyes shut. "No," I croaked hoarsely. "I'm ok. I just need to go home. I need to go home, Blaine."

"Ok, let's get you up. Do you need me to carry you?"

I shook my head once again but made no move to stand. I couldn't. I was still utterly frozen with fear. I didn't even know how I had gotten in that position on the ground. The last thing I remembered was searching for my keys then…

I couldn't breathe. My chest felt too heavy. Too tight. I struggled to fight for just the tiniest breath, yet oxygen had abandoned me.

"Breathe, Kami. Breathe," Blaine said soothingly, stroking my hair. He took deep, animated breaths as if to demonstrate them to me. I focused on his voice, his touch, those warm brown eyes, and followed his lead.

"Good. That's good, baby," he said softly. "Ok, I'm going to unwrap your arms now. Ok? Then we're going to get up."

I nodded, afraid that breath would escape me again if I tried to speak. Blaine gently placed his hands on mine and clutched my fingers. Though I couldn't willingly release my death grip, he somehow freed my knees without resistance from me. Once my hands were balled at my sides, he brought his face close to mine, searching for signs of approval. When he wasn't met with another scream or sob, he slid his hands under my arms and gently lifted me to my feet.

"Kami, I'm going to go into your purse and get your keys, ok?" he said, still supporting most of my weight. I nodded again, focusing on his soothing voice.

Not having his face to hold my gaze as he rummaged through my purse, my eyes roamed the area around us. They came upon a clump of dark clothing a few yards away, completely still in the night. I couldn't see a face, but I knew what it was—who it was. Horror rocked me again and I hunched over and vomited, my body heaving violently as it pushed away the remembrance of his hands on me. Blaine jumped back, then maneuvered his body behind mine and gathered my hair in his hands. Once I was absolutely sure that I wouldn't get sick again, he eased me into the passenger seat of my car.

"Kami…" Blaine turned to me, the steering wheel groaning under his tight grip. His face was full of confusion, pain…anger?

"You're hurt," I whispered, noticing his bloodied knuckles.

He shook his head, flexing his hands. "I'm fine. Not my blood." He knitted his brows together, and then shook his head again. "I need to know where you live. You don't want the cops, but I can bet that someone heard you screaming and called them. And that piece of shit might wake up soon. I really don't want to spend the night in jail."

For some God forsaken reason, his words sparked a memory.

"Did you hear what he did to that guy? I heard they released him from prison early for good behavior."

I knew it was the most inopportune time for the thought to pop into my head, but I suddenly had the urge to ask him about what that girl said. But I wouldn't. This wasn't the time for sharing details of our dark pasts. It would never be the time for that.

I gave Blaine directions to Angel's condo at The Madison in Uptown Charlotte. I could tell he wanted to ask questions—there was no way I could afford to live there on a bartender's salary—but he just nodded and cranked up the car. We rode in companionable silence, neither one of us wanting to discuss the events of the evening. There was honestly nothing left to say, and I was thankful that Blaine didn't push me to talk.

After pulling it together enough to greet the night doorman, we made our way to apt. 1202. Blaine insisted that he see me up to ensure I was ok, and I didn't object. Having him close distracted my mind from what had just happened. My brain had somehow gone into recovery mode, erasing the moments before Blaine found me on the concrete. I was thankful. I didn't want to know what he had found in that parking lot. I didn't want to imagine his horror when he saw me cowering on the ground next to my car, shivering and sobbing into my knees.

The lavish apartment was empty when we entered. I knew Angel would be staying in Raleigh overnight, but I had no clue where Dom was. His car wasn't parked in one of our assigned spaces, and the alarm system was set. It was unlike him to be out this late on a Sunday and I began to worry about someone other than myself.

"I'm going to make you some tea and run you a bath, ok?" he said once we stepped into living room.

"In my room," I said nodding towards the hallway. "I have a bathroom in there."

Without hesitating or thinking about his sore knuckles, Blaine grasped my hand, lacing his fingers through mine. Comfort filled me in a way I had never felt before. I wanted to believe that maybe he had sought the same comfort in my touch. Maybe he was scared too.

I led Blaine to my room, something I had never done. Ever. It was my sanctuary. My hideaway. The place I went to when the world got too big, and I felt too small. He pretended not to check it out and walked straight into my bathroom, his hand still in mine. When he pulled it away to start the water and pour in some bath salts, I nearly whimpered at the loss of contact.

"Ok, I'll let you get undressed…and, um, uh…" His eyes roamed my fully dressed body before falling to the floor. It was as if he was ashamed of feeling flustered over the mention of me being naked. But at the moment, I was glad he still found me attractive. I needed it. Knowing that part of him still desired me after seeing me so broken made me feel better, almost whole again.

"Blaine?" I said, just as he turned to exit the bathroom that had suddenly felt small and intimate.

"Yeah?"

I needed to thank him for saving me. Tell him how much it meant to me that he was there. Explain to him what happened to me in that parking lot and earlier at the bar. I swallowed, the taste of vomit a reminder of the shackles that kept me bound in anxiety.

"The kitchen? Off to the right of the living room, past the formal dining room. Tea is in the cabinet over the stove."

No, I couldn't tell Blaine no matter how wonderful he had been. He was still a man. He was still one of *them*. He had the potential to hurt and abuse and torture. I wanted to believe that he was different, wanted to believe that *I* could be different, but facts were facts. I still wasn't what he was looking for.

After he was gone, I eased open the bathroom door that Blaine had closed behind him, shakily letting out the breath I had been holding since he had left. I undressed, praying that he wasn't peeking at me through the crack in the door. Then I attempted to scrub away the disgust and fear left behind by the evening's events.

Several minutes later, after my skin was pink and raw and I had washed my hair, I heard a rustle behind the door.

"Kami? I'm, uh, I've got your tea, and I didn't know if you wanted it now or later," he said nervously, his back turned. It was almost endearing how nervous he was about me being naked just a few feet away from him.

"I'll be right out," I called, a sliver of a smile on my face. Before today, a man other than Dom in my personal space would have had me bent over, hyperventilating and trembling. Yet, having Blaine waiting for me on the other side of the door only brought me comfort. I felt cared for, even a little cherished, as I imagined him holding a soothing cup of tea for me.

I brushed my teeth furiously, then stepped out into my bedroom wearing only my terry cloth robe. Blaine was at the windowsill beside my bed looking at framed pictures of me and my roommates, and my collection of little trinkets. Ordinarily, the sight of his hands on my things, disrupting the order of each item, would have sent me into a panic, but for some strange reason, I was completely content. It only gave me the warm feelings of anticipation, eager for him to get just a tiny glimpse of Kamilla Duvall without the mask.

He picked up a paper crane, one of the many pieces of origami that littered my room. "You made this?"

I shrugged. "Yeah. Picked it up when I was a kid.

Keeps my fingers busy." I didn't have the heart to tell him that it aided in keeping my panic attacks at bay. The distraction helped me to put each worry in its own little cubby. Each fear had its place. And when life became too complicated and the fear took over, origami helped me focus them, tucking them away in the forbidden corners of my mind.

Blaine set down the crane and picked up another piece on pastel colored paper. "Thought origami was from Japan."

"Do you have to be Japanese to eat sushi?" I asked with a raised brow.

"Right," he remarked, embarrassment painting his face.

I walked over to the steaming mug on my dresser when I noticed the door. It was closed. I was in my room, alone with a man, and the door was closed. *NoNoNoNo.*

As casually as I could, my trembling hand threatening to spill the hot tea, I walked over and opened it, keeping it cracked just enough for me to know that it was open. If Blaine noticed, he didn't say anything.

"Hey, what's this?" he asked, holding up a glass jar filled with tiny paper stars.

"Just some stars I've been collecting."

He shook it then set it down. "Looks like a lot of them."

"253," I blurted out before I could stop myself.

"Huh?"

I took a sip of the tea to give my mouth something to do before it betrayed me further. "Two hundred and fifty-three. That's how many stars are in the jar."

I should have been adding lucky number 254 to that jar after what happened tonight. Hell, to be honest, my freak out at the bar warranted a star. But Blaine was here, and the impulse to record those fears was stifled for the time being.

His eyes continued to survey my space, his fingers grazing everything as if he were reading Braille. He was taking it all in, taking *me* all in. Blaine was absorbing his surroundings in hopes of getting to know me.

He made his way to the acoustic guitar in the corner of my bedroom. "You play?"

"A little," I shrugged.

He gently ran his fingers over the strings before looking at me with wary eyes, searching my expression for signs of distress. "How are you feeling?"

I tried to give him a smile, but it felt forced. I settled for a nod. "I'm ok. I'm not even really sure what happened."

Blaine approached me in three easy strides and eased the mug of tea from my hands, before ushering me to the bed. We sat side by side, our knees and shoulders touching, as he gathered his thoughts.

"I came out to try to stop you from leaving. To talk to you. I was locking up when I heard you cry. That *sonofabitch* had his hands on you," he said through tightly clenched teeth, his fists balled on his thighs. "I don't really know what happened after that. I snapped. All I saw was red. He was touching you, and I wanted to kill him."

Blaine turned to look at me, his jaw ticking violently with contempt. "I shouldn't have let you walk away. I should have seen you to your car, and for that, I am truly sorry. I just keep thinking what would've happened if I was two minutes later. I can't get the image of you standing there, frozen with terror, out of my damn head. God, Kami …I'm sorry. I am so fucking sorry."

"What happened wasn't your fault." The words fell from my lips unconsciously. I had been told the same countless times. I figured it was the go-to phrase for times like these. "I'm ok, I swear. Go on home. You can even take my car if you want."

Instinctively, I reached out and placed my hand on his, causing him to release the strain on his knuckles. I didn't know why I did it; there was just an impulse to touch him, to comfort him. I knew what it felt like to be absolutely stripped of control. Our reactions may have differed but the fear, the anger, was the same.

Blaine turned his palm and laced his fingers with mine, his fingertips massaging the back of my hand gently. "Kami…" He exhaled a breath, then his brown eyes were locked with mine. Being that we were so close, our arms, legs and thighs nearly fused together, the moment felt too intimate. I felt exposed, naked and vulnerable under his gaze, but the feel of his skin was a soothing balm to my soul. I could feel my body growing warm and damp, and this time it had nothing to do with a panic attack.

"Blaine?" I whispered. I don't know why, but just saying his name made that warmth spread. I imagined saying it over and over.

Screaming it. Crying it.

He licked his lips before rolling his tongue, coaxing the metal barbell while he contemplated his next words. "I know you say that you're ok. But shit, I don't think *I'm* ok. I have no right to ask this, but…can I stay here with you tonight?"

At the sight of my widening eyes, he quickly continued. "I don't mean like that. It's just…I know what happened to you was traumatizing. And seeing you react the way you did, seeing how afraid you were, I know that's not the first time you've been in that situation. You don't have to tell me anything; you don't have to explain yourself to me. But right now, I need to be near you. I need to see you. And if you let me, I need to hold you."

Words failed me. They were literally ripped from my brain and replaced with all things Blaine. He encompassed every one of my senses. I couldn't see beyond this moment with him.

Long seconds ticked by before a simple nod took him out of his misery, causing him to sigh with relief. I didn't know what had come over me. Was I really about to let him spend the night? In my bedroom? In my *bed*? But after what had happened, and Dom being M.I.A., I couldn't think of a good reason not to let him stay. I wanted him there. I wanted to let him hold me and chase away the nightmares I knew would visit me the moment I closed my eyes.

"Thank you," he muttered, bringing his other hand up to stroke my cheek. "Seriously, I think I would've gone crazy worrying about you if I went home. I feel horrible about what happened."

And there it was. His guilt. Blaine wasn't staying because he wanted me or was hoping something more would transpire between us. He felt guilty for letting me walk out to my car by myself. The Dive employees were religious about never walking out to the parking lot alone after closing. Dive wasn't in the best neighborhood, and drunken homeless men were known to litter the streets late at night. Maybe he thought I'd badmouth him to the rest of the staff and try to get him trouble. Or maybe he was just riddled with guilt and felt like staying would somehow make amends. Whatever the reason, it made the warmth of his touch feel like a lie.

"You don't have to. I don't blame you for what happened," I said, pulling my hand away. I stood and started rummaging through my drawers in search of pajamas. I couldn't look at him. I couldn't let him see the pain that clearly painted my face.

"But I want to," I heard him say behind me. "Hey."

His hand was around my elbow, stopping me in my mad pursuit to find the ugliest, thickest pajamas I owned.

"Kami, I want to be here. For you. Like I said, I won't ask you about what happened. I won't ask you to tell me about your past. But I sincerely hope that one day, you will tell me. That you'll trust me enough to open up and let me in."

I spun around to face him, a generic smile spread across my lips. "There's nothing to tell, Blaine. Absolutely nothing."

I excused myself to the bathroom to change into lounge pants and a tank, surrendering my pursuit of granny PJs. When I returned, Blaine was standing at my dresser, inspecting the origami that I had accumulated over the years.

"You're really good," he remarked, picking up a green paper frog.

"You think so? Feel free to take one. They just collect

dust."

I began to awkwardly fluff pillows, not really sure where to go from here. The silence stretched on until, luckily, Blaine dipped into my bathroom in search of a shower. I quickly flicked on my television and tried to distract my mind from what was on the other side of the door: Blaine, dripping wet and naked.

When he emerged, he was barefoot and shirtless, dressed only in his jeans. His hair was damp, and tiny droplets of water rested on his shoulders. Now I had a full view of the ink that adorned his skin. Vibrant, detailed art roped around his arms and extended up his chiseled shoulders. There were a few pieces that had the privilege of kissing his cut torso, and the carved V that was fully exposed in his low-slung jeans. As if that weren't enough to turn my belly inside out, I caught the glimmer of something silver gracing his left nipple.

Holy. Shit. His nipple was pierced.

I tried to take it all in without staring but I couldn't tear my eyes away. He was frighteningly beautiful; a rare work of art that needed to be admired and thoroughly explored.

"Sorry, my shirt kinda got blood on it," he mumbled, placing it with his shoes on the ground. "And I, uh, don't… um. I don't wear underwear."

I swallowed just to give my mouth something to do, because if I didn't, a whimper was sure to escape.

"That's ok," I squeaked as I climbed into bed. "But I have some Hello Kitty boxer shorts if you think you'd be more comfortable."

Blaine shook his head, a visible blush on his cheeks. He hit the light switch and advanced to the other side of the bed tentatively, his eyes trained on me the entire time.

"I'm sorry, but…is this alright? You're ok with this, right? I swear, I won't try anything."

I nodded, because oddly, I was alright with it. "Yeah, Blaine, hop on in and make yourself comfortable."

As Blaine slid between my sheets, a million fantasies played through my head of him sliding between…other places. Even over the fragrance of my body wash, I could smell his natural scent that somehow seemed concentrated in the close proximity. It made me so much more aware of every one of his breaths and sighs as he settled beside me. I lied stiff as a board, wondering what to do next.

"Come here," he demanded gently, pulling my body into his.

He placed my head on his chest, his strong arms wrapping around me tightly. I could feel his cheek against the top of my head. It was heaven. I felt like I had died and gone to paradise as my body melded with his. The feel of his skin, his scent, his arms holding me protectively as if I might be snatched away from him…it was incredible. And confusing. And tempting.

"Kami," he whispered, just as I had let my eyes close.

"Yeah?"

"I want you to know that nothing is going on with me and Wendy. She and I haven't been like that for several years. And I sent her home tonight. There was no way I was going anywhere with her."

"You don't have to explain anything to me, Blaine. That's none of my business." But I so wanted Blaine to be my business.

"That's where you're wrong," he retorted. "As the one

that I actually want to spend my time with, it is your business. You were way off earlier. I don't want some skanky-dressed chick. I don't want a woman that feels like she has to dumb herself down to be around me. And I don't someone so easy that it makes *me* feel violated."

I chewed my lip, suddenly aware of how close my mouth was to his nipple ring. "So what do you want?"

"I think you know that already, Kami."

I exhaled, and let myself settle against his body, the sound of my name wrapped around his tongue replaying in my head. And for the first time in years, I didn't need to count each fear in the jar in my windowsill. I hadn't even thought about it. With Blaine's arms wrapped around me, his fingers tracing circles on the bare skin of my arm, I drifted into sleep easily. And when my subconscious took the reins, there were no monsters. There was no fear. It was the scary-beautiful man beside me who starred in my dreams.

CHAPTER TEN

Blaine

I tried to stay awake for as long as possible. I didn't want to sleep. I didn't want to miss a single second of feeling Kami in my arms. I didn't want to forget her scent of vanilla and orchids, filling my senses as I breathed her in. I didn't want to let go of the overwhelming urge to run my hands over every inch of her petite body until she shook with need. Need for *me*.

But after working all day, then beating the shit out of that drunken asshole, I had to finally give in. I let my eyes close and tried to hang onto the edges of my reality, refusing to dream. Because my dream was right beside me, curled against my body.

Some time during the night, I felt her jerk awake and gasp. I wanted to ask her if she was ok and soothe her if she had a nightmare. But before I could, I swear I heard her moan and nuzzle into my chest like a cat finding that sweet spot on the couch. She felt incredible in my arms, but more than that, it felt like she was comfortable there. Like she was made to be there. And that made me feel 10 fucking feet tall.

I kept my breathing level and my eyes closed as I felt the very tips of her fingers brush against my arm. At first, it was just a simple touch. I almost thought she had fallen back to sleep and was unaware of what she was doing to me. Then after a few seconds ticked by, she started touching me again with the most feather-light strokes of her fingertips. There was a pattern in her touches. She wasn't trying to drive me insane, causing a deep throb inside my jeans. She was tracing my tattoos.

Her fingers outlined every curve and line with light, leisurely strokes. She worked her way up from the back of my hand to my shoulder, those delicate digits beginning their trek down to my chest. Softly, she brushed the ink next to my heart, letting her fingernails graze the ring through my nipple. I damn near bit my own tongue to keep from groaning.

After she had finished her thorough examination of the words that housed my pectoral, her fingers continued their dance down to my abs, taking the time to caress every ripple of my midsection. Her touch ignited a fire inside me, and I prayed that she couldn't see the bulge in my pants in the dark. And if she did…well, shit, there was nothing I could really do about it. She had to have known the effect she had on my body. She was sexy as hell; I'd have to be dead not to be aroused.

Just as I was about to pretend to stir awake so I could cover the massive erection that was aching to be touched, I felt it. Her lips on my chest, so soft, warm and utterly perfect. It was just the slightest brush of her mouth, but it was enough to have my heart hammering double time and my cock throbbing. Shit. There was no way she couldn't know what she was doing to me. And there was no way I could restrain myself much longer.

I heard Kami sigh, then she placed her head on the spot she just kissed. I couldn't be sure, but what sounded like a sob broke free from her chest. I could almost feel the ache in her throat as she tried to muffle it, but once I felt the warm moisture of tears against my skin, I knew she was crying.

As much as it made me feel like an insensitive asshole, I let her cry in private. Only a few tears slid onto my chest, so I knew that she was somewhat ok. At least, that's what I hoped. I just didn't understand how she could go from caressing the length of my torso and kissing me, to crying. Had I done something? Was some hidden pain inside her triggered by my presence? Whatever the reason was, it tore me in two. She was too beautiful to cry. I wanted to kiss those tears away and make it so she never had a reason to cry again. Unless it was from the overwhelming waves of pleasure that I ached to give her. Those tears were absolutely acceptable.

The telltale signs of deep breathing told me she had fallen back to sleep. As carefully as I could without waking her, I wrapped my arms back around her and held her tight. This girl had gotten to me. She was making herself as permanent as the ink already embedded in my skin. Kami had branded me with those tears.

The bright sun filtering through the curtains stirred us

from our slumber hours later. I didn't know what time it was, but judging by how tired I still felt, I knew it was early.

"Good morning," Kami whispered, her head still on my chest.

"Morning," I replied in a gruff voice, kissing her hair. It was a reflex. I don't know if she felt it but if she did, she didn't react.

After a few beats, she sat up and stretched her arms above her head. My eyes, still lazy with sleep, were fixed on the patch of exposed skin from her tank top riding up. Her skin looked so soft and delicate. I imagined licking every inch of it. Every. Single. Inch. My mouth watered.

She looked back at me, catching my appraising gaze. "Oh God. It's true. *Dammit,*" she mumbled.

I frowned, my eyes narrowing with confusion. Was she regretting letting me stay? I sat up next to her, still reclining back on my elbows. If she wanted me gone, she was going to have to say it. And judging by the way she was touching me last night, she had no regrets then.

"You're one of *them,*" she muttered shaking her head.

"Them?"

"Yeah, *them,*" she sighed. Her eyes met mine, the rosy flush of her cheeks giving away her reticence. "One of those guys who have freakishly amazing hair first thing in the morning. Those guys that don't even have to style it. Just run their fingers through it a few times, and it's magically perfect and gorgeous. *Them.*"

I chuckled to mask my relieved breath. "Them. I wasn't aware there was a club. Do I get a membership card?"

"I don't know," she shrugged. "I've never seen one in the flesh. I've never woken up beside a guy. Other than Dom, but of course, he doesn't count."

Again, my eyes widened, and my playful smile faded. Was she trying to tell me she was a… "Oh. *Oh.* That's ok, I mean, uh…"

"Oh no!" she giggled shaking her head. "I mean I've slept with a guy…like…you know. *Slept with*-slept with. But I've never slept with one for the sole purpose of sleeping."

"Never?" I asked, my brow cocked with skepticism.

"Never."

I ran my hand through my tousled bedhead without thinking, earning an eye roll from her. "Well," I smiled, "glad I could be your first."

Kami shook her head before climbing out of bed and crossing the room to the bathroom. She turned back to look at me before reaching the doorframe. "Well, why don't you and your sexy head of hair go make some coffee? Since this is the first time," she rolled her eyes again, "I should warn you: I am a bitch on wheels without my coffee."

"Yes, ma'am," I grinned, rolling out of bed.

Kami giggled as she entered the bathroom, causing the smile on my face to widen even more. "Ugh! You southern boys with your perfect manners! Kill me now!"

I popped into a hall bathroom to freshen up before heading to the kitchen in search of steaming hot ground goodness. They had one of those fancy machines that made one cup at a time. I had no fucking clue how to work one, but after tinkering with it and finding the little cups of assorted coffees, I finally figured it out. Kami walked in just as the first cup had finished brewing.

"I made you French Vanilla," I said, handing her the hot, steaming mug. "You guys have so many different flavors, and I didn't know which one you'd like. I figured it was safe."

Kami took the cup in her hands and took a sip without the use of cream or sugar. "Oh, so you thought I looked like a vanilla type of girl?"

I had to turn away from the task of trying to brew my own cup to assess her face. I didn't know if I had offended her or not, but the sweet smile on her face told me she was just teasing me. "I don't know, Kami. Do you like vanilla?"

She shrugged, then took another sip. "It's great sometimes; vanilla can be really good when it's done right. But I like it a bit bolder. Stronger."

I had to grasp the edge of the counter to keep from splaying her body across the breakfast bar and covering her with my mouth. Shit. There was no way we were still talking about coffee. The evidence was right there in her pink cheeks. Kami was flirting with me. And if she wasn't careful, she would see just how bold and strong *I* could be.

Still blushing, Kami broke eye contact and set her mug down. I took the opportunity to finish making my cup of coffee, taking it black as well.

"Are you hungry?" she asked, making her way to the refrigerator. "I can make you breakfast."

I sipped my hot brew and contemplated her question. Oh, I was hungry alright, but not for eggs and bacon. The way I was feeling at the moment, I was ready to make Kami my breakfast, and I didn't have enough time to fully savor her.

"No, thanks. I actually have to get going. CJ will be by to pick me up soon. I texted him earlier."

Her face instantly dropped though she caught it quickly, slipping on a manufactured smile. "Oh? Big plans today?"

"I don't know. That depends, Kami," I shrugged.

"Depends on what?"

"Whether or not you can be ready by 6."

I set my cup on the counter and walked over to her at the refrigerator. I eased the door closed and propped an arm over her head, gently pushing her back against it. "I have to go by the bar, but I want to take you out later. I know it's your day off so I understand if you have plans already. But if not, I want to spend the evening with you. Will you let me?"

I looked down at her big green eyes, our faces mere inches from touching. I needed to kiss her. So. Fucking. Bad. But not now. Not like this. I needed to make her believe that she needed to kiss me too. I needed to prove I was worthy of her lips.

The sounds of the front door opening and closing startled us, and I went back to where I had left my coffee. Not because I was scared or embarrassed, but because the ball was now in her court.

"Yes," she whispered. "I can be ready."

Dominic entered just as a relieved smile crept onto my face.

"Holy shit, what a night!" he exclaimed. Once his eyes fell on me, still shirtless and barefoot, his smile quickly faded, and he froze. His wide, almost angry, expression whipped to Kami, her back still flush against the fridge.

"Kam, what's going on?" he asked her, though it sounded like he was asking her if she was ok.

Kami's eyes met mine, and I took that as my cue to exit, downing my coffee and placing the cup in the sink.

"Hey, I'm gonna grab my stuff and wait for CJ downstairs. He should be here any minute."

I walked over to Kami and slowly let my hand brush her cheek. I wanted to do so much more, but I didn't need an audience.

"I'll see you at 6," I said quietly, still aware of Dom's questioning gaze. Then I let my thumb graze her bottom lip before forcing myself to pull away.

"Dom," I nodded as I passed him. He still looked confused, his eyes darting between Kami and me. I knew she was about to receive an earful, and I desperately wanted to save her from it. I heard the hushed interrogation before I even made it to Kami's room.

I slipped on my dirty t-shirt and shoes and was just about to head out of the front door when Dom stopped me.

"Hey man, wait up," he said, jogging towards me. "I'll walk you down."

Ah, I knew where this was going. Though the whole "What are your intentions" conversation was usually reserved for fathers and big brothers, I could respect Dom for looking out for Kami. I could tell he really cared for her.

"Kam told me what happened last night," he began as we made our way down the hall to the elevator. "Thank you. Seriously. I should've been there. I should've brought my ass home last night. Fuck! Dude, thank you for helping her. I owe you."

I shook my head. "You don't owe me anything. I was just glad I was there in time before…shit. I'm just glad I stopped that fucker in time." I felt my fists tighten at my sides and my face flame with rage.

"She also said you stayed with her. To make sure she was ok." Dom cleared his throat, clearly uncomfortable. "She said nothing happened."

"Yeah, and?"

"It's just…even though nothing's happened yet, I see how you look at her. And how she looks at you. And I just want you to know… Kami is special. She's unlike any chick you've probably ever dealt with. And because of how *special* she is, she needs to be treated delicately."

"Ok…?" What the hell was he trying to get at? I knew Kami was special, but he was making her sound special in a totally different way, as if she was disabled or slow.

"Bottom line, she needs a lot of patience and understanding. She needs someone that can protect her, mostly from herself. And if you're not that type of dude, walk away now. I won't judge you; I won't be upset. Don't show up for your date tonight. I can even cover for you or something. Just get out now, and don't look back."

I frowned with disgust, furious at his words. "What the fuck… Do you have this talk with every guy she dates?"

Even after seeing the violent expression on my face, Dom chuckled and shook his head. "Only with ones she actually likes."

"Hmph," I snorted. "And is she ok with this shit?"

"Wouldn't know," he shrugged. "You're the first."

His words cooled the anger I felt just moments before.

I was the *first*.

I wasn't just imagining it; Kami had feelings for me. Feelings as real as the ones that had kept me up at night for the past month, picturing those bright green eyes and pouty lips. Feelings that I needed to explore. *We* needed to explore.

"Let her know I'll be back at 6. And tell her to dress comfortably."

I stepped onto the elevator, the doors sliding closed on Dominic's nod of acceptance. I already knew Kami was special. I knew she was unlike anyone I had ever met since the day she came into Dive, blinking away tears and in search of an escape. I knew she was running then. And thankfully, she had run straight to me. And I was hell-bent on making it so she never felt the need to run again.

CHAPTER ELEVEN

Kami

"You're nervous."

I looked at Angel lounging on my bed like the princess she claimed to be and rolled my eyes. "You think?"

"Mmm hmm," she remarked, her eyes glued to a gossip magazine. It was a good thing too; she couldn't see me flipping her off.

"Maybe this is a mistake. I said I wouldn't get involved with coworkers again. I need to call and cancel. I should cancel, right? Oh, holy fuck, what am I doing?" I rambled, wringing my hands in front of me. The room shifted before my eyes, throwing off my equilibrium. A panic attack was on the horizon.

"Calm down and breathe, Kam," she gently admonished, tossing her magazine to the side. "It'll be fine. Blaine is a gentleman. You'll be fine."

"She still freaking out?" Dom asked as he entered my bedroom. He flopped down next to Angel.

"I am *not* freaking out," I insisted, crossing my arms in front of me. "And don't think I'm speaking to you again. First, you totally blow up my spot last week at my job, and now you're having secret pow-wows with Blaine? Not cool, dude."

Dom let out a heavy sigh and scrubbed a hand over his face. "I explained and apologized for last week, Kam. I just…I don't know. Got caught up in stupid guy talk. I'm not used to being around other people outside of you two. For once, I wasn't caught in a huge estrogen fest and I lost my head. Shit, you know I'm sorry."

"That doesn't explain your little talk with Blaine earlier," Angel chimed in, earning a hard glare from Dom that screamed, *"Mind your own damn business."*

"Just go into this with an open mind," Dom said, successfully changing the subject. He knew he couldn't win with us. "Don't feel like you have to rush into anything."

"Ok," I nodded, smoothing my jean skirt over my hips. "How do I look?"

"He said dress comfortably," Dom remarked, taking in my skirt, sheer, flouncy top and flats.

"This is comfortable! It's hot as a witch's tit outside!"

"Oh hell," Dom shook his head. "Angel is rubbing off on you."

"Damn right!" Angel exclaimed.

As we laughed off the tension, a buzz from the intercom caused the nerves to return with a vengeance. Angel flitted to the door, giving Blaine clearance to come up. I felt like I would break out into hives.

"Damn, girl," Dom chuckled, climbing to his feet. "You act like he's going to steal your virtue or something!"

He crooked an elbow out for me to lace my arm through. "Come on, you'll be fine, Kam. You deserve...*this.*"

"This?"

"The normal dating thing. You deserve to be swept off your feet. The flowers and candy. You deserve to be happy, Kam."

I looked up at my best friend, the man who had been closer to me than family. The only man I had ever truly trusted. "You too, Dom," I whispered, my eyes shining with unshed tears. "You deserve that, too."

"Eh," he shrugged with a grin. "One day. But no time soon. Too many chicks out there with low self-esteem and even lower morals."

I gave him a light punch with my other hand and shook my head. "Oh Dirty Dom, what am I gonna do with you?"

"I can think of a few things, but right now, you've got a guy waiting to take you out on a date. And if you don't get out there soon, I'm sure Angel will start spilling stories of drunken girl's nights involving tequila and dildos."

My eyes grew wide with shock and alarm at the sound of Blaine's deep laugh from the foyer. Yeah, Angel would totally give him an earful.

On shaky legs, I let Dom lead me out to the living room where Blaine stood with Angel, his back facing us. As if sensing our approach, he turned and my breath caught in my throat at the sight of him. Even though he wore a simple short-sleeved button up and jeans, his good looks still managed to disarm me. He was a rare, captivating work of sculpted art.

"Hey," Blaine breathed, as we were just inches from each other.

I unhooked my arm from Dom's and folded my hands in front of me, unsure of what to do with them. Part of me wanted to stretch on my tiptoes and give him a peck on the cheek, which is what I would usually do while going through the motions of a "date." But this was unlike any of those times because Blaine was different from any man I had ever known. And the way I felt about him was just as foreign to me.

"Why does this feel like prom?" Angel asked, breaking the ice.

Blaine barked out a laugh and rubbed the back of his neck. "I don't know. Should I have brought you a corsage?"

I looked up into his warm brown eyes, reflexively smiling at the sight. "I don't know. Are you gonna try to spike my punch and feel me up in the back seat of your family's station wagon?"

"Maybe," he winked.

We escaped my roommates' awkward questions and made our way down to Blaine's truck. Turned out, truck was an understatement. He drove a beast.

"Huh," I nearly snorted as we approached. "I hate to say it, but you surely live up to the stereotype."

"What?" he asked sheepishly.

I waved my hand in the direction of the gleaming black F-150 before me. "Southern guy with a big ass monster truck? If you have a camouflage cap in there, I'm going back upstairs."

Blaine laughed, shaking his head, as he opened the passenger side door. "No, sorry to disappoint you, but I don't. Looks like you're stuck with me for the evening."

Before I could respond, his hands had wrapped around my waist, and he was lifting me up into the truck effortlessly. I let out a little yip out of shock although I felt completely safe and secure with his hands on me. He even reached over and buckled me in, letting his incredible scent wash over me, as his mussed hair tickled my face. I should have known at that very moment that my fate was sealed.

"So where to?" I asked after he had climbed into his own seat and revved the car to life.

Blaine smiled that boyish grin that made even the most ornery woman forget her name. I imagined the countless pairs of panties that must have dropped instantaneously from that smile alone.

"I have to feed you before I put you to work."

"Put me to work?" I asked with mock offense.

Blaine winked a chocolate-brown eye, and I swear my heart stuttered. "You'll see."

Fifteen minutes later, we pulled up to a small diner in a rundown neighborhood. The parking lot was packed with cars, and I could hear at least five different types of music blasting from various stereo systems. The restaurant was old, nondescript, and reminded me of a hole-in-the-wall place with a chef that everyone called Cookie. I looked to Blaine with a raised brow. If this was the famous Blaine Jacobs persuasion, then he was extremely misguided and overly confident.

"Keep an open mind. I've got you; I promise," he smiled, his brown eyes smoldering under the dimming sunlight.

He jumped out of the truck and came over to open my door, nearly picking me up out of my seat. Then he laced his fingers through mine as he led me into the diner. It was packed, and I could feel the panic rising in my gut. There were so many people…so many eyes suddenly on us. The only thing that kept me from falling apart was the fact that every table was filled. I knew we wouldn't get a table and would hopefully leave. Thank baby Jesus for small miracles.

Heads turned instantly, and I heard quite a few people greet Blaine by name, including a tiny grey-haired lady behind the counter. She had a sweet face—one that reminded you of your grandma. Her eyes lit up when she saw Blaine and she flashed us a comforting smile.

"Hey sugar, you all go ahead on to your table. Mavis will be by with some sweet tea shortly, ok?" Her southern accent was thicker than Blaine's, as if she had lived in the area her entire life. For some reason, it warmed my soul.

Blaine led me to a small table towards the back, greeting what I assumed were regulars the entire way. They all seemed to know him well, especially the female patrons.

"I take it you come here often," I remarked once we took our seats.

"Yeah. I actually used to live a block away. My family and I came here all the time."

I nodded, picking up the plastic menu. "So what's good here?" I peered over the menu, noticing that Blaine hadn't even picked his up yet. He must have known it by heart.

"Everything, really. But the waffles are the best you will ever taste in your life. And it just so happens that we're here for breakfast."

"Breakfast?" I asked, giving him a confused glare. "Um, you do realize that it's nighttime, right?"

"True. But nobody does waffles like Ms. Patty. And you told me the first time I asked you out for breakfast that we'd have to do it some other time. And then I couldn't stay for it this morning. So yes, breakfast is in order. We owe it to each other."

I put my menu on the table and narrowed my eyes. "And what if I don't want breakfast?"

Blaine grinned but didn't get a chance to answer before a stocky-built young woman wearing an apron came by with glasses of iced tea.

"Hey baby, been a while since we seen you 'round here," she said to Blaine. He smiled at her politely then nodded towards me.

"Mavis, this is Kami. Kami, this is Mavis. Her family runs this old broken down joint."

Mavis flashed me a smile before smacking Blaine on the shoulder. "Hey now! If Mama hears you bad-mouthing her establishment, she's liable to send you back to wash dishes. Don't think you are above some *real* hard work, Blaine Jacobs. I knew you when you didn't have two nickels to rub together," she jibed.

We all chuckled before Mavis turned her attention towards me. "Well, you two get back to your date. Mama will be by for your order. It was nice meeting you, Kami. And Blaine, try to stay outta trouble, ya hear? And you still owe me a bike." Then she sashayed over to a table of rowdy teens.

"A bike?" I asked once we were alone.

Blaine shrugged. "She's adamant that I stole her bike and rode it into a ditch when we were eight. It was actually CJ that did it, but I never ratted him out," he winked.

"Hmph. Interesting." I picked up the menu and began scanning it again.

"Seriously," Blaine began, prompting me to lower the menu from my face. "Order whatever you want. You don't have to get breakfast."

I simply nodded and went back to perusing the selections in silence until a squeal rang out from beside us.

"You better stand up and give me a hug, you rascal!" the older grey-haired lady exclaimed.

"Yes, ma'am," Blaine smiled, standing up to wrap her tiny frame in his arms. He looked like a giant compared to her.

"And who is this beauty?" she asked, smiling at me.

"Ms. Patty, this is the lovely Kami Duvall. Kami, Ms. Patty has been whoopin' my ass since the day I was born."

"Hush that mouth, boy," she laughed, smacking him lightly with a rag. "Not in the presence of ladies. Now I know I taught you better'n that!"

"Forgive me. You certainly did, Ms. Patty."

I couldn't help but smile as she looked at Blaine with a loving pride that only a mother figure could possess. She loved Blaine, and I could tell that he loved her too. It made the walls around my heart crumble just a tiny bit more.

"It is so good to finally meet you, Kami," she said, grasping my hands with hers.

I just barely stifled a yelp from the contact and tried my hardest to transform my grimace into a smile. "It's really nice to meet you too, Ms. Patty."

"Oh, Blaine, she is just too precious," she remarked, patting him on the back. The look on his face was pure adoration, and I found it hard to tear my eyes away from his.

"Ok, what can I getcha? Blaine, you'll have your usual, right?" Ms. Patty said, pulling out a pen and pad.

"Yes, ma'am. Kami?" he nodded.

I pushed the menu away and gave Blaine a wink. "And I'll have whatever he's having, please."

The spontaneity was unlike me in every way, but the look on Blaine's face was worth it. I don't know what I would call it. Not quite joy, not quite admiration. It was something else…something warm and gratifying. Something that gave me the urge to do whatever I could to make him look at me like that again.

I must have gotten lost in those expressive eyes, because I totally forgot about Ms. Patty until she walked away, announcing that she would put our orders in right away. I shook my head, trying to regain my bearings.

"You're doing it again," I said, grasping a neon green flyer on the table advertising a car detailing shop.

"Doing what?"

"Giving me that look. Like you're studying me. Like you see something in me that's invisible to everyone else."

"I'm sorry. Does it make you uncomfortable?"

I shook my head, my fingers mindlessly tearing the paper. "No. Not really. But remember you said I distract you? And that's why I couldn't wear skirts?"

I heard him chuckle, but I was too bashful to meet his gaze. I knew the Asian flush was in full effect.

"Yet you have one on right now. Which you look incredible in, by the way. And it's distracting the hell outta me."

I chewed my bottom lip, my face flaming like a 12-

year old girl with Bieber Fever. "Well…when you look at me like that, you roll your tongue. Like you're playing with your piercing. And it's very, *very* distracting."

His hands were suddenly cupping mine, causing me to look up into his face. He was giving me that look, yet it was laced with something else. Something *more.* Something that made my insides clench with desire and my belly do somersaults. The feeling was new and unknown, and it both thrilled and terrified me equally.

"What's this?" he said just above a whisper, picking up the origami flower formerly known as a paper advertisement.

I shrugged. "It's a habit. When I'm nervous or stressed, I tend to do it without even thinking about it."

A frown marred his features, yet he never let go of my hands. "Are you nervous or stressed with me?"

I shook my head and gave him a slight smile. "No, you don't stress me out. But you do make me nervous. In a good way," I replied, repeating my words from last week.

"Hmmm, I wasn't aware there was a good kinda nervous."

We sat there for a few more seconds, his hands still housing mine, before Ms. Patty arrived with our food.

"Now here y'all go, just the way you like 'em, Blaine," she announced, placing giant platters of waffles covered with butter, fresh blueberries and whipped cream, with sides of bacon and sausage in front of us. My eyes grew twice their size.

"Now you take care of this young lady, ya hear?" she told Blaine, smiling at me sweetly. "Kami, you come by any time you like. And if this rascal gives you any trouble at all, you let me know, ok?"

I returned her smile with my own, and nodded. "I'll be sure to do that, Ms. Patty. Thank you."

Ms. Patty gave Blaine one last swat with her rag and turned to tend to the masses.

"She likes you," Blaine remarked, unrolling the silverware in his napkin.

I rolled my eyes playfully. "She probably says that to all your dates."

"Yeah right," Blaine scoffed. "First off, Ms. Patty doesn't do fake. If she doesn't like you, you will know it. And secondly, I've never brought a date here. Ever."

I tore my eyes away from the mountain of food in front of me and gave him a skeptical look. There was no trace of humor or deceit on his gorgeous face, and it quickly rendered me speechless. What could I possibly say to that?

"Eat up. You'll need your energy for later," he instructed, pointing his fork towards my plate.

"Energy?"

Blaine just chuckled and shook his head, taking a giant bite of blueberry-smothered waffles.

After nearly polishing off a plate of the best waffles I had ever had and earning an *"I told you so"* from Blaine, we said our goodbyes to Mavis and Ms. Patty and headed back out to Blaine's truck. I was beyond stuffed, so I was grateful that Blaine took it upon himself to lift me back onto my seat. I felt bad for him; I must've packed on at least 10 pounds in the past hour. Ms. Patty's food was more than worth it though.

Housing developments, strip malls, and restaurants became scarcer as Blaine drove east, the sight of thick, lush foliage whizzing by in the darkness. He turned onto a dirt-paved road surrounded by tall trees, and a niggling feeling in the back of my head set off alarm bells.

"Um, where are we going?" I asked with a trembling voice. Images of my body chopped up and stuffed into dozens of Ziploc baggies flashed in my mind. I shivered despite the warm temperature.

I felt his warm hand on my knee without even seeing him move. "You'll see. Don't worry; I won't let anything happen to you. You're safe with me."

I eased back into the seat, his touch radiating comfort and tranquility. It didn't feel like a sexual touch, being that he didn't stray from his position on my bare knee. It felt soothing…calming. It was all *Blaine*.

When he finally stopped the truck, I noticed we were at a field of some sort. I didn't really understand why he had brought me here. It was nearly pitch-black out. Suddenly, the earlier vision of my gruesome demise didn't seem so far off.

Blaine reached behind his seat and recovered two Mason jars, handing me one.

"And what do you expect me to do with this?" I asked.

"Catch lightning bugs, of course," he smiled, the lights of the dash illuminating his face.

"Lightning bugs? You mean fireflies? Why would you want to catch them?"

"Tomato, tom*a*to. I can't believe you never caught them before. I know y'all had lightning bugs down in ATL."

"I didn't grow up there," I replied, shaking my head. Without even thinking, I was telling him the truth. I was letting him in. "I'm from California, where they're called *fireflies*."

"Ah, makes sense. Ok, city mouse, time to show you how it's done."

He slid out of the truck and came over to my side to help me out. Then he took my hand and led me out into the field. "Look," he instructed, pointing out into the darkness. Dozens of tiny glowing insects swirled around us, creating a field of twinkle lights. I could hear the buzz from their wings, harmonizing with the sounds of crickets and distant night critters. The combination was oddly peaceful, and I let myself soak it all in.

"When I was a boy, my mother used to bring me out here at night so we could catch lightning bugs. We'd place bets to see who could catch the most. I think she always let me win."

I could almost hear the smile in his voice, and his accent suddenly sounded thicker. Rich with emotion. He was that little boy again, catching fireflies with his mom.

"She told me that you would always find the most lightning bugs when a summer storm was approaching. They were like a warning, illuminating the sky before the real lightning struck. They were nature's omen. The change in the atmosphere, the moisture in the air, some unseen current…they knew something big was coming. She swore she could predict the weather just by watching the lightning bugs. The more there were, the worse the storm."

"Sounds like a pretty resourceful woman," I remarked.

"She was. She knew a bit about everything. I never knew my dad, so she was all I had. And I believed every word she said."

His use of past tense did not go unnoticed by me. I squeezed his hand a little tighter and stepped into his side. "I'm sorry."

I could see Blaine shaking his head in the darkness. "Don't be. She died a long time ago. I believe I got her best years. Any more than that would have been selfish of me."

Strangled, silent moments passed between us as I digested Blaine's words. I imagined a little boy with expressive brown eyes and messy russet hair, crying for his mommy. Reaching out for the one person who he loved more than anything in the world. His lifeline. Alone, frightened and utterly helpless. He had lost his everything.

I didn't even realize how deeply his words had touched me until I felt a hot tear roll down my cheek. I don't know why Blaine shared that with me, but I was thankful. It reminded me that pain was necessary. Pain was life's curveball. Without it, we would never appreciate what it felt like to be loved.

"Come on, we've got some lightning bugs to catch," he said, looking down at me with a mournful smile. I never wanted to kiss him more than in that moment.

After Blaine taught me how to capture the bugs in the Mason jar, we spent the better part of an hour running through the field to see who could catch the most with only the truck's headlights to brighten our efforts. Despite jumping at every creak or rustle of the trees, I did pretty well for a first-timer. Blaine was a madman. I spent several minutes just watching him go crazy, nabbing the mystical little pests with a childlike fervor.

When we were both exhausted and sticky from the humidity, Blaine spread a quilt in the bed of his truck where we lay on our backs side by side. He turned on the truck's radio to a popular station, the sounds of OneRepublic, and our laughter the only noise to be heard for miles.

"Ok, before we tally up the results, would you like to make a little wager?" he asked holding up his jar of flickering insects.

"Oh please! You know you won. Betting against you would be stupid!"

I felt him shrug beside me. "You never know. Come on; humor me."

I sighed. "Fine. If I win…" I scrunched my forehead in concentration until a stroke of genius sent me into hysterics. "You have to perform at the next Open Mic Night!" Blaine's horrified expression only fueled my laughter, causing tears to roll down the sides of my face.

"Ok, ok, so you want to play it like that, huh?" he said loudly, trying to drown out my giggles. "If I win, you have to spend the night with me again."

His words quickly quieted my guffaws, and I rolled over onto my side to assess his expression. "You're serious."

"Absolutely. For some strange reason, I have a sudden appreciation for sleepovers." Blaine rolled over onto his side as well, putting us face to face. "And I do mean sleep. No funny business, young lady," he jibed.

"And here I thought you were going to wager a kiss," I said just above a whisper.

"Nah. No need," he replied, matching my hushed tone. "I was gonna do that anyway."

CHAPTER TWELVE

Blaine

This.

All I needed was *this*.

Her warm, sweet breath fanned across my face as she sighed with anticipation. I could almost hear her heartbeat stutter over the music. Hooded, sultry eyelids blinked slowly, those emerald green retinas sparkling under the moonlight.

This.

This moment was the only one that mattered. This woman in front of me was the only one that existed.

I wanted to make Kami mine in every way, shape, and form. I wanted to claim every moan, every whimper, every shudder. But for right now, I would settle for *this*. I would savor *this*. I would put every ounce of the concentrated desire exploding in every synapse like fireworks on the 4th into *this*.

This.

I couldn't see anything beyond *this*. Beyond her. Beyond us.

I just had to make her feel *this* too.

CHAPTER THIRTEEN

Kami

I always thought of myself as physically, well… normal. As emotionally and mentally fucked up as I was, I almost took pride in the fact that sex was never the issue. It was a welcomed distraction. An outlet for all the suppressed aggression and pain. I could be completely detached and let my carnal instincts take the reins. I could be as expressive as I wanted to be.

I could be fearless.

It numbed the pain and gave me a substitute for the love and affection I could never receive. My body felt what my heart could not. I knew I was damaged goods. But, it was the one thing… *he*…never took from me.

Sex, affection and love would never share the same space in the tidy little compartments of my psyche.

Until now. Until Blaine.

Everything I thought I knew about my heart and body was completely shattered the moment Blaine's arm snaked around my lower back and drew me to him. And when his soft lips fell on mine, I knew that I was far from normal. I knew I had never felt true intimacy until that very moment. I don't even know what I had been doing before.

I had kissed this man a thousand times in my head. In my dreams, he had explored every inch of my body with thorough precision. Blaine had already known me inside and out, and he didn't even know it. Hell, I couldn't even understand it. But the moment that metal barbell slid against my tongue, I knew. I knew that I was forever changed.

Blaine took me in that kiss. Right in the back of his truck with the crescent moon overhead and the forgotten Mason jars of fireflies at our sides.

With my breasts pressed against his hard chest—a chest that I had studied and committed to memory—our lips melded into one moving, tasting, teasing entity. He was gentle yet demanding, aggressive yet compliant. He was perfect. His scent, his taste, the way his lips seemed to know mine automatically. Absolutely perfect.

I allowed myself to get lost in him, wrapping my arms around his neck and back, our legs tangled together, seeking the warmth of each other's bodies. I moaned as his hand gripped my bare thigh and coaxed my leg around his waist. He groaned when my hand slid up from the nape of his neck and into his hair, tugging lightly.

I hardly registered the rumbling of thunder overhead. My tightly closed eyes didn't see thc flash of lightning that ripped through the sky. I was too consumed by him. Too overwhelmed by my own aching need for more.

Lightning sliced open the clouds, bleeding warm,

summer rain down on us in buckets. Reluctantly, we broke apart, panting, our eyes trained on each other. I wasn't done, and the seductive gleam in his eyes told me that he wasn't nearly done with me either.

"Come on," he growled, pulling me up with him.

We hopped off the truck and scrambled to shelter, laughing and squealing as the rain soaked us. I was only too aware of how my sheer top clung to my body, creating a silken second skin. But I didn't care. I would have peeled off every wet layer that very second if Blaine had asked me to.

The moment we were safely inside the cab, the heat of our humid bodies creating fog on the windows, reality set in. We had just officially crossed that unseen line between "just friends" and "much, much more." My cards were on the table. He now knew that I wanted him just as badly as he apparently wanted me. Fighting it would have been pointless and frustrating.

Just as the awkward silence had grown and swelled, filling up the enclosed space, Ed Sheeran began to belt out the words to "Kiss Me" on the radio, urging his lover to give herself over to his lips, lust and…love.

"Blaine…I…"

I don't even know what I meant to say. But as I looked at him, the longer front layers of his sandy brown hair wet and dripping into those melted chocolate eyes, and *that* song suggesting every emotion I had tried to avoid… I just had to say *something*. Because if I didn't, if I didn't keep my mouth busy, I was liable to lick every little raindrop from his face.

"Kami…" he murmured, a slight frown dimpling his

brows. But it wasn't out of anger or frustration. It was as if he was fighting his own impulses.

Thank baby Jesus that whatever they were, they won out over his restraint.

His lips were back on mine, and he was sliding my body towards his before I even knew what was happening. Still, I needed to feel more of him. I needed his heat to warm me. I needed his flavor to intoxicate me. I needed his scent to take me higher than I already was.

I straddled his lap, pinning my frame between his torso and the steering wheel without my mouth ever leaving his. The slick coolness of our rain-drenched bodies created erotic sounds of skin slapping against wet skin as we pawed at each other furiously in a hungered frenzy that I had never felt before.

This is what I had heard about, yet never experienced. The intense need. The fervent craze. The spark that combusted into an inferno when you were with that one person that you couldn't keep your hands off of. I honestly thought I didn't need it. I thought it wasn't necessary for a substantial sensual exchange.

Boy, was I wrong. Dead. Wrong.

In the midst of it all, I realized that my skirt had been hiked up to my hips, leaving my backside nearly bare in my thong. Blaine's hands were dangerously close, kneading my outer thighs. Did I want to take it there? Could I actually see myself having sex with him in his truck, out in the middle of nowhere?

As if hearing my internal battle, his lips and tongue still tasting me, Blaine's hands trailed up my hips, bypassing the exposed flesh of my ass, and rested on my lower back. But, as much of a gentleman as he was trying to be, he was still all *man.* I could feel his craving, as it pulsed with virility beneath me. He was unbelievably hard and… large. Large enough to cause me to do mental calculations, both excited and scared about the prospect of feeling every inch of him.

OhmyGodohmyGodohmyGod.

His agile fingers eased their way under my soaked top, his touch searing my skin. They massaged a path up to my bra clasp, stopping momentarily to see if I would object. When I didn't, still too lost in sensation to do more than moan against his lips and push my already pebbled nipples against him, he unfastened the clasp in a swift, stealthy move. I gasped into his mouth, causing him to pull me even closer into him, pressing my swollen breasts into his chest.

His hands slid to my front as his lips found my neck. I was already tugging at his wet, shaggy hair by the time I felt his thumbs on my nipples, rubbing them back and forth with perfect pressure. The erotic sound that tore from my chest was pure pleasure and surprise. Blaine, the man that had starred in every one of my fantasies, was fondling my breasts. I had imagined how his skin would feel against mine, had dreamt of fusing our panting bodies together, since the day I met him. And to be honest, I had never really had a fantasy before him. He was the embodiment of everything I had ever wanted.

And I could have him. Right here. Right now.

Not able to do much more than whimper as his fingers explored my chest, I shivered as Blaine kissed my collarbone, my chin, my trembling bottom lip, nibbling and licking like I was the most delicious thing he had ever tasted.

He was ravenous, like he just couldn't get enough, no matter how much of my skin he sampled.

"God, I want you, Kami," he murmured against the base of my throat. "I want you so bad."

That metal studded tongue slid up my neck to my earlobe, and I reflexively rotated my hips, feeling every inch of his arousal.

"Fuck," Blaine hissed, pinching my nipples so deliciously hard that I felt a tremor throughout my entire body. "Do you want me, baby? Tell me you want me. Tell me you feel this too."

An almost animalistic whine escaped me when he raised his hips into me, the friction of his jeans nearly undoing me through the thin lace of my thong. "Yes," was all I could find the strength to say.

"Yeah?" he rasped, finding my mouth again to suck my bottom lip. "Does that feel good to you?"

"Yesss." I felt the truck spinning.

His tongue flicked out to taste mine. "Do you want me to make love to you, Kami?"

Fuck.

My eyes popped open, trained on his hooded smolder, as I pushed back into the steering wheel. I was no longer lost in him. I was no longer swimming in a sea of sensation. I had capsized and was hurled onto shore, completely dumbfounded and terrified.

"No," I said shaking my head, my face stoic.

"What?"

"I said no. I don't want you to make… I don't want you to do that to me."

Confusion painted his gorgeously flushed face. "But

you said…"

"I do want you, Blaine," I quickly blurted out, not wanting to hurt his feelings or seem like a cock-tease. "I do. But I don't make love."

"I don't get it."

I grimaced, as I slid off his lap and sat beside him, suddenly freezing at the loss of his warm body against mine. Blaine must've felt the same chill because he switched on the heat.

"I don't make love, Blaine. I never have. In order to do that, you have to be capable of feeling a semblance of love. You have to be able to return it. I'm not. I can't."

"Kami, I didn't mean… Wait, what do you mean, *you can't?*"

I kept my glassy eyes trained on the darkness on the other side of the windshield. "I'm saying I'm unlovable."

His large hand was cupping my cheek and turning my head to face him just as the first tears welled in my eyes. I wanted to be able to love one day. I wanted to be able to feel pure bliss when someone uttered those three little words to me while gazing into my eyes. I wanted to surrender my broken heart to him so he could mend it, and make it new again.

But I couldn't. My past, my pains, had ripped that away from me. Fear had claimed me before love ever got the chance to.

"Kami, I find it hard to believe that you're unlovable. I know for a fact that isn't true."

I closed my eyes for a moment, trying to absorb the tears before they had a chance to fall. "That's because you don't know me. And if you did, I guarantee you'd agree with me."

His hand dropped from my face as his brows knitted together. It was all coming together for him. He was slowly getting it. I was broken. And no one wanted to play with the broken toy.

"It's getting late," I said turning my face away from him, so he couldn't see my trembling lip. I slid on my side of the car and reached for my seatbelt. "I better get home."

"Yeah. You're right."

I know I am, Blaine. No matter how bad I wish I could be wrong.

I heard him open his door and jog out to the back of the truck to secure it. The rain had let up, but inside I was battling a tsunami. When Blaine returned, he cranked up the truck without another word. A stubborn tear slid down my cheek, which I quickly batted away. It was an angry tear. I hated myself more in that moment than I ever had. I would have given anything to be someone else, someone normal, for Blaine.

We pulled up to The Madison without any more words exchanged. Blaine unbuckled his seatbelt, but I stopped him before he could open his car door.

"Don't get out," I said, grasping his forearm, thinking it would still his movements. Instead, Blaine slid his arm up so his fingers could tangle with mine. He looked at me expectedly, flipping the barbell in his mouth – the same one that I had sucked into mine and longed to feel again.

"Blaine," I began, worrying my lip with my teeth. "What I said… it has nothing to do with you. And because I actually *like* you, I had to tell you before we ruined everything. Before it all turned to shit before it began."

"What are you talking about, Kami?"

I took a deep breath, my eyes trained on our clasped hands. I wanted to pull mine away. I wanted to run and hide in my room for week to nurse the ache of regret. But then again, I wanted to touch him. *Needed* to touch him. I just didn't understand why that need was so strong.

"When I told you that I wasn't the girl you were looking for, I wasn't lying. I'm not. I'll never be. I can never give you more than this right here. And you don't want more. Trust me; it's not worth the hassle."

I flicked my gaze up to his warm, brown eyes and bit back the sob at the confusion he still wore. Then came a flash of resignation, causing him to pull his hand from mine. But he wasn't done with me yet. He unbuckled his seatbelt, leaned over to unclick mine, and pulled our bodies together.

"You're wrong," he whispered, his lips mere inches from mine. One arm snaked around my waist, imprisoning my frame to his, as the other raked my still damp tresses. "You're so wrong. And I'll prove it to you. I'll make you believe it one day."

"That's impossible," I replied, holding his gaze.

"It's not, Kami. Just no one has been man enough to stick around to show you. You scared them all away before they could. But I assure you, I'm not afraid. I'm not scared of whatever it is you think will send me running. I'm not going anywhere."

"For now. But eventually, you will," I murmured, pushing away from him before he could see the tears in my eyes. No one liked a chick that cried all the time.

I grabbed my purse, careful to keep my head down,

and opened the door to the truck.

"Hey," he called out, right before I jumped out. I kept my eyes fixed on the sidewalk below, afraid of completely losing it if I looked back at him.

"I mean it, Kami. I'll prove it to you. I'm not afraid of this, and you shouldn't be either."

I didn't respond. I simply nodded before swinging my legs out of the cab to hop down. Then I walked away from the only man I ever wanted. The man who had both owned me and set me free with just a kiss. The man who had broken me down and put me back together again with his touch.

Blaine. The scary-beautiful man I was terrified of loving.

CHAPTER FOURTEEN

Blaine

This was bullshit.

Complete bullshit.

I was an ass for letting Kami walk away from me. I should have stopped her. I shouldn't have let her go. But I couldn't make her stay, no matter how bad she needed to. I couldn't make her believe that I was different from all the other guys that had turned away from her. But I could show her. I could give her what they hadn't.

I just didn't know what that was.

I hadn't been able to sleep since she jumped out of my truck Monday night. I couldn't shake the image of those sad, green eyes from my head. I hadn't stopped thinking about the feel of her petite body in my arms, her full lips moving against mine. The way she tasted, the way she mewled and squirmed on my lap when I flicked her nipples.

Shit.

I needed that again. I needed *her* again. But more. So. Much. More.

I was the asshole that let her get away. I should've demanded she hear me out. I should have made her look me in the eye and tell me how she felt in return. Because though her mouth was telling me one thing, her body, her eyes, her lips…they told me an entirely different story.

Kami wanted me. And it wasn't just some superficial physical attraction. She felt how good we were together. She knew that whatever she was afraid of, whatever kept her running from me, could never win out over my feelings for her. Because, dammit, I fucking had feelings for her. And it was complete bullshit that I didn't tell her, in fear that it would scare her even more.

It was Wednesday, the first day I would see Kami after our date. Maybe she spent her day off thinking about me. Maybe she was just as tormented by her feelings as I was. And maybe, just maybe, she'd run right back to me, finally ready to let me in.

If only I could be so lucky.

I was talking to CJ when she walked in for her shift. Well, more like listening to sordid stories of his latest conquest: a 38-year-old divorcee with three kids, a sex drive that wouldn't quit and a thing for bondage.

"So this crazy-ass broad handcuffs me to the bed and leaves! Fucking leaves me butt-ass naked while she goes to pick up her fucking kids from school or some shit like that. And it wasn't until one of those little brats walked in and caught me, my dick flapping in the wind, before someone set me free!"

I shook my head. "Dude, that's fucked up. Where do you meet these women?"

"Milfs.com?" he shrugged. "It's cool. She actually has a pretty hot daughter that lives at home. She's 18, too…"

"You didn't."

"Shit! Why not? She was hot and legal! And her mom had left to go to some recital for one of her little crumb snatchers!" CJ exclaimed, downing his beer.

"So you had sex with her daughter?" Again, I shook my head in disbelief. CJ could really be a douche.

"Hey, it wasn't like she was a virgin. Not the way she hopped up and down on my…"

Before I could stop him from elaborating further, Kami walked in with Lidia, one of Dive's servers. The girls were laughing about some private joke and didn't even bother to look our way when they passed. Not even a wave or a smile. Not even a nod in my direction. Kami fucking ignored me like I wasn't even there.

"Dude, you totally just got the brush off. Damn!" CJ chortled, once they had disappeared into the back to clock in.

"Shut up and drink your damn beer," I replied, slapping one down in front of him with more force than necessary, causing it to slosh out of the bottle. I didn't care if he was right; he didn't need to point it out.

When Kami walked behind the bar, her black apron causing her tee to ride up a bit around her hips, I could feel the shift in the atmosphere. The air was thick with unspoken words and unasked questions. I'd never been the type to not say what was on my mind. Not anymore at least. But with CJ sitting just feet away and the Hump Day crowd filtering in, I didn't know when I'd get the opportunity.

"Hey, Kam," CJ shot out before I got the chance. I turned and pegged him with a murderous scowl. I knew exactly what he was doing, and if he wasn't careful, he would be outside on his ass. CJ was family, but he knew me well enough to know when to shut the hell up.

"Hey CJ," Kami smiled. Then she turned her gaze to me, her mouth settling into a tight line. "Blaine."

"Kami," was all I could muster without wrapping her in my arms and dragging her to the back, caveman style.

She flew into helping customers and straightening everything in sight, obviously trying to busy herself to avoid talking to me. I didn't get it. I thought we had left things sorta decent. But the way she barely looked at me had me second-guessing everything that went down between us two nights ago. Had I imagined it all? Had I only dreamt that she had been straddling me, fisting my hair, while I tried to slide my tongue over every bit of her neck and mouth?

She had felt it. I know she had. The craving. The need. The sheer madness of desire that made me want to rip off her clothes and taste every inch of her. She wanted me that night just as bad as I wanted her. Yet, now, she acted as cold and distant as a stranger.

Like I said. Bullshit.

It was nearing the end of the dinner rush when Lidia made her way to the bar, propping herself on a stool and bubbling with excitement.

"So guess what my boyfriend just told me?" she asked Kami. "His cousin from New York is coming into town on business and will arrive this weekend. He's some hot-shot, young investment banker and, *ohmygod*, totally hot!"

Kami poured the overly zealous waitress a soda and set it in front of her. "Okay?"

"Well, I thought it'd be a good idea if we hung out tomorrow night. You know, the four of us?"

"Kami works Friday night," I interjected before good sense could stop me. Shit.

Kami's green eyes plunged into mine, a mix of surprise and embarrassment in her gaze. They held me where I stood, testing me, challenging me to say more.

"Anyway," Lidia scowled, before turning back to Kami. "They'll be here to see A.D. play and then we're hanging out after work. So what do you say? He is really cute, Kami. And rich!"

Kami flashed a nervous smile before looking down and fiddling with the container of sliced limes. The image gave me a welcomed flashback of the night we met. Her tongue on my neck, slowly licking the salty trail. Her lips on mine, the barrier of lime the only thing stopping me from drinking her in… I got hard just thinking about it. Almost as hard as I was when she unknowingly sucked my bottom lip into her mouth.

Crimson painted Kami's cheeks as if she was recalling the same memory, and she quickly pushed the container away. "Geez, um, Lidia, that's really sweet of you to ask, but–"

"You're not seeing anyone, right?" Lidia asked, cutting her off.

Kami chewed her bottom lip nervously, as I looked on with rapt attention. "Um, no, I'm not…"

Bullshit. Total. Fucking. Bullshit.

"Good! What's stopping you?"

I waited for her answer, every second passing slower than the next. Her shaky fingers worked over a paper napkin, absentmindedly tearing and folding. She was panicky and reverting to her coping ritual. My hand flew out to hers, stilling her movements before I even knew what I was doing. Big, green eyes widened with surprise as she looked up at me, yet didn't pull her hand from my grasp.

"Lidia," I said, never tearing my gaze away from those emerald pools. "I think your customers need you."

Lidia huffed, murmuring her irritation under her breath, as she hopped off the stool. I didn't care. She could've called me every name in the book, and I still wouldn't have turned away from the contact I currently possessed.

"Kami," I breathed, stepping in closer. She angled her body towards me, her t-shirt clad nipples just barely brushing against my chest.

"Where'd you go, roadrunner? I thought you were done running," I whispered. I lifted a hand and slipped a tendril of hair behind her ear, my fingers lingering on her skin. I needed to touch her. In that moment, it had become as necessary to me as air.

"I'm not," she stammered, her voice unsure. "I mean, I am."

I smiled pensively at Kami, stepping in to close the distance between us. I wasn't going to ask her why she hadn't returned any of my messages. I wasn't even going to question her distant behavior towards me. Questions would have sent her running again. I had her now, and I wasn't ready to let go.

But the Kami that I knew, the Kami that was warm and soft and as sweet as candy wasn't in front of me. Whoever this beautiful stranger was knew nothing of dancing in a field as lightning bugs swirled around her bare legs. The sound of her laughter didn't make heat spread deep in my chest like lava. I had never tasted her lips while warm summer rain slid down our bodies.

No. This girl wasn't *my* Kami.

"Blaine," she began, the wavering uncertainty gone from her voice. The sound was harsh and foreign, and something inside me sunk into my gut. "We had fun; I'll admit. But that's all it was. We're coworkers. Let's just leave it at that."

Then she pulled her hands from mine, turned, and never looked back to see my stunned expression.

The next day brought a fresh blanket of bullshit when she came in for her shift with the same cold demeanor. But I was over it. She wanted to be left alone. She wanted to pretend like there wasn't shit between us. Fine. I'd play along. If that was what she needed, I'd give her just that. I wasn't going to keep chasing a chick that obviously didn't want to be caught.

We went hours without speaking, other than the occasional "excuse me" as we worked to avoid contact. Kami nearly sighed with relief when CJ came in after work, plopping down in his usual seat at the bar. She was so desperate to ignore me that she was actually happy for the distraction that my imbecile cousin brought. Un-fucking-believable.

"She still not speaking to you?" he asked, once Kami was out of earshot.

I shrugged. I wasn't in the mood to humor him. If I answered, he would press for more, which would result in me itching to press my fist into his face. I didn't understand it. How the hell could I? Kami had gone from scorching hot in my lap to as cold and awkward as a wet blanket. It was confusing and infuriating as fuck.

By the time Angel and her band made it in for Dive's first Open Mic Night, I was long overdue for a break. I needed a cigarette. Badly. I hadn't felt that craving since the first time Kami came barreling through the parking lot and into my life. She replaced the intense need from that day on. But with her purposely shutting me out, the taste for nicotine was clouding every sense and thought.

"Hi, Blaine!" a chorus of feminine voices greeted me when I returned to the bar. AngelDust had joined CJ at his usual spot at the bar and were chatting about the evening's events. I noticed Kami shift uneasily on her feet when she realized I was back.

I nodded and gave them a half-smirk before turning to a customer for an order. I was done being the nice guy. Chicks swore up and down that they wanted a good man, but when there was one right in front of them, they went for the douchebags and players instead. Maybe Kami was better off hooking up with Lidia's friend. Maybe she was into the suit-and-tie types. That wasn't me and never would be, no matter how badly I wanted to be her choice.

The staff kept their distance from me for most of the night. Even CJ directed his crude jokes and stories to Dom when he arrived just as the first act took to the stage. My head ached at the sound of amateur singers and musicians butchering perfectly good songs. Normally, I would have been more forgiving, maybe even shot CJ an amused look as I stifled my laughter at some of the really bad performances. But, as it was, I just didn't give a fuck. I just wanted them all to shut the hell up, drink their beer, and get the fuck out so I could take my pathetic ass home.

By the time a young guy took the stage, I was two seconds from saying, "Fuck it" and bumming a smoke from a customer. He began strumming his guitar, bypassing AngelDust's accompaniment, and I instantly picked up the tune. It was an older John Mayer song, speaking about the love between a father and daughter. His voice curled around the words as he sang of the girl who had been damaged due a broken relationship with her dad, too hurt and impaired to let anyone love her. It was a bit melodramatic for my tastes, but I liked it, and found the tension in my shoulders loosening a fraction with every profound note.

As if being pulled by an unseen force that I couldn't understand or resist, my gaze swept over to Kami who stood stock-still, her attention focused only on the man on stage. I couldn't even tell if she was breathing, though her mouth hung ajar just a bit. And, as if the same current pulled her to me, she slowly turned her head, giving me a full view of those big green eyes, shining with unshed tears.

I didn't even think about. I clapped CJ on the back, grabbing his attention and ordering him to take over. Then I scooped Kami into my arms and led her to the back office before anyone could get a glimpse of the beautiful girl who was crumbling before my eyes.

Once we were alone, the closed door muffling the song that had obviously conjured a hidden pain, I led her to the couch. I held Kami like my life depended on it—like *her* life depended on it—because at that very moment, I wanted to be her lifeline. Whatever was eating her up inside, I needed to make it right. I needed to make it better.

"Kami, baby," I whispered into her hair just as the first round of sobs wracked her entire frame, shaking us both. The ache behind the sound both startled and scared me. I had seen her cry before, but that was after her near-attack. She was in shock then, almost paralyzed with fear. This was different. There was so much anguish in her cries that it seeped into my skin. Her tears served as translucent tattoos, marking us both with the evidence of her immeasurable pain. I felt it. I broke for her too. I refused to let her suffer alone.

The semi-muted music shifted into an upbeat tempo, but I didn't let Kami go. I couldn't. Her tears had validated me. They gave me purpose, made me realize just how incredibly much I needed to be in this girl's life. And just how much I needed her in mine, no matter how hard she tried to fight it. The past few days were a distant memory. Her coldness towards me was forgiven and forgotten. I didn't give a damn about any of it. Only this girl in my arms mattered to me.

Even after she emptied all her tears into my shirt, I still didn't let go, murmuring soothing words as I kissed the crown of her head.

Kami's demons had somehow become mine without me even knowing them. And I swore on my life that I would fight every one of them. I would fight for *her*.

CHAPTER FIFTEEN

Kami

Shit happens.

I never really understood that saying. Yeah, there were certain situations in life that were shitty, but they were just that; they were *life*. So it really wasn't the shit in life that was, well, so shitty. It was life itself.

Life happens. That was much more appropriate.

Unfortunately, many of us found that out earlier than some. We found out just how awful life could really be. We found out that monsters were, indeed, real. They walked among us. They looked just like you and me. They came in the form of the people that we loved and trusted the most. The people whose only job was to love and protect us.

Funny thing about life is that it never turns out the way you want it to. It's never fair. It's harsh and brutal. It kicks you when you're down. It makes you wish you could give up and part with it just to have a semblance of peace.

I almost felt that peace unintentionally. And if I had

known exactly what I was fighting against, I would have succumbed to it. I would have traded my young shitty life for the peace that came with death.

I should have. I would have been free.

My father took me to a party when I was barely five years old. He said there would be other children there for me to play with. I was excited because he never took me anywhere. I usually stayed at home with my mother, breathing a sigh of relief whenever he was away. I got to watch television then. We didn't have to cower in my room whenever he was feeling "playful." It was the only time I didn't see my mother cry.

Yet, for some strange reason, my father took me along this time. I remember the loud music and the different colored bottles of strong smelling alcohol burning my small nose. I remember people staggering around in an intoxicated haze and the half-naked women gyrating on men's laps. And I remember the swimming pool. I had never seen one, and I was in awe.

Many of the adults kept disappearing inside to a back room. Then they would come back out, their eyes glazed and movements sluggish. My father told me he needed to go back in that room to "talk" to someone. I told him I wanted him to take me swimming.

"You wait here and I'll be right back," he told me. Then he dropped me into the pool, fully dressed, and told me to hang onto the side. I was too short to reach the bottom, and he said if I let go, I'd be in big trouble. I wanted to listen to him. I wanted to be good. I didn't want to do anything to ruin this experience for me. I was actually happy.

But I was five. And my 5-year-old intentions did not win out over my curiosity.

I let go of the edge. And I nearly drowned, finding just a slice of that peace at the bottom of the swimming pool.

I don't remember being pulled to the surface. I have no clue how long I was submerged. But when I finally regained consciousness, vomiting on the concrete as oxygen tried to combat the water in my lungs, I stupidly fought for my life. I battled for every breath, thinking that my life had to be better than the alternative.

I feared death when all along I should have feared life.

I sat on my bed cross-legged, dozens of tiny stars tickling my bare feet, as I put them back in the jar one by one. I had counted them over and over again since I broke down at Dive Thursday night. I could feel the cracks in my mask broadening into large fissures, splitting to reveal the little girl hidden underneath. The one that was so scared that it crippled her. The one that was afraid of someone finding out just how damaged and unlovable she really was.

"Knock, knock."

I looked up to find Dom standing in my doorframe, smiling his usual boyish grin full of mischief. I was one of the few people who ever got to experience this smile. It was *him*. Unmasked, free and real. It wasn't laced with pain or deceit. There was no anger in it.

"Hey you. What are you doing up so early on a

Saturday morning? I thought you had a date," I said, scooping the stars in my hand to hide them away. Of course, Dom had seen them before, but this was a personal process for me. It was something I could never share with anyone. No one would fully understand why I needed to count every single one.

Dom flopped back onto my bed, folding his hands behind his head. "Yeah. But I sent her home last night. Felt like sleeping alone."

I detected the affliction in his voice, prompting me to abandon my task. "Nightmare?"

"Yeah."

"Same as always?"

He nodded. "Yup."

I let my hand cup his cheek, hoping my warmth would soothe him. "Wanna talk about it?"

"Nope."

I wasn't offended. I knew he would decline; he always did. If I had to battle that caliber of pain and anger daily, I'd want to keep it bottled up too.

Dominic divulged his level of fucked-up-ness to me soon after we met. He was a known man-whore on our campus, and once we had established that we liked being around each other, he tried to sleep with me. I turned him down, and it wounded him. Deeply. He cared for me, and he thought that sex signified affection, both friendly and romantic.

"It's just… you're my best friend, Kam," he said to me, betrayal written on his handsome face after my rejecttion. "I love you more than anything else in this world. And this is the only way I know how to show how much you mean to me."

"Dom, do you love me like *that*? Like more than a friend?" I asked, grasping his hand. It was our thing. Dom needed constant affection, and I only found it acceptable with him.

"Well…no. I mean, I know I love you, but honestly, no. Not like that."

"Then you don't want to sleep with me."

Genuine confusion flashed across his features. "I don't get it."

I knew something dark and ugly had happened to Dom, but that moment solidified it for me. I would never, ever leave him. He was a smart, witty man, but emotionally, he was an infant. He honestly had no idea that sex and love were two totally different things.

Then he broke down and told me what happened to him, his inhibitions numbed after sharing a few bottles of wine. I cried for him. And when my sobs had grown out of control, stealing my breath, I wanted to vomit from the sheer repulsion of his account. My beautiful, dear friend deserved every one of those anguished tears.

"I didn't understand, Kam," he cried, his face buried in my neck as I held him tight. "He was my uncle, and he said he loved me. He said that if I loved him that I would show it. That I would be a good boy and show him my love. And when he invited his friends to come over and… and… *fuck!* When he let his friends fucking rape me over and over, he said it was because he loved me so much that he had to share it. He had to share his love for his nephew by letting them fuck me!"

He went on to tell me how it continued for years and

didn't stop until Dominic was hospitalized for severe damage to his rectum. His uncle had been his caretaker since a car crash claimed the lives of Dom's parents when he was just a toddler. The police investigated and arrested all the sick-fucks involved, including his uncle, the only family that Dom had ever known.

After his body had healed, Dom was sent to live with a relative in North Carolina when he was 14. The relative, a distant older cousin, was a stranger to him and only took him in out of obligation. She never helped him heal emotionally from the trauma or cared enough to get him help. So Dom coped in the only way he knew how—with sex. He slept with any girl that would have him, desperately trying to prove to himself that he was straight, that he hated everything his uncle had done to him. But he couldn't deny that he still loved him. He was the only parent he had ever known. The conflicting feelings, the abuse, it fucked with everything he thought he knew about love and sex, right or wrong.

The man that laid beside me today was still confused and outraged but he had begun to heal. He knew that intimacy wasn't a substitute for affection, but he sought it out anyway. He needed that constant reassurance. He needed the physical reminder that he was a man, that no amount of abuse could strip him of his masculinity. I still hurt for him deeply, but I was honored to love him. He of all people deserved it.

"Kam?" he said, pinching my thigh and breaking me from my morbid account. "Wanna tell me why you've been missing Dr. Cole's appointments?"

I shook my head and resumed putting the tiny origami

stars back in the glass jar. "Because I'm not going back. It doesn't help. And she thinks I'm being irrational."

Dom let out an exasperated sigh. "You have to talk to somebody, Kam. I'm serious."

"I talk to you." I got up and put the jar in its spot on my windowsill before walking over to grab my guitar. I needed a distraction.

"Bullshit. You don't talk to me. And I'm afraid that I won't be around when you finally *need* to talk to me. Please, Kam, give Dr. Cole another chance."

"Why the hell is she calling you about me anyway? You aren't my father. Doesn't that break some kinda patient-doctor confidentiality?"

"She didn't tell me what you two talk about," he replied, rolling his beautiful eyes. "Her office called to find out what's been going on."

"Mmm hmm," I said, lightly strumming the strings. I was done talking. Nothing Dom could say would make me go back to therapy. It was a waste of time and money.

Dom got the hint and sat up with a huff. He knew I wouldn't budge. "Fine. But the moment you feel yourself losing control, you come to me. Ok? Don't give me that "I'm fine" bullshit. Next week, we look for another therapist."

I nodded and just kept thrumming, getting lost in the melody that had been stuck on a continuous loop in my head for days. I hadn't played for weeks but, for some reason, I felt the need to let my emotions trickle out in song. It flowed easily, and before I even realized it, I was humming, and the story was slowly coming into focus.

It was a song about hope and longing. About wanting

something so bad but feeling too afraid to admit it. About fighting against fear and denial and letting in the unknown. The song swelled and flourished, the picture behind my closed eyelids becoming brighter and clearer. Hums turned into lyrics and the tune took on a life of its own, only using me as the vessel. And once it began to climax, the anticipation building deliciously, the picture came into focus, and I nearly broke into a sob.

Blaine. All I could see was Blaine. He was the muse for every song, every painting, every dream. He occupied my deepest, most intimate desires, and hindered my past pains from consuming me with his touch.

It had always been Blaine. I just wasn't ready to see it.

I wasn't sure what I would tell him, but I knew it was time. I couldn't keep fighting what my soul so desperately needed. Him. His presence, his smile, his words. They were all necessary. It was the thought of not having those things that sent me into a panic. It was even stronger than the anxiety I felt at the decision to let him in.

But of course, life had different plans. It always did. It never stuck to the script that you had rehearsed in your head a dozen times. It didn't give a shit about crushing your expectations, causing you to second guess what you were so certain about just moments ago.

We had been at work for a couple hours when life decided to remind me just what a bitch it could be. Things had been better since Thursday. Pleasant. Blaine insisted I take Friday off after my meltdown, and I was too humiliated to argue with him. It's not that he made me feel embarrassed for losing it behind the bar. It was the total opposite, actually. He was sweet, gentle, patient. He was exactly what I needed. What I wanted.

AngelDust had just kicked off their set with one of their newer up-tempo songs, when Kenneth approached the bar with some of his buddies. I was shaking my hips as I flitted behind the bar, serving customers with an easy smile, as I sang along to the provocative tune. The moment his eyes locked with mine, I froze, nearly sending the highball glass in my hand crashing to the ground. Kenneth looked just as surprised before his mouth turned up into a smug smile.

"So I see you landed on your feet, Kamilla," he said coolly. He refused to call me Kami, no matter how many times I corrected him.

"Yeah," I rasped, my throat tight. My heart was hammering in my chest, and I was certain he could see it through my thin, snug tee.

"I have to say, I'm disappointed. A woman with your... skill set, working at a bar? Hmph."

I was furious. At him for being such a pretentious prick, and at myself for choosing not to see that he had always been one. Kenneth Walters was a partner at one of the most successful law firms in Charlotte. His father started the firm from the ground up decades ago, and their family was known as modern day royalty.

When a temp agency had assigned me to his office, I had hoped to reevaluate my life goals. Once upon a time, I wanted to pursue a career in law. I had majored in criminal justice and had hoped to focus on family law. But as the saying goes, "The best laid plans of mice and men often go astray." Robert Burns got the memo on just how shitty life could be.

I shook off the shock of seeing him and gave Kenneth a hard glare. "My skill set? I answered phones and fetched your coffee, Kenneth. There's nothing to be disappointed about. I actually like it here."

"That's cute," he scoffed. "But if you change your mind about your future, you know I can find a place for you at the firm. Just say the word. I'm serious, Kamilla; you don't have to slum it at some rundown bar just to avoid me."

"Who's slumming it?" a smooth as silk masculine voice said from behind me. With the tension swirling between Kenneth and I like noxious gas, I hadn't even felt him approach. Usually the lower regions of my body knew he was near before my head did.

Another smug smile played on Kenneth's lips. "Well, if it isn't Blaine Jacobs. I see not much has changed since high school. Still working at the family bar?"

"What are you doing here, Walters?" Blaine nearly growled, his jaw tight with visible anger. He was not a Kenneth fan.

He shrugged. "I heard the hottest band in town played here on the weekends. Me and the guys thought we'd check it out. I didn't know the staff was just as enticing," he said pinning me with his dusky blue eyes. I couldn't believe that I had once found them gorgeous and alluring. Now they just seemed icy cold.

"Is that right?" Blaine answered flatly.

"It is," Kenneth shot back, making his retort sound more like "Fuck you." He looked Blaine up and down, sizing him up. "Congrats on beating those charges, Blaine. I heard it was a tough one, but Edward Maren is one of our best attorneys. Hopefully, you won't require his services again."

I looked up at Blaine with question in my eyes but bit my tongue. Kenneth was baiting him and I'd be damned if I aided in his extreme assholishness. But I knew something was up. I had never seen Blaine look at anyone so threateningly, and it both worried and thrilled me. Something inside me liked this side of him. It was dangerous and undeniably sexy.

Blaine stared daggers right back at Kenneth before returning my gaze, his eyes instantly softening into melted chocolate. I could see his mouth troubling the metal in his mouth, and I reflexively focused on his lips, fighting the urge to still his assault with my own tongue.

"Ahem."

Both our heads snapped back to Kenneth who looked like he had just experienced a drive-by colonic. "Hmmm, interesting," he sneered. "Looks like those… *special skills* …aren't going to waste after all, though I have to say, they could be put to better use. All the same, you know where to find me if you change your mind, Kamilla." Then he slapped a hundred dollar bill on the bar along with his business card, summoned his cronies, and turned away.

I knew that if I didn't intervene, Blaine would fly over the bar and beat Kenneth into the hardwood. His fists were balled at his sides, and his lips were drawn so tight that they were white. I could feel the heat of rage radiating from his trembling body. He was beyond pissed and if I didn't act fast, Kenneth would be leaving in an ambulance and Blaine in a squad car.

So I did what any normal young woman would do when an incredibly hot man was turning her on with his bad boy charm. I pressed my hands to his chest, stood on my tiptoes, and kissed the hell out of him.

Blaine didn't reciprocate at first, being that I had caught him totally off guard. But once his lips started working with mine, his strong arms pulling me flush against his body, I could've sworn that Kenneth, his butt-buddies and the rest of the bar had fallen away, bringing us right back to our little island off the coast of Dive. It had been a while since we had been here, but now that we were, I never wanted to leave.

Blaine let his tongue caress mine, and I felt myself melt in his hands. I wasn't worried though. He had me. Blaine had always had me, no matter how hard I tried to fight against that fact.

"What was that for?" he asked against my lips, our foreheads still touching.

I touched my lips with his once more. "You're hot when you're mad."

He squeezed me tighter to him, splaying his large hand just above my backside. I could feel the front of his jeans growing stiffer by the second. "Only when I'm mad?"

I giggled. I couldn't help it. This guy knew he was drop-dead delicious, and something about him made me feel like a damn schoolgirl.

Blaine stood up straight and looked over my shoulder.

It was his turn to smile smugly, and I let him have his moment. With my body still fused with his, he grabbed the $100 off the bar and held it up. "Drinks on this asshole!" he said, pointing at Kenneth, who was bubbling over with fury. But he wasn't an idiot. He knew he had his daddy's money and power to hide behind but he wasn't willing to suffer an epic ass whooping just to prove that theory.

The patrons around the bar erupted into cheers, and Blaine and I reluctantly broke apart to serve bottles of beer. Many gave us knowing smiles and winks while Blaine's fan-girls shot me obvious scowls. I had gotten used to them. They were like gnats—insignificant, annoying as hell, and impossible to get rid of. No matter how many times Blaine swatted them away, they just kept coming back.

Once we had distributed the beers, and Kenneth had retreated with his tail between his legs, Blaine turned to me, his brown eyes smoldering. The fire that had ignited between us since the moment our lips touched was still kindling, and the way he was looking at me only fanned the flames between my thighs.

He stepped forward, bringing his lips down to my ear. I shivered as they brushed the shell. "Care to tell me how you know Kenneth?"

"Care to tell me how *you* know him?"

He lifted his head, a small frown resting between his brows. I could see the internal battle playing out in his expressive eyes. With a resigned sigh, he nodded. "Yes. Tonight. I'm taking you home with me."

"Excuse me?" The butterflies in my stomach broke out into a choreographed happy dance, flash mob style.

"Don't get excited. I'm not giving it up no matter how badly you want it," he teased. "I just want to talk. And I want to show you something. Ok?"

I was nodding before he even finished his sentence. "Ok. I want to talk to you too."

This was it. This was my chance to tell him how I felt. But what would I tell him? How did this type of thing go? I had only been on the receiving end of those awkward conversations, and my reactions were less than gracious. Oh shit, would Blaine laugh in my face? Could I blow this thing between us with my tendency to obsess over every freakin' thing?

"Breathe, baby," he murmured in my ear, his warm breath blanketing my bitter thoughts. "Breathe, Kami. It's ok."

I listened to his words, letting them pull me back to the surface. Bringing me back to him. That's when I felt the fresh droplets of sweat on my forehead. My skin was clammy and hot, and my hands were trembling. I let out the breath I had been unknowingly holding, my lungs whining at the loss of oxygen. I had nearly sent myself into panic attack. Again. *Shit.*

Blaine rubbed the back of his neck. "Look, you don't have to do this if you–"

"No, I want to," I insisted, cutting him off. "I mean, I want to go to your place, Blaine. If you still want to talk."

He smiled, and it was pure and real. Not laced with hidden malice. Not infused with lust or desire. It was an honest-to-goodness happy smile. And his smile made me smile.

"Have I ever told you how much I love it when you

say my name?" he asked, grabbing my hips and pulling me closer.

"Do you…Blaine?" I replied sweetly. I didn't have the guts to tell him how much I loved it too. And how I craved to scream it.

He let out what sounded like a hiss between his teeth. "Keep talking like that, and I might shut this place down early."

"Sure, bud. Mick will have your head for that," I chuckled. Reflexively, I scanned the perimeter for him, not wanting to get caught flirting again.

"Yeah, right," Blaine snorted.

He opened his mouth to say something else, but CJ came barreling up to the bar, completely trashed. He tried to flop onto a stool, missed it, and tried three more times before getting himself settled.

"Holy fuuuuck, dude! I am so fuckin' wasted!" he slurred, slumping over on the bar.

I grabbed a glass and filled it to the brim with water, setting it in front of him. CJ could barely lift his head to drink it.

"Dude, drink. You know your dad is gonna flip once he sees how sloppy drunk you are."

CJ made a face, but picked up the glass and chugged. He set it down empty and hiccupped. "B, get me some food so I can soak this shit up. Please?"

Blaine let out an annoyed huff before turning for the kitchen. I went to swipe CJ's empty glass when his hand reached out to grab my forearm.

"Hey," he rasped. "You like him, don't you?"

Reflexively, my eyes went to the direction of Blaine's

retreating back that was being swallowed by the crowd. I looked back at CJ and shrugged.

"And he likes you." It wasn't a question.

I pulled my arm away from his weak grasp and turned to refill his glass.

"So what's wrong with you?"

I spun on my heel to face his sweaty, dazed face, my eyes narrowed in irritation. "Excuse me?"

"You know," CJ replied, leaning forward. "What's wrong with you? What's your sob story? Blaine likes that type."

I stepped towards him, a hand on my hip. "What type?"

"The broken ones. The ones with issues. The chicks that need to be saved and look at him like a knight in shining fucking armor." He closed his eyes, and his mouth curled up on one corner before he laid his head on the bar. "The fucked up, damaged girls. *Just like his mom*. He needs that. All part of his Captain Save-a-Hoe complex. He needs to rescue them." Then he was out like a light.

What the *hell*?

Before I could smack CJ across the back of the head to wake him so he could tell me more, Blaine appeared with a basket of food.

"Wake up, asshole. I'm calling you a cab," he said, setting the burger and fries down next to his cousin.

Shaken by CJ's words but not wanting to let it show, I plastered on my mask and gave Blaine a pensive smile. Questions ran through my head on an endless conveyer belt, each one leaving me more and more unsure of what I should do. But I needed answers. And the only way I could get them was to ask.

We finished our evening in comfortable silence, brushing against each other and stealing lustful gazes whenever we got the chance. I had to admit, I was still excited at the prospect of being alone with Blaine, despite what his motives could have been. I wanted him. So. Damn. Much. But something inside me needed more than just the physical release that I knew he could provide. A part of me that had been forced into self-preservation, blocking itself off from the love that it desperately needed to thrive. This…feeling… had nothing to do with my head. Even my lady bits had to take a backseat to the foreign emotions.

Yet CJ's words continued to replay in my head, nagging my rationality until it gave into doubt. Could I really trust Blaine? Could he only be drawn to my scarred, fragile psyche, feeling some strange, deep-seated need to rescue me from my demons? I knew if that answer was yes that I wouldn't survive it. I couldn't come back from that type of pain. I had already lived through so much. I had already reached my limit of heartache for this lifetime. I wanted to open up to Blaine, I truly did. But I wouldn't be some pet project. I wouldn't be a pathetic charity case. And because I refused to be just another broken girl in need of fixing, I knew that I could never tell Blaine who I really was.

Blaine would soon realize that, no matter how hard he tried, I was beyond fixing. Because you can't fix what was never really right in the first place.

CHAPTER SIXTEEN

Blaine

I didn't really know what to expect. I just knew that I needed to be with her. I needed her in my space, in my arms. I needed to know that she was safe for the night. It was damn pathetic, but it was my truth. And the closer we were to approaching that truth, her following behind me in her Nissan Sentra, the stronger that need grew.

I needed to have Kami tonight.

Every part of my body was screaming for her. And the way she kissed me just hours before, told me everything that I needed to know. The way her nipples hardened instantly against my chest. The way she shivered when my fingers found that patch of exposed skin just above the waist of her low-rise jeans. The way she moaned into my mouth whenever I sucked her tongue. Oh yeah, Kami needed me too.

But I wanted to do this right. I needed to give her a

reason to trust me, to never doubt me. I needed her to trust me with her heart, as well as her body. And something told me that that would be harder than trying to get CJ to go 24 hours without talking about his junk and all the sordid shit he does with it.

We pulled up to my house, parking side by side in the driveway. It was late/early and pitch-black out, but she still seemed to appraise the yard and outdoor furnishings intently.

"You live in a house?" she asked, obviously surprised. She ran her fingers over the wicker chair on the porch.

"Yeah?" I didn't know why it sounded more like a question. For some reason, her approval seemed more crucial than ever. Of course, I wanted to impress her, but it was more than that. I wanted her to feel comfortable here. I wanted her to be at home in my place, maybe even enough to call it her own…

Where the fuck did that come from?

I shook the insane thoughts from my head and grasped her hand, threading my fingers through hers. "Come on, let's go inside."

Her careful assessment of my home continued when I ushered her through the hall and into the living room. Her big green eyes danced from every piece of artwork, every houseplant, every picture. Then she would glance back at me and smile, as if trying to make the connection.

I rubbed the back of my neck nervously. I had no idea why the hell I felt so anxious. It's not like she was the first woman I'd had here. But, if I was being honest with myself, she was certainly the most significant.

"Would you like something to drink? I have wine,

beer, water, soda…"

"Wine, please," she smiled, appraising my collection of shot glasses on the special shelving I had installed to house them. They spanned most of the dining area leading to the kitchen. "Oh wow, how many of these do you have?"

"Um, I don't know. I lost count. Dozens, I suspect," I called from the kitchen, watching as she picked up a few that had caught her eye. I joined her, handing over a glass of red wine. She took a long sip and hummed her approval, causing more than one of my body parts to swell with pride.

"I like to pick up a few whenever I visit a new place."

"You like to travel?" she asked, fingering one with a red, animated crab on the side that said *Myrtle Beach.*

"Yeah," I said, before taking a sip from my own glass. "You?"

"I guess," she shrugged. "I mean, I have traveled quite a bit, so I guess I should say I enjoy it."

As if she didn't mean to offer so much about herself, Kami cringed before taking another hefty gulp. I noticed that she didn't like to talk about herself. At first, I found it a refreshing change from the normal chicks that would prattle off about any and every trivial detail of their lives. I thought maybe she was a bit shy or just a really great listener. Kami hardly ever divulged anything about herself, though. I wouldn't even know her full name, age, and birthday if it hadn't been on her job application.

Not wanting to spoil our easy banter, I decided not to push for more. I set my glass down and made my way to the stereo system. Kami loved music, and my hope was that it would soothe her enough to open up.

I was right. As Imagine Dragons crooned out the first haunting notes of "Demons," Kami began swaying from side to side, singing along softly. I couldn't really hear her, but I knew she had an amazing voice from the few times I had heard her sing along with AngelDust. She didn't think anyone could hear her—I could tell she wasn't singing for attention or praise—but Kami was a natural. Any note that Angel could hit, she matched it effortlessly. She knew every run and even incorporated her own adlibs when she was really into it. I wanted to ask her why she didn't perform with the band but I knew she would just brush me off. Either that or clam up and withdraw. Tonight was all about the opposite. I wanted Kami to open herself to me in every way.

"You like them?" I asked, situating myself behind her, close enough that her ass lightly brushed against my front, as she continued her little dance. Her wineglass was empty, and I knew she was feeling the effects. I took it from her and set it down, freeing her hands to explore further.

"Mmm hmm," she answered in her singsong voice. She picked up a shot glass with a picture of a green leaf on it and turned to face me with an accusatory glare.

"Amsterdam," I answered with a shrug.

"You've been to The Netherlands?"

I nodded and reached past her to grab one that boasted the Eiffel Tower. "It was closed when I went but it really is spectacular. Especially at night. I've heard New Years is crazy there! I definitely gotta do it."

"Wow," she said, exchanging the memento from the marijuana capital for one from the city of romance. "That'd be awesome. I can only imagine."

"Go with me."

I pinned her big green eyes with my gaze, not a trace of humor in my expression. I meant every word. I wanted to show her things. I wanted to take her places she had never been before. I wanted to create a world so safe and secure for her that she would never, ever feel the need to shut down again. And I didn't even know her. Not the way I yearned to.

"That's crazy," she muttered, putting the shot glass back on the shelf and picking up one of Big Ben.

"Why is that?"

"Well, for starters, I don't even know you, Blaine."

Gently, I pulled her face towards mine. "Get to know me."

My lips were on hers in an instant, my tongue tracing her pouty lips. I kissed her deeply before pulling back. Her eyes fluttered open, dilated and hooded from eroticism and wine.

"I've wanted to do that since the first day I met you," I whispered, my thumb stroking her cheek.

"You damn near did," she smiled.

"Hmmm, that's not how I remembered it. I believe it was *you* who tried to kiss *me*." I made a tsking sound before placing another peck on the corner of her mouth. I couldn't help myself. She had the sweetest, fullest lips I had ever tasted.

"Whatever! Don't pretend that you weren't practically wagging that metal studded tongue at me! You knew exactly what you were doing!"

I narrowed my eyes and took a tiny step back. "So you like the tongue ring?"

"What?"

"Do you like it?" I rasped, dropping my voice an octave. "Does it feel good to you?"

"Um, uh," Kami sputtered before swallowing. Without bothering to ask, she grabbed my wine glass and downed its contents.

"I'll take that as a yes," I laughed. She tried to feign offense before succumbing to her own amusement.

"Hey, where's this one from?" she asked, once we had both calmed down and diverted our attention back to the shot glasses.

I took the blank, nondescript glass from her hand and turned it over in my fingers. "Dive."

"Dive? Why would you take one from the bar you work at?" Picking up another unmarked glass, she frowned with confusion. "This one from Dive too?"

"Yep."

"O-kay. Seems kinda silly to put these up with all the other ones that are obviously significant to you."

I smiled, stepping in closer to her. Close enough to smell the vanilla and orchid scents of her shampoo. "These are significant to me too. The most significant. This is the shot glass your lips touched the first night I met you. This is the one you used when we shared a Screaming Orgasm."

She stared at me in stunned silence for a beat before clearing her throat. "So… you just go around collecting every glass I drink from?"

"Yep." I took a step forward, causing our fronts to touch. I could feel her heart beat faster with the move. "Every. Single. One."

She drew in a mortified breath, her eyes growing

unbelievably large before I broke into a peel of uncontrollable laughter.

"Oh my God! You should see your face," I howled at her confused expression. "Relax, Kami. I swear I don't creep around in the shadows, stealing your drinking glasses!"

She shook her head in disbelief. "You are such a creepy asshole, Blaine Jacobs!"

"Awww, come on now." I set the glasses back in their designated spots before wrapping my arms around her narrow waist. "Seriously, I'm not a creeper. But I did save those two. Maybe I was having a semi-creeper moment but, hey, I didn't think I'd ever see you again after you ran outta the bar that night. And when you popped back up, I knew it was fate. I wanted to commemorate that. I believe in celebrating the things that are meaningful to you, no matter how petty they may seem. If they made you feel something at one time, if their memory incites some type of emotion, then they deserve to be acknowledged."

"Wow," she whispered, her eyes low and sultry. "I must be tipsy, because that was the most beautiful thing I have ever heard."

I chuckled before placing a kiss on the tip of her nose. "Come on, let's get you off your feet."

I led her to my living room sofa, killing the music and clicking on the TV instead. "I've got the movie channels; anything in particular you wanna watch?" I asked, scrolling through the menu.

"I don't know. Any horror flicks on?"

I cocked a brow. "Horror? Seriously?"

"Yeah, why not?"

"I don't know," I shrugged. "I just pegged you for a chick flick lover. You know, guy meets girl, they fall in love, and skip into the sunset or some equally sappy shit like that."

"Blech," she replied with a mock shudder. "That's way scarier than any horror movie. Besides, the real monsters aren't stalking in the shadows with masks and butcher knives. They don't have fangs or claws. They're all around us, hiding in plain sight. That's what's scary."

Her solemn words hit me like a ton of bricks, reminding me of why we were really here. I cut off my flat screen and turned towards her. It was time to say "Fuck it" and put all the cards on the table.

"The real reason I brought you here is because there are things I need you to know about me. Things that may help you understand why I say some of the shit that I do."

She nodded. "Ok. I think there's some stuff I need to tell you too," she replied with an edge of uncertainty. She chewed her bottom lip and cast her eyes down to her hands knotted in her lap.

I took a deep breath, preparing to dive in headfirst. "Ok. I had sort of a rough patch after my mom died. I was the typical out-of-control teen, not giving a fuck about grades or my future. I skipped more than I attended. And I had a temper. Shit, honestly, I still do.

"There was this girl named Amanda. Cheerleader, blonde, perky…and I was wild, rugged and had already collected quite a few tattoos and even more piercings."

"Really?" she asked with genuine interest. "What kinda piercings?"

"Other than the ones you know about…eyebrow, lip,

septum…"

She couldn't hide the flush of her cheeks as her eyes wandered to my crotch, worrying the hell out of her bottom lip.

"Um, no. Hell no," I smiled, with a slight shake of my head. "Nothing down there is pierced. But good to know you're concerned."

Her cheeks went from pink to beet red. "Oh God."

I laughed it off and took her hands in mine before she wrung them raw. "I don't really do the piercings any more. I guess I grew out of them. Well, most of them," I shrugged. "But yeah… I was rough around the edges. Not the guy you wanted picking your daughter up for a date. Amanda was always nice to me though. We started as friends; we'd hang out, talk…nothing more. She was dating this guy—captain of the football team—and one night he beat the shit outta her. She showed up at my house, busted up and bleeding, scared to tell anyone because his dad was some douchebag politician. Anyway, you can guess what happened next."

Kami nodded. "You beat the guy up," she said just above a whisper.

"Yeah. After that, it made sense for me and Amanda to be together. She was scared to go anywhere without me, and I felt like I needed to constantly watch her. Eventually, we became more than friends. Then, after graduation, we got married."

Her jaw dropped before pulling down into a horrified sneer. She snatched her hands from mine. "You're… *married?*"

"Divorced. Amanda and I tried to make it work for a

couple of years, but we just weren't right together. We had nothing in common. We were from two different worlds. Other than sex, there was nothing to bind us." I looked away, searching for the best way to make Kami understand. "And even that faded."

My eyes met hers, and I swear I saw something soften in them. They reflected mine, so full of confusion, pain, anger, longing. Maybe she understood more than I knew. Maybe she could see and accept my past just as I had hoped to accept hers.

"Amanda ended up pregnant. But not by me."

"What?"

"Yeah. She cheated on me. I found a pregnancy test in the bathroom trash, and I asked her about it. Eventually, she admitted the affair and left me for the other guy."

"What a minute—how did you know the baby wasn't yours?"

I scrubbed a hand over my face a bit more forcefully than I intended. I hated reliving this shit. I was undoubtedly over Amanda, but that didn't make it any easier to rehash.

"I always used protection. Even with her. Amanda didn't want to get on birth control because she claimed it would make her fat or some shit. I knew condoms weren't 100 percent so I thought there was a chance the baby could be mine. But she admitted to having unprotected sex with that motherfucker."

"Blaine," Kami whispered, the sweet sound of her voice pulling me out of my past hell and bringing me back to the present with her. "I'm sorry."

I brushed my fingers across her jaw. "Don't be, baby. It was for the best. See, you can't save someone who doesn't want to be saved. They have to want to fight, too. They have to see that they're actually worth the fight. Amanda didn't see that. She went right back to that asshole, right back to the guy who roughed her up. I agreed to step back and let them be happy. I knew that we should have never gotten married. If that was her choice, I wasn't going to stand in her way."

Her hand covered mine on her cheek, and she nuzzled into the touch. "But?"

I nodded. Of course there was a "but." These stories were never cut and dry.

"The guy, Clark, came into Ms. Patty's diner one day with his friends. I would help out over there sometimes. He knew that and wanted to rouse me up. He and his shit-stain minions started being obnoxious, ordering food and sending it back, throwing shit on the floor. I approached him, told them to leave. He didn't take that too well, so I taught him some manners."

"The charges?"

"Yeah. I got carried away. Put him in a coma. I told him to leave; I told him to walk away. I didn't want to hurt him like that but he would not fucking listen." I sucked in a sharp breath, willing myself to calm down. "I was charged with 1st Degree Assault and would potentially face jail-time. I hired Edward Maren, not remembering that Kenneth Walters was such a dick. We went to high school together and never got along. I was from the wrong side of the tracks. He and I never came to blows, but there was always tension. But earlier at the bar… that was a whole new level of dickheadedness from him."

"Yeah," she cringed. "About that… I used to be his

secretary."

"Just his secretary?" I asked playfully, though my blood was boiling just under the surface. I knew what was coming next.

"And we dated for a couple months. The first day I came into Dive…I had just broken it off with him."

"I see." I swallowed the anger I felt at imagining his hands on her, touching her, kissing her…shit. I couldn't even think about him doing more without wanting to punch something.

"Being who he is, he obviously didn't take it well, so I vowed to never get involved with my boss again. I can't risk being out of a job again."

I nodded, taking it all in. If she was being forthcoming, I wasn't going to interrupt her.

She looked at the thin silver watch on her wrist, and something inside me twisted into a knot at the thought of losing her.

"Shit. I need to get home."

"Oh, no you don't. You've been drinking," I interjected, pulling her arm from her gaze.

She rolled her eyes. "Just a glass of wine, Blaine. I'm fine."

"And you just pulled a nonstop late shift. You look exhausted." *And sexy as hell.*

"Gee, thanks," she huffed. "So what do you propose? I can call a cab, I guess."

"No." I slid my grasp from her forearm and tangled my fingers with hers. "Stay with me. Tonight."

"Blaine…"

"I'm not saying we have to do anything. Just sleep,

like before. That was nice, right?"

She twisted her bottom lip before scraping it with her teeth. "I guess…yeah. It was nice."

A triumphant smile tugged on the corner of my mouth. "And you know you're safe with me, right? You know you can trust me."

Again she worried that lip, looking away from my fixed gaze. Finally, she let out a shaky breath and nodded.

"Yes."

Fuck. Yes.

That was all I needed to hear.

I squeezed her hand gently before climbing to my feet, pulling her up with me.

"Come on. Let's go to bed."

CHAPTER SEVENTEEN

Kami

What the hell was I doing? Was I losing my damn mind?

No, seriously. I had to be going bat-shit crazy.

Not only was I completely going against every rule I had ever set for myself, I had just told Blaine that I trusted him. Something I had never told any man, outside of Dom.

And what was even crazier? I really did trust him. Dammit, I trusted Blaine and wanted to spend the night with him. So much so, that I had let myself have that glass of wine, knowing he wouldn't let me drive afterward.

I was going straight to hell. But first, I'd earn the ride.

"So this is it," he said, ushering me into his bedroom. He swept an arm around the room like he was on an old episode of MTV Cribs.

"Where all the magic happens?" I asked, snickering at my own private joke.

Blaine shrugged sheepishly. "I wouldn't say that. I

mean, no magic has happened in here…ever."

I pursed my lips. "Bullshit."

"No seriously," he replied, holding up three fingers like some badass, rogue Boy Scout. "I just bought this place about a year ago."

"Sooo… where do you entertain your…*dates?*"

He shook his head. "You don't really want to have this conversation. Do you?"

"Guess not," I shrugged. I really didn't. But then again, the suspense might've killed me. I shook off the images of him and countless, faceless women sexing on the couch, and let my eyes roam his private space.

"Hey, what's that?"

I walked over to his dresser where two pieces of folded, colored paper sat side by side. Holding up the crane, I cocked a curious brow.

Blaine shrugged, rubbing the back of his neck. "You said I could have one."

I nodded and captured my lips between my teeth in an attempt to keep from grinning like the Cheshire cat. Then I traded the delicate crane between my fingertips for the lime-green flower that was once an advertisement for a car detailing shop.

"I didn't want it to go to waste," he explained without me asking. "It was from our first date, in a place that's important to me. I wanted something to remember it by. But that's it."

I straightened his keepsakes and looked up at him and smiled. "So just another semi-creeper moment?"

"Yeah," he grinned sheepishly.

Letting him off the hook, I swallowed the swell of

emotion building in my chest and changed gears. "Ok. I really want a shower, and I have no sleeping clothes. Unless you like the smell of beer and sweat in your sheets."

He flashed me a naughty smile, his eyes low and predatory. "I like your sweat."

Ok. That was it. Blaine had me—hook, line and sinker. All he had to do was tell me to get naked and assume the position.

He laughed, shrugging off his comment. "You can use my bathroom. Clean towels are in there. I'll get you something to wear."

When he turned to rummage through his drawers, I let out a sigh of relief. Then that relief quickly blossomed into anxiety. Was I really going to sleep with him? Were we actually going to cross that line? I mean, sure, I wanted to—more than anything—but could I see myself taking that step with Blaine? What would that mean for us? What would that mean for *me?*

"You ok, Kam?" he asked, breaking me from my conflicted inner monologue.

"Uh, yeah. Just tired."

I accepted the t-shirt and boxer shorts he offered me and scurried into the en suite bathroom, escaping his questioning eyes. It was immaculate, of course, much like everything else in his house. I felt like an ass for prejudging him, thinking I would be walking into the ultimate bachelor pad. It was quite the opposite, actually. Everything was neat and tidy, yet it felt homey and warm. There were no beer cans littering the countertops. No posters of nude models. Not even a crusty sock forgotten in a corner.

Blaine Jacobs was a walking contradiction. On the

outside, he looked dangerous. Exciting. Mysterious. But what I had learned about him told me a different story. He was kind, gentle, and protective. He was expressive to a fault. He smiled often, and he had the same corny sense of humor as me. Blaine may have looked scary-beautiful on the outside, but it didn't compare to the beauty of his soul. It was a concept I had only seen personified in Dominic, and that drew me to Blaine even more.

Not wanting to make him believe I was digging through his medicine cabinets—which I was actually tempted to do—I turned on the water. Then reality struck, crushing my chest and stealing my breath.

The door. The door was closed.

Ohmygodohmygodohmygod.

Cold sweat broke out all over my face and neck, the surface of my skin growing prickly with goose bumps. I tried to center my breathing, and focused on inhaling through my nose and exhaling out of my mouth. On wobbly legs, I took a step towards the door. It appeared to be moving away from me, recoiling from my reach. I took another step, the edges of my consciousness becoming fuzzy and unfocused. I had to get to the door before I collapsed. Before my lungs felt the fear and restricted precious oxygen. I could feel it sweeping over me like deep, dark water. It was drowning me. I was suffocating in my own pathetic trepidation.

I felt the coolness of the doorknob, my vision obscured with dark, fuzzy spots. I twisted until I heard a click, releasing it from the frame along with my ragged breath. I was ok. I would be ok.

Relief washed over me, pushing away the panic, as I

slid to the floor against the tub. Within seconds, my breathing became more productive. My heart rate had begun to slow, no longer thumping in my ears like a bongo drum. After a couple minutes, my vision had returned to 20/20, and the thick saliva in my mouth, preempting vomit, had dissipated.

I took a deep breath before standing and peering out of the cracked bathroom door. Thank baby Jesus, Blaine was nowhere to be found. I peeled off my now sweat-drenched clothes and stepped into the hot water.

Lathering up with shower gel that smelled masculine and fresh, I washed away the remains of my angst. It smelled like *him.* I squirted a generous dollop onto the shower puff and slid it along my body, letting his scent seep into my skin, as I rubbed the soap across my nipples, down my stomach and between my thighs. I took Blaine's bath sponge, the sponge he used to clean his own wet, naked body, and raked it against my sex slowly. Then I did it again, biting my bottom lip, as I applied a bit more pressure and massaged his smell into me with closed eyes. I did it once more, letting my fingers create little circles with the mesh barrier.

A half-whine, half-cry startled me suddenly, and I dropped the sponge. *Shit.* What was that? *Ohmygod*, no I was not… I couldn't even think it. I was too mortified at my complete lack of decency.

I rinsed as chastely as I could and stepped out. Luckily, I was still alone, but I wrapped the towel around me hurriedly, remembering that the door was slightly ajar. I picked up the pair of boxers first. They looked brand new and were a good bit too big. Then I remembered that Blaine went commando, and I nearly choked on my own saliva.

Oh God. What if he slept naked? My bare lady bits percolated, and I slid on the underwear, hoping like hell that the loss of air would stifle the throb.

The plain white t-shirt was next, reminiscent of the tees he usually wore. I brought it up to my nose and took a whiff, savoring the scent of mint and spice absorbed in the soft cotton. I quickly put it over my head with the need to be surrounded in his scent. In that moment, I never wanted to wear anything else ever again.

I stepped into the still empty bedroom, unsure of what to do next. After stowing my clothes and shoes in a neat pile against the wall, I sat on the king sized, four poster bed, and pulled my knees up to my chest.

What was I doing here? This was all wrong. Too risky, too dangerous. Totally unlike anything I had ever done.

"Hey, you're done," Blaine smiled, stepping into the bedroom. He was freshly showered and damn delicious in only thin flannel pajama bottoms. I sat, staring, my knees still drawn up, mesmerized by the sight of intricate patterns and vibrant colors over smooth, hard planes of muscle.

"You ok, Kami?"

I snapped my gaping mouth shut and cleared my throat, nodding. "Uh, yeah. Sorry. I'm fine."

Blaine gave me a devilish grin, rolling the barbell in his mouth as he stalked towards me. "You ready?"

"Uh, what? Ready?"

"For bed. You ready for bed?" he asked, stifling a chuckle. "Like I told you before, Kami, I'm not giving it up. So please, stop begging."

I rolled my eyes and snatched the comforter back to

climb in. "I take it back. You *are* a creeper. A full on, eyelash-collecting, panty-sniffing, toenail-munching creeper!"

Blaine stood at the foot of the bed in stunned silence before erupting into gut-busting guffaws. "What the fuck?" he chortled between hoots. "Eyelash-collecting?"

"Yes, creeper. Eyelash-collecting." I settled into the bed, and turned onto my side with a huff. Away from him.

"Awww, come on, baby." I could feel the bed dip as he climbed onto the bed. "I'm just teasing you. Don't get mad. If you really want me, you can have me. I swear," he snickered.

"Argh! Shut up, Blaine!" I pulled the comforter up to my face, hoping to hide my amused grin at his playfulness.

The warmth and hardness of his body against my back erased all signs of humor from my face. He wrapped his strong arms around me, pulling my frame into his. I noticed that about Blaine. He wouldn't come to me with his tail between his legs, begging for a treat. He pulled me to *him*. He made me want to melt into his body, making it known that he was in control and taking what he wanted. I loved it, and the desire to be somewhat dominated scared the living shit out of me.

His soft, warm lips were at my ear, his breath tickling my neck. "Do you forgive me?" A large hand dipped down under the covers and grasped my thigh, sliding upwards before stopping at the imaginary panty line.

"I don't know," I breathed.

His hand slowly made its way past my hip before easing under the oversized tee and splaying across my stomach. My head was swimming, and I closed my eyes just to keep from drowning. I felt him all over. The slide of his fingers along my bare skin, his rippled chest flush against my back, his lips teasing my ear, the large stiffness under his pajama bottoms pressing hard against my backside… it was all too much to take. Yet, I wanted more. I wanted to feel all of him, as I wanted him to feel all of me, inside and out.

"How about now?" The very tip of his tongue darted out and traced the shell of my ear. Then his lips were on my neck, gently nibbling.

"Mmmm. Maybe," I replied breathlessly. Every inch of me was aware and prickly, anticipating what would come next.

"Maybe? Not good enough."

The moment his hand cupped my left breast, my already puckered nipples hardened until they ached, and I cried out. I couldn't help it. He teased and rolled the pebbled skin between the calloused pads of his fingers, pulling and flicking gently as if simulating a tongue. *His* tongue. I wanted it. I needed it. But I was just too damn afraid to say it.

By the time his hand had moved to my right breast, repeating the delightful torture, I was writhing against him in a slow rhythm. He matched my movements, stroking me through his thin pajama bottoms, letting me feel how ready he was for me. I nearly gasped. I had never been with anyone quite *that* ready before. I mean, he was really, *really*… ready.

Blaine's mouth was hot at my ear, his breath as labored as mine. "I need to kiss you. Now."

In the next instant, he flipped me onto my back, and

settled his body atop mine. Blaine's inked arms enclosed my frame as his knee eased between my legs, slowly parting them. I didn't have time to protest even if I'd wanted to. His lips captured mine with a hunger I had never experienced before. It was like he needed me to survive. Like kissing me was as necessary as his next breath.

Our lips, our tongues, moved together in perfect harmony. We were music together—melodious, intense and dramatic. His low groans became the bass line as he plucked the strings of my body, producing soft moans and high mewls. My hands were tangled in his hair, as his roamed the soft expanse of my frame, exploring the valley of my waist, the dip between my breasts, the raised peaks of my nipples. We were belly against belly, the hard ridges of Blaine's midsection melting into the softness of mine.

Feeling his warmth, his body demanding my compliance, felt good. It felt right. And it felt like *more*. Not just another meaningless sexual encounter. Not a physical response to the opposite sex. Not a means to an end. Blaine was giving me more than just his body. He was filling me with his soul.

His mouth moved down to my neck, licking and sucking a trail down to my chest. The moment Blaine's studded tongue flicked my nipple, I gasped. Sensation attacked the puckered bud, as he skillfully twirled that barbell around the tip before taking it into his mouth completely. His fingers coaxed the other, simulating the delicious torment of his tongue.

Blaine moaned his satisfaction against my skin, heightening my own arousal for him. With every lick, stroke and suck, he was vocal. He let me know how hot he was for me, and it made me even hotter for him.

Just as I thought I could seriously lose it just from his mouth on my breasts, Blaine lifted his head and looked down at me with hooded, dilated eyes.

"Let me make you come," he rasped.

O.M.G.

He stared at me for long seconds, before I realized he was waiting for my answer. I didn't know what to say. What could I say? With every thought centered on Blaine and what he was doing to my body, I couldn't focus on much else. I knew I wanted him, *needed* him. But I also knew that crossing this line would only make it that much harder to keep him out of my head. Could I really do that? Could I give him part of me and expect him not to want the rest?

Before my brain could come up with a logical answer, I was nodding. I wanted what Blaine wanted. And that was the only thing that mattered at the moment. Not his past, not my scarred psyche, not the uncertainty of tomorrow. Just him.

His lips were back on me, once again tasting my mouth, my throat, my nipples, and moving south. He licked a trail to my belly button, swirling his tongue around it while easing off the too-large boxer shorts on my hips. I closed my eyes and lifted my backside to aid his efforts, hoping like hell that I wouldn't regret it.

Though I knew it was coming, the feel of his tongue on my hypersensitive sex nearly made me scream. Never in my life had I felt so utterly exposed and out of control. I didn't even try to muffle my cries of pleasure. He matched my erotic sounds with his own, the vibrations from his mouth creating a new layer of sensation. He tasted and teased my flesh, the contrast between the feel of hard, slick metal along with the soft texture of his tongue coaxing my orgasm. I knew it would do me in. I knew I would be totally vulnerable once I reached my peak, and dammit, I didn't care. I wanted Blaine to take me. To claim me. To own every one of my orgasms for the rest of my life.

Blaine didn't stop when the first waves of pleasure took me under. His tongue, his lips, his fingers… they kept moving, eliciting more tortured sounds during my dramatic downfall. I begged him to stop, yet worked my hips closer. Even as tears streamed down the sides of my face, and I cried his name over and over, he devoured me, demanding I surrender every drop of my defiance. And I let him have it. It was too weak to fight it anymore.

Finally, when I was just a mewling mess of whimpers, Blaine slid beside me, covering my half naked body with the comforter. My eyes were still shut tight, the aftershocks wracking my frame and pushing me into exhaustion. He eased my head onto his chest and squeezed me tight, kissing my face and hair.

"Sleep now, beautiful Kami," he whispered, just as the walls of my subconscious closed in on me.

Tucked under his arm, his silver threaded nipple just centimeters from my lips, I smiled and did just that.

I jerked awake, sweat covering my entire frame. I was

warm—too warm. And I wasn't alone. But the thing that terrified me beyond anything else, the thing that had me hyperventilating, fighting for my next ragged breath was the darkness. It was completely dark. And there was a body wrapped around mine.

NoNoNoNoNo

I couldn't breathe. I couldn't move. I couldn't even scream. I just knew that I had to get away from here. I had to find the light switch, but my body wouldn't follow my sleep-fogged brain's commands. It was already too late.

I was beyond losing it. I was already lost.

Weight lifted off of my chest, and hands gasped my sweat-slicked shoulders. A silent whimper passed my lips. I wanted to cry so badly. I wanted to scream for help. Someone was in this darkness with me, shaking me, calling my name… I had to get away. Bad things happened in the dark. Evil things. Things that had me plummeting toward the bleakest recesses of my mind…

Mommy told me if I stayed quiet, she'd leave a light on for me. She knew how afraid I was of the dark. How it reminded me of the times Daddy would lock me in the closet. He laughed at me. He called me names and teased me for being so scared. My cries only made him keep me in there for longer, but I couldn't help it.

Sometimes the fear would make me wet myself. Then Daddy didn't laugh anymore. He'd get his belt and beat my bare, soiled bottom until it was burning with red welts. He said he had to. He said he had to teach me, because he loved me.

Daddy's love hurts me. I don't want him to love me

anymore.

Afterward, Mommy would put me in the bathtub. Daddy would force her to leave sometimes. She would cry and beg to stay, but he would slap her across the face and tell her to shut up. Then he would close and lock the door. I hated when he closed the door. I knew what was coming. Bad things always happened when Daddy closed the door.

He said he had to give me a special washing with his hands. He said he had to because that's what daddies did when they loved their daughters. They touched them. I didn't like it. I never liked it when Daddy loved me. Mommy wouldn't let him love me for long though. She would beat on the bathroom door until her small hands would bleed. She'd threaten to call the police. Daddy hated that. So he said he had to teach Mommy too. He had to teach her with his fists because he loved her so much...

"Kami! Kami, baby, wake up! Kami!"

A muffled voice pierced the darkness, beckoning, pulling me out of the hell inside my head. I focused every ounce of coherency on his strained voice. I inhaled his familiar scent, and let the feel of his warm skin against mine be a physical reminder.

"Kami! Can you hear me? Oh my God, you're shaking. Baby, please wake up!"

I concentrated on Blaine's pleading words and tried to make sense of them. While darkness tried to pull me back under, his voice, his presence, fought to bring me back to him. He kept shaking me, kept calling my name. I wanted to fight too. I wanted—*needed*—to find my way back to Blaine.

"The lights," I rasped through an aching throat. "The lights! Turn on the lights! Please!"

Realizing what my hoarse voice was urging him to do, he bounded off the bed and sprinted to the wall. He clicked on the light switch and surveyed the cowering mess in front of him.

The secret was out. The ruse of my life was revealed. If Blaine didn't know how deeply fucked up I was before, he knew now. And that fact broke my abused heart in two.

He rejoined me on the bed, hesitant to touch me, as I rocked myself back and forth, my knees drawn up to my chin. I had to hold myself together. I had to keep it all in. If he knew the ugliness inside me—if I let it spill out like the rising bile in my throat—he would never look at me the same way. He wouldn't want anything to do with me, and that was something I couldn't accept. Not right now when I needed him so badly.

"Blaine?" I whispered, afraid to look at him. Wet strands of sweat-soaked hair stuck to my forehead, creating a screen.

"Yes, baby," he said soothingly, moving closer to me. He reached a tentative hand towards me, but let it drop before making contact. An internal struggle played on his features, as he tried to understand what had just happened.

I took a deep, shaky breath, before smoothing the hair out of my face, revealing my tear-streaked face. "Hold me? Please?"

His strong arms were around me before I could even finish my request, desperately trying to crush the fear that would undoubtedly take him away from me.

CHAPTER EIGHTEEN

Blaine

I couldn't even comprehend what had just happened. One moment we were sleeping, her body curled into mine, and the next she was trembling, sobbing in her sleep.

I heard her whimper, begging someone to let her out. Then she was shaking like a leaf, pleading, crying for that person to stop touching her. I didn't know why. I couldn't even decipher her jumbled stream of anguished sobs. But I knew one thing for certain—someone had hurt Kami. And I would fucking die before I ever let her be hurt again.

I held her tight, stroking her hair as she cried hot tears into my chest. I wanted to kiss away each one of those tears. I wanted to tell her that she was safe, that she was ok. That she was loved. But my own trepidation kept me bound, crippling my voice.

When she couldn't squeeze out another tear from her bloodshot eyes, she pulled away from me and covered her face. Was she angry with me? Did I do something to trigger whatever memory haunted her dreams?

"I'm so sorry," she whispered hoarsely. "I'm so sorry, Blaine. I need to go."

I grasped her wrist before she could scoot off the bed. "No, Kami. You're not going anywhere." She jumped, and I realized my voice was gruffer than I'd intended. I didn't want to scare her. Not when she was already so obviously terrified.

"I want you to stay, baby." Gently, I pulled her back to me though she refused to look at me. With a finger, I turned her face towards mine. Red-rimmed, green eyes full of shame and regret looked back at me, causing an ache to radiate in my chest.

"I… I…shouldn't," she stammered. "I ruined your evening. I didn't mean—,"

My lips cut off her next words, refusing to let her place any of the blame on herself. I'd be damned if she felt bad for what happened. Not when I felt so fucking helpless because I couldn't take away her pain.

"No," I whispered against her lips. "You'll stay. And you'll let me hold you. And kiss you. And if you feel like telling me what's wrong, you'll let me make it better. But no more about leaving. Ok?"

She nodded weakly, but it was enough. Kami was agreeing to stay with me, and I wasn't about to question it. I kissed her gently once more, the saltiness of her tears mingling with her sweet taste, before tearing myself from the bed.

"I'm going to make you some tea. Don't move, ok?"

I damn near broke my neck racing to the kitchen. I

didn't want to leave her side, but she needed to be soothed. Tea seemed like the right thing to give her.

Despite her agony, I wanted her badly. So badly that my cock was aching against the fabric of my pajama pants. And if I didn't leave her right then to get some clarity, I would be liable to take advantage of her frailty and bury myself inside her. Until her tears of sorrow turned to tears of sheer ecstasy. I felt like the dirtiest motherfucker alive, but I couldn't help what she did to my body. My mind was a bit more tactful, but my dick was a first-rate asshole.

"Here, drink this," I said, handing her the steaming mug after I had returned, erection under wraps.

"Thank you," she replied with a tense smile. She took a sip and closed her eyes, letting the hot liquid wash away the residual terror.

"So… are you ok?" It was a dumbass question, but I didn't know what else to say.

Kami took another sip before exhaling. She nodded. "For now." She tried to give me a reassuring smile, but I wasn't buying it.

"For now? What exactly does that mean?"

"It means that I may never be fully ok, but I'll survive. I'll be ok…for now."

"Is there anything I can do to help? I need to know how to make this better for you, Kami. Just tell me what to do." I didn't even realize that my hand was in my hair, pulling in frustration. Trying to get her to open up was like trying to steal a steak from a pit bull. That shit just wasn't happening.

"No, Blaine. There's nothing you can do."

I shook my head. I didn't want to scare her away, but I

could see that she was miserable. I didn't want her shouldering that misery alone. "Try me, Kami. You said you trusted me. Do you really think there's anything you could tell me that would push me away from you? Because I'm telling you straight up right now—I'm not going anywhere."

She met my penetrating stare, those green eyes filling with tears before she batted them away and turned her head. I felt like a fucking asshole.

"I'm…I'm fucked up, Blaine," she whispered. If I hadn't been hanging onto her every sigh and whimper, I would have missed it. "Like really fucked up. And if you knew what was good for you, you'd leave me alone."

"I don't believe that," I replied, shaking my head. My hands cupped her face, turning it back towards me. I needed to look her in the eyes. I needed her to see just how serious I was. "I'm not going anywhere. I mean that."

She pulled away from my touch and shook her head. "I'm telling you, I have problems. And you don't need the headache. I'm not like your other girls, Blaine. I can't be saved."

What the fuck?

"My other girls? What the hell does that mean?"

A hard scowl marred her soft features as if she was conjuring an unpleasant memory. "CJ. He said you like damaged girls. He said you needed to feel like you could rescue them." She looked down at the cooling mug of tea in her slightly shaking hands. "Because of your mom."

I was on my feet and pacing, fists clenched at my sides, before good sense could stop me. "CJ needs to mind his own fucking business!"

Kami flinched, and I instantly regretted my outburst. I willed myself to calm down, shaking away the fresh wave of tension. "I'm sorry," I muttered pathetically. "But he doesn't know what he's talking about. I don't have any other girls, Kami."

She nodded, though I could tell she was unconvinced. Shit.

"But you have, and that's why I'm here, isn't it? You do feel the need to fix girls like me, don't you?" Anger and disgust replaced the fear that had occupied her face. "You can't fix me, Blaine. So don't even try."

"Dammit!" I nearly flew to her side, snatching the mug out of her hands and setting it on the nightstand. "That's not why you're here, Kami. Not at all. Do I want to take your pain away? Yes. Do I want to make it so you never have to wake up crying like that again? Hell yes. But do I want you here just to satisfy some sick wounded-bird complex? Fuck no!" I grasped her face between my hands, forcing her to look at me. "I want you, Kami. I care about you, and that's the only reason why I want you here with me. Ok? Fuck what CJ said. I just want *you.* And if you need me to demonstrate just how much that is, I'd be happy to… Again."

Her face flamed red, as memories of the early morning hours came barging into the tense moment. She was remembering my lips on her, tasting, sucking, teasing. My tongue plunging into her, devouring her sweetness like it was my last meal. The feel of my barbell flicking her sensitive clit, causing her to cry out my name.

Kami was ready for me, and holy fuck, I was ready for her. But I wanted to make her feel good. I wanted her to know that I wanted nothing from her aside from her taste on my tongue. And my God, she tasted good. So good that I was ready to dive in for another round just to hear her scream my name again.

Or maybe that was just what my sick, twisted mind wanted to believe. It was hard to tell, being that all the blood in my body was centralized elsewhere.

"Do you trust me?" I asked, touching my forehead to hers.

"Yes," she nodded.

"Then stop trying to leave. Just stay, Kami. If you don't want to sleep, we don't have to. I can just hold you. Or we can talk. Whatever you want to do."

"I don't want to talk anymore," she replied with a shake of her head. "Let's just…lay here. Let's just be."

I crooked a smile and eased her head down on the pillow, positioning myself on my side to lie beside her. We stared at each other for long seconds that turned into minutes, neither one of us knowing the right words to say. I wanted her to know how I felt, but I didn't want to scare her. I also wanted to know how she felt about me, but I was too chicken-shit to ask.

"Blaine?" she whispered, breaking the ice. "Can I ask you something?"

"Anything." And she could. She could ask me absolutely anything.

"Your mom… What CJ said… What did he mean?"

Anything but that.

I rolled onto my back with a huff and scrubbed a hand over my face. Shit. I didn't want to go there. Not with her or anyone else.

"If you can't talk about it, I understand," she muttered, sensing my discomfort. She was giving me an out, and, dammit, I wanted to take it. But I had promised her honesty. And if I had any chance at cracking the mystery behind those green eyes, I had to prove myself.

"My mom died when I was 13. I was sent to live with my uncle and his family right afterward," I answered, my voice devoid of all emotion. Over the past twelve years, I had the said the same lines over and over again until they didn't hurt anymore.

"And?"

She knew there was more. I just didn't know if I could give her more than that. Not when it came to my mother.

I shook my head. "And that's all. People die. We move on. We learn to deal."

"But you haven't," she interjected, placing her small hand on my bare chest to cushion the blow. "You haven't learned to deal. You're still hurting."

I placed my own hand on top of hers and gripped it, holding on to any semblance of peace. "We all hurt, Kami. It's a part of life."

"Can you tell me about it?" she asked, her small voice filling me with foreign emotion. I couldn't quite put my finger on it, but everything about her felt sincere and humble. Like she actually cared about me and wanted to share my pain. Like maybe she felt for me what I couldn't help feeling for her.

I took a moment to collect my thoughts, sifting through the memories in the forbidden Rolodex of my mind. I didn't revisit my past if I could help it. It wasn't a place anyone wanted to stay for long.

"My mom killed herself," I finally said. There was no way around it. The best way was to tear off the band-aid as quickly as possible. "It was always just the two of us when I was growing up. She was always so happy, so free-spirited. So it came as a shock when I found her dead on the bathroom floor. She had overdosed."

Kami moved closer to me, close enough for me to feel her warm breath on my arm as she gasped at my mournful account. "I'm so sorry," she croaked, her voice thick with emotion.

"I later found out that my mother suffered from schizophrenia. I just thought she was eccentric. She'd get these hare-brained ideas, and we'd be off on an adventure. She'd pull me out of school for impromptu road trips. Let me eat ice cream for dinner. Throw me birthday parties when it wasn't even my birthday. She was my best friend, and I didn't even know she was sick."

"Blaine…" Kami stroked my cheek, letting her fingers travel up into the locks of hair that had fallen over my forehead. "You know it's not your fault, right? You know that it wasn't your responsibility to save her?"

I turned on my side to face her, revealing the ugly scars I still bore after all these years. "Wasn't it? I was all she had, and I didn't even know my mom was dying inside. I could've helped her. I could have done something to stop her and get her help. But no. I thought I had the coolest mom in the world when all the while she was suffering. Don't you see how fucking selfish that was of me? Don't you get why I hate myself for letting her die?"

I turned away from Kami, utterly disgusted with my self-loathing. "How unhappy must she have been to take her own life? How unhappy must she have been with *me*? To not at least try to survive?"

Kami hands tugged my bicep, pulling me, until my back was once again flat on the bed. Then she was straddling me, her small body pressed into mine while she buried her face into my chest.

"I'm so sorry," she sobbed, kissing my chest. She rained light pecks along my upper torso, her sorrowful eyes leaking with sympathy. "I'm so sorry, Blaine. It's not your fault. I swear it!"

I wrapped my arms around her and cradled her head against my chest, stilling her movements. It's not that I didn't want Kami to kiss me. Shit, that was all I wanted. But I wanted it to come from a place of desire. A place of affection. Not pity. I wanted Kami to kiss me because she wanted me, minus the bullshit of my past. I wanted her body to crave me like mine craved hers. Not because she felt sorry for me.

I held her soft body on top of mine until her sobs subsided and her breath grew heavy and deep. And just as the sun had begun to peek over the horizon, I let my eyes close to soak in the feel and smell of her.

Kami was in my arms, and in my bed. And for the first time since my mother's suicide, I felt like I could begin to forgive myself.

CHAPTER NINETEEN

Kami

"Oh my God, you dirty little slut! You did it, didn't you? You totally did it!"

I kicked off my shoes and stowed them in my closet before lying back on my bed. "Did what?" I huffed.

Angel put a hand on her narrow hip and slid next to me. Then she bent over and sniffed me. She *fucking sniffed me* like a dog.

"Ewww, what the hell are you doing?" I yelped, scrambling away from her curious nose.

"You had sex! I can smell it on you! You fucked Blaine last night when you swore up and down that you wouldn't!" With a goofy grin, she bounded from the bed and stuck her head out my bedroom door. "Dom! Wipe the coochie crumbs from your chin, and get in here! I won, fucker! You owe me fifty bucks!"

Won? *What the hell?*

"Angel, it's not what you think," I tried to explain. But

before I could come up with a believable story, Dom swaggered in, wearing nothing but tight, black boxer briefs, his muscled, tan body looking as amazing as ever. But he wasn't Blaine. No one had a body like Blaine. Or hands. Or a tongue…

Shit.

Dom settled beside me just as Angel hopped on my other side, wrapping her arm around my waist. "Kam, please tell me you didn't do it. I thought we had an understanding, woman! I was gonna split my winnings!"

"*Oh, Kami wants the D, Kami wants the D, ohhhh, Kami wants Blaine's big nasty D,*" Angel sang sweetly.

I shoved Angel's arm off me. "No, Kami does not want the D." (Yes, she did.) "And, no, I did not have sex with Blaine!" (But I wanted to.)

"See! I told you; I know my girl!" Dom exclaimed before kissing the side of my face. "Not everyone is totally slut-tastic like you, Angel."

"*Pffft.* Yes they are," Angel retorted, twirling a lock of blonde hair. "They are just too scared to admit it."

"I need to get ready for work," I said, climbing to my feet in an attempt to avoid questioning.

"Not so fast," Angel called out before I could make my escape. "I know something went down last night, Kam. You're practically glowing, and you look like you've had a 24-hour full body massage. And you look less… stick-up-the-ass-ish."

"*Stick-up-the-ass-ish?* Seriously? Since when do I look like I have a stick up my ass?" I scowled.

"Whenever you're *not* getting a stick up your ass," she smiled. "Which is, like, never. I think I've had more dicks than you, and I'm allergic to them."

I rolled my eyes at my friend and her colorful language before turning to my closet to retrieve a clean Dive tee and a pair of jeans. Then I spotted my favorite denim skirt hanging up nearby. Oh, what the hell. I slipped it off its hanger and stowed the jeans. Blaine never said it was against the dress code policy. And Mick so rarely poked his head out of the office when he was actually there. Plus, Sundays were slow, relaxed days. A little...distraction... never hurt anyone.

I gathered my outfit and undergarments, bypassing my roommates' conversation about their weekend trysts. Apparently, they both got lucky last night after AngelDust's set and were comparing the sordid details. They could keep the countless one-night stands with different women every other night. I didn't envy their raunchy conquests in the least. I had something much more exciting and fulfilling. I had possibilities. Possibilities with a man that was worth the risk of falling flat on my face.

I strode into Dive an hour later, my head held high and a mischievous grin on my face. For the first time in a long time, I felt good. A little tired from staying up most of the night, but good. Maybe Angel was right. Maybe I did look different now. Maybe Blaine had breathed life into me with a flick of his silver-studded tongue.

Blaine spotted me right away, his brown eyes growing wide with craving. He licked his lips, giving me a peek of that tongue ring and reminding me of what he did to my body in the wee hours of the morning. My knees nearly buckled, as I made my way to the back to clock in.

"Hey, Kami!" Trisha, a part-time day shift bartender

waved at me as she grabbed her purse from her locker. We had never worked together, but we saw each other in passing a few times a week. She was a college student/ model, and, holy shit, she was gorgeous. Tall, blonde, and tan. I thought for sure that she and Blaine had been more than friendly being that they were both equally beautiful. It only made sense, but apparently things between them were strictly platonic.

"Hey Trish, thanks for covering for me Friday night. I owe you one," I smiled as I clocked in.

"Oh, please, girl. You were doing me a favor. I've been begging Blaine to give me more weekends, so I was thrilled to get the chance. Anytime you're not feeling well, give me a call. I'm happy to do it."

Huh.

"Blaine does the scheduling?"

Trisha shrugged. "Well…yeah. I mean, I guess he could delegate the task to Mick, but he said he'd rather do it. He likes knowing who is where. Between you and me, I think he's a little OCD. Complete control freak. But he's nice and fair, so I'm not complaining."

She waved goodbye though I was too engulfed in confusion to return the gesture. Was Blaine the shift supervisor or something? It'd make sense, being that Dive was family-run. Of course he'd have to take on a bit of responsibility. And if he was making the schedule, then was he purposely scheduling all of our shifts together? I hadn't worked with any of the other two bartenders, and I never worked by myself, which was normal for slower weekdays.

Well, only one way to find out.

"Hey Kam!" CJ called out with a devilish smile before I had a chance to fully step behind the bar.

"What's up, CJ," I replied, wrapping my black apron around my waist. Before I could twist the strings together, Blaine was behind me, his agile fingers easing them from my grasp.

"Let me," he breathed, his lips grazing my earlobe. "I like your skirt."

"Do you?" I replied for only his ears. "Not too... distracting?"

"Oh, it is. But I'd gladly get lost in your distraction. Over. And over. And over."

He finished tying the knot above my tailbone before running his fingers through a rogue lock of hair. "I missed you," he whispered, as he placed it behind my ear.

"You just saw me," I said, turning to face him. The overwhelming urge to kiss him was growing by the second. And if it weren't for CJ sitting just yards away and the evening crowd trickling in, I would have done it. Well, maybe.

"I want to see you again. I want to see you in every way possible."

I crooked a playful grin. "Oh, Blaine Jacobs... are you asking me to go steady?" I jibed.

"No, I'm not." His fingers were in my hair again, as he stepped into the tiny space that separated us. "I'm telling you that I want you to be mine. Because, Kami, I've been yours since the first day you walked in here. And I think, on some level, you've been mine since then too."

The conviction of his words stole my breath, and I couldn't do more than melt under his gaze. But what was more than that, it was true. I had been Blaine's all along. I couldn't even see anyone but him since the day we locked eyes. Since he marked me over a shot of tequila and a slice of lime. Blaine was the only man that existed in my world. And at that very moment, I couldn't be entirely sure that he wasn't the world itself.

"Excuuuse me, but some of us are thirsty over here!" CJ hooted, swinging his empty beer bottle in the air.

I broke away from Blaine, hoping to regain just an ounce of my wits, and cracked another beer for CJ.

"You know, it didn't take much skill for me to do that," I said, gesturing towards the open bottle before looking back at Blaine. "Is there some special reason why you still need to babysit me?"

A small frown creased Blaine's forehead. "No. Why?"

"I don't know," I shrugged. "Trish said something about you making the schedule. And I noticed that I never work alone. Is it Mick? Does he not think I'm ready?"

"Mick?" CJ interjected behind me. "What would he have to do with it? He doesn't have any control over that. That was all Blaine."

I lifted a brow at Blaine, who was staring daggers at CJ. He was already pretty pissed at his cousin for his slip up the night before. I wouldn't be surprised if Blaine had words with him later.

"So?" I asked, hoping to break his death glare.

Blaine turned to me and quirked a crooked smile. "I like the company."

CJ snorted from behind me, but was smart enough to keep his mouth shut.

"So you do make the schedule. Oh my God, don't tell

me you're like my supervisor or something."

CJ made a coughing noise behind me like he was choking, drawing the attention of Lidia, the waitress, who began to lightly pat him on the back.

"What are you guys talking about?" she asked. I liked Lidia, I really did, but she was extremely nosey.

CJ wrapped an arm around Lidia's waist and gestured towards Blaine with a jut of his chin. "Blaine here was just explaining to Kami why he makes the schedule and not my pops."

Lidia shrugged and placed a hand on her hip. "Well, it's his bar. He can make the schedule however he wants, as long as I keep getting Wednesday nights off for my Zumba class."

His bar?

"Blaine?" I didn't need to say anymore. Either he would be honest with me, or he would lie to my face. I hoped to God it wasn't the latter.

"Let me explain, Kami," he said, rubbing the back of his neck nervously.

That was all I needed to hear. Out of sheer humiliation, I turned and went straight to the back room that housed the employee lockers. I had done it again. I had gotten involved with my boss, the very thing I had vowed not to do again. No wonder Kenneth was such a prick towards me. I probably looked like some slut that just screwed whoever was in charge.

"Watch the bar, motherfucker," I heard Blaine growl before heavy footsteps approached the room. He left the door cracked and looked down at me, remorse written all over his face.

"Were you ever going to tell me?"

Blaine worked the barbell in his mouth, contemplating his answer, while I forced myself not to watch with rapt fascination. "Yes," he finally answered.

"When?"

He took a step towards me but kept his distance. I was glad for the space. With my heightened emotions, I would either slap him or kiss him. At that moment, I wanted to do neither.

"Eventually. When it came up."

"When it came up?" I shouted, disregarding the bar full of patrons. "Blaine, we work together just about every day. We've gone out on a date. Shit, we've spent the night together twice! You've had ample opportunity."

"I know, Kami, I just didn't think it mattered. It's just a bar." He ran a frustrated hand through his already mussed hair.

"Yeah. The bar I work at. Holy shit, I'm your employee. Do you know how this would make me look to everyone else? And you claim you want me to be yours?"

He closed the distance between us in three long strides and imprisoned my face in his large, inked hands. "I *do* want that. *Fuck*, I want that more than anything. Don't you think I wanted to tell you? That I went over the scenario in my head a thousand times? Kami, if you knew I owned this place, you never would've given me the time of day. Tell me I'm wrong."

I couldn't. I couldn't disagree with him there. I took a deep breath and shook my head anyway. "But now look. Now I feel like you've been lying to me all this time. I feel like such a damn fool, Blaine! I trusted you."

"Baby, you can still trust me. I'm still the same man that is fucking crazy about you. Still the same guy that is obsessed with these lips," he murmured, running a thumb along my bottom one. "This changes nothing, I swear."

"But what will the other employees think?"

Blaine shrugged. "If they have something to say, they can walk."

Without warning, his lips were hot against mine, coaxing my mouth open so his tongue could meld with mine. His kiss was full of apology and regret. It begged for understanding. It needed my forgiveness. His lips needed me to let my guard down and free fall into the unknown with him.

"You're crazy about me?" I asked breathlessly, once his mouth left mine.

"Fucking crazy," he smiled.

"Well," I said wrapping my arms around his neck. "You better get your crazy ass out there before your cousin drinks you dry."

He chuckled, and the sound chipped at the crumbling walls around my heart just a bit more. "Yeah, you're probably right. So hard to find good help nowadays." And with that, Blaine palmed my backside and squeezed, making me squeal. After I gave his rock-solid bicep a playful smack, he grabbed my hand and tugged me towards the door.

"Oh, Ms. Patty has been asking when you'll be back by the diner."

I reached on my tiptoes and gave him a swift peck on the cheek just before we passed the threshold of the door. "Well, I have to see if my boss will give me a day off. He likes to work me for long, hard hours."

Blaine chuckled again, and the barriers in my chest came crashing down.

Yeah. I was pretty fucking crazy about him too.

The next few days passed in a blur of flirty banter, longing stares, and hidden kisses when no one was watching. I returned to Ms. Patty's diner with Blaine, subjecting him to all types of loving torture from her and Mavis. Apparently, he was telling the truth about never bringing a date to the little hole-in-the-wall restaurant that appeared quainter than dilapidated the second time around. Maybe it was getting to know Ms. Patty and the love she had for Blaine. Maybe it was being there with him, smiling around a mouthful of waffles. Whatever it was, I was thankful that he made it known that he wanted me in his life. I wanted him in mine…I just didn't know how.

"Hey babe, pass me that Grenadine," Blaine said, pointing to the bottle of red syrup.

I snagged the bottle and handed it to him, giving him a wink before sashaying towards the next customer. It was Thursday, and word had gotten out about Dive's Open Mic Night. We were busier than last week, but it was nothing that we couldn't handle.

"Hey sweets!" Angel squealed, nearly propping herself on the bar to leave a kiss on my cheek.

"You and the girls all set up? I think there will be a lot more victims—I mean—performers this week." I winked at the older gentleman in front of me and slid him his beer. He was a regular and not a fan of Dive's new themed night.

"Yup! And if there's a lag in singers, I thought you and I could try out that new song we've been working on."

I passed Angel her signature shot of tequila and light beer. "Uh, no way. You know that's not happening."

"Aw, come on, Kam!" she pouted. "I think it's ready. Just try it!"

I was already shaking my head. "Nope. Ain't gonna happen. I will not perform that song with you tonight. Ask one of the girls."

"But it's *our* song! Ugh!" She downed her shot and chased it with a swig of beer. "Fine. So you won't perform that song with me tonight."

"Nope."

"Alright… whatever you say, Kam."

I returned my attention to the growing line of thirsty customers and awaited the first singer to be announced. Luckily, she was decent, choosing to do a rendition of "Heartbreaker" by Pat Benatar. I could tell Angel was itching to grab the mic and kill it. She was a huge fan.

The acts gradually improved, and it seemed that Dive's Open Mic Night was proving to be lucrative. I was happy for Blaine. He had explained to me that he had actually bought the bar from his Uncle Mick when he returned to Charlotte a bit over a year ago. The economy hadn't been kind to the family-run business, and the place needed tons of cosmetic work. Blaine had been sitting on a large health insurance settlement from his mother's death and decided to bail his uncle out of the quickly piling debt. He fixed it up, added some new staff members, and gave it a new, updated image. Though I had only known him for a matter of weeks, I was proud of his dedication. He was young, successful and driven. He was everything people expected him not to be.

"Alright Dive," Angel's seductive voice sounded through the speakers a couple hours into the evening. "This next act is one of our own. She's a badass vocalist and crazy sexy on the strings. And, she is drop-dead lickable. Put your fucking hands together, Dive, for my girl, Kami!"

The bar erupted into cheers, every head turning to look at me with expectation. That's when I realized what had just happened. Holy. Shit. I was going to kill Angel!

I tried to shake my head "no," but the entire place was already chanting my name. Blaine had even abandoned his customers to come stand beside me, wearing a reassuring grin and nodding his support. The roar of the crowd, the lights, the dozens of eyes looking at me in expectation… I couldn't deal. But I couldn't lose it. I *wouldn't* lose it.

I looked to the man next to me, who gazed at me like I was the only person that existed in the crowded bar, and took a cleansing breath. I could do this. I could block out every face and focus on him. I could pretend like I was giving him his very own private concert in his bedroom. And afterward, he would lead me to his bed and make me sing his name in every octave of my vocal range.

On trembling legs, I made my way to the stage, the spotlights causing tiny beads of sweat to form on my nose. Angel was beaming with pride, and even Dom was in the front row, still dressed in his work clothes.

"I am sooo gonna kill you, bitch," I whispered between clenched teeth when I approached her on the stage.

"You'll thank me for it later, slut," she winked. Then she skipped to the back of the stage and retrieved my guitar. This had been premeditated! That whore was as good as dead!

I looked out at the sea of people growing restless as I tried to figure out my next move. Who was I kidding? I couldn't do this. This wasn't me. This wasn't my life. This was Angel's. People like me didn't perform in front of crowds. We didn't sing and play for perfect strangers. I couldn't do this. Oh my God, I couldn't.

My eyes swept over to the bar, finding Blaine's smiling face. He looked so proud and excited for me. There wasn't a trace of doubt on his face. He had faith in me. I didn't want that faith to be wasted. I wanted to give him a reason to be proud of me.

I looked down at Dominic, my best friend in the whole world, who wore a similar expression. He had never made me feel like I was damaged goods. He understood me, and he loved me. If anyone knew courage, it was him. And right now, he was channeling it all to me in the depths of his comforting smile. If Dom believed in me, then maybe I could do this.

A small hand squeezed mine, and I realized that Angel had never left my side. She nodded, telling me that I was ok with the simple gesture. She really was a good friend to me. She had overcome so much pain and rejection in her life, yet found a way to get on stage and belt her heart out like she didn't have a care in the world. She was fearless, and I longed for just an ounce of her confidence.

"I'll be right here with you," she whispered. "We'll do this together, ok?"

I nodded and slowly positioned myself on the stool in front of the microphone. This was it. This was what I had always secretly dreamed of doing, but was too afraid to try. This was my moment to kick fear in the ass. And I wanted to share it with the three people in this bar that had come to mean more to me than anyone in this world.

I strummed the first chords of the only song that was on my heart at the moment. It wasn't the song I had rehearsed with Angel. It wasn't a legendary classic rock anthem. It wasn't even a sappy love song. The song I chose to play was undoubtedly *me*. So much so, that I cried for days the first time I heard it. Because I wanted it. I wanted exactly what the lyrics of that song boasted.

Recognizing the intro of Paramore's "The Only Exception," Angel joined in with her own guitar as she sat in a stool to my right. We had played it before, and I knew she would pick it up. I looked over and smiled at her. Yeah, I hated Angel sometimes, but I loved her fiercely.

When I opened my mouth to belt out the first notes, I knew my voice was shaky. I was afraid, but it was ok. Fear would fuel my determination. I wouldn't let it ruin this moment. Not this song. Not when it verbalized every single emotion I was feeling but couldn't reveal.

As we entered the second verse, K.C. joined in on bass while MiMi picked up her own guitar. I smiled and let my eyes close, letting the melody completely take over me. This was the sweet spot. This was the place where everything clicked into place and created magic. I didn't even think about the movement of my fingers on the strings. I didn't even worry about remembering the next lines of the song. I didn't have to. Somewhere in those lyrics, Angel's voice harmonizing with mine perfectly, I became those notes. I was one with each chord. I let the music guide me as I recited the story of my life, stripping myself bare in front of a room full of strangers. And I didn't care. I was fearless, even if only for a few minutes.

Nessa carried us into the second chorus, the heavy drumbeats pushing us into the bridge. With my eyes shut tight, I sang for hope. For understanding. For courage. For love.

For Blaine. I sang my heart out for Blaine.

We finished belting out the notes together, as if I was a part of the band. And, in that moment, with the girls backing me up in beautiful harmony, I was. But the last verse, the lyrics that I so desperately needed Blaine to hear, I sang alone. I revealed more than my feelings for him on that stage. I exposed my soul.

I opened my eyes to a crowd of stunned faces before the entire building broke into hellacious cheers. I smiled, turning to my temporary band mates, as they all swiped tears from their eyes. Even K.C. was blotting her black-lined eyes and nodding at me. Turning my attention towards the crowd before emotion took over my own tear ducts, I jumped down in front of Dominic, who quickly pulled me into his arms.

"I'm so fucking proud of you, you know that?" he murmured, squeezing me to his body. "So fucking proud, Kam. I knew you could do it. I never doubted you for one minute."

I gave him a swift kiss on the cheek before bar patrons congratulated me with hugs and high fives. It was all scary as hell, but judging by the overwhelming praise, it was worth it. If I never did anything that impulsive again, I would always have that moment.

I was surrounded by a group of fan-boys asking to buy me a drink, when my body began to hum, the intoxicating smell of mint and spice impaling my senses. I felt his heat at my back first, creeping up over my shoulders and down my chest, before settling between my thighs. With a slight grin on my face, I turned. I didn't know what to expect. I didn't even know if he truly felt the same, but the look of pure adoration on his beautiful face said it all.

"Blai-," was all I could get out before his mouth was on mine, taking me hungrily, as he picked me up and coaxed my legs on either side of him. The bar broke out into hoots, hollers and whistles, as Blaine claimed me for the world to see. He didn't care about staying professional. He didn't give a damn what anybody else thought. And with his mouth working feverishly against mine, my legs wrapped around his waist, neither did I. It was overly dramatic, corny as hell and ostentatious, and I loved every single second of it.

"You are so amazing," he murmured against my lips. "So fucking amazing."

His tongue dove in for another taste, and I gleefully complied, squirming as his hands squeezed my ass through my jeans. My hands fisted the long layers of his hair that he so masterfully styled into unbelievably hot, "Fuck Me" hair. And that's exactly what I wanted to do.

"Get a room!" someone called out, making us chuckle into each other's mouths.

Blaine reluctantly let me slide down his body, letting me feel the hardness concealed under worn denim. I gasped and bit my lip, unable to tear my eyes away from the pronounced bulge. Following my gaze, he pulled me by my hips into his middle, giving me just a sample of what I longed to feel.

"A round on the house!" he announced to the onlookers, still holding me close to his body. "And you all can thank this beautiful woman beside me!"

We made our way back to the bar, where CJ was already distributing beer. He shot us both a knowing grin and clapped Blaine on the back. "Proud of you, cuz." Then he looked to me and winked. "Sexy and talented. B better keep his eyes on you. Big dicks run in the family, you know."

I shook my head and smacked CJ on the arm before jumping into serving, a wide grin on my face. I looked at the appreciative faces surrounding me, thanking me and showering me with praise.

All I could do was smile. I smiled for all the times I wished I could step out on faith and perform. I smiled for the friends that had been my rock and my family, and I even smiled for people like CJ that I had begun to care for, as unlikely as it may have been. But most importantly I smiled because I had finally found it. I had discovered the meaning laced between the lyrics of that song. I had finally found *my* exception.

CHAPTER TWENTY

Blaine

The best part about being the boss? I could close up shop whenever I damn well felt like it. And if there was a reason to shut down for a day, it was getting to see Kami in a bikini.

Oh. Hell. Yes.

I decided a team-building trip to Lake Norman was in order and invited the entire staff and their families for a day of fun. I had even gone all-out with food and drinks. Shit, I deserved some fun. Ever since I came back over a year ago, I was all about business. I wanted to put the bullshit of my past behind me and prove that I wasn't just some hot-tempered misfit with a record. Not for anyone else; I could give a flying fuck what people thought about me outside of my family and Ms. Patty. I wanted to prove it to myself.

But now that things were finally falling into place, now that I actually had a reason to wake up in the morning aside from the distraction of work, I was ready to slow down. And I wanted to slow down with Kami. Shit, I knew I was being presumptuous. I still knew very little about her and, honestly, there were things that she still needed to know about me. But I was ready to share them with her. Hell, I was ready to share my life with her. I just didn't think I could ever tell her without scaring her shitless.

We caravanned up to the lake late Sunday morning, BBQ utensils and swimsuits in hand. Kami rode with her friends and the rest of the AngelDust girls, even though I wanted her to ride with me. It was cool though. They were taking Dom's Expedition, and it was more convenient for her. Plus, I had agreed to drive my bonehead cousin and his random flavor of the week that had already started pre-gaming earlier that morning.

"So Blaine, do you have a girlfriend?" his date asked from the backseat, where she had been damn near giving CJ a handjob. I think her name was Mindy. Or Misty. Or something equally unappealing. "If I would've known you were coming alone, I would have brought one of my girlfriends. You are way too sexy to be all alone. We all could have had a little fun."

I glanced at her through my rearview mirror, and shook my head. Her store-bought cleavage was spilling out of her bikini top, and she had the nerve to lick her inflated lips at me. Hell no. She had nothing on Kami. Hers were the only set of lips that got me hard as steel just thinking about them.

"Nah," CJ answered, saving me from having to embarrass this broad. "He's not interested."

"Not interested?" Misty/Mindy scoffed indignantly.

"How could you not be interested in *this*?" And with that, her hand snaked around my waist and tried to grab my junk. I swerved, barely missing the guardrail.

"What the fuck?!" I shouted, scowling at her through the rearview mirror. "Don't ever do that shit again!"

Mindy/Misty waved off my warning. "Oh, come on, Blaine. I'm totally cool with taking you both, sugar. Don't be shy."

"Calm the fuck down, or your ass will be on the side of the road," CJ interjected, his voice devoid of his usual playfulness. "Now I told you he wasn't interested. He has a girl. A girl that is 10 times hotter and cooler than you could ever be. She'll be at the lake, so you might want to take notes. Now chill the fuck out, or you can get the fuck out!"

CJ's words left both Mindy/Misty and I with dropped jaws. I never expected him to speak up on my behalf. CJ and I had a reputation for sharing chicks in the past. We were the same age, and in high school, we were pretty notorious for our wild parties and sexual antics. Even when I had hooked up with Amanda, CJ was less than accepting. He thought Amanda was narcissistic and vapid. It nearly killed me to admit he was right.

When we pulled up to the lake, I couldn't wait to escape the tension of my truck and scoop Kami up into my arms. She and her roommates arrived a little while later, the three of them lugging their towels and foldout chairs. I grabbed her things from her without a second glance. There was no way my lady was carrying shit when I had two functioning hands. I was a stubborn sonofabitch sometimes, but I had been raised right.

Dive's head cook, Mr. Bradley, a 60-year old veteran

that had been with us for years, had already fired up the built-in grills, while some of the other staff prepared the hot dogs, hamburgers, steaks and veggies. Of course, I ended up playing bartender.

"Anything I can do to help?" Kami asked, making her way over to the picnic table that I had deemed the bar as I mixed a pitcher of Rum Runners. She looked incredible, a light, cotton cover-up dress concealing her yellow bikini. My cock twitched at the possibility of having her sprawled out under the hot sun, her tan skin warm against my tongue.

"Nah, babe, you go relax. I'll be done in a minute."

Kami smiled before placing a tiny kiss on my cheek, and I felt like I was on top of the fucking world. That was a big step for her. Even though everyone had seen us full-on making out Thursday night, she wasn't a PDA type of chick. She didn't like everyone knowing her business. I could respect that because I thought I was the same way. But there was something about her that made me want to show her off. I wanted everyone to know that she was mine, even though we hadn't seriously had that conversation yet. She knew I wanted to be with her and only her. And while she would sometimes show it, she hadn't said that she wanted the same.

Once Mr. Bradley announced that lunch was served, our group lined up to pile their plates high with meats, salads and sides. I let everyone get their fill, standing back to sip on a cold beer. When Kami, Angel and Dominic stepped up to get food, I watched intently. Not because I was jealous. Not because I was having a semi-creeper moment. But because something seemed... odd.

They stood side by side, Dom and Angel on either side

of Kami, as if they were glued together. As Dom distributed meat onto the girls' plates, Kami moved effortlessly around his hands to place side items on each of their plates. Angel dressed their food with condiments and grabbed silverware. They didn't speak. They hardly even looked at each other. It was like they already knew what each person wanted without even communicating. As if they were much closer than I had originally thought.

"Dude, are you seeing this?" CJ asked, suddenly beside me, watching the trio just as intently.

I took a long swig of my beer. "Yeah." What else could I say?

"Are you sure the three of them are just friends? I mean, they look like a helluva lot more."

Another swig. "Yeah. As far as I know."

"Well, there is something going on with them. That doesn't look just friendly. Pretty suspect as fuck."

I couldn't disagree with him. I downed my beer and went for another, just to give my eyes and head a break. Once they had found a place to sit—together, of course—the shit just got more bizarre. It seemed like they were always touching. Kami pushing a lock of Angel's hair out of her face. Dom wiping a smidgen of ketchup from the corner of Kami's mouth, then sucking it off his thumb. Angel feeding Dom a bite of her food. Them rubbing each other's backs. Resting their heads on each other's shoulders. What the fuck was going on? Was I the only one who saw a problem with this shit?

Thankfully, they finished their lunches, and Kami's eyes searched for me in the crowd. When those green depths landed on me, the irritation evaporated instantly. I only saw her. But, I knew that I wouldn't be able to fully have her until I understood the relationship she had with her roommates. I had unknowingly shared a woman with someone before. I'd be damned if I'd let that shit happen again.

"This seat taken?" I asked, as she was reclining in one of the beach chairs. Dom and Angel had decided to go swimming, finally leaving her alone.

She lifted her sunglasses to the top of her head and peered at me mischievously. "Hmmm, I don't know."

"I come bearing gifts," I grinned, holding up two Coronas.

"Eh, I guess. You're lucky I'm thirsty, and it's so hella hot out here."

I handed her the beer, then slid my seat closer to hers before sitting down. "That's the only reason you'll let me sit next to you?"

"Well, there are definitely other advantages." Kami placed her perfect lips around the rim of her bottle, and I prayed my dick wasn't pitching a tent under my board shorts.

"Oh? Like what?"

She took a small sip, then let the ice-cold bottle skid across the top of her cleavage. My eyes followed the movement, hypnotized by every drop of condensation that slid off the bottle and onto her plump breasts.

"Well…if I don't put on some sunblock, this hot country sun is going to burn me."

I laughed, throwing my head back. "Hot country sun? I think the sun is the same no matter where you are, babe. And Charlotte is hardly the country. I bet Atlanta was way more country-fied."

She shrugged. "Yeah, I guess you're right. Though it wasn't as bad as Memphis."

Another tidbit of info, thank you. "You've lived in Memphis?"

Kami answered with a quick nod of her head, then avoided my eyes by rummaging through her beach bag to retrieve her sunblock. "Please?" she asked holding out the bottle.

I looked her up and down and licked my lips reflexively. "You're gonna have to take that dress off."

"Not all the way. I just need a bit on my shoulders and back." She turned around to give me access, and gathered her long, thick hair in her hands. I fought the urge to kiss and lick every inch of her neck and back. Fuck, she was the sexiest thing I had ever seen, and she didn't even know it.

Slowly, I pulled at the strings of the halter style dress and let the thin fabric fall around her waist. Irresistibly smooth skin stared back at me, and, dammit, I wasn't one to let an opportunity go to waste. I leaned over and pressed my lips to her shoulder, trailing a path to the other.

"What are you doing?" she half-moaned, prompting me to repeat the ritual.

"Protecting this precious skin from the hot country sun," I answered, running my tongue along the back of her neck.

She giggled and turned to face me, her green eyes burning with lust. My gaze fell to her pebbled nipples straining against her bikini top. Shit. What I wouldn't give to have them in my mouth again. But I didn't need these other assholes getting a glimpse of what was only for me.

Hell no. Gently, I turned her around again and opened the bottle of sunscreen. My mouth would have to wait, but at least I could still have my hands on her.

"You enjoying yourself?" I asked, making small talk as I rubbed her soft skin. To be honest, I was trying to subdue my raging hard-on. I had to focus on anything but the feel of her under my fingers.

"Yes. You?"

"Yeah, I am." I knew this was the best time to ask her about her relationship with Dom and Angel. I didn't know when I would get another chance. And if she admitted to being more than friends with them, I could easily jump in my truck and drive away from the situation before my temper got the best of me.

"So you've known Dom for a long time, right?" I asked, opening the conversation I had been dreading.

"Yeah. About five years."

"And Angel? You two are close too."

"Yeah? Why?"

I was done rubbing sunscreen on her back but I kept massaging her shoulders, thankful she couldn't see my face and I couldn't see hers. "It's just…you three seem really close."

"We are close, Blaine," Kami replied with a hint of suspicion.

"No. I mean, *close*-close. Like, not-normal-close."

Kami spun around to face me, disconnecting the comfort of contact we had just seconds before. "What are you getting at?" she asked with narrowed eyes.

I ran a hand through my slightly sweat-dampened hair. "It's just…the way the three of you are, Kam, it's weird.

Not bad weird, just weird. How it seems like you always need to be touching one another. Or how you always need to be together. And how affectionate you are. I don't know… even the way you move around each other, like it's choreographed. Like you've been spending every second of every day with them for years. Like you know them inside and out. Like you aren't whole without them."

I picked up my beer and downed most of its contents in one gulp, suddenly dying of thirst. "Kami, I don't want to be jealous. But, shit, I am. I am, ok? I can't help it. Hell, I want my movements to be synchronized with yours. I want you to always need to touch *me*."

Without thinking about it, I reached out and brushed the back of my hand against her cheek. "I wanna be weird, too."

Kami stared back at me, expressionless. Hell, I couldn't even tell if she was breathing. But at that very moment, I hated my need to always speak my mind. With each silent moment that ticked by, I felt like someone had dropped me in the middle of Lake Norman and left me to drown. And for a second, that scenario seemed much more comfortable.

"Take your shirt off and turn around," she finally muttered.

Confused, I did as she requested, happy to escape her disapproving gaze. Fuck. Had I just totally messed up everything?

Kami grabbed the sunscreen, and seconds later, her small hands were massaging my shoulders gently. Even though the tension was as thick and unforgiving as quick-sand, I couldn't help but be wholly aroused.

"Dom was there for me when I had no one. When I wanted to give up and lie down and die, he wouldn't let me," she said quietly, her hands still working the lotion into my skin. "He helped me learn to put one foot in front of the other. He still helps me. We help each other."

Whoa. I didn't know what explanation I was expecting, but I sure as hell wasn't expecting that. I kept my mouth shut though. I knew she needed my silence right now. Anything I would say would be misconstrued as a judgment.

"And Angel… Angel was rejected by the people who were supposed to love her the most, simply for being who she is. She can't help that. She did nothing wrong. She has no one, just like me and Dom. Those two are my family. Their love is the only kind that is safe enough to accept and return."

She was alone? Safe enough? I bit the inside of my cheek to keep from interjecting.

"Blaine, I told you before that I was unlovable. That hasn't changed. But I know we all need love. Even people like me. And those two have found a way to give me just enough to keep me waking up in the morning. Without it, I don't know where I'd be. So no, we don't have some freaky poly-amorous relationship. There is nothing sexual between any of us. They are my family. Nothing more, nothing less. And while we may be a fucked up family to the outside world, we are a family nonetheless. I'm sorry if you can't understand that."

Fuck it.

I turned around to face her, grasping her lotion-slicked hands in mine. She lifted her head, revealing the pain that she tried to keep hidden right underneath the surface. I had hurt her feelings. I was being a jealous asshole and made her feel bad, like the insensitive prick that I was.

"Baby, I understand, ok? You don't have to explain anymore. They're your family. I accept that. And I love that they care about you so much. Ok? Don't you dare apologize. I should be the one apologizing to you for being such a douchebag."

A small smile crept onto her face. "Well, I wouldn't call you a douchebag…"

"Oh yeah?" I jibed, trying to bring back our lighthearted banter. "Then what would you call me?"

"I don't know," she shrugged. "Ok, maybe a tad bit douchey."

I chuckled, pulling her close, so I could plant a kiss on her forehead.

"Ewww, stop, Blaine! I'm sweaty!" she squealed.

"Well, lose the cover-up, and come swimming with me."

"No thanks. You go ahead," she said shaking her head.

"You're not going to swim? It's scorching, and we're at the lake. What did you plan to do?"

Kami reached into her beach bag and retrieved what looked to be a big ass smartphone. "I've got a date with my Kindle."

I took the eReader from her and powered it on. "So let's see what kind of smut you read while fantasizing about me."

"Smut? I don't read smut!" she giggled. Once again, my dick was straining against my shorts.

I pointed to one of the book cover icons and held up

the Kindle. “What’s this one about?”

A sly smile spread across her pouty, pink lips. “A con artist and a sexy tattoo artist with lots of ink and piercings. Lust, deceit, redemption. All very tragic and beautiful. And hot. Very hot.”

I licked my lips and peered down at her heated expression. “So you like guys with tattoos and piercings, huh?”

Sucking her bottom lip into her mouth and capturing it with her teeth, Kami gave me a naughty look that had my balls aching. “Oh yes. I find them to be extremely sexy… on the right guy, of course.”

“And what’s the right guy?” I didn’t know where this game was headed, but I sure as hell wanted to play.

“Hmmm, tall, tan, brown eyes, gorgeous smile. A hard, chiseled body. And hair that looks like he just had crazy hot sex with someone who likes to pull it. Know anyone like that?”

Fuck. *Me*.

“Babe, if you don’t stop it, I’ll be forced to take you out in that water and help you out of those bikini bottoms.”

Kami laughed, but I was dead serious. I had no plans for our first time together to be in public, but if she kept this up, I would be driven to betray my good southern manners.

“Ok, ok,” she chuckled, holding up her hands in surrender.

I diverted my attention from the way her breasts bounced when she laughed, and looked back down at the Kindle, which was the only thing keeping me from adding an indecent exposure charge to my rap sheet.

"How about this one?" I asked, pressing another icon.

"Mafia romance. Good guy with a rough past meets a nice girl with her own demons. He tries to leave *the family,"* she explained, as she made air quotes with her fingers. "But, of course, it's not that easy. She tries to break it off, but they can't live without each other."

I pointed to another, thankful that blood had started to flow to my other extremities. I just had to keep her talking.

"Oh, you'd like this one. It's about a motorcycle club. Well, actually about this one girl who falls for the head of an MC and all the crazy drama their lifestyle bring. Really gritty and just…*ugly*. I mean, it's beautifully written, but some shit is just not pretty."

"Like life," I murmured, not even realizing I was saying the words aloud.

Kami nodded appreciatively. "Yeah. Like life."

Handing her back the eReader, I let my fingers linger against her hand, brushing tiny circles against her knuckles. "Life may not be pretty, but it's always beautiful. We may only see the ugliness on the surface. The shit that only the world chooses to notice. But, if we dig deep, if we get to the heart of life, where there's no pain or fear, where we can just be who we are and love freely without judgment, it's really beautiful."

She cocked her head to one side and narrowed those dazzling green eyes. "There you go with the words, Blaine Jacobs. Always tempting me to break my own rules."

"What's the fun in following the rules?" I shrugged. "Breaking them has always been much more appealing, if you ask me."

"That's the problem; you may end up breaking me

instead." The slight smile on her lips didn't match the intensity of her gaze. She was serious. She actually thought I had it in me to hurt her when all I wanted was to protect her.

"I could never break you, Kami. Not unless you wanted me to."

Heat surged between us, elevating the already scorching temperature and causing our conjoined hands to become damp with sweat. Before any more words were exchanged, CJ came bounding up, smacking me on the back. "Come on, B! Get your ass out there!" Then he and Mindy/Misty raced into the water.

"Go ahead, Blaine," Kami waved towards the lake. "Go swim. I have a book I really want to finish."

"You sure?" I asked, already standing. It was hot as hell and I was sweating bullets.

"Yes, I'm sure. Go. I'll be right here waiting when you get back. I need to work on my tan." Then she eased her dress down past her hips and thighs, kicking it off when it reached her ankles.

I knew Kami's body was amazing, but…*damn.*

"Well, how do you expect me to leave you *now*?" I needed to though. If I stood there any longer, I was liable to poke her eye out.

Her gaze blatantly roamed my torso and arms, as she slowly licked those plump lips. "Well, I was hoping to get a glimpse of you dripping wet…" she cooed with a devilish grin.

"Yes, ma'am," I nodded, turning just in time to conceal the sight of my swell that was aching to be released. Maybe I should've let her get an eyeful. It was, in fact, her fault.

Moments later, I was cooling off in the refreshing lake water, letting the chillier temperature alleviate my stiff predicament. The majority of the female employees and A.D. were scantily clad in teeny tiny bikinis, splashing and flirting with the guys. CJ had Mindy/Misty wrapped around his waist while she kissed his neck. Even Dom and Angel were chatting up with some cute chicks. I was happy for all of them, but I couldn't help but feel a bit lonely. Yeah, Kami sat only yards away, but I wanted her wrapped around my waist. I wanted to hear her squeal when I splashed water at her. I wanted to flirt and kiss her while my hands roamed the exposed skin that her itty-bitty yellow bikini couldn't cover. Shit, maybe even dip inside that bikini under the water.

"Hey, B, watch this," CJ murmured suddenly beside me, sans date. He trudged out of the water, casually making his way over to the beer cooler. But instead of grabbing a brew, he changed course and crept up behind Kami who was still engrossed in her eBook. Aw, hell. I knew what he was up to and that Kami would be pissed. I should have warned him, but I secretly wanted to see her reaction. If she hauled off and punched CJ in the face, it would serve him right.

Before she even knew what was happening, he snatched the Kindle out of her hand and flung it on a towel. In the next instant, her slight body was slung over his shoulder, and he was running towards the water, laughing like a madman.

"No, CJ! No, please!" she shouted. But the roar of his laughter obscured the seriousness in her voice. Even I was chuckling at the sight of Kami's tight little ass in the air.

Instead of letting her down next to me, CJ tossed her into the chest-high water a few yards away, sending her crashing in with a splash.

"No!" came Angel's shrill scream the next moment. She and Dominic were frantically wading towards the scene, both donning furious expressions.

I looked to Kami. She still hadn't surfaced from the water. Shit. Was she just joking around? Or maybe she couldn't swim?

"Kami! Babe, just stand up. It's shallow," I called out, wading towards her. Still nothing.

"Do you know what the fuck you've done?" Dom hollered, shoving CJ as he reached Kami just as she finally floated to the surface.

Face down and unmoving.

Alarm bells wailed in my ears, as I struggled to get to her unresponsive body. Fuck! Had she hit her head on a rock at the bottom of the lake? Had she choked? What the fuck was going on?

Dom scooped her up into his arms, her limbs flailing limply like a ragdoll. I reached out to take her from him, my protective instincts kicking in. Dom angrily shoved me with his shoulder. "Get away from her!" he barked, his hostile glare bringing me up short. What the hell?

The rest of our group was making their way to shore as Dom laid Kami's limp body on a beach chair. She was pale and eerily still, and her body looked frail and tiny. The back of my eyes prickled with fear and I took a step back, frozen in panic. This wasn't happening. Not again. I couldn't do this shit again.

Angel wrapped a towel around her wet body while Dom checked her vitals. He opened her mouth with the tips of his fingers and pressed his lips to hers. I understood what he was doing, I knew he was trying to save her life, but I couldn't help the sudden flash of jealousy that flooded my chest. I pushed my way through the onlookers to her still motionless body.

"There's no way she could've drowned; she was only under for a few seconds," I said, kneeling in front of her. But I couldn't touch her. I was...scared. I was scared that history was repeating itself.

Dom worked to bring her to consciousness, talking to her, shaking her, opening her eyes for any sign of coherency. "Don't you think I know that?"

"We need to call 911," one of the waitresses said.

"No!" Angel shot back. "Nobody call. She'll wake up in just a second. Just get back! Give her some damn room!"

I helped her push back the crowd before turning to a shame-faced CJ, his frightened eyes rimmed with tears.

"Dude, I had no idea. I was just being a dick. *Oh my God,* did I kill her?"

"No!" Dom answered without looking up, still shaking Kami's lifeless body. "But you could have, asshole. Don't ever touch her again. Do you hear me?"

CJ grimaced as if physically pained, then let his head drop. He really was mortified, but I couldn't comfort my cousin. I couldn't do more than worry about the woman lying still before me. The woman that I was losing before I could even possess her.

In a gut-wrenching gasp for oxygen, Kami awoke, her delicate hands grasping the air like she was fighting for her life.

“I’m here, Kam. I’m here,” Dom said soothingly, tentatively pulling her into his chest. She continued to fight until she realized who he was. Then, she broke into a heart-stopping sob, clutching his back like she would die if he let go. Dom squeezed tighter and began to rock her, tucking her head under his chin to shield her from onlookers. Angel covered her with more towels before embracing her from behind, wrapping her arms around both Kami and Dom. And I just sat there. Stunned. Silent. And stumped. Had I missed something?

Kami continued to wail, her body shaking so badly that the tremors vibrated the beach chair.

“Shhhh, it’s ok, Kam. You’re safe. It’s over. You’re safe now. I’ve got you,” Dom chanted over and over in her ear.

The trio sat there for long moments, as I observed like some sick spectator. I wasn’t wanted here. I wasn’t what she needed. But I couldn’t turn away from her.

“Come on, let’s get her to the car,” Angel muttered, once Kami’s cries had decreased to painful whimpers. The two pulled away but kept Kami’s face and body obscured by towels.

“Kam?” I said reaching out to grasp her trembling hand. Dom smacked it away before I could make contact. *What the fuck?* I jumped to my feet, fists tight at my sides. “What the fuck is your problem, man?”

Dom stood, taking the same offensive stance. “My problem is you and your cousin fucking around with some-one you don’t even know. You have no idea what you’ve done. No fucking clue what damaged you’ve caused with your little joke. Well, consider playtime over. You're not playing with her anymore."

"Who the fuck said I was playing with her?" I snapped through clenched teeth. "And who are you to tell me what *I'm* going to do with her?"

Angel stepped between us, lightly pushing against both our chests. "Guys, cut it out. This isn't the time."

"You're done with her," Dom replied, moving Angel aside. "Do you hear me? Done. Leave her alone."

"Fuck that! I'm not done until she says we are." I looked to Kami again. Her head was down, yet angled towards us. I advanced towards her again before Dom blocked my way with his arm. I shoved him back, bringing up my fists in preparation. Dom did the same.

"Stop!" Kami's small, shaky voice called out below us, drawing both our attention. I kneeled before her, my anger towards Dom temporarily forgotten.

"Baby, are you ok?" I asked, grasping her hands gently.

Her slightly blue lips trembled as her bloodshot eyes searched my face. She opened her mouth as if to say something, but sighed in resignation as she looked away.

"For now," she whispered.

No. Hell no. I wasn't going to let her lie to me. Not this time. I needed to make this better for her. For both of us.

"Kami, talk to me," I urged. "Let me know what I need to do."

She shook her head and brought her gaze back to me, her eyes rimmed with fresh tears. And with pain etched in every inch of her beautiful face, her body quaking uncontrollably, she cracked a sad smile. "There's nothing you can do. Just let me go."

"No," I all but growled. "You don't mean that. Talk to me."

"Blaine, she said…"

I gave Dom a murderous scowl before he could even get the words out. This was between Kami and I, and I'd be damned if I let her friends scare me away.

Her quivering hand gave mine a small squeeze, and I turned back to her, my expression softening at the sight of her solemn face. "I wish I could."

"Then do it. You trust me, right?"

Kami's big green eyes fell to our clasped hands, and she nodded faintly. "Just…give me time. I'll call you, ok?"

I didn't argue. Kami was giving me a chance, even if it was a half-hearted one, and I'd be a fool not to take it.

Slowly, I leaned forward and pressed my lips to her forehead. I knew it very well could have been the last time I ever felt her skin against mine, and that thought ripped me to shreds. But, I would do as she asked; I would give her time. I would have done just about anything for her at that moment.

As I watched Angel and Dom usher her away, all the little pieces of my reformed life, the parts that had finally fallen into place, were left scattered in disarray.

Kami said she couldn't be saved, but I still needed to save her. She said she was broken, and I desperately wanted to fix her. She claimed she was unlovable, but… shit…

I needed to love her.

CHAPTER TWENTY-ONE

Kami

I once was a believer in wishful thinking. I thought if I told myself that I was ok enough times that I could actually start to believe it. That somehow, I would eventually morph into the perfect picture of normalcy. That I could be somewhat happy.

I was wrong.

I wasn't ok.

Not even a little bit.

This…sickness. This affliction… it ensured that I'd never be normal. That I'd never find contentment. That I would live out my days alone and unloved. And I honestly thought I was fine with that realization. I was resigned. No one deserved to have to deal with my shit. I wouldn't wish that upon my worst enemy. Especially since my worst enemy was me.

I lay curled up in a ball on my bed, humiliated and mortified beyond belief, staring at the glass jar of tiny paper stars.

253.

I know I should have added one. I know I should have brought that number to an even 254, but I wasn't afraid. It wasn't fear that consumed me. It was rage.

Why couldn't I have just fought through it? Why did I have to freak the fuck out like I always did? Why couldn't I be normal for one damn day?

Angry tears leaked from my tired eyes, trailing saltwater over my nose and onto the comforter. I brushed them away furiously. I was so sick and tired of crying. Of feeling sorry for myself.

Fuck me. That's right—fuck *me!* Fuck my stupid, hurt feelings. Fuck my inability to get over my past. Fuck my fear and all the things it crippled me from doing. Fuck it all!

I punched the pillow in frustration, wishing I could be brave enough to take my anger out on the person who deserved it. It was all *his* fault. All *his* doing. If he hadn't been such a disgusting, sadistic piece of shit, I wouldn't be like this. I could lead a normal life. I could find happiness. I could find love.

That was a lie. I had found happiness. Hell, maybe I had even found love. I just couldn't accept it. I couldn't let myself believe it. I couldn't feel it. Bad things happened when I let myself feel. There was ugliness in love, at least for me there was. It wasn't the same for regular people as it was for me, Dom and Angel. We were exempt from the romantic type of affection that movies and books boasted about. Life had ruined us for that type of ardor. Now we could only love each other. It was better that way. There was no pain or deceit in it. There were no expectations or regrets. It was safe. It was selfless. It was all we had.

No, that wasn't true either.

"Kam? You awake?" Angel whispered from my doorway. I ground my teeth. I wished I could close and lock that damn door.

"No."

As if my answer was an invitation, Angel entered and climbed onto my bed, spooning me from behind.

"You ok, love?"

"No."

"But you will be, sweetie. You will be," she replied, squeezing me tight. I wanted to pull away from her embrace, but I knew it was more for her comfort than mine. I had scared her today. Dom had witnessed more of my meltdowns than he could count, but Angel was still new to them. Sure, she'd learned the hard way when it came to enclosed spaces and darkness, but she had never experienced my reaction to water. We had warned her about it so she was somewhat prepared. She and Dom had made it their mission to make sure I was comfortable all day, but I couldn't do that to them. I couldn't allow them to babysit me in the hot sun while everyone else enjoyed themselves in the water. Why should they have to suffer for my idiosyncrasies?

Maybe Dr. Cole was right about my fears. Maybe they were irrational.

I hated that know-it-all bitch.

"Don't blame yourself," Angel said suddenly, disrupting my diabolical plan to key the good doctor's car. Or egg her office. Or just suck it up and admit that she was right all along.

"I'm not." *I was.*

She held me for a few more silent minutes before the elephant in the room plopped its big, ugly ass on my avoidance.

"Blaine call you yet?"

A lump attacked my throat, taunting the sob I had been swallowing for the last six hours. "I don't know. I don't know where my phone is." I knew where it was. It was with my Kindle and the rest of my things, abandoned at the lake in my haste to escape. But even if I did have it, I doubted he'd call. Who would call after witnessing a scene like that? Who the hell would want to deal with a total basket-case?

"I think you may have left it," Angel remarked, reading my thoughts. "I'll go call one of the girls to see if they grabbed it." She slid off the bed and made her way to the door, turning to shoot me a sympathetic smile before disappearing down the hall. In that moment, I wanted to slap her. I was so tired of people looking at me like that.

Some time during my wallowing, I had drifted off to sleep, only to be awoken by noises outside my cracked door. Shuffling. Voices. Male.

Blaine.

I heard my bedroom door open wider but decided to feign sleep, too chickenshit to face him.

"Naw, man, she's still asleep," Dom whispered.

"Ok. I'll just leave her stuff," Blaine replied in an equally hushed tone. I heard him pad across the room and set down my things on the dresser as quietly as he could. Then his footprints grew louder as he made his way towards me. I tried not to flutter my eyelids and kept my breathing heavy and deep. Oh shit, I must look horrible. After showering, I had thrown on a pair of old cotton shorts and an oversized t-shirt, not even bothering to brush out my ratty hair. Great. I was just a hot mess all around.

His scent hit me first, causing my mouth to reflexively salivate. It had grown familiar to me. Comfortable. Safe. It made me feel…home. Something I had never had before. Something I had always craved.

When he drew close enough to me that I could feel his warm breath, I thought I might break. I still wanted him. Dammit, this wasn't supposed to happen. I wasn't supposed to feel like this. Not this strong.

Warm, soft lips accompanied with a bit of stubble brushed across my forehead ever so lightly. I bit the inside of my cheek to keep from melting into the touch. I wanted to pull him down onto the bed with me and nuzzle into his arms. I wanted him to squeeze me tight and tell me he'd never leave me, no matter what. That no matter how fucked up I was, he wouldn't abandon me. Then I wanted him to make sweet love to me for hours and hours until I was too exhausted to do more than smile…

No. I didn't want that. What was I thinking?

As I was losing my internal argument, Blaine retreated from the intimacy of my bedroom, closing the door behind him.

No! I can't…breathe…God…no

Before panic seized every muscle and joint, the door quickly clicked back open. I breathed an audible sigh of relief, clutching my chest to ease the jolt of my heart rate.

"Hey man," Dom began on the other side of my

bedroom door. "Sorry about earlier. I panicked. Emotions were high, and I jumped to conclusions. We good?"

A pregnant pause before what sounded like a hand clap. "Yeah man. We're good."

"Thanks for bringing her stuff back. Appreciate it."

"No problem," Blaine answered. "I would have come sooner, but I wanted to give her space since she said she'd call…"

"Yeah, um. I wanted to talk to you about that."

Oh no, Dom. Don't. Please don't.

He took a deep breath. "I don't know how much Kam has told you about her past…"

"She hasn't told me anything," Blaine interjected.

"Ok. Well…I think there are things that you need to hear from her, if she wants you to know. Outside of Angel and me, plus…professionals, she hasn't told anyone. But you…you're different. Well, she's different with you, I should say. I've never seen Kami with anyone. Like really *with* them wholeheartedly. Not like she is with you."

"Sometimes I can't tell if she really is." I could hear the pain in Blaine's voice. Was he hurting in all this? Did he even care enough to be hurt?

"She is, dude. She's with you. You have… *her*. No one gets her—not the real Kami. But with you, she's natural. She's carefree. She laughs because something's funny, not because it's expected. She smiles because she's happy, not because she's trying to hide her pain. She can be herself. That's pretty major for her."

Silence passed, and my strained ears were aching to hear a response from Blaine.

"What happened to her?" he finally whispered.

"Not my story to tell," Dom answered. "But I will tell you this: that girl is the strongest person I know. It may not seem like it, but if you knew the heavy burden she carries every single damn day and still manages to crack a smile, you'd understand."

"Well…help me understand. Help me be what she needs me to be," Blaine urged.

"I can't. Only she can show you that part of her. But something tells me the pieces are finally coming together. You've seen what happens to her, right?"

"Yeah."

"And you're still here."

"Yeah."

Another beat of silence.

"Do you love her?" Dom asked quietly.

I held my breath in expectation. Seconds ticked by. Then a minute.

No answer from Blaine.

"Well," Dom muttered. "I just hope you realize what you're doing."

"I do," Blaine answered assuredly. Footsteps started to move away from my door, taking the voices with them. "Can you have her call me when she wakes up? I really want…"

I know I should've been happy that he didn't say he loved me. I all but told him not to from the beginning. So why wasn't I relieved over his omission? Why were confused tears sprouting at the corners of my eyes, making me even more frustrated than I was before? And why the hell did he kiss me, knowing that he wouldn't stay. He couldn't stay. He'd be a fool to.

"Kam?" Dom whispered, popping his head into my bedroom.

I fluttered my eyes open and feigned a yawn. "Yeah?"

Dom eased himself next to me, giving me a tentative smile. "You didn't happen to overhear a conversation I just had, did you?"

"What conversation?"

"Blaine was here."

I worked to keep my face blank, hiding the excitement at just the mere mention of his name and the memory of his lips. My forehead still tingled. "He was?"

"Yeah. He brought your stuff, and he wanted to see if you were ok. He wants you to call him."

I nodded.

"But you're not going to, are you?"

I looked at Dominic, my best friend and the only man I could totally be honest with. "Nope."

He let out an exasperated sigh. "Kam…"

"What's the use? Why should I call him? Why not make a clean break? Why drag this out when we both know that it won't work?"

"How do you know it won't work? Have you ever tried to have a relationship?"

I lifted a brow. "No. Have you?"

Dom's mouth twisted as he digested my words. He had never tried either. He slept with anything on two legs in an attempt to mask his insecurities and shame. After years of being raped by someone who proclaimed to love him, Dom had been confused about his sexuality. He thought being violated by a man meant he was gay, yet he didn't find men attractive. He was undoubtedly good-looking, almost pretty. Both men and women found him exotic and enticing. His uncle even tried to use the defense that Dominic had indeed enjoyed it since he had ejaculated. Luckily, the jurors in Dom's case saw his bullshit for what it was.

"You don't want to be like me, Kam. Different chicks every night—hell, I couldn't even tell you who I brought home last week. That's not you. You're not a slut. You deserve someone who is going to cherish and love you. You need someone to build a life with. Maybe even start a family."

"And you think that someone is Blaine," I said incredulously.

"I think he could be. But you won't know that until you try, Kam." He handed me my cell phone that he'd been clutching. "Call him. Maybe he'll understand. Maybe he'll be exactly what you need. You owe it to yourself to at least try and find out."

Dom brushed away a wayward lock of hair from my forehead before leaving me alone to make my decision. I looked over at the jar of colorful origami stars in my windowsill. They were laughing at me. Taunting me. Reminding me why no one would ever be able to accept me. Not the way that I needed them to.

I powered down my cell phone that was hanging on to its last bar of battery life and set it on my nightstand. No. I couldn't call. I had 253 reasons not to.

CHAPTER TWENTY-TWO

Blaine

I was off for the next two days, so I was able to properly wallow in my misery. I was pathetic. It was bad enough that I had played every sad song in existence on a continuous loop, but I had also played my own renditions of dejection. I had no right to be sad when my unhappiness was self-inflicted. But I was a masochist. I needed the pain. I needed the constant reminder of what…*he*…had done to me.

By Tuesday, fed up with the doom and gloom of my bedroom, Angel stormed in with a determined expression.

"That's it! Enough already, Kam! You are obviously miserable, and it's making *us* miserable. Call him, please!"

I propped my guitar against my bed and frowned at her. "Why should I? He has officially seen me at my worst. Do you really think I can just bullshit my way out of a freak out like that?"

Angel fingered her blonde hair and flopped down onto my bed. “No. But I think you can be honest with him. And I think he would be ok with it.”

“Ok? *Ok?* Angel, how is any of this ok? How is screaming bloody murder in the middle of the night ok? How is hyperventilating to the point of fainting whenever a door is closed ok? How the fuck is nearly drowning because I can’t stand up in a pool of shallow water ok?”

Angel’s big blue eyes glazed over with emotion at my outburst. “Kam…” she croaked, before swallowing down her hurt. But there was nothing left to say. There was no answer to my questions.

“He wouldn’t understand.” I looked away to keep frustrated tears at bay. “He thinks he would. He thinks he could be with me despite it all, but I know it’s impossible. And when he finally sees that, it will kill me. I have no room left in me to be hurt, Angel. I’m barely hanging on as it is.”

I looked back to Angel’s solemn face and sighed with resignation. “And how could I ever forgive myself for subjecting him to all my shit? He doesn’t deserve that. No one does.”

Angel’s slender arms were around me instantly, squeezing me as if her life depended on it. Fresh tears on her cheeks wet my shoulder. “Don’t you dare fucking think that! Do you really think you are undeserving of happiness? Of love? That’s bullshit, and you know it! Blaine would be lucky to have you, Kami. It would be a fucking dream come true to love you, scars and all.”

I clutched her arms that were wound across my chest, and let my own tears fall freely. I didn’t wipe these away.

They weren't just for me. They were for Angel, who wanted nothing more than to be loved for all that she was. She had experienced rejection of the worst kind. Her own parents had disowned her for being gay and tried to buy her off to keep her hidden. Her father was a US senator and an unrelenting conservative. Having a homosexual rocker for a daughter just didn't fit his agenda. So, she had been sent away with a trust fund and a condo as long as she kept hidden from the media. She wasn't allowed to visit for holidays or special celebrations. Birthday gifts were sent in the form of a wire transfer. It was as if she didn't even exist in their lives anymore.

"I'm sorry," I whispered, feeling like a jackass. I really was. I was carrying on like someone had died because I was too stubborn to face my fears.

"Just try. Please. Do it for me. And for Dom. And for you—do it because you deserve it. You do, Kam. You deserve to be loved. Out of the three of us, you have the best chance."

"Ok," I choked out between silent sobs. "Ok, I'll try. But you deserve it too, Angel. There's someone out there for you. You are loved. Do you hear me? You. Are. Loved."

We held each other for a few more minutes, trying to stifle the surge of emotion threatening to drown us. When Angel finally pulled away, she gave me a pensive smile. "Dom is meeting us at the bar in an hour. You're coming too, no exceptions. This is your chance. Don't let it get away."

I nodded, though a big part of me desperately wanted to get out of going. I couldn't do that to her. She needed hope. She needed to believe that there was still beauty in a world so full of ugliness. And if I needed to be the sacrificial lamb to restore that hope, then I would gladly take one for the team.

I put myself together as best as I could, considering my face was still a bit splotchy, and my eyes were a little red. I even slipped on a sundress and espadrilles, hoping it would give me a boost of confidence. No such luck. I still was terrified to walk into Dive after what went down Sunday. Everyone had seen me lose my shit. They knew something was terribly wrong with me. They would look at me with pity. They'd whisper. They'd see me for what I was.

Angel grasped my hand as we approached the entrance, and gave it a squeeze. "If anyone says anything, I'll kick them in the nuts."

I tried to twist my frown into grin. "And what if it's a girl?"

"I'll cunt punt the bitch," she deadpanned.

A real, genuine chuckle broke through my lips as I let her lead me inside. I loved the awesomeness that was Angel Cassidy. And one day, someone else would too.

My eyes zeroed in on the bar, only to be met with a pang of disappointment. Trisha smiled at us as we approached, already preparing Angel's signature tequila shot and light beer.

"Hey, Kam. What brings you in tonight? I thought you were off?"

My gaze ghosted in the direction of the back office. "Oh, um, just hanging out," I stammered, swinging my attention back to her. "And I need to speak with Blaine. Is he here?"

"He was, but I think he went home. Everything ok?"

I knew she was just being friendly, but I couldn't help but grow annoyed at her question. It was none of her business, and I was just sick of people asking me that.

"Yeah. Everything's fine. Can I get a Coke, please?"

Minutes later, the A.D. girls filtered in, securing a booth tucked away in a corner. Dom arrived shortly after them, still dressed for his day job at a local center for at-risk teens. After everything he had been through, Dom had still found the courage to help others in need. Sometimes his job put him face to face with his demons, yet he fought through them in order to help others. His strength and selflessness knew no bounds, and I was proud to be his friend.

"I need a drink," he stated sliding in next to me.

"Rough day?"

Dom shrugged before signaling for Lidia. "No rougher than usual. Just so sick and tired of kids getting bullied. It's seriously getting out of hand. A kid came in, 15 years old and gay. The guys at have been really laying into him, and he's reported them several times with no results. One of his tormentors—you know the type, asshole jock with something to prove—corners him and tries to force himself on the poor kid. He said that if he told, no one would believe him because the little prick has a girlfriend. Anyway, the kid got away with a busted up eye and a bloody lip. I called the police and had him report it. Hopefully it helps to stop these little shits from torturing him, but we know how it goes..."

Dom's eyes grew dark and desolate, the way they always did whenever certain triggers resurrected his own painful memories. I laid my hand atop his clenched fist and gave it a squeeze. He blinked rapidly and turned to me, his dazzling smile replacing the grimace that had marred his handsome face.

"So Kam, you call Blaine?" he said, low enough to escape curious ears.

I shook my head. "I was hoping to see him here."

"Well, maybe CJ knows. He just walked in."

I looked over in time to see CJ sauntering over, a nervous, tight-lipped grin on his face.

"Hey, uh, um…" he stuttered. "I just wanted to say, that, um…"

I held up my hand, halting any further explanation. "It's all good, CJ. Nothing to worry about. Pull up a chair and join us. Better yet, you can have my seat." I nudged Dom to let me out, earning a half-frown from him.

"And where do you think you're going?" he asked, sliding out of the booth.

"To do what I should have done a long time ago."

Minutes later, I was in Angel's Lexus Coupe, cruising down the highway towards Blaine's house. I had to do this before I lost my nerve, and with the sun setting behind me, I was running out of time.

The squeaky hamster wheel of scenarios in my head drowned out the subdued sounds of The Civil Wars on the stereo system as I tried to prepare myself for the worst. What if he wasn't alone? What if one of his groupies had already taken my place? What if he was currently losing himself in her in an attempt to forget me?

The possibilities weren't enough to get me to turn back. I needed to see it. I knew the scene would be enough to hurt me into never letting myself feel again. I needed that pain to be my constant reminder, to help me return to indifference. I had apparently forgotten about the agony I already harbored, allowing Blaine to take up space in my heart and mind. They had both been destroyed, but somehow Blaine had begun to repair the damage.

They say that a broken heart never really can be fixed. Yet his touch had sealed the gaping wounds and even filled the tiny fissures that couldn't be seen. My heart may have not been completely healed, but Blaine had nurtured it with lingering smiles, whispered words and soft kisses. It had been out of order for so long, and over the past weeks, had slowly but surely begun to function again.

I pulled up to his house, palms sweaty and breath shallow. I could do this. I had to do this. I owed it to Angel for every lonely night she spent longing for someone to love her. I owed it to Dom for all the pain and suffering he had endured at the hands of someone who proclaimed to love him. And I owed it to myself for all for the love I had been too afraid to feel.

Love. It was the thing that bound us and tore us apart. It was our disease and the remedy of our shattered hearts.

It was a sonofabitch.

I counted down from 10 with every step I took towards his front door. I didn't see his truck, but it could've been in the garage. I didn't know what I walking into, and the uncertainty seized my joints, making me work for every single movement towards my fate. It felt like I was walking the green mile rather than the paved stone path to Blaine's porch.

My pressed the doorbell before my brain could talk me

out of it. No answer. I hit the button again and waited another 30 seconds. Shit. All that worrying and he wasn't even there. I shook my head at the absurdity and rummaged through my purse. Then I left a folded piece of paper on his doorstep. At least he'd know I'd been by. And if he had moved on, maybe this would make him think about me. Maybe even enough to not want to forget the memories of our time together that I clung onto like a lifesaver.

"Kami?"

I slowly spun around, the air in my lungs abandoning me at the sound of his voice. Blaine stood just feet away from me, shirtless, and dripping wet with sweat. Black athletic shorts and running shoes were the only thing gracing his magnificent body. His tanned skin glistened underneath the setting sun, and his sandy brown hair stuck to his forehead. A single, solitary drop of sweat hung onto one of the longer layers over chocolate-brown eyes that watched me with appreciative surprise. I suddenly grew incredibly thirsty—parched, even—and only that drop would ease my dry throat.

"Kami?" he repeated, pulling the earbuds from his iPod out of his ears.

I didn't realize that I still hadn't said a word to him, too wholly captivated by his near nakedness. Blaine was gorgeous. Magnificent. The prototype of what a man would look like if fantasies were realities.

"Oh, um, sorry I didn't call…"

"That's ok," he interjected, stepping towards me and bringing the dark ink adorning his body into focus. Intricate patterns and script kissed his fingers, arms, shoulders and torso. I had discovered more on his legs at the lake but never got the chance to study the designs. Now I was close enough to glimpse the reds, yellows, greens and blues that crawled up his left calf. Every piece was stunning and sophisticated.

"Is that for me?" he asked, pointing towards the abandoned piece of paper tucked in the corner of his doorframe.

"Uh, yeah. Figured it'd be better than leaving a note," I shrugged.

He reached past me and squatted down to retrieve the little origami frog, giving me a whiff of his sweat slicked skin. His scent, coupled with the trace of mint and spice that I had grown to crave, was masculine and erotic. It was exactly what I imagined his sweat to smell like, and I wanted to bathe in the tiny droplets.

Blaine fingered the delicate paper and looked down at me with a half-grin. The heat from his body enveloped me, igniting fire in my belly. "Or you could've called me."

I worked to keep my tight-lipped smile even. "Some things need to be said in person."

He nodded, fishing out a key from the iPod armband that hugged his sculpted bicep. "Come on in."

Blaine's house was immaculate, just as it was before. Seeing it again brought back memories of his hands and lips caressing me, his strong arms holding me, and the tender words he uttered after I awoke in the dark. The look on his face when he shared his past with me, the intense feeling of wanting to take away his pain—it all came crashing back.

Blaine and I may have not known each other well, but we had grown close where it counted. He had witnessed my demons and revealed his own. Our connection wasn't like the solidarity I shared with Dom or even Angel. But, something had bonded us, and I needed him in my life just the same.

"I need to take a shower," he said from behind me as I took in the shelving that held his shot glass collection. My eyes zeroed in on the two blank ones, the ones he claimed were the most significant to him.

"That's fine," I breathed, feeling almost high from his scent.

"You can stay down here and watch TV if you want." He made his way to the kitchen and grabbed a bottle of water from the fridge, downing it in just a few gulps. "You want some wine?"

"Sure." A little liquid courage was just what I needed.

After handing me a glass of chilled white wine, Blaine clicked on the TV. He still had the little paper frog between his fingers, holding it like it was a precious gem. I smiled inwardly. Who knew a tough guy with tattoos and piercings could be so quirky and sentimental? It made him that much more attractive.

I surveyed the area once I was alone, sipping my wine as I looked at framed pictures of him and CJ, and even a few of Mick. I noticed several of a woman I knew was his mother. She shared the same sandy brown hair and warm brown eyes as Blaine. Of course, she was stunning, and her bright, beaming face brought a smile to my lips. When I stumbled upon a photo of her and a young Blaine, my breath caught. He looked so happy and innocent, the perfect picture of a young man with his whole life ahead of him. Even then, he was incredibly good-looking, and I imagined his mother having to beat the girls off with a stick.

"Her name was Amelia," his rich voice said behind me, a touch of southern drawl conjured up with the memory of his mom.

"She was gorgeous," I smiled at Blaine. He was dressed in low-slung cargo shorts and a sleeveless tee. The smell of his body wash filled my nostrils, bringing back memories of the suds all over my naked skin as I touched myself, imagining it to be his fingers. My face flamed, and I turned back to the photos. Shit. Leave it up to me to think about sex while talking about Blaine's deceased mother. *Class-y.*

"She was," he nodded. "Most of the men in town would try to date her, but I wouldn't have it. No man was good enough for her. So, I mastered the art of being a sneaky little shit, and making their lives hell."

"Not you, Blaine Jacobs! Look at that angelic face," I chuckled, pointing to the younger version of the scary-beautiful man in front of me, sans tattoos and piercings.

"You'd be surprised," he answered rubbing a hand behind is neck.

I took a deep breath and turned around to face him, resigning to confront the real reason I was there while the wine was coursing through me.

"Before you say a word," Blaine interjected, "I want you to know that you still have a place at Dive. Just because things may not work out for us, doesn't mean you have to leave. I can schedule you with Trisha or Corey, or you can work alone. Or…"

"Wait…what?" I frowned, taking a step back. "You… you think I came here to break things off with you?"

Blaine shrugged. “I don’t know. What was I supposed to think, Kami? I haven’t heard from you in days, and now you just show up, looking… fine. Better than fine. *Shit,* you look amazing. And here I am, going out of my fucking mind worrying about you. So please, tell me what I was supposed to think.”

He didn’t sound or look upset. He seemed hurt. And I felt like a huge asshole for making him worry.

“I’m sorry, I, uh, just needed some space and time to get my head together.”

“And now?” he asked with a raised brow.

“Now? Shit… I don’t know what. I, uh, you know…” Words failed me. Even the conversation I had on repeat in my head on the way over was long forgotten. I didn’t know how to do this. I didn’t know how to make him see that, though I was damaged, I still wanted him. And dammit, I wanted him to want me too. Not out of pity or obligation. But out of love.

Fuck. There’s that word again.

“You know…” I began chewing my lip nervously. I couldn’t do this. I didn’t even understand why I thought I could. No one could truly love a person like me. I was broken beyond repair. It would be selfish of me to expect him to be placated when I knew he deserved so much more. Someone normal and healthy. Someone who wasn’t afraid to love him as furiously as I wished I could.

“Shit, I’m sorry, Blaine. I can’t do this. I’m sorry.” I shoved my empty wine glass in his hands and turned towards the door before the first tears could be seen. I had to get away from here. I had to get away from him. With the impulse to stay and fall into his arms growing stronger by the second, I knew that my resistance wouldn't hold much longer.

"Stop, Kami!" he called out.

I forced my legs to carry me to the door though my heart crumbled with every step. It was breaking, the new fractures disrupting its previously restored state. It was all my fault this time. I would have rather suffer alone than throw him into the thick of it.

I pulled the doorknob open, only to have Blaine slam it shut before I could escape.

"Dammit, Kami! Stop this shit! Will you stop trying to run from me all the time? It's obvious that you came here to say something, so just say it. If you want to tell me how you feel, say it. If you want tell me I'm an asshole, say it. If you never want to see me again, then fucking say it! But I'm not just gonna make this easy for you. So if we're done, you have to say the words."

He pressed his front into my back, the heat of his anger seeping into my skin and causing sweat to break out all over my body. My breath caught at the feel of his hard body encapsulating mine.

"Blaine…I… I ca—,"

"Yes you can," he gritted. "You came all the way here. Spit it out, so you can go back to not giving a shit about me, and I can start not giving a shit about you."

I pushed against him and spun around, pinning him with my own angered glare. "What? You think I don't give a shit about you? You think I came here because I don't have feelings for you?"

"It's obvious you don't."

I let out a frustrated huff, causing my nipples to brush

his chest. "You don't know a damn thing. It's because I care that I'm even here. Do you think this was easy for me? Do you think this shit doesn't kill me just to think about?"

Blaine took a step back and ran a hand through his wayward locks before stalking back into the room. "How am I supposed to know that, when you shut me out?" He looked back at me with enraged confusion. "Kami, I know nothing about you. All I see is this gorgeous girl who looks like she is carrying the weight of the world on her back. And every time I try to help shoulder that burden, every time I get too close, you try to run. So please… help me understand what I'm missing. Because I'm tired of trying to figure this shit out on my own."

With my hands wrung tight in front of me, I stepped back into the living room. "You don't know what you're asking for, Blaine. You don't want this."

"Don't tell me what I don't want just to get out of talking. What are you so afraid of?"

Every tortured emotion that had been bottled up for the past month came rushing to the surface, bursting out of me like a violent volcano.

"Everything!" I screamed, tears streaming down my hot cheeks. "Everything! I am fucking afraid of everything, Blaine! Don't you see that? Don't you see why you shouldn't be with me? I am twenty-three years old, and I'm scared of the dark! Or how about this—I can't even close the fucking bathroom door. Do you realize how embarrassing that is? And let's not forget about the best part…how I can't even step foot into a body of water. That's what you want to hear, right? You want to fix the broken girl. You want to make me a little pet project so you can feel better about yourself. Well, newsflash… I can't be fixed. This is *me*. I'll never be what you want, Blaine."

Blaine was stunned into silence for long moments before he took a step towards me, his expression unreadable. "Why?"

Huh? What was he asking me? I glared at him through wet lashes and smeared mascara.

"Why?" he repeated.

"Why?" I snorted turning away from him. "Life happens. This is life, Blaine. And I don't care what you say. That shit isn't always beautiful. It's ugly. And hurtful. And abusive." I tried to wipe my leaking eyes, but the dam had broken. I couldn't stop. If he wanted to know me, then he would. He would see the loathing that festered inside me. And when he realized just how scarred I was, he'd do what any sane man would do. He'd walk away.

"Life is cruel and evil, Blaine. There's nothing pretty about being beaten repeatedly for no apparent reason other than existing. There's no joy in being locked in a closet in the dark for hours on end while being taunted. There's no happiness in being called every vile name you could imagine before you're too young to even know what they mean." My voice broke, quieting my tirade into a hoarse whisper. "There's no beauty in being tortured and hated by the one man that was supposed to love you the most."

He was in front of me before I could collect my bearings, brushing away my tears with the pads of his thumbs. "Your father did this to you?" he whispered.

I looked up at him through watery eyes, and could clearly see the compassion etched in his face. "Now do you see why you don't want me? The *real* me? My own father despised me from the day I was born. And my mother was so messed up herself that she forgot I existed. She forgot to love me. I live in a world of constant fear where monsters exist, and there are no happily-ever-afters. Only pain. And sorrow. Hatred. You don't deserve that."

"And neither do you," he uttered with a wavering voice. He pulled me into his hard chest and squeezed out another fresh wave of tears as he stroked my hair. "Neither do you, baby."

"Blaine, please don't do this. Please don't be nice to me. Please don't act like you want me when you don't. It's ok; I'm used to it."

"Dammit, Kami," he growled pulling me from his chest and grasping my shoulders. "Stop trying to push me away. Stop trying to make me not want you. Because guess what? I care about you. And I do want you. So fucking bad."

Before my mind could dissuade my heart, I looked into his brown eyes and let myself free fall into him. "Show me."

Blaine's hungry mouth captured mine as he pulled my body up into a kiss that shattered all other kisses. We were a mosaic of lips, tongues and teeth, drinking in each other's agony. I wanted to kiss away his guilt and pain. He wanted to swallow my fear and loathing. And, as my legs wrapped around his waist, the hardness of him pressing into my heat, I let him. I let him because I wanted to be better for him. I wanted to give myself to him freely without worry or hesitation. I wanted Blaine to take it all away.

Our mouths still fused together and moving furiously, Blaine carried me to the staircase. With one hand fisted in my hair, the other grasping my backside, he walked us to his bedroom with ease. I didn't even know we were there until he laid me down on his bed, settling on top of me. When his lips abandoned me, I nearly cried. Kissing him was finding bliss for the first time. And now that I had finally found it, I never wanted to let it go.

"You are so beautiful, Kami. And so strong," he murmured against my neck as he dotted it with kisses. "If you only knew how amazing you are… I'll make you see it. I'll make you *feel* it."

He stroked me through our thin layers of clothing, my dress bunched up to my waist. I didn't care. I wanted it off. I wanted to feel his skin against mine. I wanted Blaine to fill me with the same bliss that fell from his lips.

As if hearing my unspoken plea, Blaine eased the straps from my sundress off my shoulders, revealing my bare, heavy breasts. He instantly palmed both before drawing a pebbled nipple into his mouth and sucking, swirling his tongue ring around the hardened skin. I cried out as sizzling heat engulfed the area before shooting down between my thighs. I squeezed his waist tighter, locking my legs around him at the ankles. I ached for him. I needed Blaine to put out the flames that each flick of his studded tongue ignited.

He teased the other nipple until the skin was so sensitive that it hurt. Then he eased up on his elbows and gazed down at my writhing body. "I know you said you don't make love," Blaine uttered, his gaze branding me with smoldering passion. "But I want you. I need you. So. Bad. *Shit*… Kami… I need to fuck the fear out of you."

The air left my lungs in a rush as I absorbed the

delicious blow of his words. I was nodding furiously; out of control with my own desire for him to do any and every thing he pleased. "Yes," I answered breathlessly. "Please."

A long beat passed as we just stared at each other, our anticipation preluding frenzy. Blaine took my mouth again and claimed it with every stroke of his tongue as he slid my body up farther onto the bed. Gently, he placed my head on a pillow before pulling my dress down the length of my body. I lay before him unashamed and unafraid, in only my panties, as he appraised my body like a rare jewel.

"So fucking gorgeous," he muttered, as those hooded, chocolate-brown eyes took me in.

"I need to see you too," I whispered unabashedly.

Without hesitating, Blaine pulled his shirt off with one arm, revealing the masterpiece that was his torso. If I hadn't felt the warmth of his skin, I would have sworn it was cut from marble, the smooth hard planes and ridges a true work of art. I ran my fingers over his abs and chest, stopping to caress the small silver hoop in his nipple. He groaned and closed his eyes, motivating me to lift up on my hands and kiss it. I felt Blaine's body tense and tremble as I licked and sucked gently, careful not to get too eager. Touching him was a practice in restraint because God only knew how badly I wanted to push him down and mount him.

Feeling the excitement growing too thick, Blaine pulled away, sitting on the heels of his bare feet. His gaze was molten as he eyed the scant lace thong covering my sex. When his fingers finally hooked underneath the waist-band and pulled them down my legs, we both moaned. I was so ready for him that the throb was painful. The sight of my swollen clit must've told him the same.

"God, you're so beautiful," he said, before his face disappeared between my thighs.

The first flick of his tongue made me cry out. The second made me scream his name. By the third, I was coming, pulling his already disheveled locks as he continued to devour me. He groaned his appreciation for my taste, sending vibrations through my sensitive flesh up to my belly. By the time he was finally done sliding that magnificent barbell through every delicate fold, I had come again.

As I lay mewling and shaking, Blaine leaned over me to retrieve a condom from the nightstand. We both stared at the foil packet for an awkward beat before our eyes flicked back to one another.

"I've never been with anyone without one," he finally said, a tiny crease settling between his brows.

"Me neither." I chewed my lip, conjuring up the confidence to ask for what I wanted. And I wanted Blaine. All of him. "I'm on the pill."

Blaine swallowed before a small smile spread across his full lips. "You sure?"

I knew what he was asking, and I was. I had never been more certain about anything in my life. "Yes."

He was lowering himself onto my body in the next instant, rejoining our mouths as his hands continuously explored my body. I reached down for the fly of his shorts, desperately needing to feel every part of him, inside and out. Blaine sat up a bit, giving me access to the buttons that sheathed his hardness. And once he was free, my eyes grew wide with delightful shock as I took in the sight of his beauty. Because, dammit, he was beautiful. Every long, hard, swollen inch of him.

He settled between my thighs. "I'll go slow," he murmured against my lips as if he could feel my tension. Relief flooded my joints. Blaine was incredibly well-endowed. Hell, he was flat-out big. Bigger than I had ever had.

The tip of him teased my slick entrance, slowly pushing through the barrier of tightness. Even through the slight pinch, I welcomed him inside me, my walls hugging him after adjusting to the intrusion. Blaine pulled out a bit before sliding in deeper, causing me to gasp at the foreign feeling of pure pleasure. I couldn't focus on my insecurities. Fear was a distant memory. All I could focus on was the man cradling me, kissing me, as he filled me to the brim.

Blaine worked himself into me, stroking me deep and slowly. I caressed his back and shoulders before taking his face in my hands to look at him. His expression was a mixture of strain and ecstasy as I gazed at him though glassy eyes. He felt so…good. So good that he had conjured emotions I had never felt before. Emotions that I wanted to feel everyday from here on out.

I moaned and whispered his name while Blaine echoed my pleasure with sounds of his own. He was vocal as he rocked into me over and over, groaning, telling me I was beautiful, saying how good I felt, even growling as he sped up the tempo and pressure began to build. It was the sexiest thing I had ever experienced, and it heightened my arousal even more.

Tears sprouted at my eyes when the telltale signs of orgasm began to sweep over me, tightening my belly before blooming into an inferno that scorched each nerve ending. I clenched around him, matching the pulsing of his hardness inside me. Blaine shut his eyes tight and hissed as he pounded into me harder, melding pain with the intense pleasure, pushing me into another devastating climax. My back arched off the bed, and Blaine grabbed my hips until only my shoulders and head remained grounded. He surged into me harder and faster still, my garbled screams meeting the sounds of his own building orgasm.

Blaine's body finally went rigid as he held still inside me. I pulled him down on top of me and wrapped my arms around his neck. I was spent, but I wasn't ready to let him go. The feel of our wet arousal and sweat was slick between us, but I didn't care. I wanted him close. I wanted to hold him like he had held me so many times. Like he was holding me now, kissing me, smiling down at me lazily.

"You are amazing. So fucking amazing," he whispered.

"You're not so bad yourself," I grinned.

He nuzzled my neck and nipped my skin, causing me to squeal-moan with him still twitching inside me. I squeezed him tight. I never wanted to let him go.

Just as the glory of afterglow began to sweep over me, my tired eyes ghosted over his shoulder.

The door.

It was closed.

But with Blaine on top of me, kissing my nipples, and working me back into a frenzy, I was too incredibly happy to even be afraid.

CHAPTER TWENTY-THREE

Blaine

"I was seven when my mom and I left."

At hearing her confession, I reflexively squeezed Kami tighter, her soft, naked body curled around mine while she traced the ink on my torso and arm. I still couldn't believe she was here. And even more than that, I couldn't believe she had given herself to me after divulging the horror of her past. Hearing those words, seeing her tears, stirred an insane feeling of desperation inside me that I had never felt before. I was beyond outraged, but my need to comfort her outweighed my need to hunt down the sick fucker who hurt her. I knew at that point that I would do anything for her. I would risk my life to protect her, and give anything to ensure that she never felt that type of pain again.

"My mom is from a very strict, traditional Filipino family. My…father…is American. He was a musician and met her at one of his concerts when she was just a teenager.

My mother's refusal to stop seeing him was a huge show of disrespect, and her parents kicked her out when she was only 16. He took her back to LA with him, and they were married within a year."

She stopped her account to kiss the inscription on my left pec, conjuring my own demons. But they would have to wait. Kami was the only thing that mattered in that moment.

"I don't remember when things got bad. I think they were always like that. The lifestyle he led…the drugs, booze, women…my mother had no business being a part of it. Neither did I."

I kissed the top of her head, encouraging her to continue. Kami turned to look at me, giving me a sad smile that knocked the wind right out of my chest.

"I used to try to rationalize what he did to us. He had a tough upbringing; his dad would kick the shit out of him and rape his little sisters. He was sick. Sick to his core until he finally put a bullet in his brain in front of his wife and kids." Her green eyes glossed over with fresh tears before she blinked them away and placed her head back on my chest. "I thought it was possible that that sickness could be genetic. Maybe I'd be like them and get sick too. So I figured if I never let anyone in, if I never cared enough to want that for myself, I would be ok."

"You're not like them, baby. Not even a little bit," I said, guiding her head back up by her chin so she could see the conviction in my eyes.

A genuine grin pulled at the corners of her luscious mouth. "I know." Another soft kiss on my pierced nipple. "But maybe, in ways, I'm worse."

"How can you say that?"

Kami shrugged before running the very tips of her fingers up and down my stomach. "The way I am. So devastatingly afraid. It goes beyond fear, you know. It's like my body shuts down completely. I'm not normal. I'll never be. Which makes it impossible to have a normal relationship."

"I don't believe that, Kami. Not for a second." I brushed the hair away from her face, letting my fingers trail down her spine. "And what relationship is really normal?"

She nodded, and I could almost hear the proverbial "but" on her tongue. "Still…no one deserves to be bogged down with all my baggage. Can you understand why I kept all this from you? It wasn't just to protect myself, Blaine. It was to protect you too."

"From what?"

"The end. What always happens when I've gotten involved with other guys."

I let my hands roam the mounds of her ass and down to her thigh, pulling it over mine. "I'm not other guys. I don't need protection from you, Kami. I want every part of you. Even the parts you think are too painful or ugly to share. I want it all. I want all of *you*."

She nodded again as she silently contemplated my vehement declaration. Every word I said was steeped in truth. I not only wanted to possess Kami's demons as if they were my own, I wanted to completely free her from them. I never again wanted fear to consume her, and I would do anything I could to alleviate her anxiety.

"When my mom returned home to her family with me in tow, I thought we were finally safe," she whispered, returning to the story of her tormented past. “But I was so wrong. So very wrong…”

“Baby…” I kissed the top of her head, a piece of me breaking at the sound of her wavering voice. I knew whatever she needed to say would kill me. Just the thought of her hurting pushed me to the brink of violence. But I quelled my own emotions for her sake. Kami didn’t need my shit piled on top of hers.

“He found us six months later. We were staying with my grandparents up north. And he made it known that we would never be safe. We would never be free of him.”

I felt warm moisture slide onto my chest, heating my body with anger and sympathy. I hated that she had ever shed a tear for that piece of shit. He didn’t deserve them. But I wouldn’t stop her. She needed to let it out, and I was honored to be the one she had opened up to. I was her choice. Kami could have any man she wanted, yet she trusted me with her darkest secrets.

“As soon as he busted down the door, my aunt tried to pull me to the back bedroom to spare me. I kicked and screamed for her to let me go. I knew if someone didn’t help, he would kill her. When I finally wriggled free, I instantly regretted it.”

She took a deep breath, prompting me to stroke her hair. “My grandparents had a wall that was covered with a huge mirror. He…smashed her head into it repeatedly. Over and over again until she was a pile of blood and torn flesh on the floor. Even after he had beaten her unconscious, he just continued to kick her and call her disgusting names. And when his wild eyes flicked up to mine, he just…smiled. He smiled at me as if to say I was next; as if the thought of slicing me up until I was unrecognizable pleased him."

"Fuck. Oh my God…" I had no words. Nothing could sum up the horror and fury I felt. I just squeezed her tighter. I never wanted to let her go.

Kami sniffled before pressing her lips to my chest. "My mother spent weeks in the hospital. Plastic surgery may have repaired her face, but she was never the same after that. He killed her. Whatever was left of my mother was murdered that day. She never smiled again. She never kissed or hugged me. She never told me she loved me. She just existed. I think a big part of her wished he really did kill her."

"I'm so sorry, Kam. Shit, I'm…"

"Part of me wished he killed her too," she whispered through a sob. "I could have mourned her. I would have been given the chance to grieve the loving mother that I once had. Not the empty shell that forgot I existed."

"You don't mean that."

"I was alone with my memories, Blaine. I had no one to help me through them, no one to tell me it would be ok. I had nightmares every night, and no one soothed me. No one told me I had nothing to be afraid of. Fear became all I knew. It was all I had."

I pulled Kami until she was on top of me, and we were chest to chest. I needed her to see the severity in my face. "Kami, I swear to God that you will never feel that way again. As long as you'll let me, I will be there to comfort you through every nightmare. To hold and kiss you every day so you never feel lonely again. To dry every last tear." My thumbs brushed away the ones trickling from her impossibly green eyes. "Fear isn't all you have. You have me. If you want me, you have me."

Before she could answer, I covered her mouth with mine and swallowed the last of her sobs. Her hands gripped my hair while mine palmed her ass, slowly grinding her against my hardening cock. Kami placed her knees in either side if my legs, sliding slickness against hardness. I teased her opening with my erection, the friction to her clit causing her to moan and squirm. Fresh wetness covered my stiff length.

"I want you inside me," she mumbled against my lips. "Now."

"Yes, ma'am," I replied, lifting her hips and easing her onto me as I delved into the softest, sweetest place on earth.

An hour later, after a shower that nearly led to me thrusting into Kami against the tiled wall, hunger steered us to the kitchen. Kami sat cross-legged on the counter, wearing my t-shirt and boxers. Though the clothes swallowed her petite frame, she looked unbelievably sexy, and it was all I could do to keep from taking her right there.

"How do you like your eggs?" I asked, pulling out a frying pan.

"Isn't it like 11 at night? A little late for breakfast, don't ya think?" she asked, stealing a grape from the bowl of freshly cut fruit I had placed in front of her.

"It's never too late for breakfast. Besides, it's my

favorite meal. And the only one I can cook successfully."

Kami smiled around a mouthful of plump grape. "So you mean to tell me that you live off of breakfast food alone?"

"Mostly," I shrugged. "I eat at the bar a lot. And Ms. Patty or Mavis drop by with food throughout the week. I think there's some leftover fried chicken in the fridge."

Kami nodded while sucking fruit juice off her fingers. I was on her before she could even blink.

"Maybe one day I could cook for you," she said breathlessly, feeding me a small slice of peach.

I sucked the juice off her fingers slowly, twirling my barbell against the soft pads of her fingers. "You can cook?"

"Mmmm," she moaned, as I nibbled the inside of her wrist, lapping up the juice that had dribbled down her hand. "Yeah. I'm pretty decent. I used to watch my mom in the kitchen. I think it was what she considered quality time—her cooking and me watching."

I abandoned her wrist and fished a piece of melon from the bowl. Teasing her tongue, I glided the fruit across her lips before sucking the nectar from her mouth.

"You keep this up, and we'll never get any food made," she giggled once I released her lips. I rewarded her with the slice of melon.

"Would that be so bad?"

"Not at all. Especially since my hunger for food has suddenly been eclipsed by my hunger for something else," she smirked, her eyes flicking down to the bulge in my shorts.

My cock jumped to attention, straining against the

fabric. I turned back towards the stove to hide the evidence of my weakened willpower. When it came to Kami, self-control went completely to the left.

"I'd love for you to cook for me one day. But I must warn you: I may not let you go after that."

Kami smiled and slid a wedge of tangerine between her pouty lips. "That's what I'm counting on."

I struggled to throw together a decent meal for Kami and me, too distracted by her presence to focus on much else. Once we had both filled up on cheese omelets and toast with Ms. Patty's homemade boysenberry jam, we lounged on the couch with glasses of wine. Kami tucked her body under my arm and laid her head on my chest. She felt good in my arms. It felt natural, like she was made to always be there. It was presumptuous as hell, but shit… I didn't believe in playing games. Not when it came to her.

"What does this mean?" she asked, running her fingers over the tattoo on my chest.

I grasped her hand gently and placed it over the words forever etched in my skin. *"Alis Volat Propriis*. It's Latin for *'she flies with her own wings.'"* I guided her fingers to the cluster of roses adorning the lettering. "These are Amelia roses. My mother's name was Amelia Rose Jacobs."

"It's beautiful," she smiled, as I brought her fingers up to my lips.

"I got it when I was 16. Even my ornery old uncle got a little choked up when I showed him."

"I love your tattoos. I never really was into them before, but on you…it just sorta fits. Like I couldn't imagine you without them."

I released her fingers so she could explore further. "When did you get this?" she asked, pointing to my right sleeve.

"Different pieces from over the last few years," I explained as she traced a finger over the mural that covered my arm. "I like to get something done whenever I travel to a different place. Sorta like the road map of my life."

"How do you find time to travel the world and run a business?"

"I wasn't always the owner of Dive," I shrugged. "After shit went down with me and my ex, then with that asshole Clark… I kinda fell off the grid. As soon as my probation was up, I hit the road. No cell phone, no email, just the world mapped out in front of me. I needed to get away, just escape all the bullshit that was waiting for me here. And I really had no plans to ever return."

I ran a hand through Kami's hair while she continued her study of the lines and colors embedded in my skin. "I was gone for almost two years when I heard about my uncle's situation with the bar. I knew what I needed to do. He took in his sister's little badass kid and treated me like his own. Even moved to a better neighborhood to try to give me a new start. I owed it to him to help out. So, about a year ago, I came back."

"Family is important to you," she smiled up at me, her face completely devoid of sorrow. There was something else there. Admiration? Pride? The way she looked at me…I don't know…it stirred something inside me. Like maybe she could see the man that I desperately wanted to be. Not the guy covered in ink with a reputation for being too quick with his fists. Not the guy that used to bang different chicks every night just because he could. Not the man that had tried to run from the shitty hand that life had dealt him.

Maybe Kami could see straight into my soul just as I tried to see into hers. With those green eyes penetrating flesh and bone, awakening the parts of me that I had kept hidden from the rest of the world, I silently vowed to make life beautiful for her again. To erase the ugliness that her father had left behind years ago. To restore her faith in humanity and make her believe in happily-ever-afters.

To *be* her happily-ever-after.

CHAPTER TWENTY-FOUR

Kami

They say God laughs when you make plans.

I had planned to survive. I was resigned to not having any emotional attachments other than Angel and Dom. I could float from job to job, refusing to lay down any roots in order to stay detached. I'd even move every few years, hoping to just coast under the radar. Life would be…easy, filled with inconsequential interactions just to squelch the need for intimacy. Shallow. Insignificant. And lonely.

God was flippin' hysterical right now.

I knew Blaine was different. I wasn't naive to the fact that I had feelings for him. Feelings that I never thought someone like me could ever harbor. I just didn't know how deep those feelings could run. And holy shit…they ran deep. So deep that the impulse to stay and make Blaine the center of my universe was just as strong as the one to run like hell and escape the unknown.

Even as I made my way through the doors at Dive after

waking up in his arms just hours before, sentiments of both bliss and dread overwhelmed me. I counted to 10, but the queasy feeling in my gut didn't subside. My hands were clammy, and tiny beads of sweat broke out on the back of my neck. Still, something kept my feet moving farther into the building. Towards him. Running away wasn't even an option.

The moment his deep brown eyes bore into mine, I knew exactly what that impulse was. It was all him. All Blaine. My affections for that scary-beautiful man had won out over reason and rendered me absolutely dumbfounded. I knew I was a fool, but dammit, I was a deliriously happy one.

"You're not gonna make this easy, are you?" I asked, after I eased behind the bar.

Blaine narrowed his eyes, one side of his mouth curling into a knowing smirk. "Make what easy?"

I looked around to make sure no one was in earshot. "Playing it cool. Trying to act like nothing happened."

"And why would I want you to do that?"

I frowned. "You don't really want everyone knowing that we… slept together, do you?"

"Why not?" he shrugged. "I mean, no, they don't need details. But Kami, what happened between us was more than just sex. You get that, right?"

"Um…yeah?"

"Not convinced that you do."

Without saying another word, Blaine hopped on top of the bar and towered over the Dive Hump Day Happy Hour crowd. Everyone looked up at him like he had three heads.

"Attention everyone! You see this beautiful woman

behind the bar? Well… I am pretty much crazy about her. Like fucking insane. And whether she wants it or not, Kami's got me. *All of me*. And, all bullshit aside, I just want her too."

Half the bar erupted into cheers, most of the patrons raising their glasses to Blaine and me in an air-toast while the other half ignored us completely. When Blaine hopped down from his makeshift soapbox, I was already seven shades of red and completely mortified.

"*Oh my God!* Why did you do that?" I screeched, covering my face.

Blaine gently tugged my hands and wrapped them around his waist before grasping my flush cheeks in his large tattooed hands. "Because, Kami, when you know, you know. And you don't fight it. You don't deny the inevitable. You free fall because you know there's someone there to catch you on the other side."

His face inched closer to mine, close enough for the scent of mint and spice to intoxicate me as his earnest words entranced me. "You don't have to be afraid of falling. Just close your eyes, let go, and know that I'll always be here with arms outstretched, ready to catch you."

"So Blaine, what's going on with you and my girl?" Angel asked, before taking a bite out of her French fry.

It was Thursday, over a week since Blaine and I had officially crossed the line from friends to lovers, leading to a mortifying declaration to the entire bar. Open Mic Nights were quickly becoming just as popular as nights when AngelDust ruled the stage, especially since my performance two weeks prior. Luckily, I had successfully reiterated to Angel that it was a one-time deal. She promised not to spring anymore surprises on me though I did have to throw her a teeny tiny bone and confess my real feelings for Blaine. To most, it was obvious. But me actually saying the words out loud to another living soul? Major.

Blaine swung his gaze to me and smiled. "You'll have to ask Kam."

"Ugh. Don't you think I tried? I even bribed her with promises of shoes and handbags. Nothing. I swear, that girl is a steel vault," Angel griped, rolling her eyes.

"Get over it," Dom chimed in, swiping a chicken tender from her plate. "Not everyone is as shameless as you. Or slutty."

"Slutty? Oh you're one to talk! I'm sorry…I believe I ran into one of your "dates" this morning after you left for work. What was her name again? You know…the one with the butterfly tattoo?"

"How the hell should I know?" Dom munched away before whipping his head back to Angel with wide eyes. "Wait! How would you know about her tattoo? A tattoo that's on her *ass?!"*

I watched as the pieces fell into place for Dom, while Angel gave him a devious grin.

"Dammit, Angel! Not again!" he scoffed.

Angel shrugged and resumed nibbling her fry. "Not my fault you left her unsatisfied, and she found her way to my room. Don't be so sensitive, Dom. It's not like you cared."

Dominic shook his head before turning to pin me with an accusatory glare. "And you knew about this?"

"Why are you asking her?" Angel interjected before I could even open my mouth to answer. "She spent the night at Blaine's. *Again.*"

My mouth dropped. I didn't know what to be more mortified about: Angel announcing my newly revived sex life to the entire bar, CJ snickering beside her as he looked me up and down, or Blaine's cocky grin. I decided a little friendly retaliation was in order.

"Thank God for that," I shot back. "I sure as hell don't want to witness you running to Dom's room to borrow lube while wearing a strap-on. *Again.*"

Dom's face was as red as Angel's cherry red lipstick. "Ang, keep that shit in your room! I don't want plastic dicks flying around where I sleep! And get your own damn lube!"

I shook my head at my shameless roommates, leaving them to bicker, before looking back at Blaine.

I returned his smile. "Still wanna be weird?" I asked, nodding towards the raucous scene before us.

He rolled the metal barbell inside his mouth, causing the delicious ache that still lingered between my legs to grow into a throb. "If it means I get to be with you? Yes. Weird as hell."

Within the next hour, the crowd inside Dive had doubled, and we were swamped. I was glad for the distraction. With Blaine near, all I could think about was being pressed against him, feeling his hips settle between my legs, his tongue tracing a path down the length of my throat down to my hardened nipples…

"Kam?"

I looked up at Blaine, who was wearing a knowing smile. "This morning *was* incredible," he whispered, causing my face to flame as hot as the fire in my belly.

"There you go again, giving me that look."

Noticing my blush, Blaine stroked the apple of my cheek with the back of his hand. "The one that makes you nervous?"

I looked away, embarrassed by my wayward thoughts. "No. The one that makes me want to take you in the back and let you…"

"How you doin' this evening, Dive?" Angel's voice bellowed through the speakers, drawing my attention. Blaine's eyes stayed focused on me, waiting for me to finish voicing my fantasy.

"This next performer is a repeat, and a damn good, musician. And ladies… he's pretty fuckin' hot, right?"

Shrill catcalls and estrogen-fueled hoots answered Angel as a familiar face climbed onto the stage. I couldn't say I knew him, but something about him piqued my interest enough to keep my eyes trained on the guitar-toting blonde.

Then the memory hit me like a 2-ton boulder, stealing my breath and causing the prickle of new tears to sting my eyes. It was the same guy who had performed weeks ago, singing the song that had me running to the back before I burst into uncontrollable sobs. The song that had summoned the painful reminder of the man who had wounded me to my core. And when my tears had breached the dam, Blaine was right there, pulling me into his chest, wrapping his strong arms around me as I emptied 23 years worth of heartbreak and anger into his t-shirt.

My eyes met Blaine's, hoping he would understand and let me slip out before emotion drowned me. I couldn't revisit that dark headspace. I couldn't keep letting him see me broken and defeated.

"Just wait, baby," he said, his warm eyes devoid of alarm, despite my expression. "It's not what you think. You'll be ok."

He turned me back to face the stage, just as the guy situated himself behind the mic.

"Good evening," he said, his voice smooth and rich. "My name is Taylor Hart, and I have a special song, dedicated to a very special lady, from someone who is…" He smiled as he paused, scanning the crowd, "…fucking crazy about her."

He spotted Blaine and I stationed at the bar and nodded, a mischievous grin on his face. "This is "Your Guardian Angel," originally by The Red Jumpsuit Apparatus. Hope you enjoy."

My eyes instantly flicked up to Blaine whose appreciative gaze was enough to make my stomach start break-dancing to the beatbox of my thrumming heart. He stepped into me and pulled my hips into his unabashedly, a crooked smile gracing his lips. "I can't sing worth a damn and like the saying goes, turn about is fair play."

Blaine's inked fingers stroked the length of my jaw, and I reflexively nuzzled into the touch. "I don't want you holding onto the memory of what happened last time. I know it'll hurt you every time you hear him sing. So, let me help you create a new memory, ok?"

As if on cue, Taylor began his song, capturing my attention with the haunting sounds of his guitar. His voice was as sweet and melodic as I remembered, but even more so now that they were laced with the tender words that Blaine had deliberately wanted me to hear. The words that had my eyes misting with happy tears, something I had never understood until that very moment.

Blaine moved behind me and wrapped his arms around my waist, giving me full view of the stage as Taylor belted out words steeped in promise, hope, and security.

And love.

There was pure, concentrated love in the lyrics that fell from Taylor's lips. And though Blaine may not have been singing them, I heard them echoing loud and clear from his soul.

"I will never let you fall..."

The words could not have meant more than if Blaine had sung them himself. He didn't need to. I felt it. I felt him. Every last bit of the scary-beautiful man that was Blaine Jacobs. The emotion behind every note and chord awoke things inside me that I never knew existed. Beauty bloomed inside my sheltered heart with each harmonious seed the music planted.

Just as Taylor was finishing the second chorus, the girls of A.D. joined in with their own instruments, rocking him into the dramatic climax. The crowd cheered, pumping their fists in the air while Blaine slowly swayed me side to side, his face buried in my neck. Tears ran down my cheeks without shame, yet I was too captivated to bother wiping them away. I wore them like a badge of honor, wanting to hang onto the feeling of bliss for as long as possible.

"That was… Wow," I whispered, after the crowd had erupted into a standing ovation. I turned to Blaine with watery eyes and smiled. "Thank you. So much. Thank you."

Blaine wiped my wet cheeks, his warm brown eyes heating me from the inside out. "I'm glad you liked it. And I hope you realize that I mean it… I mean it, Kami. Don't be afraid of me. I could never hurt you."

I believed him. Within my fractured, tattered soul, I knew it was ok to fall for Blaine. He would catch me; he always had. So I looked into those deep, chocolate eyes and surrendered the fear I carried around with me like a coat of armor, protecting the secrets that had been festering inside. I was afraid to love Blaine—dreadfully so. But I knew, undoubtedly, that he was the only one worth the risk.

CHAPTER TWENTY-FIVE

Blaine

"Are we almost there?"

I looked over at Kami seated in the passenger seat of my truck and shook my head, giving her bare knee a squeeze. "Patience, baby."

"Ugh, I don't like surprises. The anticipation is killing me," she whined, as she watched the trees zipping by. "I would have just let you blindfold me like you wanted to, if I wasn't such a freak."

I gently pulled her face back towards me, giving her a quick, pointed glare before returning my eyes to the road. "Hey, you are not a freak. Don't say shit like that about yourself."

Kami shrugged dismissively. "It's true. Know any other grown-ass women that are afraid of the dark?"

"No, I don't. But that's just a tiny part of you. A small, insignificant detail. It doesn't define who you are."

"Now you sound like Dom."

"Well, then…if two totally normal, sound men see you for the amazing, beautiful woman that you are, then it must be true," I smiled.

"Hmph. Only one of you is actually normal…" she murmured under her breath.

"Huh?"

Kami shook her head before reaching for the knobs of the radio. "Nothing."

"You ok, babe?"

Since I picked her up at her apartment, Kami had been noticeably preoccupied. A bit distant, and moody even. We had spent the entire weekend together, both at the bar and at my place, completely wrapped up in each other. But an imaginary switch had been flipped overnight; something was wrong.

"Yeah," she answered, but shook her head in contradiction. "I don't know."

"Kam," I said, pulling her hand out of the knot of her fingers in her lap. "You know you can talk to me. There's nothing you can say that will make me feel differently about you. I'm here. I'm not going anywhere."

Kami took a deep breath, steeling herself for the words she obviously didn't want to say. "Um...I just didn't sleep well last night. And then I woke up to an email. From… *him.*"

"Him?"

Kami swallowed, before barely whispering the words, "My father."

I nearly swerved off the road, narrowly missing a ditch just off the shoulder. "*What?* He's contacted you?"

"He's still around. I moved; I changed all my email info. Hell, I'm not even on Facebook. But somehow, he always finds me." Her hand grew hot and clammy, prompting me to squeeze it.

"What the hell does he want from you? Shit, hasn't he done enough?" I asked through a clenched jaw. Those weren't the words I really wanted to use. If I had my way, I would have been busting a U-turn and hunting down that prick myself.

"Money."

"Money? Why would he hit you up for money?"

"Because…" she sighed with resignation. "I have his money."

My head snapped to her solemn expression before I forced myself to look back at the asphalt stretched out in front of us.

Kami pulled her hand away, and her fingers deftly began to work over an old receipt from my cup holder. "About five or six years ago, my paternal grandmother died in an accident involving a bus. Since it was the city's fault, her family was left a hefty settlement. Being the eldest, and her administrator, most of the money went to my father. But, since he owed so much money in back child support, the state went after him and seized the funds, giving them to my mother."

"As they should have," I added. I gripped the steering wheel until my knuckles turned white. If there was one thing that made me shake with anger, it was a deadbeat dad. I had never known mine, but considering what Kami was still going through with hers, I was relieved I never had the displeasure of knowing the spineless sonofabitch.

"My mom moved back to the Philippines with her family, as soon as I graduated high school. She didn't even care where I ended up. Hell, she didn't even ask what my plans for college were. She just gave me the money and left."

I shook my head, feeling helpless. I wanted to erase all the bad that had ever happened to her. I wanted to give Kami the life she deserved. I wanted to love all the hurt away.

"Kam…baby…" was all I could coherently form.

"It's ok. I'm over it." She continued mindlessly folding, her glazed-over eyes hardly looking at the paper.

"So…he wants it back?"

"Yeah," she nodded. "And I would give it to him if it meant he would be out of my life for good. Dom said that wouldn't work. He'll just keep coming back. It's not really the money he wants; it's the control. He knows that I still fear him, and once he knows where I am, he'll never leave me alone. He'll just keep tormenting me."

I contemplated her words before nodding my agreement. "He's right. Shit, Kam, he's right. You need to get the police involved."

"They already know. He's violated every restraining order, but no one can pinpoint his whereabouts." Kami sat the tiny paper heart on the dash before looking to me with misted green eyes. "There's not much I can do, Blaine. Other than leave."

"No," I was growling before I could stop myself. "No. You're not going anywhere. Fuck him, Kam. He doesn't control you."

"But he does!" she shrieked. "He absolutely does. Do

you know how small and disgusting I felt when I read the words in that email? Him calling me a whore? A slut? A stupid little thieving bitch? I wanted to run away, Blaine. I wanted to hide and never be found."

"Babe…" I responded, my tone softer. "That's a natural response. He hurt you deeply, and he's still finding ways to hurt you. You can't let him. You're here…with me. I won't let anything happen to you."

"He found me in Atlanta," she deadpanned.

"What?"

"He found me. It started with emails. Then text messages and phone calls. Then he sent a letter to my address. My address, Blaine! He found me! That's why Dom and I moved here."

I ran a free hand over my face and cursed under my breath. "Shit, Kam, I…"

"Blaine, I failed my last semester of college two months from graduation. I was too afraid to go to class. I moved in with Dom and never left. For fucking months, I hid in my bedroom, too terrified to even walk outside."

I fought the urge to punch a hole through my own windshield. "I'm so sorry, Kam. Fuck! I am so fucking sorry."

Her small, delicate hand grasped the taut tendons in my forearm, squeezing away the rage coursing through my veins. "Hey…don't be. It's not your fault. I'm sorry for ruining the mood. I feel like such a jackass. You had something planned, and here I am being Debbie Downer again with all my bullshit."

Glass and steel enclosed the heat of our combined tension as I sucked in a breath through clenched teeth.

Beyond being pissed, I hurt for her. This girl had lived through so much, yet here she was, trying to soothe *me*. I wanted to pull over on the damn freeway, pull her into my lap, and kiss her senseless. Kiss away the anger, kiss away the pain. Kiss every part of her that that bastard had ever touched.

"Can we just drop it?" she asked in a small voice, prompting me to cover her hand with mine. "I don't want to ruin this day. I know you planned something special, and I just want to enjoy it."

I brushed her knuckles with my lips before nodding. "Yeah, babe, that sounds good. Because we're here."

The moment I pulled into the gravel pathway, Kami's eyes grew twice in size and her jaw dropped. Although my attention was on maneuvering through the tall trees on either side of us, I could feel her confused glare burning into the side of my head.

"Here? Why would you bring me back *here*?" she shrieked.

I pulled into a parking space facing Lake Norman and killed the engine before turning to her, ready for the onslaught. "Because I don't want your last memory of this place to be a negative one."

She cringed as if being here physically pained her, making me feel like a total ass for thinking this was a good idea. Having Taylor perform for her had proven to be a great idea, so I assumed that theory would work here as well. Well, you know what they say when you assume…

"Just try, ok? If you don't want to go in, we won't. But at least let me try to make this better for you."

She narrowed her eyes, the small space between her

brows crinkling with question. "Why?"

"Why?"

"Yeah. Why do you want to make things better for me?"

Releasing her from her seatbelt, I pulled Kami's body close to mine. "Because you deserve it. Because there is nothing on Earth more beautiful than seeing you smile."

And because I love you.

Whoa. *What?*

As if hearing my internal confession, Kami's lips spread into a knowing smile before connecting with mine for a swift kiss. "Ok, Blaine Jacobs. I'm all yours."

Thirty minutes later, we had devoured the lunch I had packed and were laying side by side on a blanket, watching a group of kids splashing around a few yards away. Kami looked at them intently, small smiles twitching her lips and silent chuckles shaking her shoulders. I couldn't help but be taken by her fascination.

"You want kids?" I heard myself ask before good manners stopped me.

Kami shrugged without taking her eyes off the children. "Would be nice, but I more than likely won't."

"Why not?"

She shuffled her bare feet against the sand and dropped her gaze. "Having children isn't really ideal for someone like me."

"Someone like you?"

Kami sighed heavily. "In my condition. My… sickness. My fears." She turned so I could glimpse the severity in her expression. "We are all products of our pasts, Blaine. My father was a disgusting prick because his father was.

Who's to say that I won't turn out just as bad? And I don't know how to be a mother. My own mom was too broken to be one. I know she loved me, I truly do. But I can't remember her telling me. And because of that, I can't picture saying those words. Ever."

I tried to digest the bitter pill of her words without letting it show on my face. But I had never been good at masking my emotions, especially when it came to Kami.

"Kinda fucked up, huh?" she smiled, though I could feel the painful undertone in her words.

"Well…yeah. But you're not fucked up. Not at all."

She shrugged, then looked back at the boisterous children. "What about you? Kids?"

I looked away before I grimaced as the memory of Amanda's swollen belly came barging into the forefront of my mind. A belly that was swollen with another man's child.

Though she admitted to being unfaithful, it wasn't until months after the discovery of her pregnancy. She led me on to believe that I was about to be a father, filling me with pride only to steal it with the ugly truth. I hated her, and for a while, I hated the thought of fatherhood.

But that was then. Now… now I had a reason to want that feeling back.

"Yeah, one day. A whole basketball team of 'em."

"Oh God!" she laughed. "Little tattooed, pierced baby Blaines, wreaking havoc on the poor citizens of Charlotte!"

Her smile was infectious, wiping away the foul taste of painful memories. All I could see was Kami. She made everything better. She made me want to *be* better.

"Living up to the stereotype again? Southern guy with

a pick up truck full of wild kids?" I asked, nudging her with my arm.

"Oh, God, yes! I wouldn't be surprised if you already had their names picked out. Let me guess: Cash, Cage, Gage…"

"Nah. I don't. But you're right about one thing."

Kami turned to me and narrowed her eyes with question, but didn't say a word.

"We are products of our pasts."

Kami inched closer. "Elaborate."

I nodded, diverting my eyes to the blue, cloudless sky. "After my mom passed, I was out of control. It was hard enough to be 13 with raging hormones and the bullshit of peer pressure. Losing her sent me into a really dark place. I was angry all the time. I didn't listen to anyone, I didn't care about anything. The fights, the mood swings… no one knew how to reach me. So, they ran some tests to see if I could be suffering from the same thing that killed my mom. To see if I had schizophrenia too."

A beat passed before Kami released a slow breath. "And?"

I turned and smiled before pressing her to my side. "Only crazy as hell over you."

Her body relaxed in my arms, giving me the opportunity to pin her body with mine. My tongue darted out and sampled her bottom lip, tasting her strawberry lipgloss and the delectable flavor that was uniquely Kami. I couldn't help myself. I needed all of her. I was addicted to this woman, and I needed a fix badly.

"Ummm, I think we have an audience," she murmured against my lips.

I turned my head to spy the group of kids snickering at us and pointing. I smiled and winked at them before planting a quick peck on Kami's lips and sitting up. The girls giggled and blushed while the boys made gagging gestures.

"Ready to change?" I asked, swiping the light sheen of sweat on my brow. It was warm out, and feeling Kami's body under mine had taken the temperature up a few notches.

"Change?" She looked down at her denim shorts and tank top. "Into what?"

I fished out the gift bag I had stowed with the supplies for our picnic and handed it to her. Kami took the pink and white striped bag and raised a brow. "Victoria's Secret? A little presumptuous, aren't we, Mr. Jacobs?"

"Just open it, *Pervy Pervison.* It's not what you think. Besides, lingerie is overrated. Just an unnecessary obstacle keeping me from what I really want," I replied, waggling my eyebrows playfully.

She rolled her eyes before tearing into the bag, pulling out a teal, jeweled bikini.

"The sales girl helped me pick it out, so if you don't like it, blame her," I shrugged, when she didn't say anything.

"No. I love it. It's beautiful, Blaine. Thank you." She rewarded my shopping efforts with a soft kiss. "But how'd you know my size?" she asked checking the tag.

"Kami, I'm pretty sure I have seen every inch of you naked. And that's not an image I could ever forget easily. The taste of your lips, your scent, the silkiness of your skin, the little sounds you make when you come…" I tapped my forehead with a single finger. "All committed to memory.

Detailed memory."

She blushed bright red before slapping my arm. "Creeper."

"Only a semi-creeper where you're concerned."

Kami fingered the soft fabric nervously before meeting my gaze. "I don't know if I can. I don't know if I can get in, Blaine. You shouldn't waste this on me."

I shook my head. "Nothing is wasted on you, Kam. And you don't have to get in if you don't want to. Just put it on and see how you feel, ok? We'll take this slow. Together."

"Ok," she nodded. "I'll try."

I knew Kami was gorgeous, but seeing her in that bikini had me wanting to say *"Fuck the lake,"* so I could drag her back to the car and rip it off her with my teeth. Luckily, I had changed into my board shorts after cleaning up and could somewhat hide my enthusiasm under the looser fabric. *Down boy!*

"Well, you got me all but naked," she said, after returning from the bathroom clad in the skimpy teal fabric adorned with faux jewels. "Now what?"

I grasped her hand and pulled her body flush into mine. "You know you're safe with me, right? That you can trust me?"

Kami looked up at me with clear, unblinking eyes. "Yes."

With my gaze still trained on her, and my arms wrapped around her waist, I slowly led Kami to the edge of the water. "Just look at me. Don't think about anything else. Just me and you. The second you say the words, we'll stop. I just want to show you what you're capable of, how strong you really are."

"I'm not a total spaz, Blaine," Kami remarked, rolling her eyes though her hands clutched my back tightly as the water met our feet. "I'm not afraid of water. I just don't want to be submerged in it."

Inch by inch, I walked our bodies into the water, my arms still wrapped around her protectively. Every few seconds she would tense or gasp, yet Kami didn't resist. She let me take her in deeper until we stood waist-deep in the lake.

"This is nice, right?" I asked smiling down at her.

"Nice?" She raised a slender brow and narrowed her eyes. "Yeah sure. About as nice as a colonoscopy."

"Aw, come on. There are advantages to being in the water, you know."

Kami tilted her head to one side and asked, "Like what?"

"Well," I replied with a lustful grin, picking her up and pulling her thighs around my hips. "We can do this."

"Hmmm," she smiled, wrapping her arms around my neck. "I guess this is nice."

"And we can also do this." I drew her closer to the hardness under my shorts and discreetly grinded into the soft flesh that was covered only by a thin strip of nylon.

"Mmmm, yeah," she murmured breathlessly, pressing her face into my shoulder to hide the flush of her cheeks. "Nice."

Still moving, I walked us deeper into the water, leaving kisses along her shoulders and neck. Kami reciprocated with little whimpers and sighs, too caught up in what our lower halves were doing to notice. I stopped just before the water hit our chests. I didn't want to alarm her, plus I was damn near too hard to even walk.

"Blaine," she whispered against my shoulder.

I let my hands slip under her bottoms and palmed her bare ass. "Yeah, babe?"

"Ah," she moaned at the contact. "I know what you're doing. I know you're trying to distract me."

"Is it working?"

She sucked my neck lightly before nipping my skin with her teeth, causing me to push myself into her softness even harder. "What do you think?"

"Shit," I hissed. "Why does it feel like you're the one trying to distract me?"

"Maybe I am," she replied, looking up at me and smiling. "Maybe I really just want to get you home and show my gratitude."

"Gratitude?"

"For this. For believing in me despite all my crazy. You're a good man, Blaine. And I really am thankful for you, even if it doesn't always seem like it."

I flashed a crooked grin. "Are you trying to tell me that you're falling for me, Miss Duvall?"

Kami rolled her eyes and shook her head, her pouty lips curved into a smile. I couldn't help myself. Before she could protest, I was devouring those lips with uncontrollable hunger, kneading handfuls of her backside. Still, I couldn't get close enough, couldn't kiss her deep enough. I needed her. And by the way her nipples strained against her bikini top as she moaned into my mouth, she needed me too.

"As much as I want to get out of here at this very

second," I mumbled, between pecks. "If I don't put you down, I'll probably get arrested for concealing a deadly weapon."

She giggled, though I could see the seriousness creep onto her face. "Hey," I said, grasping her chin to look into her eyes. "I'm right here. I'm not gonna let you go, ok?"

"Ok," she said just above a whisper.

I kissed her deeply before letting her body slide down mine. With the height difference, the water was at her breasts. Panic flashed across her face just as I wound my arms around her tightly.

"Blaine…" she panted.

"I got you, baby. I got you, and I'm not letting go. You're safe. I'm never letting go, Kami."

The feel of her heart hammering in her chest vibrated through mine as I squeezed her even tighter, hoping to still her trembling. Minutes ticked by before the tremors began to cease, and I slowly pulled her away to access her face. Even through terror stricken eyes, I could see the strength in Kami clawing to the surface. She was so incredibly resilient that I couldn't help but be amazed by her.

"What I wouldn't give to let you see yourself through my eyes. To see what I see. There is so much beauty and courage in you, Kam. See, your fears don't own you. They don't define who you are. You just made this lake your bitch. Do you see how fucking crazy that is? You're a fighter, babe. You aren't afraid. You aren't crazy. You. Are. A. Fighter."

Her eyes misted, making me believe that I had crossed some unseen line, but before I could console her, she crushed her lips to mine. "Thank you for giving me something to fight for," she said when she pulled away, claiming my next breath. "Now about that show of gratitude... Take me home."

More than just my chest swelled when I looked down into those gorgeous green eyes. "Yes, ma'am."

CHAPTER TWENTY-SIX

Kami

Fear #38

The unknown.

While most people would argue that the unknown would easily make the Top 10, it was what I knew, and what I experienced, that was much scarier.

Now, I feared it for an entirely different reason. There was one thing I knew for certain, but not knowing if I could ever truly accept it and reveal it in turn…terrified me.

I had never been good with words. Not the spoken kind, that is. Where Angel was bold and brash, and Blaine was sometimes overly expressive, I was closed and guarded. It wasn't that I didn't want to tell him how I felt, because I did. I just didn't know how he would react. And then what? What would that mean for us? Would it change everything? Would he feel the same?

Dammit, Kam. Don't start this shit. Not tonight. Tonight is special.

I refocused on the task of assembling individual rolls of meat and vegetables, and tried to block out the doubt screaming in my head. I wouldn't listen to it. I couldn't. I was already two seconds away from scrapping my plan and skipping town, but I owed it to Blaine to be honest with him. Hell, I owed it to myself.

"Score!" Dom boomed, as he entered our kitchen. He lifted the top of one of the pots simmering on the stove, allowing the scents of soy sauce, garlic and chicken to waft through the apartment. "Hell yes! I'm starved!"

"Hands off, this isn't for you! You and Angel are going out for the night, remember?" I said, swatting him away.

"Yeah, yeah," Dom replied, nabbing a Lumpia. "Send us off to eat crap while Blaine gets to savor all *my* favorite dishes. Yeah…*that* doesn't seem unfair at all."

"Awww, you'll survive. Plus, I'm sure we'll have plenty left over."

Dom took a bite of the hot, crispy-fried goodness with closed eyes. A deep throaty groan erupted from his slightly greased lips.

"Fine," he said around a mouthful of shredded cabbage and meat. "Make me a plate, and I'll go quietly."

"Deal," I winked.

After a few more minutes of watching me nervously flit around the kitchen, Dom finally addressed the thing that had my stomach tied in knots. "So, tonight… you think you're ready?"

I frowned, but didn't look up from the rice noodles sizzling in the wok in front of me. "I don't know what you mean," I lied.

"Come on, Kam. You cooked for the man. And, you spend almost every single day together. I've never seen you this happy. This…free and unafraid. You opened up to him, and he's still here, still completely into you."

Dom walked over and stood at my side. I could almost feel the heat of his penetrating gaze boring into me though I refused to meet his eyes. "You love him, Kam, and I know for a fact that he's in love with you too."

Until that moment, I hadn't audibly digested those words. Yeah, I had thought them before quickly pushing them away, but hearing it out loud… that was a different beast. I had planned to tell Blaine how I felt that night, but was I prepared to tell him *that?* Could I even do it?

"You don't know what you're talking about." *When in doubt, deny, deny, deny.*

"Sure, Kam. But you're not fooling anyone. Just because you can't say the words doesn't mean you don't feel it. What are you going to do when he tells you? Are you prepared for that?"

I shook my head. "Well…he won't. You're reading this all wrong. We're just hanging out, just having fun. And if it ever came to that, I'd deal with it."

"Ok, Kam, whatever you say." He reached over and plucked a piece of chicken from the wok. "Just know that when he says it—and he will say it—that it's ok if you want to say it back. It won't make you weak or stupid. It won't hurt you."

He placed a kiss on my cheek and exited the kitchen, leaving me to ponder his words. My own skewed vision of love had kept me from accepting it. It was what made me break Kenneth's heart when he told me how he felt. It was what caused me to push people away whenever they got too close. It was what left me to feel unwanted and alone for years.

Until now. Until Blaine.

I never wanted to go back to that. I never wanted to go without feeling Blaine's arms wrapped around me as I fell asleep. I never wanted the warmth of his smile to abandon me. I never again wanted those stars on my windowsill to hold my thoughts hostage, not when I wanted to dream of only him. I had gotten just a taste of how good…*this*… could be, and I wanted more. I wanted it all.

I wanted *love.*

An hour later, Blaine was at my door, wearing his usual panty-melting smile. "Hey babe, something smells incredible," he said greeting me with a kiss. Though we were the only two people in the vast condo, his presence filled the space with authority. Blaine engulfed every one of my senses, and I was only too happy to let him. I couldn't even smell the food sitting on the dining room table, too intoxicated by the scent of mint, spice and pure seduction.

"Well, let's hope it all tastes good," I said pulling him by the hand to lead him to the feast I had spent all day preparing.

I sat Blaine at the head of the table and placed a linen napkin on his lap before picking up his plate to pile with food. It was all very subservient, and probably set women back several decades, but something inside me warmed. I remember watching my mom, aunts and grandmother cooking for hours together. When the food was ready and every mouth watered with anticipation, they would serve their family first, waiting on their men with rapt attention. I can't even remember my grandfather ever getting his own food. Or my father.

I knew I should be ashamed, maybe even a bit disgusted, for wanting to serve Blaine, but I wasn't. Part of me craved this. I liked feeling wanted. *Needed.* And no one made me feel those things more than him.

"You cooked all this?" he asked with wide, hungry eyes as he licked his lips.

"Yup. Now, we have Pancit, Chicken Adobo with white rice, barbeque pork and Lumpia. Should I give you a bit everything?"

"Yes, please," he answered excitedly. "You don't have to do that, you know. I can get my own food, Kam."

"I know, but I want to."

Blaine nodded and watched me intently, a small smile on his lips. "I can't believe you did all this. What's the occasion?"

I shrugged, avoiding his gaze as I spooned out the food. "Nothing special. Just wanted to do something nice for you. I've never cooked for a guy other than Dom so if you don't like it, just don't tell me. I probably would never cook again."

"Baby, I'm sure I'll love it all."

There was that dirty little four-letter word again.

My hands began to sweat a bit, so I put the plate down to finish loading it before sliding it in front of Blaine. He dug in enthusiastically, moaning around mouthfuls of meat, noodles, vegetables and rice.

"Oh my God. Oh my God," he mumbled, closing his eyes in ecstasy. "This is amazing, babe. I'm in heaven. No bullshit, I think I just died and went to culinary heaven."

I laughed as I took a bite of my own meal. "Good?"

"Good? Are you kidding me? This is the best food I've ever tasted. Seriously. Now if you tell Ms. Patty I said that, I may have to take an ass-whooping, but it'd be worth it. Yeah, babe…so damn good."

I smiled as I watched him devour everything on his plate. I felt…domestic. Nurturing. Secure.

Home.

Not because we were at my place instead of his; it was Blaine. I felt at home with Blaine. And I never wanted that feeling to leave me.

What was I so afraid of? This was *Blaine*. Good-natured, uncomplicated, fun-loving Blaine. I was letting my imagination get the best of me. He would never try to get too deep with me. He knows about my past. A guy like him could have any woman he wanted. Why on Earth would he fall for someone like me—a total nutcase with more baggage than she could carry?

And if he did—so what? I could handle that. We were having fun. Just getting to know each other. Things were… comfortable. It's not like he'd ever expect anything more than *this*.

Right?

"Hope you left room for dessert," I said, once he had polished off another serving. I brought over a covered cake stand from the buffet behind us and set it before Blaine. Then I pulled off the top with a flourish, revealing a Leche Flan adorned with fresh blueberries and raspberries.

"Oh my God," he breathed. "I think I love you."

Thank sweet baby Jesus the cake cover was plastic,

because it was on the floor.

We both scrambled to pick it up, though Blaine beat my shaky hands to it. I stood up straight, putting every ounce of my attention into cutting the flan. The knife shook between my clammy fingers.

"Kam?"

I couldn't respond. I could hardly think beyond sinking the knife into the confection without losing a limb. I thought I was ready for this. I thought I wanted to hear those words. Hell, I thought I was strong enough to say them too.

But I was wrong. *This*…was wrong.

Love wasn't for me. Fear eclipsed that possibility a long time ago.

"Kam, say something." Blaine's hand was over mine, slipping the knife from my trembling grasp.

I forced myself to meet his gaze. "Like what?" I croaked, my throat suddenly parched.

"I don't know. Anything. I can see you're freaking out, and I need to know you're ok. That you're still here with me."

"I'm ok," I whispered through the sand in my mouth.

Blaine pulled me closer to him. "No, you're not. Talk to me."

I looked away. I couldn't look at his gorgeous face and mar it with the ugliness of truth. Because I wasn't ok. I never would be, no matter how wonderful Blaine was. All the love in the world couldn't undo the damage left behind by my past.

You could cover shit with roses; you could hide all the vileness and make it seem beautiful and good. But no matter how badly you wanted to mask it, underneath it all, it was still shit. Putrid, disgusting shit.

"Blaine…" I wasn't sure what I wanted to say. What do you say to the man you know you have to destroy?

A finger slid under my chin and gently guided my face to his. "Kam, I just told you that I think I love you, and it scares you, doesn't it?"

"No," I lied. I wasn't even sure if any sound came out.

"Well…I'm sorry. I was wrong. I shouldn't have said that."

Huh?

Reflexively, I frowned, though I should have been relieved. Blaine said he was wrong. He really didn't feel that way. That fact should have erased my unease, but all I felt was a hollow, endless ache in my chest.

"I was wrong, Kami," he continued, taking in my expression. "I don't think I love you."

The empty ache spread into the pit of my stomach, twisting like the knife in my crumbling heart.

Blaine pulled me into his lap, and though his words were ripping me to shreds, I let him. I was too weak from the assault to stop him.

"I don't think it; I *know* it," he murmured into my hair, his warm breath fanning down my neck. "I love you, Kami."

Again, I waited for the relief that I was sure to come. Blaine loved me. *Loved. Me.* But the knife kept twisting. The pain kept spreading. Sorrow blanketed the joy that I should have felt when he uttered those words. I was so unbelievably conflicted about my feelings, and I didn't know why.

Yes I did. I knew exactly why.

Fear #2.

Falling in love.

The only thing that terrified me more than falling in love, and the very reason I was so afraid of that magnitude of affection?

Fear #1.

My father.

"No," I said in a hoarse whisper. It was my voice, but it sounded strangled. As if it hurt just to say the word. "No."

"No?"

Against my better judgment, I turned around to face him. Maybe I was a sadist. Maybe I needed to see the pain that I would undoubtedly cause.

"You can't love me, Blaine."

"Why not?" he frowned.

"Because I told you; I'm unlovable. I don't *do* love. I'm incapable of accepting or returning it."

He shook his head. "You don't mean that."

"And why's that?"

He grasped my shoulders, pegging me with his unforgiving glare. "Because I know you love me."

I jumped out of his lap and was across the dining room before he could blink.

"You don't know what you're talking about," I sneered.

Blaine climbed to his feet and crossed the room to face me in four wide strides. "Yeah, I do. We both know it. You love me, Kami. And dammit, I love you too. More than anything."

Angry tears pricked the back of my eyelids. "No."

"*Yes.* And it's ok. You know I could never hurt you. You don't have to be afraid."

Blaine went to grab my hands but I quickly pulled them out of reach. "That's ridiculous. I hardly know you. And with what you *do* know about me…how could you feel that way?"

"You know me, Kami, better than anyone else. And yeah, I get that you're dealing with a lot of shit. And honestly, that makes me love you even more. It makes me want to take away all the pain and ugliness so you never have to feel that way again."

I pursed my lips and placed a hand on my hip. "So that's it; you pity me. Well, newsflash, Blaine: You can't fix me. You can't save me. So just stop trying."

"I don't pity you, Kam," he replied shaking his head, taking a step towards me.

"Then…why?"

"Why?"

He took another step forward, causing me to back into the wall. Rational thought abandoned me, as I went into defense-mode like a wounded, frightened animal, cornered by its predator. A predator that was fashioned to be beautiful and alluring, deeming its prey susceptible to its charms.

"Why even deal with all my bullshit?" I said, squaring my shoulders, preparing for the emotional battle. "What is it, Blaine? Does it make you feel good about yourself? Does it validate your manliness to save the broken girl? Or do you just get off on going after the damaged ones?"

I sucked in my bottom lip before I went for his jugular.

I wanted to stop myself. I wanted to fall into his arms and tell him I loved him too, and let him kiss away the hurt. But, we fear what we don't understand, and I didn't understand the feelings I had for Blaine. I couldn't fully grasp that depth of devotion and trust. I had never had it before and experiencing it now…scared the living shit out of me.

"Does it make you feel less guilty about not saving your mother?"

Blaine glared at me through the narrow slits of his eyes, and his jaw ticked with irritation. Good. He should be mad. He should be utterly disgusted with me. Hate me even. At that moment, I surely did. Maybe he'd even loathe me enough to get out now. To leave and never look back.

No. Please, don't go. Don't leave me.

"I know what you're doing," Blaine gritted, interrupting my contradicting inner monologue. "I know you're just trying to say anything to push me away. Well, it's not going to work, Kam."

"You don't know anything," I snarled, though my heart totally agreed with him.

"Oh, I think I do, Kam. I know you're afraid of this. I know you think that you're too messed up for someone to love you. You think that I'll hurt you. That I'll end up being just like your dad. I'm here to tell you that you're wrong on all accounts. You're wrong and I plan to spend every day proving that to you."

I pushed against his chest but it was hard as stone and just as immovable. "You don't know anything! I don't think any of those things."

Blaine raised a brow, a smug half-smile on his lips. "Really?" He looked down at my hands still on his chest. I hadn't even realized I was still touching him and I quickly pulled them back and balled them at my sides.

"Kam, why are you so afraid of love? Do you really think I would do something to hurt you? I'm not *him*. You have to know that by now. I'm. Not. *Him*."

My mouth went dry, making it impossible to form a response as I looked up into his intense brown eyes. Eyes that shone with warmth and understanding. Eyes that exuded patience and gentleness. And love. Eyes that made me believe that, without a shadow of a doubt, the scary-beautiful man in front of me loved me.

I tried to blink the image away. Gazing into those chocolate depths only made it hurt more. It only made the jagged pill of the inevitable that much harder to swallow.

Blaine cupped my cheeks, forcing my eyes back to his face. He wouldn't let me hide. He wouldn't let me find solace in denial and avoidance. He made me face my fear head on, and I wanted to hate him for that.

"I love you, Kami. And I'm going to keep saying that until it stops being scary. Until you accept it. Until you believe me when I tell you that I will never, ever hurt you. I. Love. You."

His thumb brushed along my bottom lip as he searched my face, his brows furrowed and eyes glassy. "The only one that should be afraid is me," he whispered. There was pain there. Pain and fear and vulnerability. The same things I felt at that very moment.

I didn't know what was stronger—the guilt of knowing that I was hurting him, or the fear that made me continue the charade. But, I knew one thing for certain: Blaine was too good for me. He deserved so much more than what I could give him. There was no way he could be happy with my pseudo heart. Eventually, he would see that for himself. He would need more. I just had to make him realize that before it was too late.

"Don't. Please. Please don't love me."

He frowned. "Why not?"

"Because…"

"Because what?"

"Just…because."

Blaine let out an exasperated breath and shook his head.

That's right. Get frustrated. Get upset. Tell me I'm stupid and petty. Tell me that I don't deserve your love. That I'm a lost cause. That I'm unlovable, just like I knew all along.

"You're gonna have to do better than that, Kam."

Desperation turned to irrational rage, and I shrugged out of his touch, pushing him away. "Because! Because I don't fucking want it! Because I don't need it. So just stop, ok?"

I turned on my heel and tried to escape to the refuge of my bedroom. I needed to get away, but of course, Blaine was right behind me, utterly perfect with the patience of freakin' Job. I wanted to scream until my lungs collapsed.

"You don't mean that," he retorted shaking his head. "Everybody needs love, including you. *Especially* you. And I know you want it. You're just too afraid to admit it."

My balled fists shook at my sides as fury misted my eyes. "I'm not afraid of love, Blaine. *I loathe it.* Love is cruel and unforgiving. It beats you. *Tortures you.* Smashes your face into a mirror and tells you that you're disgusting and ugly. That no one else will want you. Love whips you with a belt until giant, red welts are left on every inch of your body, leaving you too sore to even sit for days."

Hot tears streamed down my face, leaving me blind to Blaine's reaction. It was too late to stop them. He had opened the floodgates.

He wanted the truth. He wanted a reason for all my crazy. Well, now he was getting it.

"Love rapes your mother right in front of you while she weeps, telling you that Mommy's ok," I hoarsely whispered, my throat strangled with years of emotion. "It touches you in ways and in places that it should never, ever touch you, trying to murder the last bits of your innocence. It kills you, cripples you. It leaves you damaged beyond repair."

I stood before him, naked and bleeding, my impaired soul exposed for him to witness every ugly scar. "That's love, Blaine. Why the fuck would I want that? Why would anyone want that?"

Blaine stepped towards me, his arms outstretched, ready to fix the broken girl. But I didn't want his sympathy. I didn't need him to save me. I wanted him to save himself.

"Kam, baby…" he rasped, his horror-stricken eyes glazed with tears. "Baby, I'm so sorry. Please, let me…"

"No," I deadpanned, moving out of his reach. "No, don't try to make this better. You can't make it better. And I don't want you to."

"Just let me…"

"Seriously! Stop it, Blaine! I don't want your charity! I'm not your little pet project! Stop trying to push me into being what you want me to be! I am not your mother!"

Blaine stopped his advance and looked at me with confusion and pain marring his face. He was just as open and injured as I was, plagued by my horrid account. I had him right where I needed him. And, as excruciating as it was, I said goodbye to the man I loved more than I hated myself before slipping on my cold, unfeeling mask and I went in for the kill.

"I am not what you want, and I don't want to be. I don't love you, Blaine, and I never will. So let's stop wasting our time and face the inevitable," I spat as I gestured between us. "This is over. Done. There was never a future for us. Never a happily-ever-after. And the more we keep pretending there is one, the more I despise the thought of it. Goodbye, Blaine. It was fun while it lasted. But let's not keep forcing something that's not meant to be."

Blaine's expression was completely solemn as he looked back at me, waiting for the punch line to a cruel, tactless joke. But he knew just as well as I did that it would never come. He knew that what we had had crumbled into a heap on the floor leaving nothing but a mess of ashes. In a matter of minutes, I had managed to taint countless tender kisses, heated caresses, and longing stares. Things that we both held onto like lifesavers in the tumultuous storms of our pasts. Things that gave us hope for a future without pain and guilt and fear.

All of it. Gone.

I had successfully pushed away the only man I ever gave a damn about because I was too afraid to love him. But not only that, I was too afraid of what his love would do to me. I knew how shitty life could be. I knew, sooner or later, his love would hurt me. And being that I was now so vulnerable to him, my heart exposed and on display for him to see and crush in the palm of his ink-adorned hand, there would be no coming back from that. I would have no chance of survival.

Without a word, Blaine turned and walked out of my room while I stood there, steeped in my own hatred and affliction, numb and completely still. I didn't move after I heard the front door close. I didn't even blink as reality began to set in. I couldn't. I couldn't feel it. I couldn't let myself believe it, even though it was what I caused.

Blaine was gone. And he was never coming back.

CHAPTER TWENTY-SEVEN

Blaine

The mind is a tricky thing.

You can tell it to ignore the signs. To play dumb and let shit happen, even though you know it will only screw you in the end. To continue on like a damn fool, setting yourself up for failure.

Ignorance is bliss.

And the mind is a bliss-seeking, stupid motherfucker.

I knew all along that it was coming. I knew Kami would selfishly hang on to her insecurities like a shield in an attempt to protect herself. And in the process, she would hurt anyone that attempted to penetrate the armor.

She was smart. That was what I should've done. But instead, I was a sucker. The sucker that fell in love with the girl who was terrified of the mere mention of the word. The fool who sacrificed his heart time and time again, thinking someone would actually see that he was so much more than the rough exterior.

Love was a bitch. And she was squeezing me by the nuts.

I didn't realize I was at Dive until the smells of beer and fried food assaulted my nostrils, making me even more aware of my afflicted state of mind. I bypassed the questioning looks and whispers, grabbing a beer from the cooler and slid onto a barstool without so much as a cordial greeting. I didn't care. I was done caring. Caring got you nowhere. And that's exactly where I was. Nowhere.

Uncle Mick spotted me and furrowed his brow, not expecting to see me in on my day off, especially alone. I pretended not to notice him but I knew he was already making his way towards me.

"Didn't expect to see you here tonight, son," he said gruffly, clapping me on the back. "Everything ok?"

I took a swig of my beer, not even bothering to face him to answer. "Fine."

Maybe it was the flat, dead tone of my voice that served as an invitation, because the next thing I knew, he was climbing onto the stool next to me. I kept right on staring at nothing. Thinking of nothing. Feeling like nothing.

Minutes ticked by without either one of us saying a word. I was used to it. Silence I could deal with. It blanketed the words I didn't want to say. It numbed the ache that seemed to radiate from my chest like a gaping bullet wound.

"You always did feel more than anybody else," he said out of the blue, his voice rough and permanently hoarse from decades of smoking. "Couldn't help taking on everyone's pain like it was your own. Would even bring home old, banged up strays when you were just a youngster. Your mama used to say you were empathetic. Said you had a heart bigger than your brain."

I continued to sip my beer, trying to block out my uncle's mindless ramblings. What was his point? Did it look like I was in the mood to take a walk down memory lane?

I knew coming here was a bad idea. There was no way I could sit undisturbed to wallow in my misery, but I only had two other options: Ms. Patty's or my place. Ms. Patty's was out of the question. She would no doubt expect me to spill my guts and wouldn't take no for an answer.

Going to my place first had been a huge mistake. It just didn't feel like home anymore. Not without Kami there. She had ruined it for me. Every surface and corner was laced with a memory of her. Her warmth and light had given those bricks and wood life. Being without her, knowing that those four walls would never exude peace and happiness again, seriously had me thinking about moving.

Uncle Mick cleared his throat and scrubbed a hand over his face. "You're a lot like she was. We used to fight like cats and dogs when we were kids. Hell, she was a scrappy little thing," he laughed, his voice echoing with nostalgia. "But she had a heart of gold. Like you. She couldn't help it and neither can you. Sometimes, loving people can be just as much of a gift as it is a curse. Because some people…you can't help but love. Even when you know it will hurt you in the end."

I couldn't tell if he was talking about my mother, or me, or even himself. But I knew that every word was true.

Some people you couldn't help but love. You loved them without reservation or fear. You loved them hard and fierce, because they deserved it. They deserved to be loved just as much as you deserved for them to return it.

But life—love—didn't work like that. It was rarely rational or just. It destroyed relationships and brought even the strongest people to their knees in agony.

It was exactly what Kami believed it to be.

"Is there a point to all this?" I snapped, suddenly annoyed by his presence. I still refused to look at him. Seeing him, a face that housed features similar to my mother's, similar to mine, would only bring my tormented emotions to the surface. It would make me *feel.* I couldn't have that. Not now. Not anymore.

"The point is, son…everyone has baggage, some more than others. Some people have a tote bag. Others have an entire trunk full of drama. You, Blaine, have a carry on. And that girl of yours has a full set of luggage. You know that as well as I do. And the type of person you are, the type of man that you have grown to be, you expect to be able to shoulder all that baggage alone. You can't; that's not your job. You can't take away all her problems. No matter how bad you want to, you can't carry it all and expect for that heavy burden not to crush you under its weight."

I felt his hand on my shoulder. "Stop trying to carry it all alone. Taking it away doesn't make it any less hers. It just weighs you down, son. You're only one person. One man. You can't expect to save someone that doesn't want to be saved."

I swallowed down my next gulp of beer through the

tightness in my throat but the foul taste of rejection remained. I knew my uncle was right. Hell, he usually was. But I wasn't ready to hear that. I wasn't ready to accept that Kami just didn't want me.

She didn't want me to save her. She didn't even believe she was worth saving.

The booming sounds of my cousin's boisterous laughter flooded my ears, drawing my attention from the harshness of truth. I hated to admit it, but his presence was welcomed. CJ was a distraction. And right now, I needed that the most.

Tinkling feminine laughter accompanied him, stopping right beside me. Uncle Mick snorted before climbing to his feet. "Remember what I said, son," he said before heading to the back, shooting his son and his company a frustrated look.

I could feel CJ's eyes on me, but I continued to look ahead. CJ was a lot of things but he wasn't stupid. He knew when no words were necessary. Too bad his entourage didn't get the memo.

A small hand slipped over my shoulder, squeezing the tight tendons. I was too numb to even care enough to brush it off. "Hey, Blaine, it's so good to see you again."

I recognized the voice as Wendy's, but I didn't bother to offer my own greeting. Judging by the way her manicured fingers raked down my arm, it didn't seem to offend her.

Without saying a word, CJ slipped behind the bar, earning a frown from Corey, the other bartender. He bypassed the liquor displayed on the shelves and dipped down to a hidden cabinet where we stored the premium alcohol reserved for big spenders aka pretentious douche-bags.

Two glasses and a bottle of Johnnie Walker Platinum were placed before me. The girls behind us nearly shit themselves when they saw it, until they realized there were no glasses for them. Luckily, CJ handed them apple martinis to shut them up before opening the scotch and pouring a good amount in each glass.

"To not giving a fuck," he said holding up his glass.

Another petite arm snaked around my shoulders, and Wendy pressed her double Ds into my back. I could almost feel her hardened nipples through the thin barriers of clothing. I looked down at the amber liquid before me and picked it up. Wendy giggled and ran her fingers through my hair.

"To not giving a fuck."

CHAPTER TWENTY-EIGHT

Kami

The familiar buzzing of my cell phone grew louder and more annoying as I worked to ignore it. I couldn't acknowledge it. Couldn't even begin to let myself wonder who it could be. That involved feeling and right now with my emotions pressing at the dam of my resolve, feeling was out of the question.

I packed away the food on the table including the uneaten flan—the flan that I had made especially for Blaine that he would never try. My stomach twisted and roiled as my heart dropped into my gut.

Don't go there. Don't do that to yourself. He's gone. He's done with you. That's what you wanted. Don't start that pity party shit now.

I shook my head, trying to quiet my cynical, inner asshole, and focused on washing each dish with thorough precision. I wanted everything spotless, everything beautiful and sparkling. I could control this. I could clean and make everything neat and tidy. But my life? My life was shit. Dark, vile, filthy shit. I couldn't change that. I couldn't control it. And every time I felt like I had gotten a handle on it, fear bitch-slapped the taste of hope right out of me.

I fingered the jar of tiny iridescent stars between my fingertips and sat down on my bed. 253. Two hundred fifty-three reasons why I couldn't let Blaine love me.

I hated these fucking stars and everything they represented. I hated that I couldn't just throw them away and never feel the impulse to count them again. But most of all, I hated myself. I hated what *he* created, what *he* left behind …and what *she* forgot.

The jar shook in my hands until I let it tumble onto the comforter. I flexed my fingers, staving off the trembles that preluded the panic attack on the horizon. I couldn't do this. I couldn't revert back to some pathetic, wounded bird every time this shit happened. This was how it would be; this was my life. There was no reason to cry about something that I couldn't control. I needed to just suck it up and stop letting it affect me.

The buzzing started back up again, and this time I jumped up to stop it. Anything to distract my mind from the breakdown that was on its way in 5…4…3…2…

"Hello?"

"Kam? Damn, girl, it's about time," Angel shouted from the receiver. Rock music blared on the other side, accompanied with random peals of raucous laughter. "We've been calling you all night!"

"Why?"

"Well…um…we came into Dive, and…"

"*And* if you don't get your ass down here *right now*, I *will* be spending the night in jail," Dom's voice boomed. Angel furiously whispered for him to calm down and shut up before she was back on the line.

"Kam, sweetie, uh, I just think you should come by. Like, the sooner the better."

"No."

"No? But why not?" she whined.

"Because I don't feel like it." That wasn't entirely true.

"Please? Um, I'm really drunk. So is Dom. We need a ride home."

I knew she was lying. I just didn't have it in me to call her on her bullshit. Not when I was currently up to my elbows in my own.

I took a deep breath and gazed at the alternative. Shimmering stars laughed back at me, taunting me, holding me their captive.

Fuck them.

"Be there in 20."

I sat in the Dive parking lot, scraping together the last bits of my courage before entering. I knew Blaine was here; his truck sat in its usual space as it did most nights. So why the hell was I here? Why was I walking into God-knows-what when I should be running away to hide? Why was I torturing myself by going straight to the man that I needed to avoid?

Because I was stupid, that's why. Stupid in love with him, and tired of running.

I was sick of playing the victim. Sick of depriving myself of the only thing I wanted. Dammit, I wanted to be with Blaine. I wanted to love him fiercely and unabashedly and just dive right into this crazy, mixed up whirlwind of emotions with him. I wanted to give the middle finger to fear and let him kiss away all my reservations.

Maybe he could do it. Maybe he could make me forget what I was. Blaine had the ability to make me face my fears and kick them in the nuts triumphantly. I wanted to be a better person with him. I wanted to be a better person *for* him.

I picked up the red paper heart I had brought along as a peace offering. I smiled, imagining the spot he would reserve for it on his dresser. Blaine made even the silliest things meaningful and significant. That's exactly what he did for me. He gave me meaning. He made me feel like I was an important piece to his puzzle. Like I belonged. I shook my head at myself. How stupid of me to push him away when all along he was exactly what I needed.

He wasn't just my exception. He was my reason.

Tears clouded my eyes as I made my way inside. Not because I was afraid or sad. But because I was ready. I was ready to love that scary-beautiful man and give him my whole, broken mess of a heart if that was what he wanted. He wasn't the one to reject me. I rejected *him*. I rejected myself. I couldn't even see a logical reason for all the drama I had caused. I just knew that I had to make it right.

"Hey, Kam," Corey greeted me with a tight smile. "What brings you in tonight?"

I quickly scanned the bar. It was oddly crowded for a Tuesday night and music was blasting from the jukebox. I could tell Corey was swamped so I didn't want to keep him too long. "Hey, is Blaine here? I saw his car."

Corey looked up from the drink he was preparing with

hesitation etched in his face. His blue eyes darted to the right then back to me before he cringed and mouthed, "Sorry." I turned my head to see just exactly what he could possibly be sorry about, but part of me knew without looking. The hope I had felt just minutes before had already dissolved.

Blaine sat in a dark corner booth with two girls on either side of him. I noticed one of them as Wendy and it seemed like her plastic knockers were getting the attention they craved as she tucked a full shot glass between them snugly. Blaine was laughing hysterically at CJ who sat across from them, entertaining his own eager guests as he licked salt from some chick's cleavage. Then he plunged his face into her silicone-filled boobs to retrieve his own shot of tequila with his lips and teeth. Throwing his head back, he downed it in one swift move. Then he sucked a slice of lime that was nestled between another girl's lips before probing her mouth with his tongue.

It looked like some freaky alcohol orgy and was tacky as all hell. I thought I had been propelled into a raunchy dating show on VH1 involving a washed up musician and 20 penis-pawing groupies. I instantly felt sick.

"Your turn, Blaine!" one of the girls called, gripping his t-shirt with neon pink acrylic nails.

Two booths down, Angel and Dom stared daggers at Blaine, both too consumed with rage to notice I had walked in. I should have told them I was here. Hell, I should have been snatching handfuls of cheap, blonde extensions and staking my claim on Blaine, but I couldn't. I wouldn't. I was that scared, meek little field mouse thrown into a pit of lions, too crippled by fear to do or say anything at all. I would be eaten alive.

I tried to swallow down the sour taste of betrayal but my throat was too tight with an unleashed sob. Prickles assaulted my eyes, signaling rapid approaching tears. With a shaky hand, I laid the folded piece of red paper on the bar among a sea of dirty glasses, spilled beer, and crumpled napkins. At that moment, I felt just like that paper heart: lost, alone, and in a place where I didn't belong.

I knew what would come next, and it was stupid to torture myself further. I didn't need to stick around to watch Blaine lick salt off Wendy's tits. I didn't need to witness him sucking the lime from another girl's lips, not when I still could taste him on mine. I forced myself to walk swiftly yet steadily from the bar. If my body had its way, I would have burst into a full sprint to my car with tears streaming down my face the entire time. I was a coward of the worst kind—afraid of seeing the truth.

I didn't let myself process the scene back at Dive until I hit the doorway of my bedroom. Then I broke. Piece by piece, bit by bit, I fell apart. I cried until my soul hurt, until the ache of loving and losing had me on my knees. I wrapped my arms around my middle tightly, as I struggled to breathe through the pain. Air fled my lungs like the tears that ran down my face. I was empty. Completely devoid of the wholeness that I had once felt with Blaine.

A while later, quick raps on the front door startled me from the overwhelming sobs that had me shaking uncontrollably on my bedroom floor. My clouded mind knew I had to get up. The way I had been wailing like a wounded animal, it could very well be one of our elderly neighbors wondering what the hell was going on. I had to stop this shit. I had to pick myself up and dust myself off. I had been down this road before. I knew how it felt to not get what you wanted.

Then why did this time hurt worse than anything I had ever experienced? Why did I feel every jagged shard in my chest break, stabbing me from the inside out with years of regrets and disappointments?

The knocking resumed, forcing me to abandon my thoughts and focus. Slowly I made my way to the door, working to wipe away my smeared makeup. The collar of my shirt was drenched with tears. There would be no denying that I had been crying. And honestly, I didn't have two fucks to give. I was beyond hurt. And masking it wasn't an option. Not anymore.

The moment my hand grasped the doorknob, intuition should have hit me. But something else entirely hit me instead. Something hard and brutal enough to force me to abandon the edges of consciousness and slip into cold, desolate darkness.

Bad things happened in the dark. I'd had the displeasure of finding that out the hard way. But this time was different. Because before the darkness could fully claim me, I saw *his* face.

Him.

My father.

CHAPTER TWENTY-NINE

Kami

"Mommy, why does Daddy hurt us?"

Mommy's eyes got real watery, and she blinked a lot. She smiled but it didn't look right. Not like a real smile. It looked like it hurt her to do it.

She began to brush my hair again. "Daddy hurts us because he loves us."

I frowned. That didn't sound right. "I don't understand."

Mommy nodded like she didn't understand either. "He has to. To make sure we act right."

"But I do! I promise! I try to be a very good girl."

"I know, Langgा. *I know."*

I heard Mommy sniffling. She cried a lot. Usually when Daddy was home. He laughed at her when she cried. He laughed at me when I cried too so I tried not to do it. I didn't like it when he noticed me. That always led to pain.

"Mommy, I don't like it when Daddy loves me," I

whispered, though he was nowhere in sight. Daddy didn't always come home. I liked that.

Mommy was quiet. Maybe I had made her sad. Maybe she thought I was bad.

"I don't like it either, Langga,*" she whispered back.*

I turned around to face her. "If you don't like it, then why doesn't he stop? Can't you make him stop?"

"No," she said, shaking her head as tears rolled down her face.

Seeing Mommy cry made me sad. I didn't mean to upset her. I reached out to wipe them away. "Why not?"

"Because...because I'm scared."

My face grew hot, and my own eyes got watery like Mommy's. My throat felt funny, like something was stuck in it. I tried to swallow it down, but it only made it harder to breathe. To breathe through the pain.

"I'm scared too, Mommy."

A stinging sensation on my cheek and a muffled voice tugged at the seams of my consciousness. Then pain. So much pain. My head. My neck. It all felt stiff, as if I had been sleeping awkwardly for hours. But when my hand grasped my forehead and felt warm stickiness, I knew that an uncomfortable night's rest was not the cause of my unease. I couldn't be so lucky.

"Wake up, you little bitch!"

A palm struck my cheek, engulfing it in pricking

flames. I tasted blood from the flesh inside my mouth that had ripped open from the impact. I coughed and sputtered, too stunned to cry out.

"I said wake up!"

I knew this voice. I knew it like I knew the fears etched on each star on my windowsill. Knew it like the monsters that haunted my dreams. Knew it like the ache that spread through my chest from years of loneliness and rejection.

He was the reason for it all. He had created those fears. Had spawned those monsters, and had left behind that debilitating ache.

Him.

He was here. He had found me.

Pure, undiluted fear raced through my veins and seized every sense. I was paralyzed with it, rendered completely useless against him. Screaming, fighting, crying—it was futile. He stole it all from me.

"You thought you could run from me," he sneered. "You thought you could hide, and you would be safe. Ha! You'll never be safe. I'll always find you."

Against my better judgment, I opened my eyes. They stung from the blood that dripped from my forehead, blurring my vision. Green eyes, wild with rage, yet so similar to mine, stared back at me. Full lips, resembling my own, were tightened into a murderous sneer over yellowed teeth.

He was me, and I was him. Features so alike that there was no denying that he was my father, and I was his daughter. Features that made my mother hate me because I was the living, breathing reminder of the man that killed her.

"Now that I have your attention, you little cunt, time

for you to give me what I want," he growled.

I could hear the words but I didn't understand. I didn't get what he wanted from me. Hadn't he done enough?

You answer Daddy when he speaks to you. Don't hesitate. Daddy doesn't like it when you do that.

"I don't know what you want," I croaked, around my swollen tongue. My lips felt foreign. Puffy, like the rest of my jaw, the way they did when pumped full of Novocain from the dentist. But I wasn't numb. No. I felt everything. I writhed in overwhelming pain.

My father knelt in front of me. "Don't play dumb with me!" he spewed, grabbing a handful of my hair and yanking my face close to his. I took in his crazed features, trying to focus my senses. He was obviously older, and the years had not been kind to him. Drugs and alcohol had corroded his once dashing face, leaving his jaundiced skin marred with pockmarks and scars. Some of his teeth were missing, and the ones that were left were yellow or rotten. His brown, once full, shiny hair was thin and matted. And his eyes—eyes that once shone brightly whenever he picked up a guitar, eyes that had occasionally exuded kindness and love, eyes that looked exactly like mine—were dead and cold. Lifeless.

My father was dead inside. He was gone, just like my mother. He had taken their lives in a murder-suicide a long time ago. I had been an orphan all this time; I just hadn't realized it.

"Please," I begged, my voice no more than a strangled whisper. "I don't know what you want from me. I'll give you anything. Anything! Just please don't hurt me."

He shoved me back, releasing the tight grip on my hair

before breaking into a full-belly guffaw. "You stupid little bitch. My money! You *will* give me my money! Where is it? I want it now! Give it to me! *Now!"*

I winced. Not from the stinging in my scalp. Not from the oozing gash on my forehead that was dripping blood down the side of my face. Not even from the cuts inside my mouth that made it painful to talk. It was *him*. Seeing him so crazed and delusional. So desperate and out of control.

I hated this man. Hated him with everything inside me, yet, I couldn't help but hurt for him. He was a broken boy once. His father did to him what he had done to me. What he was doing to me now.

This man was once my father. No matter how much I despised him, he was half of me. But the man before me right now was a stranger. A cracked-out, sickening stranger that I had never seen before.

"I'll give it to you, I swear! But I don't have it here. It's at the bank. If you let me go, I'll get it for you. I promise. Just let me go, and I'll get it all!"

Fury washed over his ugly face, and he bared his decayed teeth, taking a step towards me. "No. I want it now!"

I scurried back, colliding with the couch. My hands searched for something – anything—that I could use as a weapon, but the closest lamp was feet away. I whimpered in desperate resignation. "I can't get it to you now! I have to get it from the bank!"

"Well, if I can't have it now, then I'll take something else."

His hand went for his belt buckle, and I felt a brand of terror that I couldn't even imagine. It was the kind of inconceivable fear that spawned nightmares. Reprehensible dread that forever ruined you. Murdered your spirit. Slaughtered your soul.

My stomach roiled violently, causing the taste of bile to invade my mouth. Cold sweat blanketed my skin, mixing with the blood that ran from my face. Tremors assaulted every inch of my body, and my senses were overwhelmed with panic.

No. Please don't. Please don't do this.

I wanted to say the words. Wanted to beg him to spare me, but fear had seized my vocal chords. It had stolen my breath as well as my sanity. I had to be hallucinating. This couldn't be happening. No. I refused to believe this was real.

"You're a little slut, aren't you? A little slut that opens her legs for any guy. Well, now it's time to open your legs and that nasty little mouth for Daddy."

"No!" The word ripped from my throat in a sob. *"NoNoNo!"*

"You've been a very bad girl, Kamilla. A whore, just like your slut mother! So, first I'm going to beat you. Then I'm going to take what's mine. I'm going to fuck you like the whore you are."

He took another step towards me, unleashing his belt from his pants. He folded it in half and slid the leather between his fingers slowly, a ritual I had seen him do dozens of times. A ritual that sucked the breath right from my lungs and demolished the tidy, fragile compartments of my psyche…

"You've been a bad girl, Kamilla. A very bad girl. And now I have to punish you."

"No! Please, no, Daddy! Please! I'm so sorry. I promise to be good! Please, no. Don't hurt me!"

"See what you make me do, Kamilla? I have to. I have to hurt you because I love you."

"Please. Please, don't."

"Don't make me angry. Your mother made me angry, and you see what happened to her. Do you want to be like her? Do you want to be a dirty whore like your mother?"

"No, Daddy."

"Then come here and get what you deserve. It's your fault; you make me do this, Kamilla. You make me hurt you."

He stood before me, his pants unfastened and his brown leather belt at his side. He smelled of stale beer, and filth as if he hadn't showered in weeks. "This is what you deserve, Kamilla. You're a dirty, filthy whore. And whores need to be beaten. You make me do this to you. You make me hurt you. I wouldn't do it if I didn't love you."

Before I could utter a semblance of a plea, he raised his arm up over his head and brought it down in a blur of haggard skin and worn leather. I didn't even have time to brace for the attack, let alone shield myself from it.

The first blow landed across my shoulder and face, setting it ablaze, bursting with reds and oranges. I felt my skin split open with the impact. My eye suffered the worst of it, and I couldn't tell if it was swollen shut or if the blow had taken out my eyesight. It was all pain. All fire. I couldn't differentiate it. Couldn't tell where the agony ended and relief began.

The second one made me see stars. Not the beautiful,

twinkling ones that inhabited the night sky. The ones that appeared in blurry splotches behind swollen eyelids. The ones that told you that unconsciousness was near, whispering promises of vivid dreams, if you just succumbed to it. It hurt too much to scream, and I was too weak to even cry. I was tired. So tired. I wanted to sleep and escape this pain. I wanted those dreams that the stars boasted. I needed them.

The third slash across my face claimed me. Dragged me under in a deep sea of numbness and detachment. A place where pain was no longer felt, fear was not my captor, and my father's love did not rip me apart and scatter each piece of me, making it impossible to ever be whole again.

I almost felt this peace once. I was five, and it was waiting for me, beckoning me to the bottom of a swimming pool.

And now… now I had found it. I found the peace that came with death. And this time, I didn't fight against it. I ran to it with outstretched arms.

CHAPTER THIRTY

Blaine

"Can't you drive any faster?"

"If you have a problem with my driving, maybe you should've driven your own car. Oops! You can't, can you? Because you're fucking *drunk*. So just sit back and shut up," Angel sneered from over her shoulder.

Normally, I would've shot back with my own ass-holish comment, but she was right. I was fucking drunk. But I had miraculously sobered up quite a bit once I saw what was lying amongst a clutter of shot glasses and peanut shells almost fifteen minutes ago.

I had to get away from CJ's groupies, and had only marginally escaped the pressure to suck a shot of tequila from Wendy's rack. They were nice tits; I couldn't deny that fact. But they weren't Kami's tits. Kami had great tits. Perky and soft. Perfect, sweet nipples. Just the right size to fit in my hands…

Fuck. Even my thoughts were drunk and stupid.

I slumped back and tried calling her again, hoping the reminder would defog my mind. I screwed up. I know I did. But I really hadn't done anything with those chicks. I didn't want to.

I had just been about to grab a bottle of water and a cab home when I saw it. A small, red paper heart. It felt like a bucket of ice water had been dumped over my head, and I immediately woke the fuck up. Kami was here. At least she had been. And if she glimpsed what was going on over at CJ's table, I knew I had some serious groveling to do, whether or not she wanted anything to do with me.

I couldn't let her believe I was *that* guy. The guy that got drunk and stupid whenever shit hit the fan. The guy that hooked up with any girl with a warm hole and a wet mouth. Ok, maybe I was that drunk and stupid guy. But Random Hookup Guy? That wasn't me. Not anymore. Not since Kami.

I don't know how long I stood there holding that red paper heart in my hand, looking as if I had been tasered in the nuts in the middle of that crowded bar. But I knew I had royally fucked up.

"Where did you get this?" I snapped at Corey just as he passed by to grab a bottle of vodka.

His brows knit together, and he shrugged. "Oh, uh, I can't be sure but I think Kami had it in her hand when she…"

"Kami's here?"

"Yeah. Only for like a second though. Then she just left."

"When?" I asked stepping into his personal space. I

was tempted to grab his collar to shake the shit out of him, cheesy soap opera style. Maybe a dramatic backhand to drive my point home.

"Like maybe 5-10 minutes ago?"

"And you didn't think to tell me?" I shouted, drawing the attention of just about every bar patron. I didn't care what they thought about my behavior. Not where Kami was concerned.

"What the hell is going on?" Angel said, sauntering up to the bar with Dom in tow, looking like he was ready to break some skulls. Probably *my* skull.

"Kami was here." I lifted the paper heart for her to see, but I didn't hand it over. It was mine. It was meant for me.

"What? I didn't see her come in," Angel frowned.

"Probably because she took one look at you and your table of bleach blonde cum dumpsters and left," Dominic nearly growled, taking a step towards me. "I swear to God, if you fucking hurt her, if she shed one fucking tear over you, I will…"

"I didn't do shit, and you know it," I interjected before Dom's mouth started writing checks that his pretty boy ass couldn't cash. Yeah, he may have been stockier but I was a good two to three inches taller and known for my quick fists. Besides, if anyone was worth fighting like hell for, it was Kami.

Shit.

I should've fought for her. I should've stayed and made her see that she had nothing to be afraid of. That being with me—loving me—could never hurt her.

SHIT!

I *had* hurt her. Instead of staying by her side, despite

the bullshit she spewed to push me away, I got drunk and let her witness a couple of grab-happy broads damn near dry-hump my leg. I had let her down. I had proved to her that men couldn't be trusted. That *I* couldn't be trusted. I had to change her mind. I just hoped she'd hear me out long enough to let me do just that.

I wanted to book it to the apartment as soon as we parked, but I needed to be patient long enough to get past the doorman. However, he was nowhere to be found, and a few food delivery guys were waiting to be buzzed up. That should have been a red flag. I should have sensed something wasn't right, but I was anxious to get upstairs to Kami and plead my case. Anxious to just be in her presence again.

An inexplicable sense of dread twisted my stomach into a giant knot as we approached their door. That should have been the second sign. That should have put me on high alert and made me barge into the apartment, figurative guns blazing. But I chalked it up to alcohol and nerves. I had to make this right. Knowing that I had a small window of opportunity had me worried as hell.

"Well, playboy, it's your funeral," Angel sniggered as she placed her hand on the doorknob. "I'll just come back after Kam is done making earrings out of your nuts. I'm sure she'll want to go shopping for a matching handbag."

What happened next was beyond incomprehensible. Not because the scene in the living room was something out of a horror film. Not because there was a man perched over Kami with his dingy pants around his ankles while she lay on the ground, lifeless, in a pool of her own blood. And not because the stench of death instantly permeated our skin and clothing.

It was because I couldn't understand it. I couldn't describe what I did to that sick fuck that had tortured her. I couldn't express the feeling of holding her still, limp body in my arms as I cried into her blood-matted hair, apologizing for leaving her. For not saving her.

There was blood on my hands. Blood everywhere, saturated into the cream carpeting and blanketing the side of the leather couch. I looked over at Dom who was just as coated in the red, sticky substance as he spoke to a police officer. I didn't know why he was speaking to him, his horror-stricken eyes red and puffy. I couldn't remember.

"She's fading fast. We have to get her to the hospital."

"I'm riding with her!" Angel cried, her body shaking with uncontrollable sobs. She was covered in blood too. Her hands, her clothes, her...knees? Like she was kneeling in it. Like she had been on her knees in a pool of blood. Cradling her. Begging her to wake up. Crying her name over and over again.

"Ok, but only one of you can. We have to go now."

I wanted to go. I wanted to be the one to ride in the ambulance, but I couldn't say the words. I couldn't do much of anything. I sat in my own slow motion sequence while the rest of the world zoomed by me on hyper speed. I looked down at the blood covering my hands. Felt the ache in my knuckles as I flexed them.

I needed that pain to remind me. To remind me of her.

"Sir, I need to get your statement."

I looked up to see that the officer was now in front of

me. Dominic stood beside him, his bloodied fists shaking at his sides.

"Sir? Your statement?"

"Sure," I nodded.

"OK, your name?"

"Blaine. Blaine Daniel Jacobs."

"Relation to the victim?"

The victim. *Victim.*

Kami.

It all came crashing in like a wrecking ball, demolishing the single slice of sanity I had left. The knot of emotion in my throat swelled and erupted, spilling its bile down into my stomach. I felt sick. Dizzy. Out of control and unable to get a grip on reality.

"He's her boyfriend," Dom spoke up, gripping my shoulder to steady me. He gave me a reassuring nod before mouthing *"Breathe."* I did as I was told. Breathing was all I *could* do.

"Hey, can we do this at the hospital? We need to hurry up and get there," Dom asked the police officer.

He gave us both a sympathetic look and nodded. "Sure. I'll meet you guys over there."

Less than twenty minutes later, we were racing through the entrance of the emergency department, demanding that a nurse, doctor, technician, *anybody* direct us to Kami.

"She's in surgery," we were told soon after we found Angel pacing in the waiting room.

That's all we were offered. We weren't family. No. Her *family* was handcuffed to his own hospital bed, courtesy of Dom and me. Her *family* had abandoned her when she needed them the most.

We were her family. Hell, at least Kami was ours.

"We should call her mother," Angel said, fishing her cell phone out from her bag.

"What the fuck for? That woman wouldn't know what to do. Do you think she'd even care?" Dom scoffed.

"But it's her mother," Angel tried to reason. "Of course, she'd want to know what happened to her daughter."

Dom snorted and continued his incessant pacing. I resumed looking at my hands. No matter how hard I scrubbed them, I couldn't get the blood off. It had seeped into the tiny cracks of my cuticles and stained my fingernails. I still felt it all over me. Still smelled the metallic scent on my clothing and skin.

Kami's blood. *His* blood.

And while I knew they were genetically linked, I hated that his blood had tainted hers. That he had touched her. *Abused* her.

And I had let him.

If it hadn't been for me leaving her apartment, he would have never been able to get inside. If it hadn't been for me getting drunk with a bunch of bar sluts, Kami would have never left Dive and gone home alone.

This was my fault. I had failed Kami when I had vowed to protect her. To never hurt her. To never leave her. I failed yet another woman that I cared about.

I didn't save my mother from the sickness that ate away at her sanity. I didn't save Amanda from her weakness. And I didn't save Kami, the woman I loved more than I loved myself.

I had failed.

I didn't deserve her. I knew that now. I would just keep hurting her. Would just keep fucking things up. Kami deserved someone who could protect her. Someone to love her enough to heal her. And I had proven that I wasn't equipped to do either of those things.

Without a word or look in Angel and Dom's direction, I stood up and walked right out of that hospital. Away from the woman I loved. Away from the woman I failed. And I didn't look back.

CHAPTER THIRTY-ONE

Kami

"Young lady, what the hell is this?"

I stepped all the way through the front door while trying to steady my wobbly legs. Holy fuck, I was buzzing. Shit! But at least I wasn't late for curfew.

My mother stood before me, her face screwed into a scowl, one hand on her hip, the other holding up a little white rolled piece of paper.

"Well? You want to explain what you're doing with marijuana in your room?"

I walked farther into the room, making sure to kick my shoes off first. That was a must. My mom could care less about the nightmares I had every night, but all hell froze over if I wore shoes in the house.

I shrugged and tossed my purse onto the couch. "Not really."

"Excuse me?"

"I said 'Not really.' I don't feel like explaining it. You

don't care anyway."

"Langga, *you know that isn't true," she deadpanned with a flat voice. Even the use of the term of endearment was more out of habit than anything else. There was no emotion behind it, no truth.*

"Mom, give it up. You don't have to pretend to care. Not now, when you didn't care when it counted."

She rolled her eyes and let out an annoyed breath. "What are you talking about? Of course I care."

"Really, Mom? Did you care about my 4.0 GPA for the past six semesters? Or my early acceptance letters to half the colleges I applied to? Or how about the fact that I miss-ed my class trip to the water park because I am freakin' terrified of what could happen? Did you care about any of that?"

"Don't try to turn this around on me. You still need to explain why I found a joint in your sock drawer."

"It's not mine," I lied. I was just glad she hadn't found the rest of my stash. Lately, it was the only way I could get through the night without jerking awake from another nightmare.

"And what were you doing in my sock drawer?" I glared at her.

"Never mind that," she said, her accent sounding thicker than usual. "You can't get out of this one, Langga. *You can't manipulate me like you do everyone else."*

"Manipulate you?" I glowered. "Like everyone else? What the hell are you talking about?"

"Mmm hmm. Want to make everyone believe your lies. Want them to think I'm a bad mother. Now you're on drugs? And don't think I don't smell alcohol on your breath

every weekend."

I rolled my eyes. She was doing it again. She was imagining things, being paranoid. Sometimes I thought she was seriously delusional. "What lies? You aren't making any sense."

"I see how they look at me. I see your friends' mothers whispering about me. You've told them. You've told them about me, haven't you? You can't say things like that. We'll have to move again. Is that what you want?"

I took a step towards her with the intention of soothing her. She really was losing it. "Mom, I swear. I haven't said anything."

She turned from me to make her way back to her bedroom. Back to her side of the apartment where she could wallow in her misery alone and forget the burden of my existence. Before she made it to the doorframe of her room, she looked back at me and shook her head, disgust and pity in her slanted, brown eyes.

"You're just like him, Langga. *Just like your father."*

Slow, concentrated pain surrounded me at every angle. I couldn't escape it. It held me prisoner and refused to let me go, sluggishly creeping over every inch of my body. The shit just wouldn't pass, just wouldn't move on. It just kept slowly driving its way deeper into my skull, making the task of opening my eyelids seem flippin' impossible.

"She's waking up!" I heard Angel gasp. "Dom, go get the nurse. Hurry!"

Light pierced my eyes, its intensity serving as tiny, razor-sharp daggers to my retinas. I wanted to cry or at least cringe, but even that hurt.

“The lights,” I hoarsely whispered. God, my throat was sore. “Kill the lights, please.”

Once the lights were comfortably dim, I slowly peeled open my eyelids. The room was bare. Sterile. Cold. I was in the hospital.

Angel looked at me with a hopeful smile. She looked horrible as if she hadn’t slept nor groomed in days. If she looked like that, then I must’ve looked like Death with PMS on a Monday.

“What happened?” I managed to croak. What the hell was wrong with my throat? It wasn’t just scratchy; it was sore and stiff.

“You don’t remember?” Angel asked with horrified eyes.

I shook my head just a fraction but it felt like I had just given myself whiplash. “I remember…what happened. But…what happened to me? What did he…”

“Here she is,” Dom beamed as he walked in, a man in scrubs right behind him. A young woman dressed in penguin-adorned scrubs followed.

“Miss Duvall, how do you feel?” the man I presumed to be a doctor asked, picking up my chart at the foot of the bed.

“Ok, I guess.”

Doctor Lovett, who had been the one to perform the surgery to repair my small, yet worrisome, skull fracture two days ago, performed a series of simple tests to ensure there wasn’t a lag in brain function. The bandages hugging the circumference of my head, as well as the ones on my face, were itching like a bitch, but he insisted I leave them be.

"Dr. Ramini, our resident plastic surgeon, will be in to talk about your options."

"Plastic surgeon? My options?" I wanted to frown but the medical tape pulling my skin was like cheap, bootleg Botox.

"Miss Duvall, you suffered quite a bit of cosmetic damage to your face from the attack. Since the swelling from your head injury has subsided drastically, I think it's safe to go ahead and proceed with Dr. Ramini once we get the appropriate scans done. I assure you; he's the best in the state."

I sat staring at him like he was speaking a different language, unable to fully digest his words. My face? *He*…had ruined *my face?*

"The police have been waiting to speak to you for quite some time. They should be up shortly. In the meantime, try to relax and I'll be back shortly to get those tests started. Nurse Claire will give you something for pain management," Dr. Lovett said, gently patting my shin before exiting the room. Well, at least *that* didn't hurt.

My eyes darted between Dom and Angel as soon as we were alone again. "What happened to me? What's wrong?"

"Nothing's wrong, sweetheart," Dom said softly, leaning over to kiss me on the forehead. I wanted to swat him away, but one arm was in a sling and the other had been skewered with an IV line.

"You know what I mean. What did he do to my face?"

My roommates looked at each other before returning their solemn gazes to me. I could see the sympathy welling in their eyes.

"Well? Is somebody going to talk?"

Dom cleared his throat. "Kam, babe...*he*...uh..." He took a deep breath before grasping my hand. "Your father used a belt on you. And, uh, the impact, plus the buckle, tore some of the skin from your face, neck and shoulder." Tears spilled from his eyes as he awaited my reaction.

"I see," was all I could say. What *could* I say to that?

"Part of your ear was torn off, and you have some bruising along your cheekbone."

I nodded, letting understanding seep into my groggy, Morphine-riddled brain. My father had finally done it. He had taken everything from me. Everything...

"Did he rape me?" I deadpanned, not a trace of emotion in my voice.

"Um, Kam," Angel chimed in. "A psychiatrist will be in soon to talk to you about the attack. We were able to convince the staff here to let us break the news about everything else because of how...fragile you are..."

"Fragile?" I snorted. "I'm not fragile. To be fragile I'd have to be breakable. You obviously can't break what's already broken."

"Kam, you aren't broken," Dom interjected.

"Aren't I? Look at me."

Dom and Angel both let their eyes drop to the floor.

"I said look at me, dammit!" It hurt to shout, but I didn't care. I didn't care about anything. Not the pain, not my face, nothing. I felt nothing. I was nothing.

My friends brought their gazes to my torn face and simultaneously cringed, confirming my suspicions. I was a freak show.

"Now tell me: do I look like someone who is put together? Who has been repaired? Do I look like I'm ok?"

The two of them didn't answer. They didn't have to. The horror was written all over their faces.

"Again…did he rape me?"

A long, torturous beat passed before Angel shook her head. "He tried, but he didn't get a chance to, uh…go all the way before we found you."

Relief washed over me in waves, but I didn't show it. I kept my expression stoic. Detached. Cold. "Well, it's a good thing you showed up in time to stop him."

"Actually, we have Blaine to thank for that."

Blaine?

Oh no. *Blaine.*

"He knows?" I screeched. I wanted to widen my eyes in terror, but they wouldn't budge. *Fuck.*

"It was because of him that we found you in time. He insisted we drive him back to the apartment to…"

"He saw me like *this?!"* I damn near screamed. "He saw what he did to me?"

"Kam," Dom said softly, stroking my arm. It was the only exposed part of me that wasn't bandaged. "Blaine was the one to tear him off of you. I mean, yeah, I helped but Blaine…he just went crazy. Like a deranged madman. I ended up having to pull him off before he killed the fucker. Still, he nearly did."

"He'll be here soon to see you. We sent him home just to clean up and get a quick shower," Angel added with an encouraging smile.

I turned my head away as much as the bandages allowed. I didn't want them to see the tears welling up in my eyes. I didn't want them to see me *feel*. "I don't want him to see me like this."

"Honey, he's already seen you. He's been here waiting for you. He wouldn't even allow himself to doze off. I damn near had to force him to take a break."

I turned my head back to my friends. "He's been here the entire time?"

"Well, he left at first," Dom replied. Angel shot him a furious look and whispered for him to shut up, like I wasn't right there. "Well, he did. He just had to get his head right. It was a lot for him to take in, but he came back the next morning."

I nodded, just to give my body something to do. Anything but what I wanted to do. Cry.

"Well…I don't want him to see me," I said in a broken voice. "Not like this. Not now."

"Too late."

Every head turned towards the door where Blaine stood smiling, looking even more perfect than I had remembered. He held an elaborate flower arrangement that he walked over to place on a nearby table. That's when I realized there were quite a few bouquets, teddy bears and Get Well cards cluttering the room. I couldn't focus on them though. The movement caused his comforting scent of mint and spice, and just *Blaine*, to sweep over me. Emotion knotted in my throat.

He came to stand at my side and looked down at me, a smile still illuminating his beautiful face. "Hey baby," he said just above a whisper.

Words abandoned me, leaving me silent and dumbfounded. Part of me wanted to fall into his arms and thank him for saving my life. For stopping my sick fucking father from stealing the tiny piece of me that I still controlled. For loving me just as fiercely as I loved him.

But that part of me was stupid. Weak. Naïve.

If I thought that we couldn't continue before, I knew it without a shadow of a doubt now. My father had killed any hope for a future with Blaine. He had killed *me*. Just like he did my mother.

I couldn't hold Blaine captive in the fucked-up-ness that was my life. He was a good guy; he'd stay because he'd feel obligated to. Because that's what good guys did—they stayed and fought for you no matter what.

Blaine had done enough fighting for me. I wouldn't let him waste his life on someone who had no more fight left in her.

"Blaine…" His name stung my tongue. The day we met, it had felt as smooth as silk in my mouth. Now it hurt. It hurt because I knew I didn't have a right to say it anymore.

"I think you should go," I whispered.

"What?" He took a tiny step back as if I had slapped him. "Why?"

I swallowed the words I wanted to say. I locked them all up and stored them in the dark, empty corners of my mind, hoping to rebuild the tiny compartments. My father had destroyed them when he propelled me back into my childhood. Never again. I wouldn't let anyone get that close again.

"Nothing's changed, Blaine. How I feel…that hasn't changed. Thank you for being there for me but that doesn't mean things between us are different."

I met his stunned, hurt expression with nothing but cold dispassion. My mask was easier to slip on now. My father had ensured that I was never able to take it off again. It was permanently etched into my torn, battered skin.

Quietly, Dom and Angel slipped out of the room to give us privacy. It wasn't necessary though. I wouldn't continue the charade any longer. I'd make sure that Blaine stayed away for good now.

I turned away from the pain etched in his face. I couldn't look at him. I had enough of my own to deal with. "Look…let's just consider this my resignation. I know it's short notice, but I think under the circumstances, this is the best thing. Sorry for the inconvenience."

"Sorry for the inconvenience? What? Kami…baby… talk to me."

A warm single finger grazed my chin, causing me to flinch. I glared back at Blaine. Why couldn't he just stay away? Why did he make me have to hurt him?

"See what you make me do, Kamilla? I have to. I have to hurt you because I love you."

A gasp caught in my throat as my worst fear came to fruition. My mother was right. She was right all along. And that only solidified my decision.

I covered my mangled face with my only free hand and turned my head away. "Get out."

"What?" I could hear the confusion that weighted that tiny, insignificant word.

"I said get out!" I shouted louder than was necessary. But I needed to make him see how wrong this was. How wrong *I* was.

As I had hoped, Dom, Angel, a police officer and a nurse came rushing in, all displaying varying levels of alarm. Blaine took one last wounded look at me before dropping his gaze to the floor. He was defeated. I had broken him down. I really was my father's child.

I didn't face him as he walked away. The truth was ugly enough.

CHAPTER THIRTY-TWO

Blaine

Fuck it.

Fuck it all.

Fuck feeling like this. Fuck trying to find a reason for this pain.

Fuck fucking, sick-fuck fathers. Fuck them to the nth degree.

Fuck the scars they created. Fuck the pieces of a person they left behind.

Fuck the tiny glimpse of happiness only to have it snatched away. Fuck wanting someone so bad that you continuously put yourself out there, knowing that you'll be demolished in the blink of a gorgeous, green eye.

Fuck it all.

Fuck me. Fuck her. Fuck this.

Fuck it.

CHAPTER THIRTY-THREE

Kami

3 months later...

The body was a miraculous thing.

You could tear it apart, rip it to shreds, and somehow, it healed. Collagen formed scar tissue that sealed the gashes. Bones could be reset, and cartilage could regrow. Pain subsided until you didn't feel the deep ache every time you breathed. Even the brain could heal, blocking out the horrifying details that woke you up at night, covered in sweat and crying. It, too, could be soothed and coaxed into healing through time and intense therapy.

But the heart? That organ never fully healed itself. It could never be right once it had been damaged. But no matter how broken it was, no matter how badly it hurt every time a memory slipped through the cracks and gripped you, it just kept on beating. You kept on moving, kept on living. Even when you wanted to curl into the fetal position and die, it wouldn't let you. Those jagged fragments pulled themselves together and continued to pump blood through your body.

Every heartbeat killed you, but you were alive. Even if you didn't want to be.

I placed the jar of vibrant stars back on my windowsill and smiled. It was a big deal for me. To smile again. To find a reason to want to smile again. It had taken months to get here. To find just a tiny bit of peace from the hell that was my life. Not anymore. I wouldn't live like that. I wouldn't let *him* take that away from me.

I didn't do it alone, although sometimes it felt like I had been banished to the tiny island of Me. I became a recluse. I didn't talk. I didn't eat. Hell, sometimes it felt like I didn't breathe. I existed.

For weeks, I stared at the stars on my windowsill, silently cursing them, hating them, but still needing them. Each one served as an individual reminder. They reminded me why I still breathed. Why I still kept moving forward no matter how badly I wanted to give up. They reminded me of the love I had, the love I shattered, and the love that kept me tethered to this life.

One day I wouldn't need those stars. I wouldn't need

the crutch of my fears to keep me from leading a full, healthy life. I'd be able to kiss them goodbye and never look back. And I'd finally be free.

The pieces of my life were finally coming back together. My father was charged and convicted of attempted rape, attempted murder, and trespassing. That, along with the slew of warrants out for his arrest, resulted in him being sent to prison for no less than 20 years without the chance of parole. That gave me a small slice of peace, but it didn't make me happy. Who could really be happy about having to relive your own personal hell in front of a room full of strangers? Yeah. That earned #254.

Sometimes it took tragedy to make you see the things that were staring you right in the face and breathing down your neck. I knew I had problems, but I kept them tucked away, smothered with denial. After many nights spent on my bedroom floor, shaking, rocking, and crumbling right before their eyes, Dom and Angel finally persuaded me to get help. I went back to seeing Dr. Cole and, as much as I hated to admit it, the know-it-all bitch was right. My fears had become irrational. I was collecting them like coins or stamps. Like tiny paper stars. Like shot glasses from all over the world.

My body and mind weren't the only things that were on the mend. My mother had made the trip from The Philippines to help with my care after I was released from the hospital. We talked. We screamed. We cried. And I finally told her everything that had been festering inside me like a disease.

My mother had lived through the unthinkable. She had been beaten and tormented beyond anything I could ever imagine. He took everything from her, leaving nothing but the hollow carcass of a woman. And, being birthed into a traditional Asian family that didn't believe in counseling or exposing dark family secrets, my mother never got the help she needed. Therapy was taboo. Talking about your problems with loved ones, let alone a stranger, just wasn't the norm for them.

My mom never got a chance to heal. She didn't have a Dom or an Angel. She didn't even have a Blaine. But she had me. And together, we would fix what had been broken between us. It would take time, and probably enough tears to fill the Grand Canyon, but we would get through it. She was my mother. She was *me*. Repairing our relationship was helping me come to grips with what had happened to me. What happened to *us*.

I looked over at the guitar sitting on its stand in the corner of my room. I hadn't touched it since…since before the attack. Since Blaine. When I let him go, I let go of music. I said goodbye to the one thing that made me feel whole. That made me fearless.

Music made me remember, and I needed to forget. It was damn hard. Shit, it was impossible. But it was getting easier to breathe everyday. I could think about him without breaking into a million pieces, sobbing so hard that my chest ached. I'd even been able to say his name aloud. And when Angel would update me on AngelDust's weekend shows at Dive, she didn't have to omit him from the story. Shit, he wasn't Voldemort. Still, I insisted they keep all Blaine-related news to a minimum.

I missed him. Missed him like hell. But this was better for him. He deserved a healthy, loving relationship. One where the girl worshipped the ground he walked on and showered him with affection. Someone who didn't break down when fear swallowed her whole. Blaine deserved normal, and I was far from that. And that was ok. I had come to grips with that fact. I could want the best for him and know that it wasn't me, and still manage to be happy for him. Eventually.

That was the noble thing to believe. But loving someone, yet knowing that you could never be with them, doesn't make them any easier to forget. If anything, it just made you want them more.

You see, the heart was a stubborn, selfish bastard. It didn't let go easily. It never did what the brain commanded, no matter how badly you tried to push it into detachment. It kept on feeling just like it kept on beating. And the more you tried to deny it of what it wanted, the more it pined for that forbidden piece of fruit, the stronger the craving grew. So while it became less painful to accept that Blaine and I could never be, it felt like my heart would explode every time I thought of his playful smile. Or remembered the way he smelled. Or daydreamed about the feel of his bare skin against mine.

I didn't let myself wonder if he missed me too. I wasn't a total glutton for punishment. I knew Blaine wouldn't stay single for long. It had been months. Months without any contact whatsoever. He never tried to see me after I dismissed him at the hospital. No phone call, not even a text. He was done with me, and I should have been satisfied with that result. I had been right all along. I told him I wasn't the girl he was looking for. I just hate that I had let myself try to be.

I'd probably always love Blaine Jacobs. But I also loved him enough to let him go.

"Hey Kam?"

I looked up from the piece of paper I had been mindlessly folding into a crane. In the past few months, my collection had tripled in size. Luckily, Dom had suggested I donate most of the pieces to the center where he worked. The kids loved them so much that he arranged a special origami class once a week. Of course, it took many hours of begging to persuade me to do it, but after I saw how much those children enjoyed it, I was sold. Many of them were suffering from self-esteem and anxiety issues. Origami gave them an outlet. It was therapeutic. To be able to take a blank sheet of paper, something that is often discarded or ripped to shreds, and create something beautiful and graceful with it…it really put things in perspective for me.

I smiled at my best friend and roommate and waved him in. "'Sup? How was work?"

Dom strolled in, loosening his tie. His brownish green eyes looked weary though they still sparkled. "Tiring. Had a young girl come in today, probably around 11 or 12, and already very sexually active. Her mom can't get through to her and if she doesn't get help, that girl is gonna be sitting on Maury's couch within a year."

"Yikes. That's tricky."

"Yeah," he replied, flopping back on my bed. "But that's not the worst part. I'm pretty certain she's been sexually abused."

I tossed the crane on my nightstand and gave Dom my undivided attention. "What? Are you sure?"

"Yeah. All the signs are there. And if I'm right, her

promiscuity is a result of whatever trauma she's experienced. So talking to me won't help. It will only scare her more."

"Have you tried?"

"Of course! At first, she clammed up. Then—and I swear, I did nothing to provoke it—she came onto me. This *child* was trying to proposition me for sex!"

I shook my head. "Oh my God."

Dom reached over and grasped my hand the way he did when he was about to ask me for a favor. I braced myself. "I need you on this, Kam. Please. Maybe you could talk to her?"

"*Me?* How could I be of any help?"

"Because you can relate. She needs another female to talk to about this. She'd be more open with you. Plus, you're amazing, Kam. No bullshit. You've overcome so much and have turned out better for it. And whether you want to believe it or not, you are warm and nurturing. Kinda like how I imagined my own mother would have been like. You'd put her right at ease."

Tears glazed my eyes as I shook my head. "Damn you, Dominic Trevino. Playing the Mother Card. That's a low blow."

"You're sweet and comforting," he continued, knowing he had hit my soft spot. "The sound of your voice just draws people in. Makes them listen. You're absolutely the most selfless, good-hearted person I have ever met."

"So not true," I mumbled.

"Please, Kam? This girl needs you. You could potentially save her life."

I let out a resigned sigh. I imagined myself in one of

those old cartoons where Elmer Fudd morphs into a giant lollipop after Bugs Bunny makes a total sucker out of him. "Fine, fine. See if she'll come to the next origami class. I'll stay after and talk to her then. But I can't promise anything."

Dom attacked me with a huge, wet kiss on the cheek. "Thank you so much, Kam. I swear you won't regret this; you'll see." He climbed to his feet and stretched his broad, muscular body and yawned. "I'm gonna try to grab a nap. Gotta date tonight. Thanks, Kam. Love you."

He was at my door when I called out to him, stopping him in his tracks. "Hey, Dom?"

"Yeah?" he asked, spinning around.

"I love you too."

Even from across the room, I could see the tears shining in his eyes. He smiled and looked away, trying to compose himself, then nodded. Moisture was already bathing his cheeks before he could turn and escape my bedroom.

I was cooking an early dinner on a Friday night when Angel entered the kitchen before heading to Dive to perform. Her expression was unreadable though I knew something was bothering her.

"Spit it out," I finally said, as she munched on a slice of the red bell pepper I was slicing for the stir-fry.

"What do you mean?" she answered with her best doe-eyed guise. I could see right through those big baby blues and pouty, glossed lips.

"The thing that you're just itching to tell me. Go ahead and say it. What happened? Seduced another lonely housewife in our building? Corrupted someone's daughter?"

"Now why do you always think the worst of me? I'm not some sexual deviant!" she scoffed with a hand on her narrow hip.

"Could've fooled me," I laughed.

"*Hmph.* Well, for your information, it's about you. So there!" She turned on her heel to make her dramatic exit.

"Wait! What *about* me?"

Slowly, again for dramatic effect, Angel turned to face me, wearing a mischievous grin. "I don't know if I should give it to you. But I'm running out of time, and, with what Dom and Dr. Cole said, it could really get me in trouble. And you've been doing…"

"What? Ok, back up. What are you talking about? What did Dom and Dr. Cole say?"

I set down the knife I was holding and sat down at the breakfast table, motioning for Angel to do the same. With a deep breath and a quick glance over her shoulder, she reluctantly did the same.

"Now spill it. And start from the beginning."

Angel took a deep breath, as she nervously fingered her blonde hair. "After what happened to you, after the attack, you were adamant about us not mentioning…um… Blaine. Like you really wanted nothing to do with him. So we tried to just act like he never existed. You know, anything to help you get better. So when, uh, Blaine gave me something to give you a few weeks later, I went to Dom about it. To ask him what I should do."

"Wait a minute. Blaine gave you something for me?" I squeaked. It was a miracle that I could even get the words out. Just hearing his name nearly stole my breath.

"Well…yeah. But it's weird. I don't know; I just don't get why he'd want you to have that. But anyway, let me finish. So I tell Dom about it, and he told me not to give it to you. Said that Dr. Cole thinks that any reminder of what happened to you or the events leading up to that could trigger some mental breakdown. I had to agree. I mean, you were pretty scary for a while there."

I couldn't argue with her there. The weeks following my attack had been a blur. Like a total out of body experience. I wasn't all there. It was like my subconscious had created this steel cocoon that no one could penetrate while my mind digested what had happened to me. Between the drugs from the surgeries to fix my mangled face, and then accepting the new me, I was a zombie. I was dead inside. I didn't want to feel. I didn't want to think. And I damn sure didn't want to talk about it. Only the arrival of my mom, the only person that was probably more broken than me, snapped me out of it. Seeing her face opened the floodgates. All the emotions that were battling to reach the surface came bursting out. And for days, they didn't stop.

"So now you feel like you're running out of time to give it to me?"

Angel shrugged. "Yeah. I kinda am."

I chewed my lip, wondering if I wanted to open this door. Yeah, my heart was still undoubtedly Blaine's, but I had accepted the end of us. I was moving on and getting better. I needed to stay on this path. Straying from it could seriously be dangerous for my recovery.

"Well…let's see it."

Yup. Sucker. A 5-foot 6-inch sucker, complete with long, white stick and plastic wrapper. Probably cherry flavored.

Angel opened the oversized, designer handbag on her shoulder and revealed a glass Mason jar. Inside was a piece of paper. I took the jar in my hands and examined it with unwavering concentration.

"See," Angel remarked, though I could hardly hear her voice over the sound of my pounding heart. "Weird, right? Who gives someone a jar? So…you gonna read the note?"

Was I? Should I?

"I don't know," I whispered. It was true. Being honest with myself and with others about my feelings was something I had been working on in therapy.

"Well, don't wait too long to make up your mind. He's leaving."

My head jerked up so fast that I felt my mended skull rattle. "Leaving?"

"Yeah. He's taking off. To like, Australia or something. Tonight is actually his going away party and A.D. is performing. I asked him if he wanted me to invite you…"

"And?"

"Sorry, Kam," she replied with sympathetic eyes. She didn't have to say anymore. Blaine was over me. He didn't want me there.

I nodded, both in understanding and conclusion. I was done with this conversation, just like Blaine was done with me.

"Ok, well… I gotta run." Angel climbed to her feet and

kissed me on the forehead. I just sat there, still staring at that jar, unable to acknowledge much else.

Before Angel could make her way all the way out of the kitchen, she turned to face me. "Kam? Can you do me a favor?"

I forced my eyes to hers, though I really couldn't see her. "Sure."

"Whatever's in that jar, promise me you won't be afraid of it. It's just a piece of paper. Nothing on it can take away everything you've achieved these past few months. It doesn't change who you are."

I sat in silence for a few beats before nodding. "I promise."

I lied.

It was too late. I was already terrified.

CHAPTER THIRTY-FOUR

Kami

Kami,

I've written this letter in my head a million times. Shit, I've scribbled it down more times than I feel comfortable even telling you about before balling it up & chucking it across the room. But the truth is, I don't know what to say. I don't know how to fully explain what I'm feeling right now. Confused? Yes. Upset? Hell yes. Hurt? More than you could ever know.

I know I'm a selfish bastard for feeling like that. After all you've been through, I know I have no right to be hurt. But I am. I can't help that. It's been nearly three weeks, and all I can think about is the look on your face when I last saw you. When I lost you. So please, hate me for that. Say I'm a self-centered prick and an asshole. But don't say what we had wasn't real. Don't take that away from me. Because, Kam, to me it was everything.

Yeah, I get that it's over. And I know it's what needs to

be done for you to heal. But, know that being without you is killing me. Fucking killing me every damn second of every damn day that I can't see you. Or feel you in my arms. Or hear your sweet voice singing softly. Baby, I miss you so much and I feel bad for it. Like missing you won't be conducive to your recovery. Like feeling this way will only make things worse. And that's not what I want. Not at all.

So I'm telling you, Kami, I won't miss you anymore. I won't hurt for you. I won't need you like I do. And I won't love you. Loving you is what caused all this. It's what ruined us. And I am so sorry for that. I hate myself for failing you. For not being enough to save you. But I won't fail you again. If this is what you need—for me to never think of you again—then that is what I am going to do. I'll forget you. I'll stop loving you like I do. Because, dammit, I do. So much it fucking tears me apart.

I hope this is what you want. I know I didn't get it right the first time, but I promise to try like hell to make it better.

Always (Never),

Blaine

P.S. The jar is for you. Maybe before a big storm rolls in, you'll use it to catch fireflies (see, I did remember something, city mouse. But they're still lightning bugs down here). And if you do, just remember, the storm doesn't last forever. It can scare you; it can shake you to your core. But it never lasts. The rain subsides, the thunder dies, and the winds calm to a soft whisper. And that moment after the storm clouds pass, when all is silent and still, you find peace. Quiet, gentle peace.

That's what I wish for you. Even if you couldn't find it with me.

I read the letter a second time. Then a third. Each word jumped off the page and slapped me in the face. Each sentence stabbed me straight through my fractured heart.

I won't miss you anymore.
Loving you is what caused all this. It's what ruined us.
I'll forget you.
I'll stop loving you.

I repeated it over and over like a mantra, seeing if it would start to make sense. If the words could somehow form coherent thoughts for me to digest. Because I couldn't understand. I just didn't fully get it.

Blaine stopped loving me. *For* me?

I had really lost him. It was really over. And though we hadn't been together in months, knowing for sure that he no longer had feelings for me just drove the knife in deeper.

Maybe somewhere in the back of my convoluted mind, I thought we would find our way back to each other. That we were really meant to be. He told me that we were inevitable. That when you knew…you just knew. Maybe I had been holding onto that this entire time.

The thing that probably disturbed me the most was Blaine's belief that he had failed me. That he was somehow responsible for what happened. The thought of him carrying around that immense guilt, thinking that history had repeated itself, had me choking back a sob. No. I couldn't let him think that. I couldn't let him take the blame for my father's actions.

Blaine was a good man. The best kind that there was.

He was the kind of man that women dreamt of taking home to their mothers. The kind of guy that opened doors and pushed in chairs. The kind of man that fairytales were written about and songs were sung for.

And I had pushed him away. I had destroyed the man whose only crime was loving me. All of me—phobias, insecurities, and scars included.

What the fuck was wrong with me?

I folded up the piece of paper and slid it back into the Mason jar before setting it on my windowsill. Right next to those little stars, so small and delicate in size, yet the weight of their burden had crippled me for so long. I picked up the glass that contained their cynical smiles and taunting laughter.

Those insignificant little things had held me prisoner for years. And now they had cost me the only man I had ever loved.

I had never hated them more, so much so that I wanted to be done with them for good. It was time. I was ready to live.

The roar of the crowd was louder than I had remembered, though the only thing I could hear was the steady, rapid pounding of my heart. I wiped my sweat-slicked palms on my cotton dress. Shit. My dress was white; I really hoped it didn't become see-through from the spotlights. Would I look stupid? Would people be pissed?

Hell, could I even do this?

Stop it, Kam. Breathe. You got this. Everything else, all the bullshit you've been through...it was all for this. *This moment. Prove that you're strong. That you're a fighter. That you can be fearless. Because if anyone is worth the risk of falling, it's him.*

The sound of Angel's voice signaled my entrance, and with trembling legs, I forced myself from the safety of backstage. I shielded my eyes to adjust to the bright beam of the fluorescents and stepped forward. Luckily, the packed audience was still too wrapped up in their drinks, food, and conversation to even notice my approach. Good. Maybe I'd remain safe and hidden, overshadowed by the powerhouse that was Angel Cassidy and the rest of the A.D. bombshells.

But Lady Luck was a bitch in too-tight stilettos that liked to do the Electric Slide on my glimmer of hope. The only thing I could be thankful for was the fact that his back was turned. But even in the crowded bar, I instantly zeroed in on his heavily inked arms and messily styled, sandy brown hair. Every synapse jolted to attention then tingled with remembrance. My stomach coiled into a knot that Popeye himself couldn't get out of. My body knew him, had felt him. And undoubtedly missed him.

Even with the hushed whispers of my return swirling about, Blaine remained in deep conversation with his cousin, CJ. The crowd around them, mostly comprised of scantily clad girls, vied for their attention, yet the pair seemed totally oblivious. One chick in particular was damn near trying to force feed Blaine her tits.

Maybe this was a mistake. Blaine didn't want me here;

he even told Angel that. He was leaving. If he felt anything for me, why would he move to the other side of the world?

The room quieted a decibel when I stepped up to the mic with my guitar, yet Blaine still didn't turn around. I looked over at Angel, who shot me an encouraging smile with a nod of her head. I shrugged. I was here. Getting to this point was half the battle and I'd be damned if I turned back now.

Without saying a word to even introduce myself, I began to play. At first, the strings felt foreign under my fingertips. Almost like a lover that you hadn't kissed in ages. But soon, familiarity kicked in, flooding me with feelings of comfort and serenity. Angel was right—this was where I belonged. Nothing made me feel more fearless… more like *me*. Nothing could hurt me here. That broken girl had been fixed and set free.

With my eyes trained on Blaine as I belted out the first notes, I could see his body stiffen. He knew my voice. He had heard me. But I needed him to really *hear* me. To listen to the words that I had penned just for him months ago. The words I was too afraid to tell him.

In pieces when you found me
Shattered like broken glass
So scared that you would see
What hid behind this tattered mask

Slowly, he turned around, and his stunned gaze sought mine. The moment our eyes locked, I knew that my fate was sealed.

I had fallen into forever.

I would never be able to move on from *this*, from him. From that scary-beautiful man that I was hopelessly in love with. And fear bloomed into exhilaration. Anxiety morphed into sheer joy.

I sang every word to him as if no one else existed. In my world, no one did. He was my all. *My everything*. He was the only thing that could save me. He already had.

The thought of loving and losing
Baby, it terrifies me
Didn't know what I was doing
Just wanted to be free

The entire bar fell silent as Angel and I continued to play, our voices blending in perfect harmony as we fell into the chorus, as seamless and steady as one voice. The music wrapped around us, guiding our fingers and tongues. The rest of the A.D. girls caught onto the melody and began to improvise with their own instruments.

I was there—that sweet spot where everything came together. The picture was no longer blurry; I could see it—I could see Blaine—as clear as day. And I no longer played my guitar; I became it. I no longer sang; I was song.

But now you see
The mess that I've made
Feeling so desperate
Just wanted the pain to fade
Time and time again
Tried to push you away
I know that I'm crazy

But you make it okay

Blaine's eyes never strayed from mine as he sat as still as stone. Even when some bleach blonde bimbo tried to grab his attention, he was unmovable. Unshakable. Just as he had always been. Blaine was a constant. *My* constant. Somehow he had become just as necessary to me as Dom or Angel. He had become my family.

As we neared the conclusion, I let my eyes close and just…*felt.* I let the emotions those lyrics evoked flood through me. I let the truth of those words set me free from fear and worry.

This wasn't only for Blaine. No, this was the Emancipation of Kami Duvall. The once broken girl who had put herself back together. The scared child that survived even when she didn't have the will to. I kissed that little girl goodbye. I let go of the fear that had been my only friend at times. I didn't need it anymore. I had love.

I'm not afraid
Of monsters and ghosts
But the thought of losing you
Is what scares me the most

I opened my eyes once the song ended, and Blaine was right below me, standing at the edge of the stage. His cheeks glistened with tears, and his deep brown eyes were rimmed with red. The sight of him sent a surge of courage through my veins, and I stripped off my guitar and handed it to Angel before jumping down to join him below. I didn't even hear the raucous cheers and claps. I just needed to hear his voice, telling me that it wasn't too late. That I hadn't lost him.

"Hey, roadrunner, where'd you go?" he asked in a raspy voice.

I smiled. "I thought I told you not to call me that."

"I thought *you* were done running."

I nodded. He was right. He always called me on my bullshit, and that's exactly what I had been afraid of. He saw me for what I was.

"I am. I have nowhere else to go. Nowhere else I'd rather be."

Blaine rolled the barbell in his mouth as I had seen him do a hundred times. The temptation to suck that tongue into my own mouth blossomed in my belly.

"So, where do you want to be?" he asked.

"With you." There was no hesitation. No fear.

"But you said…Kam…" he stammered. Blaine took a deep breath and took a step towards me, filling the air between us with scents of mint and spice. He lifted a hand and stroked the length of my cheek where a faint scar had been left behind. I didn't even stop myself from closing my eyes and reveling in the feel of him.

"Kami…" he whispered. "Why? Why now?"

I opened my eyes so he could see the conviction in them. "Because you're the exception, Blaine. And, honestly, I was a coward. I was terrified of feeling this way about you."

He cocked his head to one side and narrowed his eyes. "And how do you feel?"

A flush crept up my cheeks as I reached up on my tiptoes and softly kissed his lips, catching him off guard. "I love you," I murmured against them. "I love you so much it scares me."

He pulled his mouth from mine just far enough to meet my eyes. "Scares you?"

"The magnitude of what I feel for you, the thought of losing you for good? Yes. Scares me to death."

My hands found his and I pulled them up between us, holding them to my chest. "Blaine, the scariest part about love isn't love itself. It's letting go and plunging into the unknown. It's trusting someone with the very most sacred part of your heart. It's allowing yourself to feel something foreign and uncharted, despite how much it terrifies the hell out of you.

"The scary part isn't loving you, Blaine. That part's simple. It's the fall. I fell a long time ago, and you know what? I'm not afraid anymore."

I didn't have a chance to utter another word, as he pulled me into him and claimed my mouth.

Yes, *claimed.*

This was no kiss. Blaine marked me for life. Branded me like the vibrant artwork that covered his magnificent body, making me his forever. Every stroke of his tongue soothed the lonely ache inside me, erupting a new ache that had me quivering in his arms. My knees went weak and buckled, causing me to sway. But Blaine had me. He had never let me go.

Reluctantly, I unraveled my arms from around his neck, and shimmied out of his tight grasp. "I have something for you," I said, turning to grab my purse that was strategically stashed nearby. That's when I noticed Dom, Angel, and even CJ, watching us from across the room, their faces wearing varied looks of joy and pride. I smiled at them before turning back to Blaine's curious expression.

"Hold out your hand."

A questioning frown dimpled his forehead. "Huh?"

"Just hold out your hand."

Blaine did as he was told, and I filled his palm with tiny, colorful origami stars. Many of them spilled onto the floor, and he scrambled to cup the overflow with his other hand.

"Uh, babe, thanks, but I think you could've just left these in the jar."

I shook my head. "Each one of these stars represents a fear of mine. I started collecting these years ago, and soon it became less of a ritual and more of an obsession. And now…now they're yours. Because, Blaine, the day I met you was the day that these began to lose their power. I had finally found something else to live for. So I want you to have them. I want you to take these from me for good. I never, ever want fear to keep me from the man I love again."

A smile spread across his full lips before he crushed them to mine. "You're kinda fucking amazing, you know that?"

I matched his amused expression. "Just kinda?"

"Yeah. Just a little bit. And I love you. So damn much."

And once again, Blaine staked his claim on the part of me that only he had moved. Holding those tiny stars, he captured every fear, every reservation, and crushed them in the palm of his inked hand.

EPILOGUE

Blaine

"Babe, where can I put this one?"

I damn near drop the box I'm carrying and rush to Kami's side, snatching the crate full of books in her hands. "Nowhere. You can let me deal with it. Kam, we've been over this. Stop it, ok?"

Kami rolls her big green eyes and shakes her head. "I'm pregnant, not handicapped."

Yeah, that's right. You heard her. Kami is pregnant. With *my* child. Cue the fucking marching band and flaming baton throwers. Kami is pregnant with my child.

And ever since we found out two weeks ago after we got back from spending nearly a month in Australia, I haven't been able to shake the stupid, Joker-esque grin off my face.

Kami, of course, had a totally different reaction. Naturally, she was shocked as hell. We all were. She was still on birth control but, hey, I guess things got a little crazy Down Under. Couldn't say I was pissed about it. Hell, I was elated. Guess my little tadpoles were more like fucking sharks!

She ran the gamut of emotions: shocked, afraid, angry, sad, until she finally decided to be happy about it. This was a new start for us, a new beginning. We had a chance to finally write our own story. And I want to write it in bold, bright Sharpie for the world to see.

Kami is mine. Our baby is *mine*.

I give her a swift peck on her pouty lips before putting down the crate of books and ushering her to the couch. "I know you're not handicapped, babe. But the mother of my child isn't going to be lugging around boxes when she has an able-bodied man to do it for her. Now you relax, kick your feet up and let the men take care of the rest."

Kami sighs her resignation before propping her sandaled feet onto the coffee table. "Great. My baby daddy is a male chauvinist cave man." Then she cradles her flat stomach while looking down at it, a peculiar gleam in her eye. "Aren't we lucky?"

I stand there, completely mesmerized and bursting with pride. The way she touched her belly, how she smiled at it as if she was actually gazing at our little bundle of joy…that image will forever be engraved in my mind. It's the type of thing that wars are fought and won for. That people live and die for. The kind of look that brings 300 pound, badass brutes to their knees, reducing them to sniveling pussies.

The look of love.

Not everyone gets to experience it. But if you're ever so fortunate, remember it. Hold onto it and never let it go. Because you've been given a gift.

"Dude, you just gonna sit there and fucking daydream or help us move this shit?" CJ scorns, nudging me with his shoulder as he and Dom maneuver around me with more boxes. "Fuck, how much shit does one chick need?"

"Welcome to my world," Dom chimes in, dropping a box labeled 'Shoes.' He claps me on the back. "You'll soon be the proud owner of shower drains clogged with hair, bathroom sinks sprinkled with makeup, and the occasional wish-I-didn't-know-you-did-that moment that leaves you with a permanent *what-the-fuck?* face."

"Nah, man," I chuckle. "I'm ready. Bring it on."

Yup, you heard that right, too.

After much persuasion, both in and outside of the bedroom, I finally convinced Kami to move in with me. We knew we wanted to raise our child together, and, hell, she was already over most nights, but Kami still had serious reservations about it. She had never lived with a man outside of Dom, and not having the crutch of her friends was seriously freaking her out. But she was getting used to the motherhood thing—you know, putting your own needs aside for your kid—and finally admitted that moving in would be the only logical solution. Plus, there was no way I was letting my newborn go back to the brothel known as Angel's condo. That place had a revolving door of pussy, and some of it was pretty sketchy.

A shrill wail grabs our attention and we all look towards the door in time to see Angel stumble in, her face streaked with tears.

"Oh, Kam, I'm going to miss you so much!" she cries, falling onto the couch with her friend. "I can't believe you're leaving me with Dirty Dom and his band of glitter-wearing gutter sluts."

"I think you're mistaking my dates with your Wednesday night stripper conquests. There's still a layer of edible body dust on the furniture. I feel like Elton John every time I sit on the damn couch," Dom retorts.

Angel waves him off, yet doesn't deny his accusations. "So Kam… you'll still visit, right? We can go get massages and pedicures—Oh my God, can you still get those? Isn't there like some bacteria you can get that's not safe for pregnant women? And I read you can't eat sushi. *Sushi!* But we love…"

Kami cups Angel's damp cheeks and smiles warmly. "Angel, honey, *breathe*. You'll still see me. Hell, I'll be at the bar almost everyday, like always."

"The *bar?*" CJ scoffs. "A bar is no place for a baby. Not *my* little cousin."

We all whip our heads to his stern expression. "What?" he shrugs.

Hmph. My cousin, Craig Jacobs, the guy that made it his mission in life to sleep with the entire volleyball team in high school, the same guy who bribed the AV geeks to set up hidden cameras in the girl's locker room, the very same man that vowed to never commit to one woman ever since his mom walked out on him and his dad, actually said something not centered on tits, ass or all things oral.

Maybe things are changing for the Jacobs men. Hell, maybe there's a chance that CJ could one day be as deliriously happy as me.

After every box of shoes, clothes, books, and knick-knacks is carried into the house, and Angel has cried herself dry, I kick everyone out. Finally, Kami and I are alone. In *our* home.

Kami's head rests in my lap as I play with her hair and massage her scalp. The TV is on, but I can't seem to tear my eyes away from her. The woman of my dreams. The woman that will make me a father.

Damn.

I can't keep my hands off her. And knowing that her body is now more than just my personal playground, I can't help but be in awe of her.

God, she's beautiful.

My hand trails down to the edge of her jeans and up her shirt. I rub the bare skin of her belly, so soft and warm under my fingers. Without even thinking, I begin to hum softly, angling myself closer and closer to her stomach. It's a bittersweet song for us. The song that touched Kami in a way that had her fleeing from the bar with tears streaked down her face. The song that prompted me to follow her, so I could wipe away those tears and hold her tight.

I think that was the moment I fell in love with Kami. The moment she had branded me down to my soul.

"Interesting song you're humming. What makes you think we're having a daughter?" she smiles at me.

"A man can dream," I beam proudly.

"What? No bouncing baby Blaine to carry on the Jacobs name?"

"One day," I shrug. "But for now, I just want to be our little girl's hero."

Kami places her petite hand on mine, lacing our fingers together as we cradle our baby tucked safely in her womb. Then, she looks up at me with that same peculiar gleam in her eyes, causing warmth to spread to every limb, and my heart to swell twice its size.

The look of love.

"I'd like that," she whispers before leaning up and placing those pouty lips on mine, kindling the warmth into scorching white-hot heat. "Because you're already mine."

Dear Reader,

If you're reading this, I want to say thank you. Creating *Fear of Falling* was an extremely emotional journey and sharing it with the world has been just as nerve-wracking. But I did it. And by choosing to purchase and read it, you have helped to expose something that occurs all too often.

Though *Fear of Falling* is partly fictional, the issue of domestic violence is very real. There are far too many Kamis in the world, and most of them never meet their Blaine. And as the story reflects, it affects everyone. Friends, lovers, and especially, children.

One out of four women experience some type of domestic violence in their lifetime. 50% of men who consistently abuse their wives also abuse their children.

I urge you, please, if you or someone you know is a victim of domestic violence, get help. You don't have to live in fear. Ending the cycle of abuse is in your hands.

The National Domestic Violence Hotline: 1.800.799.SAFE
www.thehotline.org

Do it for you. Do it for your children. Do it because everyone deserves a happily-ever-after.

FEAR OF FALLING PLAYLIST

The Story – Thirty Seconds To Mars
Chin Up – Copeland
Save Me – Muse
Nobody Knows – Pink
Beneath Your Beautiful – Labrinth
Stay Awake – Lydia
Counting Stars – OneRepublic
Kiss Me – Ed Sheeran
Daughters – John Mayer
Demons – Imagine Dragons
Edge of Desire – John Mayer
The Only Exception – Paramore
Fix You – Coldplay
Love Affair – Copeland
Hospital – Lydia
Fix A Heart – Demi Lovato
All I See – Lydia
This – Ed Sheeran
Your Guardian Angel – The Red Jumpsuit Apparatus
Let Me Love You – Glee Cast version, originally by NeYo
A Modern Myth – Thirty Seconds To Mars

Sparks – Coldplay
I'm Ok – Christina Aguilera
For The Love of a Daughter – Demi Lovato
Hurt – Christina Aguilera
Get It Over With – Rihanna
Heart of Stone – Iko
Alibi – Thirty Seconds to Mars
Poison & Wine – The Civil Wars
All I Wanted – Paramore
Un-thinkable (I'm Ready) – Alicia Keys
Just Give Me A Reason – Pink, Nate Ruess

ACKNOWLEDGMENTS

I recently told a fellow author that creating a book was like raising a child- it takes a village. We'd all like to believe that we are brilliant enough to hatch these stories on our own, but the reality is, we draw inspiration and ideas from the people around us. And there are quite a few key people that have influenced me in the creation of *Fear of Falling*, through kind words of encouragement, critiques, suggestions, support and, most importantly, friendship.

First and foremost, I have to thank my family. My husband and children have had to endure their fair share of frozen pizza and takeout (even a few Fend for Yourself nights) in order for me to find time to write. Thank you for picking up the slack so I could throw myself into this story. Without your love and patience, I would have never found the strength and courage to pen FOF. This book is just as much yours as it is mine. I love you all so much.

I must thank my amazing betas that put up with my anxiety-filled messages for the past 2 months. Ashley Tkachyk, L.B. Simmons, Kari Acebo, and Calia Read, I honestly could not have done this without you ladies & I am so incredibly grateful for all the chats, rants, vents & tears we've shared.

To my literary partners in crime: Gail McHugh, Emmy

Montes, Cindy Brown, Claribel Contreras, Gail McHugh, Madeline Sheehan, Karina Halle, Trevlyn Tuitt, and Mimi Abraham, thank you for all the pep talks and advice. You all are rock stars and it is such an honor to know you. Love you all.

Thank you to the amazing girls of SLJ Books that blow me away daily with their enthusiasm and support. You all are crazy awesome & I am so grateful for all that you do!

Thank you to girls at THESUBCLUB books for arranging a kickass blog tour & being so amazingly supportive.

I have to thank the design genius known as Regina Wamba of Mae I Design for the amazing cover for FOF. Working with you has been a dream and I hope we can create many more beautiful covers in the future.

To my editor, Tracey Buckalew, thank you for reaching out & taking a chance on me. It was down to the wire, but we did it! Thank you so much!

To my awesome formatter, Julie Titus of JT Formatting, thank you for being so patient with me and going above and beyond to create such a beautiful interior. You rock!

To all the amaze-balls blogs and book pages out there that have supported me from day one: THESUBCLUB books, Mommy's Reads & Treats, First Class Books, The Book Blog, Natasha is a Book Junkie, Kindlehooked, Smut Book Club, The Rock Stars of Romance, Swoon Worthy, Angie's Dreamy Reads…there are honestly too many to name! I want to thank you ALL for everything you do for the indie community. Without you, we'd all be crazy people, peddling our books on the side of the road.

Most importantly, and I mean that from the bottom of

my heart, I want to thank the readers. YOU all are why I do this. YOU have given me the platform to tell my stories. Thank you. A hundred times, thank you.

-S

Books by S.L. Jennings

The Dark Light Series

Dark Light

The Dark Prince

Light Shadows – Winter 2013/2014

Nikolai, a Dark Light Novella – Fall 2013

For more information about S.L. Jennings and her books, visit:

http://www.facebook.com/authorsljennings

http://www.facebook.com/darklightseries

http://www.goodreads.com/SLJennings

Twitter: MrsSLJ

29811068R00237

Made in the USA
Lexington, KY
08 February 2014